T0171579

Thread of Faith

Olive Boettcher

WestBow
PRESS
A DIVISION OF THOMAS NELSON

ISBN: 978-1-4497-3385-8 (e)
ISBN: 978-1-4497-3386-5 (sc)
ISBN: 978-1-4497-3387-2 (hc)

WestBow Press books may be ordered through booksellers or by contacting:

WestBow Press
A Division of Thomas Nelson
1663 Liberty Drive
Bloomington, IN 47403
www.westbowpress.com
1-(866) 928-1240

Scripture taken from the New King James Version. Copyright 1979, 1980,
1982 by Thomas Nelson, inc. Used by permission. All rights reserved.

Library of Congress Control Number: 2012901265

Printed in the United States of America

WestBow Press rev. date:1/24/2012

Chapter 1

Nicole's shift at the hospital was over at long last! It had been a demanding twelve hours with some very challenging patients.

As she climbed into her blue Jeep, she felt like the wind had been knocked out of her. How could she be so tired? She wasn't registering streets as she drove the five city blocks home; she was on auto-pilot. It was like her car drove itself home. Good thing she didn't live far!

She drove into the basement of her building and the garage door closed behind her. Parking in her slot, she sat there, thinking of her day. Then, with a sigh she climbed out of her car and retrieved her belongings from the back seat. Walking up the stairs to her second-floor condo, one slow step at a time, Nicole wondered how much longer she could go on like this. She found this tiredness suffocating.

Unlocking her front door and walking in, she took off her coat and kicked off her shoes. Shadow, her gray, shorthaired, male cat greeted her by pushing against her legs and calling out his brand of cat "hello". Nicole bent down to pick him up and walked into the living room. As she flopped onto the couch, Shadow jumped out of her arms and onto the armrest. He languidly sauntered to the back of the couch where he sat and began grooming himself.

Nicole wondered at this exhaustion. However, this time it was more than just fatigue. She was lonely too. "I miss him, Shadow," she whispered to her cat, as her lower lip quivered and two big tears pooled in her eyes. Before she could gain control, she was overcome by sobs that seemed to tear through the very fabric of her being.

Gradually, the sobs eased to a few shuddering sighs, and Nicole pulled her legs up onto the couch and lay down, emotionally and physically spent. Beside her on the floor was a small mountain of used tissues. She reached for the fleece throw that was at the other end of the sofa and covered herself.

Shadow watched her for a few minutes. When he was satisfied that she was going to stay there, he jumped down and curled his body tight against Nicole's abdomen. Just before falling asleep, she stroked him on the back, so grateful for his comfort and his sensitivity to her when she needed him.

Chapter 2

Ellen was putting the final touches on tonight's stir-fry dinner. With only one child left at home, she still found it a challenge to switch from cooking large meals to smaller ones. Humming a popular Christian song she had just heard on the radio, she chopped the carrots to add to the onions in her wok.

Suddenly Nicole came to mind. Just as quickly came sadness which settled onto her soul. Her eldest daughter had been through so much pain lately, and yet she continued to act as though everything was fine, refusing to talk about her feelings with her family. But Ellen knew better: Nicole was still grieving.

Wiping her hands quickly on a towel and turning down the heat on the stove, Ellen discerned that her daughter must need her prayers right now. She sat in the living room and bowed her head. She knew her heavenly Father was with her and listening to her every word as she began interceding for her daughter.

"Lord God I pray that You would send Your heavenly angels to minister to Nicole, even right now. Lord, that You would guide her through this darkness and grieving, and bring her into a place of peace and rest in You. Only You can satisfy, dear Jesus. Only You can fill the deepest longings in her soul. Have mercy on her and fill her with Your comfort."

Ellen prayed some more until she felt a release in her spirit. Then, standing up and drying her tears, she went back into the kitchen to finish making dinner. As she filled the rice cooker, she pondered on the event that had shaken her family to the core recently. Nicole's handsome young husband Greg, an officer in the Vancouver Police Department, had died while on the job. He had been working as a bike officer patrolling Stanley Park and other areas in Vancouver's West End, and had been struck by a drunk motorist that fateful day three months ago.

Ellen scooped up the carrots and dropped them into the wok on the stove, along with chopped celery. The stir-fry smelled wonderful, but her appetite was quickly disappearing as she reflected on those days of pain and grief.

Nicole had called from the hospital, distraught and crying: Greg had been hit by a car while on patrol. He was on his way to St. Paul's Hospital by ambulance. Clay, Greg's partner, had called to inform her and get her to meet them in Emergency. And now she was asking if her parents could come and be with her. She had been working upstairs on the surgical ward when the call came in. She sounded panicked and her voice rose as she told them where she would meet them.

Ellen's heart felt like it was in her throat as she answered Nicole. "We're in Richmond with our friends the Pattons, and we're leaving right now, honey. We'll be there as soon as we can!" Ellen grabbed her purse while she and Stan ran for the car, saying a hurried goodbye to their friends. As Stan drove, Ellen called Nicole's siblings Julie, Steve and Matthew. Julie was still working and answered on the first ring; she would check with the others so they could drive in together. Steve was playing soccer with his kids outside, and Ellen quickly gave Jennifer, his wife, an account of what happened. Jennifer was shocked to hear the news, but promised to get Steve right away and send him into Vancouver. Matthew had just finished his last class of the day and was on his way home. He opted to drive straight to Steve's house and drive in with him. "Please Mom, tell Nicole we love her; I know you'll get there before us but we'll be there as soon as possible!" They all assured her they would be praying.

Ellen then called their pastor as Stan's car ate up the miles, bringing them closer to St. Paul's Hospital. Pastor Adam promised to pray and inform the other church members. Their church would turn out to be a great support and strength to them during what would end up being the challenge of their lives. "Keep me informed of what's happening, especially if there are any changes, Ellen. I'll be there as soon as possible." Closing her cell phone, Ellen noticed they were nearing the Burrard Street bridge; St. Paul's wasn't far now.

"O God," she prayed out loud, *"preserve Greg's life I pray! Protect him right now wherever he is. And Father, place Your loving arms around Nicole and comfort her".* Stan said an absent-minded "amen" to her prayer, concentrating on his driving.

When they arrived in the emergency room they saw a distraught Nicole begging two nurses to let her be with Greg. "Please, I'm a nurse here too. Let me see my husband!" Greg had been there only a short while and the trauma team was working frantically in an attempt to save his life. One of the nurses put a comforting arm around Nicole's shoulders, leading her slowly toward the staff break room.

Turning around and catching sight of her parents, Nicole was overcome with a fresh onslaught of tears as they enveloped her in their arms. When her crying eased, they led her to a quiet area. Sitting down together, Nicole told them what little she knew: there had been an accident.

While she was talking, Clay, Greg's partner, poked his head in the door. Catching sight of Nicole, he came into the waiting room, police cap in hand. His uniform shorts and shirt were spattered with blood and his usually healthy complexion was quite pale. "Nicole", he faltered, "I'm so sorry!" He reached down to give her a hug. Sitting down, he took in a shaky breath and raked his hand through his disheveled hair. Haltingly he gave them his account of what had taken place. While on patrol in Stanley Park, Greg had stopped his bike to speak with some pedestrians who needed help. As they walked away, he nodded to Clay to carry on. Clay had taken off first, expecting Greg right behind him. Suddenly he heard a crash from behind and a dull thud. As he swung his head around to see what had happened, he realized Greg had been hit by a car. Jumping off his bike, he had run to his partner's crumpled body sprawled on the grass beyond the embankment: his body had flown through the air after being hit. Grabbing at his radio as he ran, he had yelled, "Officer down, officer down!" He had arrived to Greg's broken body immediately after directing dispatch to where they were located in the park. The car had hit a tree trunk thirty feet away. "I still don't know how it all happened..." Clay faltered as he ended his account of the accident.

Nicole's eyes suddenly registered that there was blood on his uniform. "That's Greg's blood!" she exclaimed, reaching out a hand to Clay's shirt, as if touching it might bring her a little closer to her precious husband suffering in the next room. Tears coursed down her cheeks.

About that time Julie and Matthew had run in through the door, looking wildly around till they saw Nicole and their parents. Steve, their older brother, was just parking the car. Gathering about her, they reached out touching a hand here, a shoulder there. Steve rushed in minutes later accompanied by Pastor Adam; they found the family huddled around Nicole.

When they had been brought up to speed on the account of the accident, Pastor Adam vocalized what each one was feeling. "Greg needs our prayers right now. We don't know the extent of his injuries, but God does. Why don't we pray together?" Holding hands and bowing their heads they each one cried out to God while their pastor prayed. "Heavenly Father, You are the Great Physician. You know what's wrong with Greg and what needs to be fixed to make him well again. We pray for Your loving hands to guide the doctors and give them skill as they work on him. We speak Your life into Greg's body, in Jesus' name, amen."

Now all they could do was wait. For over an hour they sat, each lost in his or her own thoughts. What were they doing in the trauma room? Each time someone came out, they looked grim-faced, but no word had as yet been spoken to Nicole or the Graham family.

At last a haggard looking doctor came out of the trauma room and towards their group. "Mrs. Philips?" Nicole jumped to her feet, "Yes, that's me," she said anxiously. The rest of the family gathered around as the doctor began to speak. "I'm very sorry to have to say this, Mrs. Philips, but your husband didn't make it."

"Noooo!" Nicole shrieked, arms flailing out towards her parents for support.

"I'm so sorry. We did all we could. Greg sustained massive brain injuries as well as internal injuries which were causing bleeding inside. But it was the brain damage that was the worst of all. I'm so very sorry." The young doctor's face had looked like he was carrying the weight of the world on his shoulders. Clearly he had given this kind of news to family members before, but it never got easier.

Nicole shook her head and wailed, "But it can't be. He was with me for lunch just five hours ago; I spoke with him at three o'clock! It can't be him in there! Mom, you tell him he has the wrong person!" She looked beseechingly at her mother, tears streaming down her face.

Even as the nurse had led them in to see the still body on the trauma table, Nicole had refused to believe it was him. "Maybe I should just call his cell; he'll answer, you'll see! It's not...."

There was a collective gasp as they entered the trauma room. Laid out on the stretcher, covered by a sheet, was the body of their dear friend and Nicole's husband. The nurses had attempted to cover the damage on his head with part of a sheet. Nevertheless, Greg's beautiful red hair poked through, covered here and there with matted blood. His bruised face showed them the extent of the blow he had suffered at the scene of the accident.

Grief-stricken they stood rooted to the spot, each one weeping silently as they gazed at Greg's lifeless body. Suddenly there was a thud as Nicole's body slumped to the floor in a dead faint.

Coming back to the present, Ellen roused herself to put the finishing touches on tonight's dinner. With a deep sigh, she set the table and made it ready for her two men to be able to eat as they came home. She knew Nicole needed time to grieve properly, but somehow Ellen knew she was struggling. Why had she not come home since that week after the accident? And she never seemed to want to talk on the phone. She continued praying even as her hands worked.

Chapter 3

Nicole woke up to find her cat meowing and rubbing his body on her arms. The sun was streaming in through the balcony doors and as she shook off the last vestiges of sleep; she had been on the couch all night. No wonder she had a kink in her neck!

Getting up, she fed Shadow then made coffee. Good thing today was the first of her days off. Suddenly nausea gripped her and she felt the familiar taste of bile in her mouth. As she hung her head over the toilet bowl, she couldn't help but think that grief had messed up her body something fierce. If she didn't get back to normal soon, she might have to consider getting checked out by a doctor. After all, it had been a while since Greg had died. Surely the grieving shouldn't still be affecting her body this severely!

She rinsed her mouth, then walked into the kitchen. Maybe a couple of crackers would help to settle her stomach. Nicole reached into the cupboard for the box and helped herself. Before long her stomach did indeed feel better, so she poured a cup of coffee, adding a little milk to make it just the right colour. Today was Thursday and she was off till Monday morning. How would she occupy her time?

Turning on the television, more for company than to watch what was on, Nicole settled on the couch to drink her favourite brew. Finishing it off with a sigh and looking down, she saw she was still wearing yesterday's scrubs. Walking back into the bathroom, she peeled off her clothes and climbed into the shower. The hot water streaming down her body felt so comforting. She stood there for a few minutes, allowing the warmth to come back into her bones and nudging away the kink in her neck. Finally she roused herself and finished washing off. As she dressed in jeans and long-sleeved t-shirt, she began thinking about her family. They had always been there for her. Maybe it was time to go home and spend a few days with them, knowing they would love to see her again.

As the plans gelled in her mind, there was a knock on the door. Annaliese from next door stood there in all her five foot glory, carefully holding on to a plate covered in a dish towel. Lovely smells were coming from under that towel. "Good morning, Nicole! I was up early and felt like baking a coffee cake, but I need someone to eat this with. Care to join me?" Her blue eyes twinkled as she smiled at Nicole.

Warmth filled Nicole's heart as she looked at Annaliese. What a sweet neighbour she was! She had been such a support during those first weeks after the accident, praying for Nicole and just being there for her. "It's so lovely to see you, Annaliese! Please come in. I could use a little company and your coffee cake might just be reviving my appetite." She sniffed the cake; the heavenly aroma put a smile on her face and made her mouth water. "Mmmm, blueberry!" Nicole loved blueberry coffee cake!

There was still half a pot of coffee, so Nicole poured some for both of them, then carried the mugs to the coffee table where Annaliese had placed the warm cake. Nicole set down her tray and placed the mugs, dessert plates and cutlery onto the table.

Annaliese sat down comfortably in the easy chair. "How have you been, honey? You've been so heavy on my heart lately."

Sitting close by on the couch, Nicole looked at Annaliese and wondered how much she should tell this lovely neighbour who was watching her with kind blue eyes. She looked quite appealing today with her gray wool slacks and light blue turtle neck. There was still a chill in the air. "I've been fair," replied Nicole. "I'm still working full time, so it's pretty busy." She got up and flicked on the gas fireplace. As they continued chatting, warmth from the fire enveloped them. They munched on their coffee cake and drank their coffee. Yum! What a delicious way to start the morning.

As Nicole listened to Annaliese speak about her volunteer work at St. Paul's Hospital, she thought back to when they had met. It was the day Greg and Nicole had moved into their new apartment.

Sweaty from the hard work and laughing with joy that they were finally together, they were interrupted with a knock on the door. Standing there was Annaliese, an engaging smile on her face and homemade cookies in her hands. "Welcome to our building! My name is Annaliese and I live right next door."

Greg and Nicole had introduced themselves and invited the spry, petite lady in. "We've just returned from our honeymoon in time to move in," spoke Nicole, her eyes dancing with pleasure. She looked proudly at Greg. "Greg is a police officer with the Vancouver Police, and I'm a nurse at St. Paul's Hospital."

"That's wonderful!" said Annaliese. "We certainly need more good nurses and police officers. Here's a little gift to welcome you to our building," as she handed them the chocolate chip cookies.

"Why don't we take a break?" Greg inquired of Nicole, rust coloured eyebrows raised as he spoke. Looking at the cookies he continued, "These smell too good to pass up right now. How about I make us all coffee? I even know where it is!" They all laughed because the apartment was still such a shambles. But apparently the coffee maker and coffee were already where they belonged. Priorities!

So they had all found a seat somewhere in the living room– Nicole on the floor, Greg on the couch beside a mountain of clothes for their closet, and their new friend on the easy chair. "Mmmm, these are fantastic!" exclaimed Nicole, as she quickly caught a chocolate chip that was threatening to fall off the edge of her cookie. They ate in comfortable silence for a few minutes.

Annaliese spoke as she put her coffee mug down, "I've been praying for the new owners of this apartment ever since I learned someone would be moving in. Tell me, do you young people know Jesus Christ?"

Greg's eyes softened as he answered her. "Yes, Annaliese, Nicole and I are both Christians. We'll have to find a good church here soon. Where do you go to church?"

Annaliese, delighted with the news, began telling them about her church which just happened to be only three blocks away. "But there are other good churches in town. The important thing is for you to go where God is telling you to go. You could try each one out and then make your decision, if you like." This seemed reasonable to Greg and Nicole.

"I should go so you folks can keep working, but first let me quickly pray for you." Closing her eyes, she began praying out loud. "Heavenly Father, I praise You and thank You for bringing me these new neighbours. Guide them now by Your Spirit as they continue with this job of moving. But I also pray, Lord, that Your Spirit would direct them to the church family You have prepared for them. Thank You for new friends who love You, in Jesus' name, amen."

She stood and smiled at them both. "We'll be seeing each other again soon." And before they could respond, she had let herself out the door.

Greg and Nicole had gone to several churches and they had had good intentions, but their jobs had intruded into their desire to be part of a church family. Shift work for both of them just didn't seem to work too well with that. Eventually they had just given up; on the odd occasion they were both home on Sundays, they chose to go together to one of the churches they had visited but they had never joined, always thinking there would be a better time later. As it had turned out, their church attendance had been very sporadic in the past two years.

Returning to the moment at hand, Nicole realized Annaliese had just asked her a question. "How have you really been lately, dear?"

"Oh, I'm fine," Nicole responded without thinking, not wanting to burden Annaliese with the physical problems she'd been struggling with.

Annaliese tilted her head ever so slightly, gazing at Nicole with her clear blue eyes. "You look thinner. Are you sure you're okay?" The kindness reaching out to Nicole broke her defences. Looking down at her hands in her lap, Nicole began to speak. "I...I'm still having problems physically. I didn't know grief could cause such turmoil in the human body."

"What kind of problems do you mean?"

"Well, I'm not able to eat much. And every now and then I throw up." Nicole stopped and picked up Shadow, who had hopped onto the coffee table. She absently stroked his head and under his chin. He in turn lifted his head back so she could better caress him. His purring was a balm to her frayed nerves.

"Is there a pattern to your throwing up? Have you noticed any special time of the day when it's worse?"

Nicole thought for a few minutes, then said, "Well, first thing in the morning is not good. But as the day wears on and there's a bit of food in my stomach, it's not as bad." Stroking Shadow she looked up and the pain was etched in her eyes. "Emotional upheaval can do strange things to the human body. I've actually been wondering if I should go see a doctor."

"Hmm," said Annaliese. "It's certainly true that grief can throw your body out of kilter." They sat in companionable silence for a few minutes, each lost in her own thoughts and staring at the fire.

Changing position to better face Nicole, Annaliese cleared her throat. "How's your relationship with the Lord these days, Nicole?"

Nicole looked down at Shadow so her eyes wouldn't meet Annaliese's clear innocent ones. "I wish I could say it's just fine, but to be honest with you, I find myself not wanting to talk to Him these days. I mean, if God is supposed to be love and all that stuff, why did He let Greg die?" She angrily wiped at a tear running down her face. "It wouldn't have taken much for Him to have Greg be somewhere else, even a few feet ahead, when that drunk driver lost control!" She swallowed a sob and turned away from Annaliese's compassionate eyes. "I hate Him for that!"

Sneaking a peek at Annaliese's face, Nicole was surprised to find no anger or judgment there, but love and compassion. She was such a good Christian; how come she wasn't trying to defend God after an outburst like that?

"I understand where you're coming from, Nicole. It's sometimes very difficult to comprehend why certain things happen. But even if you don't feel it right now, God does love you. Do you believe that?"

Nicole was silent as she considered the question. "I grew up in a Christian home. That was a lifestyle for us as a family because that's who we were: good church people and law-abiding citizens. But around the time I met Greg I was ready to break out of that. Oh, I don't mean turn my back on God, but I wanted more freedom. And now? Well, I don't find Him to be the loving God the Bible talks about."

Annaliese was nodding her head, letting Nicole know that she understood. "Maybe going to church just wasn't enough for you."

Nicole turned sharply to her, "That's exactly what I mean! Who needs all those rules and regulations anyhow?"

"That's not quite what I meant, Nicole. It's not ever enough for children to think they can ride on the faith of their parents and for it to bring faith to their own hearts. It's a life-changing relationship with Jesus that brings the difference."

Nicole was uncomfortable with the topic, but Annaliese's non-judgmental way of speaking with her was a consolation, even if the subject-matter was somewhat frustrating. Where did all this "God-talk" take you anyhow? At the end of the day it didn't help you deal with grief any better.

"One thing I do know," continued Annaliese. "God knows what it feels like to have a loved one die. His own Son was in that very position at one time, and it wasn't an accident that brought Him there, but the sin of the world. You can go to Him with your anger, your fears and frustration. Be honest with Him. As you release it all, He will guide you into the peace that passes all understanding...that peace that stays even in the most devastating circumstances. It's only His peace and comfort that can help us in times like that."

She stood up and smiled at Nicole. "I'll be praying for you, honey. Know that you are very much on my heart every day." She bent down to give Nicole a hug. "Call me anytime if you need to talk." And with that, she turned and let herself out the door.

Nicole felt curiously deflated. She sat there, stroking her cat, looking at the fire and lost in her thoughts.

Chapter 4

Ellen, Stan and Matthew were chatting in the kitchen as the last preparations for dinner were being made. Stan was making a salad and Ellen was cutting the garlic bread. Matthew was leaning against the counter, watching their progress from his vantage point.

"It's such an awesome class and everybody loves this teacher. I'm pretty excited I made it in because it sure didn't look like I'd get in for a while! But I guess somebody decided to opt out of the class after all, and 'ta-daa' – yours truly got a shoe-in!" Matthew stuffed a raw carrot into his mouth and chomped happily. At twenty years old, he was quickly becoming the tallest of the Graham men.

"That's terrific, son!" Ellen gave him a hug and smiled up fondly at her youngest. "God answered our prayers, didn't He?" You wanted to get in, so we asked Him to work it out for you."

Matthew agreed, "He sure did, mom. I don't think I would have gotten in otherwise."

"That's great," Ellen said as she took the lasagne out of the oven. "Could you please set the table? We're nearly ready to eat."

Matthew set out the dinner plates and cutlery while Stan put the salad on the table. They all loved eating in the large dining room when the whole family came home for a meal. But for now it was much cosier eating at the smaller kitchen nook.

As Ellen placed the hot dish on the table, Matthew leaned in and sniffed appreciatively. "Mmmm, this smells so good!"

Just as they were about to sit, they heard the doorbell. Stan was on his way to answer it when the front door opened and Nicole popped her head in. "Yoo-hoo, anybody home?" she sang out.

"Nicole!" They all rushed over as she closed the door behind her. Ellen got to her first and enveloped her in a warm hug. "What a delightful surprise! Can you stay for dinner?"

Stan was next. "Honey," he said, "I've missed you!"

Matthew hugged her last and pulled her, laughing, into the kitchen. Nicole loved their eagerness in seeing her. "As a matter of fact, I can and I'm starved!"

"Super!" Matthew said as he quickly re-arranged the dinner table to add another place setting.

Ellen beamed at her loved ones. "In that case, let's not waste another minute. We can talk while we eat."

They all held hands as Stan prayed the blessing over the food. *"And thank You Lord for this unexpected pleasure of seeing Nicole again,"* he ended. He squeezed her hand as everyone said, *"Amen."*

Nicole felt warmth fill her heart and knew it was good that she had decided to come for a visit. The deep freeze around her heart, which she had contributed to since Greg's death, was beginning to thaw.

The next few minutes were filled with dishes passing around and happy chatter as they ate their meal together.

"What time do you have to go back, Nicole?" Stan knew it was a long drive back to Vancouver from Abbotsford, so she probably wouldn't stay long.

"Well actually," began Nicole. "I'm off for three more days, so I brought an overnight bag and thought I might stay a couple days if that's okay." She looked at her parents, eyebrows raised in query.

"Oh what a treat! Of course you can stay," Ellen answered her. "Any time you want to come home is fine with us, right Stan?"

"Absolutely," he affirmed. "You've arrived at a good time because we're all off now for the weekend. This way we can spend time with you."

While the others were chatting away, Ellen watched Nicole. She looked like she had lost weight, and her complexion was pale. She wondered if anything was wrong. Nicole's healthy glow was gone; could it be she was still suffering from grief? Well, if she was going to be staying a couple days, the subject would eventually come up. This was the first time Nicole had come to stay overnight since Greg had died three months ago. Was there something else wrong, or did she just need to be loved for a while? No matter, she decided. Nicole was here now and they would enjoy her company.

"Thank you for the delicious dinner, Mom." Nicole sat back and sighed as she put down her knife and fork. "It's nice to get a good home-cooked meal for a change. I haven't been doing too much cooking lately, what with work and all."

"What have you been eating then?" Ellen was curious. Greg had loved Nicole's cooking, so Ellen knew she had it in her to cook a good meal. Being alone though might have curbed her desire to spend too much time in the kitchen.

"Oh, I've been grabbing a sandwich in the cafeteria when I'm working. And when I'm home it's just easier to open up a can of soup than cook a whole meal." Nicole stood and began gathering the dirty dishes. "I'll help clean up." There was a flurry of activity as they all got to work.

Matthew had been speaking to Stan about school and Nicole listened in while she was filling the dishwasher. "But seriously Dad, getting in is the best thing that could have happened to me. There's just something about it that's clicking with me. I'm into my third year of business education and still enjoy most of it."

Stan moved in closer and gave Matthew a loving pat on the back. "That's amazing, son. Do you remember how undecided you were to apply for this business program?"

"I sure do. And in the end I didn't really know if I'd like it or even do well. I knew I should go to school, but it could have been so many different things."

Stan looked thoughtful. "Do you remember the verse in the Bible that tells us not to lean on our own understanding but in all things to acknowledge God? I think it's in Proverbs 3."

Matthew reached over for his dad's Bible sitting on the window sill at the nook. He flipped over to Proverbs 3 and scrolled down. "Here it is in verse 5."

"Why don't you read it out loud, son?"

"Sure."

"Trust in the LORD with all your heart, and lean not on your own understanding; in all your ways acknowledge Him, and He shall direct your paths."

Matthew looked up, "Well, I definitely was in a position where I had no understanding when I was trying to decide what to do with my life, that's for sure! Do you think God directed my path?"

"Well, we're seeing the fruit of it now, aren't we?" Stan leaned over his shoulder to look at the Bible verse.

Ellen hung up the dishcloth and turned to them. "There's another verse that fits here too. It's in Psalm 37 somewhere around verse three.

Matthew flipped the pages back and found where she had directed. "Hey, listen to this!

"Trust in the LORD, and do good; dwell in the land, and feed on His faithfulness. Delight yourself also in the LORD, and He shall give you the desires of your heart. Commit your way to the LORD, trust also in Him, and He shall bring it to pass."

"That's a good one," said Stan. "At the beginning you weren't sure what to go into, but you prayed for direction. You kept your eyes on Him, allowing Him to work and direct you as to where to go. It's a tough decision when you're getting ready for university and have so many possibilities for career choices."

"Yeah," Matthew reminisced. "I remember being so tempted to worry about it all. But then around the same time Pastor Adam was preaching about putting your faith in God and not to allow worry to sidetrack you. Worrying just made me more confused, so what's the good of that?"

Nicole stood with her back to them, drying the last dishes. How could this scripture possibly apply to her? She thought she had put her trust in the Lord, and look what had happened to Greg!

"So," Matthew wondered aloud. "What exactly does it mean that He will give you the desires of your heart? It's not like I had a desire to go to business school or anything. I didn't have a clue!" He looked up with a quizzical look on his face.

"Well, that's the whole beauty of it, honey," Ellen said. "As you put your eyes on Him and refuse to give in to worry, He is able to place the desire in your heart and then He works it all out for your good! But He plants the desire there first – the desire that is in line with what He has for your life."

"Huh," Matthew said. "That's pretty cool. He worked it all out and I wasn't even aware of what He was doing!"

Nicole leaned back against the counter, arms folded across her chest in a defensive position. This kind of talk made her uncomfortable. It was one thing having Annaliese talk to her about the Lord, but when her family did, she just rebelled. Too much had happened in the past few months. Her heart felt hardened. She was so confused about God these days. For instance, how could Psalm 37 apply to both Matthew and her? Their lives were so different. His was just starting, and hers felt like it had ended! With Greg gone, she didn't really want to pursue God like she once had.

But she couldn't deny that the more they discussed God, the more she somehow felt drawn into it. She wanted to believe that God would be faithful like that in her own life, but He had already shown that she didn't deserve it. Isn't that what Greg's death was all about? At one time in her life she would have easily said that God was faithful. She could see it for other people now, but not for her own life. As she pondered that, sadness filled her soul. "It's just too hard," she muttered, not knowing she was speaking out loud.

All three stood still and looked at her with surprised expressions on their faces.

"What's too hard, Nicole?" asked Ellen.

With an embarrassed look on her face, Nicole started to turn away, then thought better of it. Why not tell them what she was thinking? "The Christian walk, it's too hard. I can't do it anymore."

Matthew had a quizzical expression on his face. "What is it about the Christian walk that you find so difficult, Nicole?"

She watched her brother for a heartbeat, then jumped in before changing her mind about telling them. "We have to be so perfect, and I'm not like that. God expects so much from us. I just find that I can't live with those expectations anymore, that's all."

Stan's eyes gazed at his daughter with compassion. "Nicole, nobody can do it. That's the whole reason that Jesus had to come to earth and die for us. No one is able to live the holy life that God wants from us. But when we come to Jesus, He takes over; He changes us from the inside out, so that our hearts and minds become more like His." Changing tactics, he asked, "Do you think I'm a perfect Christian?"

When Nicole didn't answer, he continued. "No, I'm not a perfect Christian. I make mistakes like everybody else, and there are times when I sin. But when I blow it, Jesus is there to remind me that He shed His blood for my forgiveness. It's the condition of the heart He's after, not whether or not you are able to be perfect."

Ellen spoke up. "If God wanted us to be the ones to do it, then people would be getting into heaven through their own works. But nobody is able to do that. There can be no pride in anybody's heart, for them to say they did something special to get into heaven. Jesus was the only One who could fulfill the Father's demands, and because of what He did, we can all rest in the fact that it is done. Nothing else we do can change that."

Nicole was standing with her back against the stove, her arms crossed in front of her chest. So she didn't have to be perfect! That was a consolation. But still, she'd heard enough for now. Time to stop all this God-talk. "Okay, well uh, thanks." Looking at her brother, she smiled and directed her next question at him. "Are you full time at school, Matthew?"

"Yes I am. I've been taking courses every summer in the hopes that by next year I'll be able to graduate earlier than planned."

As the conversation continued around her, Ellen thought about what Nicole had said. She had heard the gospel many times before. Where could these thoughts of doubt be coming from? Ellen was concerned about her daughter.

Nicole was still speaking. "Oh, wow. That's cool." She sauntered over to the living room and flopped on the couch. Stan sat beside her and the others joined them, now that the dishes were taken care of.

"So Nicole, do you have any plans or anything you would like to do while you're in Abbotsford for a few days?"

"I guess it would be nice to hook up with everybody in the family again. It's been months since I've been here. I'm sure I've missed a whole bunch of new things. Steve's kids are growing. I miss them all, especially Leila." She was the baby in the family.

"Hey, would you like it if we invited everybody here for dinner tomorrow night?" Ellen asked. "It's been a while since we had everybody around our dining room table! What do you think, Nicole? I don't mind putting on a nice dinner for you."

Nicole looked at Ellen with a smile on her wan face. "That would be super, mom. You'll have to let me know how I can help."

Matthew was slouching on an easy chair, long legs on the ottoman in front of him. Suddenly he jumped up. "Hey, I know what we could do now, Nicole! We could mosey on down and visit Julie in her coffee shop. That way we could get a few free cookies for dessert!"

They all laughed at his enthusiasm. Matthew always seemed to be hungry.

"Well, that's not a bad idea," answered Nicole. "I've never seen where she works. Is it far?"

"No, it's near the five corners in the middle of town. It should take us about five minutes to drive there."

"Okay, let's go, then!" Both Matthew and Nicole got up and said a quick goodbye to their parents, then went out the door to Matthew's truck. As he drove he brought her up to speed with all that had been happening in his life. He still didn't have a girlfriend, but enjoyed spending time with the other girls in their young people's group at church. It's just that there wasn't one special girl for him...yet.

Before they could get onto another topic, they had arrived at the coffee shop. It was bustling with activity inside with people lined up at the counter to buy Julie's famous cookies. "Hi Matthew," smiled Angela at the cash. "How've you been?"

"Just great," grinned Matthew. "Is Julie in?"

"Sure, I'll get her for you in a minute." She finished ringing up that sale and poked her head in the kitchen door. "Julie," she sang. "You're wanted in the front by a handsome young man!"

Nicole snuck a peek at Matthew's face and was amused to see him blushing. She hid a smile behind her hand as she looked past the counter where her sister would soon appear.

Julie came out the door several seconds later, wiping her hands on her apron. When she caught sight of Matthew she beamed. And then she saw Nicole standing beside him and let out a whoop of delight. "Nicole!" she cried as she rushed over to hug her. "When did you arrive in town?" She pulled away from her sister, holding her at arms' length, and took a good look at her. "Hmm, you've lost weight. Maybe we need to give you a few cookies to fatten you up a bit, huh? What do you think, Matthew?"

He answered her with a comical expression on his face and both thumbs up in approval. "I'll never say no to your cookies, you know that."

Julie went behind the counter and grabbed a bunch of cookies and put them on a plate. "I haven't had a break for a while, so I reckon it's time, now that I have this terrific company to sit with!" She led them to a booth near the kitchen door and they all sat down. Matthew began chomping on the cookies, his eyes closing in delight as he chewed. "Mmmm, so good!"

Julie and Nicole looked at him fondly. They didn't look much like him, nor did they look too much like each other except they had the same body build. Nicole's hair was honey-blond and she had brown eyes like her father. A few freckles were sprinkled across her nose to make her look younger than her twenty-four years. Julie, on the other hand, had long light brown hair swept up in a ponytail, and her eyes were blue-gray like her mother. Even though she was younger at twenty-two, she was a couple inches taller than Nicole's five foot four. Matthew's light brown hair was curly and would be downright unruly if he didn't keep it short. His grey eyes twinkled as he finished eating his cookies.

The three siblings had been very competitive growing up. Even so, there had always been an air of protectiveness about them, always watching out for one another. At six feet tall, Matthew enjoyed the fact that he now was taller than the girls and could pat them on the head like good little puppies. This, of course, was all in good fun.

"So what's new with you?" Julie directed her question to Nicole. "How long are you here for? Do you have some time off work? Can you stay for the weekend?"

Nicole laughed at Julie's excitement and barrage of questions. "I'm off work for a bit, so I'll be staying at Mom and Dad's for a couple days."

"That's wonderful!" Julie was delighted. "Maybe we can spend some time together before you go. How about if we meet together tomorrow morning for coffee? Would you like that?"

Nicole looked at Julie and smiled. "That would be great. How about we go to Starbucks on Sumas Way? Would it work out for about ten o'clock?"

Julie was already standing to go back to work. "That sounds perfect. I'll still be able to sleep in a bit after working this evening shift." She straightened her apron and said, "See you tomorrow at ten, then." With that settled, Julie turned and went back into the kitchen to bake more cookies.

Matthew and Nicole chatted a little longer, then gradually got up to leave. "That was the perfect end to our great dinner," Matthew opened the door for Nicole and she sauntered through.

"Still a gentleman, I see," she commented. Looping her arm into his, they walked back to his truck.

∞ ∞ ∞

The next morning Nicole woke up early out of habit. Looking at the clock, she saw that it was seven o'clock. Slumping back down she wished her body would not wake her up so early on her days off. Lying there quietly for a while, she gradually tuned in to the rhythmic sounds of machines working in the next room. Her parents had found themselves with an empty room when Steve got married, and turned it into a gym. Getting up and stretching, she decided to go look. Peeking into the room, she found both her parents working hard at keeping their bodies fit and healthy. They both saw her out of the corners of their eyes, and slowed their workout so they could talk.

"Good morning, Nicole. Did you sleep well?" Her mother was always concerned about her comfort.

"Actually I did. It was nice being in my old bed again. But I can't seem to sleep in anymore. I guess my body is used to getting up early and that doesn't change even if I'm off." Nicole perched on the weight bench and watched her parents as they finished their routine. Suddenly she felt the familiar bile rise in her throat and ran for the bathroom. Stan and Ellen looked at each other, eyebrows raised, and listened to Nicole vomit in the toilet. When she returned to them, looking pale and tired, concern was on both their faces. "What made you throw up, honey? Do you think you could have a flu bug?" Stan asked her. He pulled her into a hug and she stayed there for a few minutes, loving the warmth and comfort offered there.

"Well, it's been going on for a while now, so I don't think it's a bug. I was actually going to talk to you about it, dad. I can't figure it out. You know, after Greg died my body was kind of messed up. I know grief can do odd things to a person, but do you think it could be causing this incessant vomiting as well?"

"Hmm." Stan looked thoughtful. "How's your stomach right now?" he spoke, ignoring her question for the moment so he could be sure she was all right and wouldn't throw up again.

"Oh, now that I've puked it's okay, sort of. Maybe some dry crackers would help."

"Well, let's go to the kitchen and find you some." Ellen and Stan threw towels around their necks and they all walked into the kitchen where the coffee was brewing with the most delicious aroma.

Ellen opened the pantry door and found a box of crackers. "Here you go, honey. Would you like some coffee? It's just done."

She poured a cup each for Stan and herself, then settled herself at the nook.

Nicole sat and took a cracker out of the box. Munching on it, she said, "I think I'd better wait for the coffee. I'm sure these crackers will do the trick and in a little while I can have a cup. Thanks, Mom."

Sipping on his coffee, Stan questioned her. "So tell me about this vomiting, Nicole. Does it happen every day? And when exactly did it start? Do you have it all day?"

Looking thoughtful for a few minutes, Nicole answered him. "Well, it must have started about a month ago. I was never feeling all that great after the funeral anyhow, so I wasn't really surprised when this all started. I figured that grief had messed me up something fierce. Don't you think this kind of thing could happen dad? You're the doctor; what do you think?"

"Well for sure grief can do strange things to a person. Would you like to come over to the office with me today and I could give you a bit of a check-up? I wanted to go in there anyhow sometime to pick up some files."

"Huh. I was going to go to a doctor in Vancouver, but I guess it's easier just to see you today. After all, you were my doctor until I got married and moved away." she said with a smile.

"All right. How does around two o'clock sound to you?"

Nicole thought for a moment. "That's perfect, dad. I'm meeting with Julie for coffee this morning, and I was thinking of running over to Steve and Jennifer's for a bit after that. This way I can see everybody before they all come over for dinner. What time will that be at, mom?"

Ellen looked at her watch. "I called Steve and Julie last night and they agreed to six o'clock. So we'll eat shortly after they all arrive."

"Okay, that works out well for me too then. So I'll meet you at the office at two then dad?" she enquired as she got up from her seat. "I should go shower and get ready for my date with Julie."

"I'll be there," Stan confirmed. With a smile on her face, Nicole gave them each a kiss on the cheek and went back to her room to get her shower things. She was relieved that her father was not going to have a busy schedule today. It would certainly be easier for her if he was the one to check her out. And wouldn't it be nice to have some answers, Nicole thought.

In the meantime, Ellen and Stan were already on their second cup of coffee and discussing Nicole's health. "I'm concerned for her, Stan. She looks so pale. Will you do a few tests on her at the office? I know you can't say now what you think is wrong, but I have my suspicions."

"I know, Ellen. But for the moment, let's keep our suspicions to ourselves till I examine her for the answers, shall we?" He placed a hand on hers. She knew she could trust him to do the right thing, and he would be careful to get to the bottom of Nicole's physical problems in order to help her. They continued sipping in peaceful silence.

Chapter 5

"So, how goes your job these days?" Nicole asked Julie while sipping her tall caramel macchiato. They were sitting in Starbucks, watching the bustling Saturday traffic through the large windows.

"I do love it there," Julie didn't sound too convincing. "You know, it was such a blessing that Diana offered me a position as a baker at her coffee shop. Now I have a commercial kitchen in which to do all my experimentation! You know I love coming up with different recipes for cookies, and it's been really good for the coffee shop that I'm there."

"Why do I feel like there's a 'but' at the end of that sentence?"

"Yeah, well lately I've been feeling like I would like to venture out in a business of my own. I know all the clients love my cookies, and business has grown since I started working there. The problem is how to start."

"Do you know what kind of business you would like? I mean, do you want to open up a coffee shop too, or do you want to do something different like a bakery where you just sell pastries and cookies and stuff?" Nicole was intrigued by the possibilities.

"I think if there was coffee involved I would certainly attract more clients. But I wouldn't want to open up a business close to Diana's; it just would be wrong to steal her customers, don't you think?"

"Hmmm, I see your point. But don't forget you are a big draw for those customers. If you weren't constantly coming up with new cookies, many of those people wouldn't think twice about going somewhere else."

"True. Still, I want to be careful. In any case, I'm not anywhere near close to venturing out on my own. I'd need a whole lot more money to start up my own business, that's for sure!"

Nicole flipped her hair behind her ear and sat back against the chair, taking a sip of her drink. "While you're thinking it through, why don't you pick Matthew's brain? He's the one getting a business education, and I'm sure he could be a great help to you."

"Hey, that's not a bad idea." Julie took a sip of her caramel frappuccino, eyes looking distant as she considered her possibilities. The Graham girls did love their caramel!

"And maybe Mom and Dad could give you a loan to get you started," Nicole continued. "Do you have any idea where you would like to do this?"

"Well, I think I would like to stay in Abbotsford. I know a lot of people here, and it would be fun to continue in my home town. Do you think there might be a way to build up a clientele for myself while I'm still working at Diana's Coffee Shop?"

"What about making a web page? You could start selling your cookies online while you are building up your recipes and customers. Then when the time is right, you could incorporate your new business into the web page. Do you have any idea what you'd like to call it?"

Nicole knew if her sister found the right location, she could do quite well at something like this. She had proved that with the popularity of her cookies in the past year.

"I actually had thought I would like to name it 'Sweet Tooth'. I don't want to be limited to baking only cookies. What if I want to bake other things too? So it wouldn't do to have cookies in the name of the business."

"Hey, I like that name!" Nicole's enthusiasm brought a smile to Julie's face. "I bet Matthew could get you started on a web page; he's so good with computers! And if you want to have a coffee shop, you could maybe include Coffee somewhere in the name, something like Sweet Tooth Coffee Shop." She sipped her drink and leaned back into her seat. "Or not, whatever you want to do."

Julie leaned forward and crossed her arms on the table. "I'll ask him. I'm sure if he can't help me he can point me in the right direction to get this started. And if I get lots of orders, I'll still have the commercial kitchen at the coffee shop to bake them. I'll have to ask Diana if I could come in when I'm off to bake for my own business." Julie's eyes glowed. She was delighted at the possibility of starting her own business soon, even without having enough for a down payment just yet. It would be interesting to get started and see what happens!

Nicole looked at her watch; it was after twelve o'clock! "Well, I guess I should get going," Taking one last sip of her drink, she gathered up her purse and car keys. "I'd like to pop in and see Steve and Jennifer before I run over to see dad at the clinic."

"You're going to the clinic?" Julie was surprised at Nicole's news. Her father never worked on Saturdays. What was that about?

"I've not been well since Greg died. Lately it's been getting worse. I know that grief can do strange things to a person, so I'm thinking I just need my body jump-started back in the right direction. Maybe I need vitamins or something. Anyhow, dad is going to check me out and he'll decide what needs to be done." Nicole stood and together they walked slowly to the door.

"Dad will get to the bottom of your problems, I'm sure of that," Julie gave Nicole a sideways hug. "I don't like to see you not well. I knew there had to be something wrong...you've lost weight and don't look as healthy as you used to. Vitamins just might do the trick for you."

Standing at their cars, the girls continued chatting for a few more minutes, then they climbed into their vehicles and went their separate ways.

∞ ∞ ∞

Steve and Jennifer were doing yard work, while watching their energetic children play with the dog. Clearing away the dead brush from their bushes and trees, they filled wheelbarrow after wheelbarrow as they talked. Nicole had been delighted with their hugs and kisses as she appeared at their home that day, and sat nearby on a lawn chair while they worked.

"It's so great to see you again, Nicole", Steve said, looking her way. He grunted as he hauled a particularly heavy branch to the wheelbarrow.

Jennifer peeled off her garden gloves. "Well, I don't know about you folks, but I'm famished! How about I fire up the barbecue and we can have hot dogs outside?"

The older children stopped their playing and jumped on the spot. "Yeah! Let's have a picnic, mom!"

Jennifer smiled indulgently at her family. Looking back at Nicole, she said, "How about joining us, Nicole? It's been such a long time since we've seen you. Have you got time to stay for a bit?"

Jessie and Andrew gathered around her, grabbing her hands and attempting to pull her out of her chair. "I guess I do have the time. I just have to leave shortly before two, so we have a while yet."

"Yay!" While the older kids danced around Nicole, the dog, wanting to be part of the excitement, barked joyfully.

"Okay, who's going to help me get everything ready for our picnic?" Jennifer walked toward the house. She looked back at Nicole with a grin on her face. "Never a dull moment!" she said over her shoulder, as she helped Jessie and Andrew remove their shoes prior to walking into the house. "We'll be back soon!"

Nicole watched her brother continue his work for a few minutes. Then flopping into the chair beside her, he wiped the sweat off his brow. "Phew, gardening is harder than I thought!"

"Your yard is looking beautiful, Steve. You and Jennifer have done some great work here."

"We really like our yard. But I didn't know how much work it would require, every single year!" He went on to explain to Nicole all the plans they had, and how they were going to change their backyard. "We'll clear that area over there and put in a trampoline for the kids next year. We just have to wait for Leila to get a little older. But Andrew and Jessie will love it, even if Leila has to wait a bit to get on."

"How old is Leila now?" asked Nicole. She felt like the child had grown up in the months she had not seen her. She reached down to the baby walker and pulled Leila up onto her lap.

"She just turned nine months. She's a lot of fun." Steve smiled lovingly at his daughter perched on Nicole's knees.

They chatted for a while until Jennifer came out carrying a tray loaded with plates, cutlery, condiments, buns and hot dogs. Nicole handed Leila to Steve and ran over to help her; together they unloaded the tray on the table. Onto the barbecue the hot dogs went and pretty soon they were all practically drooling with the delicious aroma that filled the air.

Their lunch was a fun-filled one, with the children rambunctious and each wanting to tell Nicole stories of their own. Clearing away the dirty dishes some time later, Nicole thanked Steve and Jennifer for asking her to stay. "I guess I should come out for a visit more often. I've missed you guys, and I don't get to watch the kids grow if I'm not around."

"It would be good to see you more. Hey, I have an idea! Why don't you consider moving back to Abbotsford? We have a brand new hospital here now, and it's certainly nicer than the old MSA Hospital was. I'm sure they must be in need of nurses there."

"That's right! I had forgotten all about it. What's it called? Is it still MSA Hospital?"

"Actually, it's called Abbotsford Regional Hospital and Cancer Centre; ARHCC for short. Dad says some people call it the ARC. Funny, huh?" Steve looked amused. Leila was standing holding on to his legs. He reached down and picked her up, rubbing his nose in the warmth of her little neck as she squealed.

Nicole looked thoughtful for a few minutes. "I'll have to look and see what's available. I've been at St. Paul's now for a couple years. It sure would be nice to get out of the 12 hour shifts if I could though; they're so tiring these days! I wonder if AR... whatever it's called, has any 8 hour shifts at all..." she mused.

"We'd all love to see you come closer to home, Nicole. We've all missed you." Steve said warmly and leaned down to give her a hug. "Too bad we have someone in our suite. It's quite nice and would be big enough for you. If it became available would you be interested?"

Nicole looked at Steve with surprise. "I've never thought of it before, obviously, but now that I've had some independence, it wouldn't work for me to move back with Mom and Dad. I just might be interested in your suite. Keep me posted, will you? If Roseanne decides to move out, I'd love to know." Roseanne had been Steve and Jennifer's tenant for three years.

Nicole walked toward the door and blew kisses at the kids. "I must run. I'll see you all tonight, okay?" Getting in her car, she sat there thinking about her conversation with Steve before starting up the engine and driving away. Would she want to move back to Abbotsford after having been in Vancouver? There was always so much to do in the city! But...with Greg gone, it's not like she was busy. She went to work and on her days off found she mostly did laundry and housework – if she had the energy. She didn't really want to go out on the town anymore, so for that matter she might as well be closer to her family! It certainly was worth thinking about.

∞ ∞ ∞

"Before I examine you Nicole, why don't you give me a urine sample and I'll check it later?" Her father had been waiting for her in his clinic, when she appeared. "I'll wait for you in my office."

"Sure thing, dad." Taking the bottle with her, she went to the washroom at the end of the hall. It was strange being in the empty clinic. She had only really seen it bustling with activity and full of people. But her dad had cut back on his hours and so they weren't open on Saturdays anymore. That was better for him; after all, he *was* getting on in years!

Joining him in his office when she was done, Nicole suddenly felt nervous. Would they come to the bottom of her problems?

Putting her at ease with his easy banter and professional manner, her father took her blood pressure, then began checking her from head to toe. Asking questions all along the way, he proceeded through the examination in good time. When he was done, he excused himself to go check the urine sample Nicole had left in the little cubicle.

She sat in the chair and waited for him to return. She was reading the paper on the wall for the patients which had a cute drop of blood with a happy face in it when her father walked in; the humanized drop of blood was holding a big stop sign. Beneath the endearing picture was printed, 'Your cooperation in helping the doctor run on time is appreciated. Most appointments are only 10 minutes.'

"That's cute, dad," Nicole said, while pointing to the poster. "Is it helping you to stay more on time with your appointments?"

Stan looked over to the paper on the wall and smiled. "It's not only a reminder to the patients, but also for me. I was going way overtime on some visits. Now when I see that, I know I don't have too long before I have to move on to the next patient. Mind you, there are some who come in here and all they really need is someone to listen to them. I still find it hard in those cases because I don't want to turn them away or rush them." He sighed. "I guess it's typical of the 'trials' of a family physician."

Walking over to sit in the chair beside Nicole, he took her hand in his. "Nicole, I think I know what your problem is." Nicole looked at him with a query on her face.

"You're pregnant."

She gasped and pulled her hand out of his. "You're kidding, right dad? I can't be pregnant now, Greg's gone! My problems are all because of this grieving, aren't they?" Tears filled her eyes as she mulled over his news.

Stan pulled her into a hug and patted her on the back. "Grieving sure can do a number on your body, that's for sure. And there might still be some residual problems because of this. But I can confidently say that all the vomiting is because you are definitely pregnant. Think about it – the timing is right, isn't it?" He held her at arm's length and watched her face, which was filled with confusion.

"I...I guess the timing is about right. I never thought of it, that's all. I was sure it was grief." Then with emotion washing over her, Nicole cried out, "But I can't have a baby on my own, dad! This was supposed to be happening with Greg here, not me alone!" She clung to him and sobbed while he held her. She was so precious to him. He didn't like to see her hurt. He let her cry till she had no more tears. Giving her a hanky to blow her nose, Stan reassured her, "We'll all be here to help you, honey. Maybe now would be the time to start thinking about moving a little closer to home."

Sighing deeply and looking down at her hands, Nicole responded. "Steve was talking about that this morning. I'll give it some thought. Right now I'm still kind of in a daze. A baby! I'm going to be a mom...and a single one at that!" as another wave of tears came coursing down her face.

"You know, Nicole, this might just be a good reminder of Greg for you. And think about it: God is giving you one last gift from him!"

"But I'd rather have him!" she wailed. She still would have preferred Greg to be here to hear this news and to help her through it all. He would have been so happy to have a baby. But now everything was messed up. A huge sigh escaped her lips, pressing upon her in a heaviness she couldn't seem to climb out of.

Stan gave her some papers. "Take these to the lab and they'll draw some blood. I've requested all kinds of things in there, so if there are other problems, we'll get to the bottom of it. I also want you to start taking a prenatal vitamin. You can get them at any drug store; you'll need some folic acid too." Standing up he pulled her into his arms. "Don't worry, honey. It'll all work out. I've also included a request for an ultrasound in those papers so you can find out when you're due and if everything is okay."

Nicole looked discouraged. "I guess I just need some time to think about all this, dad." She gathered up her belongings and gave him a kiss. "Could you please not tell the family yet? I need more time to think before they all know. I mean...a baby?" She shook her head in discouragement.

Smiling at her gently, he agreed. "You'll be the one to tell them all. We'll all be together for dinner tonight, so you can do it then if you like. Or if you need more time, that's okay too."

"Thanks, dad. I think I'll go to Mill Lake for a while. I need to walk and think."

"You do that, honey. I'll see you later."

Chapter 6

Nicole had walked all around the lake, at first angry at God for the situation she found herself in. How long had it been since she had allowed herself to really think through Greg's death and how it affected her? She sat on the bench and watched the ducks for a while, lost in thought. Being home with her family again had stirred up something in her. Watching and listening as they spoke of the Lord so easily, at first she had been annoyed, but the more she heard, the more she found her anger slipping away and a longing take its place. She hadn't spoken with God for such a long time because she blamed Him for Greg's death. But she had missed the close relationship she had once had with Him.

She threw a pebble into the lake and watched it ripple out. The longer she stared at the ripples, the more she saw her own life in the picture.

When I am angry with someone, it is similar to the pebble that hits the water. The single action of the stone hitting the water causes an after-shock of sorts, and the ripples grow in ever increasing circles around the pebble. Anger does that to me. If I allow that initial moment of anger, if I don't check it and deal with it, it grows in my heart and brings other sin, like judgment, criticism, even fear. The answer is to not allow the stone to hit the water in the first place, or to deal with the anger before it brings destruction to my heart.

Nicole sat there on the bench, mesmerized as this truth sank into her heart. And before she knew it, she found herself talking to God, something she hadn't done in quite a while.

Are you there, Lord? She knew she couldn't expect a bolt of lightning or a sign that He really was listening to her. She had learned as a child that God is always there when she wants to speak with Him.

Why, Lord? Why did you have to take Greg away from me? It would have been so easy for You to just have him be somewhere else when that car came around the bend. Why Greg? Why not Clay? He's not even married! Just as quickly as the thought came, she felt guilty for thinking it. She saw for the first time that she was being unreasonable and selfish, wishing Clay had been the one taken. After all, why *not* Greg? There was pain and suffering all over the world; why should she be shielded from it? With the thought came a feeling of shame for her self-centeredness and selfishness.

Once again Nicole was engulfed in tears, and she was oblivious to the stares of the people nearby as she sobbed into her dad's handkerchief. Eventually her tears eased. As her eyes lifted to snow-covered Mount Baker in the distance, she was suddenly reminded of something she had heard at one time: God is the author of life, and Satan is the author of death and evil.

I haven't spoken with you in a long time, Lord. Is it possible that You are not the one responsible for Greg's death?

Her breath caught as she pondered this thought. But that would mean that Satan was responsible, and she wasn't sure what to make of that. Did she really believe Satan was busy in this world, bringing evil wherever he could? Hmm, she would have to think about that more.

I've blamed You for Greg's death, Lord. I've been angry with You. I'm sorry for that anger; that was wrong. I am just so lonely! I miss Greg so much! And I miss you, Lord Jesus. I haven't spent time with you in so long...I'm sorry! Could You fill that emptiness in me? I don't know how to deal with it. I know I need You; I've just been so caught up in the sadness of all this, that I didn't come to You. But I need You now more than ever!

No sooner had she directed this to the Lord than she felt a curious weighty warmth spread on her right shoulder, like someone had put a comforting hand on her. She was so surprised she looked around to see if there was someone standing behind her. No one. Huh. Just a gentle breeze. Was that the Lord who had just touched her? Or an angel? Peace flooded her soul for the first time since Greg had died. Surprisingly, it didn't matter what had just happened or Who was responsible. She had felt His presence. Suddenly she knew beyond a shadow of a doubt that He understood what she was going through. He knew what she was facing and He cared! Covering her face with her hands, she let the tears fall once again. This time they were not so much tears of grief, but tears of gratitude. It was curious how she felt lighter inside somehow, but it felt so good. She had so missed being close to God. She had been wrong to cut Him out of her life in her grief. The first place she should have gone was to Him, but how to do that when she blamed Him for what had happened?

Peace filled her soul.

Nicole sat on the bench near the water's edge and considered what was happening to her. Her eyes followed the antics of the ducks. They looked so funny when they were looking for food: their rear ends wiggling in the air when their heads went underneath the water, fishing for something to eat. As she watched them, she pondered the strange things which were happening to her today.

Unexpectedly she thought of ostriches sticking their heads in the sand. She had been doing the same thing where her relationship with God was concerned: she hadn't wanted to move ahead but was stuck in the anger and pain, and so she refused to hear Him. She preferred to say that the Christian walk was too difficult, but she had known that this was not true when Jesus is the One guiding you, changing you. She figured she had just been using this as an excuse for her anger all these months.

Father, I'm sorry that I was so angry with you about Greg's death. Why shouldn't this happen to me? I certainly am no different than anybody else in the world. I think I've had the wrong attitude in this. I'm just really scared for what's ahead; will You be with me through it all?

As she spoke with the Lord, she found herself pouring out her heart to Him. But just as sure as she knew He was listening, an assurance flooded her soul. He would guide her through.

Nicole sat there for some time, caught up in her conversation with God. It was amazing how easily she fell back in to praying. She had pushed it away for so long. Now was the time to at least let Him know how she felt. She had so much to talk to Him about! Finally, she roused herself and walked back to her car. But this time there was a new lightness to her step. She didn't feel like she had the weight of the world on her shoulders anymore. Sure, life wouldn't be easy, but she felt cautiously optimistic now. She had a lot of decisions to make in the next little while.

∞ ∞ ∞

Walking into her parents' house, Nicole was enveloped with the wonderful smell of roast beef cooking. Mmmmm, how she loved her mother's cooking! Throwing her purse onto the side table near the door, she walked into the kitchen and found her mother peeling potatoes. Picking up an extra peeler, she began helping her.

"So how was your day, Nicole? Who did you see?" Ellen had covered her jeans and pink, long-sleeved t-shirt with a colourful apron. Every now and then she looked up at Nicole as they worked together side by side.

"I saw everybody, well, all except Matthew. I had coffee with Julie and lunch with Steve and Jennifer. Their kids are so cute! I love their ages; each one is such a treat." Nicole told her mother about a funny incident that had happened at Steve's regarding the dog and the two older children, Andrew and Jessie. Together they laughed at the amusing antics children can get up to. Putting the last potatoes in the pot and placing them on the stove, Nicole's face became sober. "I have something to tell you, mom."

Ellen wasn't sure what to make of Nicole's strained look. "What is it, dear?" She pulled Nicole to the table where they both sat down while supper continued cooking.

"Dad found out why I've been throwing up so much. I'm pregnant!" Nicole's eyes filled again. Would she never stop crying?

Ellen sucked in a breath. Her face glowed with pleasure and she clapped her hands in delight. "Oh my dear! I am so happy for..." she came to a stumbling halt. Nicole was not jumping for joy. She thought of Greg and how difficult this must be for Nicole, seeing they had wanted to have children together. "Oh honey!" She reached out and pulled her into a long hug. They swayed together for several minutes, their tears mingling as they pondered the situation.

Finally Nicole pulled away and took a shuddering breath. "It's just so hard not having Greg here. He would have been so happy to hear this news!" Nicole broke down as she spoke about her deceased husband. "I'm not sure how I feel about being a single parent; this is not what I had thought I'd do! There are so many things I have to think about." She wiped her tears with a tissue and blew her nose.

Understanding the situation her daughter was in all too well, Ellen took her hand to comfort her. "It's never easy being a parent, and being a single parent certainly has its challenges, that's for sure. But a new baby is always a reason to celebrate. As for the rest, I believe God is faithful and He won't let you down. He'll guide you through every situation that comes up. You don't have to have all the answers right now."

"How is His faithfulness shown to us through things like this?" Nicole knew what she had learned in the past about God and His faithfulness to His people, yet she couldn't think of how this would all work out. As the conversation continued, Nicole told her mother about what had happened to her at the lake. "I wouldn't have thought too much about that if it hadn't been that peace flooded me like a warm, comforting blanket. It might just have been the wind or something, except I know something happened to me inside because of it."

Here was the answer to Ellen's prayers. With shining eyes, she told Nicole she believed every word. Somehow God had revealed Himself to her and brought her back into a relationship with Himself, even if ever so fragile. "You know, as far as the pregnancy is concerned, He is able to meet all your needs, even after the baby comes. It's because of God's great love for you that He led you to a place where you could tell Him your attitude had been wrong. That's repentance! By the way, that's found in Romans chapter 2. *"The goodness of God leads you to repentance."* He loves you very much and wants what's best for you. Do you believe that?"

Nicole's head was tilted sideways, gazing at her mother with a thoughtful look on her face. "I'm not sure. I just never really thought too much before about it, you know, because of what happened to Greg. How could that be His goodness?" Her lower lip began to tremble as the emotion flooded her again. With an obvious effort she reined it in.

"Well, for sure these trials come in our lives, but God is always there to guide us through them if we want Him to. Let me show you something." Ellen reached over for her husband's Bible sitting on the window sill of the nook. She flipped to the book of Deuteronomy and found the place she was looking for. "Here in chapter 28 it says,

"Now it shall come to pass, if you diligently obey the voice of the Lord your God, to observe carefully all His commandments which I command you today, that the Lord your God will set you high above all nations of the earth. And all these blessings shall come upon you and overtake you, because you obey the voice of the Lord your God."

"But Mom, that was written to the children of Israel. We don't have to follow all those commands today because Jesus came to set us free from all that!"

"Well, He did, but He didn't. Let me explain. God gave us the Bible for a reason. He knew that man's fallen nature would eventually bring him to a place where he would have to choose from right and wrong. It happens every day! We no longer have to worship Him in a temple and we don't make animal sacrifices. But Jesus didn't abolish the Ten Commandments. He meant for us to continue following them. But obeying the Ten Commandments can't save us; they were meant to show us how we should live, but in our own strength that's impossible. Only as we guard our hearts and minds in these things can we come to God with a clear conscience. And you know, even with that, we all fail."

Ellen looked down at her hands. "God is very gracious to us. When we come to Him and repent, He is so quick to forgive!" She looked up and smiled at Nicole. "But the important thing I wanted to show you in this is that if we set our hearts toward God, His blessings will overtake us! You won't have to ask for His blessings; they will automatically come and rain down upon you as you seek to do His will, as you set your heart and mind on His Word."

"Wow, I never knew that before." Nicole continued to read quietly.

Ellen spoke passionately as this subject was so dear to her heart. "Today you made a start by talking to God and repenting for your attitude. As you continue to walk with Him, you will find that you no longer feel alone. He will work out the details of your life for you in ways you never could imagine."

"I'll certainly give this some more thought, Mom. Thanks for praying for me. I know you have been, but up until now I wasn't sure if that was a good thing!" She smiled shyly at her mother and reached over to give her a hug as the doorbell rang and the door opened with much chatter. "Oh and mom," Nicole said urgently but quietly, "nobody else knows about the pregnancy. Please don't say anything!"

"I'll let you tell them in your own way."

Ellen stood up to greet her enthusiastic grandchildren as they ran up to give her a hug. Andrew, Steve and Jennifer's middle child, was four years old and cute as a button with his freckled nose and blond hair and big brown eyes. As he bounced into the room, Nicole and Ellen laughed and ruffled his hair. Jessie, the oldest and wisest at six, grinned to show them her missing front teeth. She was carrying flowers from their garden and offered them to Ellen. Ellen crouched down to Jessie's level and gave her a hug, thanking her for the beautiful flowers. Right behind them came Steve carrying a diaper bag and baby Leila, already getting bigger at nine months. Jennifer was carrying the baby's assorted paraphernalia as she came up the rear. "Hi, Mom!"

The next few minutes were taken up with the chatter and excitement of the children as they regaled their grandmother and aunt with stories of their recent adventures.

Julie and Matthew walked in to the pleasant confusion of voices, and off Andrew ran to find grandpa in his study. "Papa, come into the kitchen! We're all here!" exclaimed Andrew when he found Stan working on the computer on his desk. Stan reached down and picked Andrew up to give him a hug, and they walked hand in hand into the kitchen to join the rest of the family. The noise eventually came down to a more acceptable level as the last touches were made to dinner.

Andrew reached up to Stan and whispered in his ear, "Papa, can I ring the chimes?" Ellen had a beautiful set of chimes in the kitchen, and Andrew had discovered they made a melodious sound. They had become their way to call everybody to dinner when the whole family was there, a tradition of sorts.

"Okay everybody, let's all sit down! Dinner's ready!" called out Ellen when the chimes were still tinkling. The children were all seated with their parents, and the other family members completed the oval of the dining room table. They all held hands as Stan prayed the blessing over the food. Everybody laughed as Andrew put his arms up as though cheering at the end and loudly proclaimed, "Amen!"

The familiar bustle of dishes passing around created a comfortable atmosphere as the aroma of roast beef filled their senses. The conversation hopped back and forth as one person, then another, spoke. "Dad, lots of 'tatoes; I love 'tatoes with gravy!" Andrew encouraged Steve as he placed food items on Andrew's plate. The sound of cutlery touching the bone china plates was interspersed with the conversation. Eventually they all sat back and one after another pronounced they were full. It had been a satisfying meal.

Ellen stood up to make coffee. Speaking over her shoulder, she said, "I hope you're not all too full for dessert. I made strawberry rhubarb pie; shall we have it with ice cream?"

A collective groan went up around the table; none of them had left much room. Matthew, however, never one to turn down dessert, answered her, "I'll have a double portion and with ice cream, if there's enough Mom. I love your strawberry rhubarb pie!"

"Oh, I guess you have to fill that other hollow leg now, do you?" asked Julie teasingly. She was very familiar with Matthew's love of sweets. He was often available to test-taste her latest concoction whenever a new cookie idea came to her. Matthew grinned back at her. "Never too full for dessert! Hey Julie, maybe that could be the next cookie you create: strawberry rhubarb! What do you think of that?" Matthew enthusiastically ate his dessert.

"Not a bad idea. I'll have to give it some thought," Julie answered.

When dessert and coffee was nearly finished, Nicole suddenly grew quiet. Would this be a good time to tell them? As the conversation continued all around her, she was very grateful for the family she had.

She cleared her throat and spoke up, "Um, I think this is a good time to make an announcement." Everybody stopped talking and they all looked at Nicole expectantly. Hesitating for a fraction of a minute, she looked at each one before going on. "It turns out I'm pregnant."

Jaws dropped in surprise and confusion. Suddenly the room erupted with happy shouts and congratulations. Julie jumped up and gave Nicole a hug. Jennifer and Steve gave each other a look that spoke volumes about their delight in being parents. Nicole received hugs and pats on the back. Matthew, the clown, stood up and danced with his hands in his armpits, flapping them back and forth and pretending he was a chicken. He crowed, "I'm going to be an uncle again, yeehaw!" They all laughed joyously.

At the same moment their smiles turned to grief as they thought of Greg; he would not be around for the pregnancy, birth and beyond. A hush came over the group as they struggled with their emotions.

Nicole was the one to bring up the subject. "You know, the only thing I regret in this is that Greg is not around. He wanted so much to be a daddy!" Two rivers of tears coursed down her cheeks. "I'm not quite sure how this is all going to pan out, I mean, I just found out today and it's all a bit of a shock. It certainly is a relief though to know why I've been throwing up so much!" Stan, who was sitting beside Nicole, put his arm comfortingly around her shoulders.

"How far along are you?" asked Julie.

"I figure I'm a little over three months now. I must have gotten pregnant a little while before Greg...." She stopped speaking and looked down at her hands. Taking a shaky breath and looking up, she continued. "Hopefully the throwing up will stop soon."

"Wow," said Steve. "I imagine you have a lot to think about now. Being a parent isn't easy, and being a single parent will be even more of a challenge. But the joys you get as a parent far outweigh the challenges and difficulties." He looked fondly at his children sitting around the table. "And we'll do everything we can to help Aunt Nicole when she has her baby, right kids?"

"Maybe I can help by babysitting sometime!" enthused Jessie. She loved playing with dolls and helped Jennifer quite a bit with Leila.

Nicole smiled at her, "Of course you'll help with the baby." She looked soberly at the others. "I'll need every one of you to support me through this. I can't do it alone!"

They all agreed they would be there for her and she could call anytime she needed help. But they all knew the help would be a little more difficult if she was still living in Vancouver.

Apparently Ellen was thinking along the same lines. "Nicole, if you want you can move back home with the baby. Maybe we could make a suite for you in the basement or something."

Nicole looked at her mother. How generous of her to offer this! "Thanks Mom. I'll give it some thought."

As she gazed at each one, she came to the conclusion that it wasn't all that important to be living in Vancouver after all. It would be better to move closer to home, wouldn't it? But where would she live? Should she move back home with her parents? And where would she work? Or would she work at all?

Chapter 7

Nicole was back at work. She had spent a lovely few days visiting with her family. That had been a welcome break. But more than that, she had received answers to some of the things that had been puzzling her recently. Her health, for one thing. Even though now she continued to feel nauseated and still vomited each day, she saw it differently. Now there was a purpose for all the suffering, so somehow it was more bearable.

The other thing that had happened was that she began to see Greg's death differently. She was no longer blaming God, thinking He had had a hand in this. She knew she had not been faithful in her relationship with Him lately, but she had felt His touch, so now there was a measure of peace where there had previously only been anger and despair. She had begun reading her Bible once again. Oh, she wasn't spending a lot of time with that, but she was reading a few chapters at least every other day. It was a start.

"I'm heading down for my break now, Chloe!" she called out to her partner and waved. Today she really needed a cup of coffee. Usually she made do with the cup she had at home before going to work, but it had been a tough morning and she knew she needed a pick-me-up. With the money jingling in her pocket, Nicole ran down the stairs to the cafeteria. She bought her coffee and walked to the library so she could do some research on the hospital computer, sipping as she went. Logging on to the hospital internet, she looked up the jobs available for registered nurses throughout the Fraser Valley. She was curious to see if there were any available at the Abbotsford hospital. She would prefer to get a job before making plans to move.

And moving did appear to be a good plan, didn't it? She sat back in her chair, sipping her coffee, lost in thought. Her family had been wonderful this weekend. They had doted on her and loved her in such a way that had begun to thaw the frozen wall she had built up around her heart after Greg's death. But would they still be like that if she was close by and they saw her all the time? She wondered if their love would stand the test of closeness. After all, she had been the one to leave. And they all knew that she had also been easing up on her walk with the Lord. Some of them had spoken to her about it through the years, but she hadn't wanted to listen. She was happy with Greg, and their life was their own. She hadn't wanted to talk about 'religious' things. She had plenty of time for that sort of thing.

As she searched for any available jobs at the Abbotsford Hospital, part of her was still not sure if that's what she should do. After all, if she moved, she'd lose the memories of their first couple of years together as husband and wife. There were so many happy pictures in her mind of days gone by at their apartment, their favourite coffee shop, their favourite restaurant. She still hadn't been able to sort through Greg's clothes. His well-used running shoes in their closet reminded her of days he would go for a run after work. His shaver on the bathroom counter reminded her of his auburn whiskers. There were even some of his red hairs still on his hair brush. How could she remove these items and lose all the precious memories?

But the touch she had received on her shoulder this past weekend had warmed her heart and given her hope. Once again she began to include Jesus in her everyday life, remembering that touch, and believing He loved her. Wasn't it strange how things changed? Her relationship with Him right now was kind of tentative; would she be tempted to walk away from Him again?

And what would she do about this pregnancy? Certainly she would go for the scan her father had arranged for her. She had asked that it not be at St. Paul's, but elsewhere. She just knew so many people at her hospital, and she was feeling insecure about them knowing. She felt they would all pity her...the one with the dead husband! So she wouldn't tell anybody until she absolutely had to.

She wondered if Chloe would guess. She was a pretty smart cookie. She, out of all the people who worked on her floor, would see the changes happening in Nicole. No matter. She wouldn't be showing for some time anyhow. She would deal with that when the time came.

Nicole logged off with a sigh, partly relieved that nothing interesting was available. Oh, they needed more registered nurses in full time lines at ARHCC on the surgical ward, but she was hoping to get out of 12 hour shifts. With the pregnancy and all, she found herself getting too tired when working a stretch of four days. The days off were nice, but by the end of two days on, two nights on rotation she could barely think straight. She took a last swallow of her coffee and threw away the cup. She sighed; time to go back to work.

At the end of the day she stopped by the grocery store to pick up a few essentials before heading home. Arriving at her door, she dumped the grocery bags on the floor so she could get the key out of her pocket. Just as she was opening the door, her neighbour Annaliese came out of hers. "Nicole! How lovely to see you! Did you just finish work?"

Nicole deposited the bags inside her door, then turned to Annaliese with a smile. "Yes, it's been a long day."

"Well, you do look tired, so I'll let you go. But would you be interested in getting together for coffee on your days off? I'd be happy to provide coffee and treats." Annaliese was looking enquiringly at Nicole, poised at the door to go down the stairs, waiting for an answer.

"Well now, how could I refuse? I work days tomorrow, then two nights. After that I'll be off. How about I give you a call when I'm off and we can arrange it?"

"Suits me well. Bless you dear. Have a wonderful sleep tonight." With that she opened the door to the stairs and walked down to the ground floor.

Nicole was so grateful to have Annaliese nearby. She had certainly been a big help whenever Nicole had gone to visit her family; she had come in daily to feed Shadow and change the litter whenever needed. Moving to Abbotsford would be even harder than Nicole had imagined. She would miss Annaliese's friendship as well as her memories of Greg!

The next day she found the nausea wasn't there when she woke up, and she didn't even throw up! Glory be! Maybe she was turning the corner on this incessant vomiting! Nicole was encouraged by the happy thought and went to work with a new lightness in her step. Chloe noticed right away that Nicole was a little happier. Looking at her curiously, she contemplated what that might mean. Nicole had been looking so wan lately. Was it only grief, or was there something else disturbing her? She'd wait for the right moment to ask her about it. After all, they had developed a good friendship working together, and she wanted to be there to help Nicole if she needed it. Even if she just wanted someone to listen to her.

Later that afternoon when they were both sitting down doing their charting, Chloe looked tentatively at Nicole. "Say, Nic?"

Looking up, Nicole met Chloe's eyes with a question in hers. "What's up?"

"Well, I've been watching you lately. Have you been unwell?" She tilted her head to the side, looking at Nicole. "Today you look a little better though."

Nicole hesitated for a few minutes as she looked at Chloe. Should she tell her? "It's been a difficult few months, you know, since Greg died."

Chloe's eyes filled with compassion. Softly she replied, "Yes, I can imagine."

The concern in Chloe's eyes encouraged Nicole. She threw her pen down on the chart she was working on and sat back. Crossing her arms in front of her, she decided to tell Chloe. "There's more though. I've been really sick for a while and I thought it was grief playing with my body."

Chloe's eyebrows rose in surprise. "I didn't know, you never said. But I should have guessed because you have lost weight. Did you find out what's wrong?"

"Well, I did. It just so happens I'm pregnant."

Chloe gasped. But of course! The timing was right, wasn't it? "Wow! Are you okay with that? I mean, are you okay that Greg isn't around anymore to help you with this?"

"Of course I would much prefer to have him here. But if I have to go through this alone, so be it."

"Really? You mean you're planning on going through with the pregnancy?" Chloe had a look of disbelief on her face.

Startled with what Chloe had just insinuated, Nicole felt the small amount of joy she had quickly dissipating. "What are you implying?" she asked. "Are you saying I would be better off having an abortion?" she asked incredulously. Nicole's back went rigid with anger.

"Well, I don't know," Chloe stammered. "I love my kids and you know I would never do anything to change my situation with them. But to go through this alone? I don't think I could do it. In this day and age you don't have to. You can just get rid of it. One day you'll meet someone else and at that point you might want to have a baby with him, but are you sure you want to do it alone?"

Nicole didn't believe she was hearing this. She had thought Chloe was such a good friend! She never thought she would be the one to counsel her to have an abortion. "I don't believe what I'm hearing!" She had automatically thought that anybody who was so happy with her children would never condone abortion. She was seeing a different side of Chloe, to be sure! She turned back to her chart and picked up her pen. "There's something you need to know," she said to Chloe. "I believe that all life is sacred. I don't have the right to 'get rid' of my baby because it's not a convenient time for me." She took a shaky breath and continued. "I believe that God created this baby, and no matter how difficult a time it may be for me, He will be there to help me through it."

Chloe looked at her with pity. What a backward way to look at this when in this day and age there was so much freedom available for women! "Are you serious? I can appreciate that you might want to keep the baby, but how on earth is 'God' going to help you?"

Nicole looked up in surprise. "But I thought you believed in Him!"

"Well," began Chloe, "I think I do. But He doesn't come to earth and 'help' me with stuff. He's up in heaven."

"So you don't pray? You don't have a relationship with Him?"

Chloe laughed. "A relationship? How can you have a relationship with someone you can't see?" She looked at Nicole like she had lost her mind.

"When you reach out to Him and believe in Jesus, He is there. He somehow makes you know in your heart that He is listening and is there for you. Oh I know I haven't always been a keen follower, but this past weekend something happened to me to revive that relationship I once had with Him. And He gave me such a peace about it all."

Chloe looked doubtfully at her. This girl had lost it! "Uh, well, if you say so."

Nicole was sorely disappointed in Chloe. For her to suggest an abortion was something she had never considered. She might be in a difficult squeeze, but she would never kill this baby! Anger welled up inside her towards Chloe, and she found herself unable to continue. She felt this was not the best time to speak about these things. Maybe one day she would get the opportunity to tell her more, but right now she had to finish her work. As if on an unspoken cue, they both turned back to their charting.

The rest of the shift was uneventful. As she was driving home, Nicole remembered all that Chloe had said to her. How could she suggest such a thing? After all, hers wouldn't be the only single-parent household in the world! Somehow this would work. It's not like she was forced to continue working. Greg's life insurance with the Vancouver Police had left her with a substantial amount of money. She was working now just to keep her mind occupied and not to dwell on how her life had changed overnight.

Climbing into her Jeep, she decided she would go for a drive tonight instead of just going home. She felt really irritated at Chloe and needed time to think. She headed toward Stanley Park, the green jewel of Vancouver. She hadn't been here since Greg had died, but she still loved walking through this park which jutted out into the ocean from the edge of the busy West End where she worked. It was still early enough in the evening that it would continue to be light for a little while. Something about this public rainforest filled her with peace. Everywhere were towering western red cedars and Douglas fir, manicured lawns, flower gardens, calm lagoons and walking trails. Her favourite place was the sea wall, which ran along the waterside edge of the park. Every time she went, there were cyclists and pedestrians on the sea wall, enjoying the magnificent panorama of forest, sea and sky.

She parked her Jeep and paid for parking. She wouldn't stay too long, but she would allow herself to walk part way on the sea wall. She loved watching all the boats on the ocean. Sometimes she just sat on the rocks near the water and gazed at the activity.

As she rounded the bend, she found herself thinking of Chloe's suggestion again. Could she ever go for an abortion? The Women's Movement had certainly helped to make things easier for women if they didn't want a baby right now...or had it? She had heard that the women who aborted their unborn babies grieved that loss and thought of what the baby could be at every stage of their lives. So, from that perspective, this wasn't making it easier for women, was it?

So if she didn't agree with abortion, was there another option for her? How about adoption? Could she give her baby up for adoption? To give birth and then to never see the baby again? Nicole placed a protective hand over her abdomen as if to shield the baby from her thoughts. Her family said they would help, but they wouldn't be there 24/7. Would they be angry with her if she decided to give her baby up for adoption?

Nicole gazed out at the sailboats. She sat down on a nearby bench, lost in thought. How would Greg respond to this kind of thinking on her part? Would he support her in this if he was here?

What a stupid question! Nicole was annoyed with herself. If Greg was here, they would be having the baby together! These questions would never enter her head if he was here. *Oh Greg, why did you have to die! I don't want to be alone; I miss you so much!* Nicole angrily brushed away the tears that were falling.

Taking a deep breath and groaning with the agony in her heart, she pushed away the grief and resumed her train of thought. So now that Greg was gone, should she consider anything other than having the baby and taking care of it herself? A deep sigh escaped her troubled soul. Nicole blew the hair out of her face and released the elastic she had trapped in her ponytail. Shaking her honey-coloured mane out, she once again found herself talking to God.

What do You think of all this, God? I never really entertained the thought that I would have a choice to make regarding the pregnancy. Or do I?

Even as quickly as Nicole thought this, she was reminded of a verse in the Bible she had once read. It said something about children being a reward.

I guess I've known before that You see all life as precious. But what happens to the woman who has been raped? Is her baby precious too? I always thought abortion would be all right for someone who had been raped or something. I never thought of abortion being available to a woman whose husband had died and left her alone to take care of it. I feel so confused in all this. Show me how to walk through this, Lord.

As the sun was setting, Nicole once again thought of the pebble she had thrown into the water at Mill Lake. All at once she saw that her anger towards Chloe was like those waves. But could she forgive her for what she had said? As she thought of Chloe, sadness filled her heart. Poor Chloe didn't know that God wanted a relationship with her. No wonder she could think this way! Coming to this conclusion, Nicole forgave Chloe for her repulsive suggestion. *Lord, I'm sorry I was so angry. I don't want that to ruin what little joy I have right now. Chloe needs You. Remind me to pray for her and maybe one day tell her more about Your love for her.*

Nicole roused herself and walked back to her parked Jeep. She felt bone-tired. She was glad she could sleep in tomorrow. She would work her first night of two shifts tomorrow, then she'd be off. She could hardly wait.

∞ ∞ ∞

Walking in to work from the parking lot the next evening, she thought of how her body was changing. Her breasts were tender, and her belly felt more swollen than was normal for her even though she still fit in her clothes. The best part was that she had only thrown up once since Sunday, so already things were improving. Somehow, though, Chloe's suggestion had left her curiously devoid of joy. She had continued to think about it, but she still wasn't sure what to do. It was like every time she thought of the changes that would have to take place in her life, the suggestion of abortion came right on the heels of that. Surely at this stage the pregnancy wasn't just a piece of tissue, was it?

Putting her purse in her locker, she walked over to the kitchen to park her lunch in the fridge. The ward was quiet as the patients rested after their dinner. She would get report and then get started on her work. Sometimes night shift on surgical was not easy; some of the patients returning from surgery were a real handful, with many physical and medical problems to sort out.

She waved at Chloe when she saw her at the nursing station. Chloe didn't know Jesus personally, so Nicole was glad she had forgiven her for her suggestion yesterday. Still, how could any mother recommend the killing of an unborn baby?

During report, Nicole found out that one of her patients this evening was a young lady who had lost her baby to a miscarriage at twenty weeks. Nicole popped her head in the door to see if all was well; her patient was lying on the bed with her eyes closed. She wouldn't disturb her now, but would return a little later and introduce herself as her nurse. When Nicole was turning away, Jenna the care aide pulled her aside. Pointing at the room Nicole had just come out of, Jenna spoke in a whisper. "Did you know she wants to properly bury her baby? We have it in the utility room if you want to see!"

Nicole's surprised look showed Jenna she hadn't heard. Jenna pulled her to the utility room and let Nicole walk in ahead of her. Laying in an ice cream bucket on the counter was the tiniest little baby she had ever seen, resting on a folded blanket. She figured this one was about the size of a grapefruit, with miniature arms and legs. She stood there in awe, gazing at the baby, taking in all the details already evident in this miracle. Emotion washed over her. How could those who preached abortion call this a piece of tissue? Here was a flawlessly formed baby, not just tissue! Backing up and leaning against the wall, Nicole took some steadying breaths. With her eyes still glued to the bucket, she knew that abortion was not an option for her. In the same instant, she remembered her prayer for God to show her what to do. Had He worked it out for her to get this patient so she would see the miscarried child? Sadness filled her heart. How could she have even entertained the thought of killing her own baby? *Forgive me, Lord! I was wrong to look for a way out!*

Never mind what had gone through her mind. Now she knew better. Wiping her tears with the back of her hand and stepping away from the wall, she left the utility room, her head held a little higher for the decision she had just made.

As the evening wore into night, Nicole determined at some point to bring Chloe into the utility room to show her the baby. When she had a free moment, she did just that. Chloe took one look at the twenty week old fetus and her jaw dropped. Emotion rippled across her face as she looked at Nicole, then at the baby. Nicole spoke softly, "So if this was a single mother and the fetus was alive, would you recommend abortion? It's a perfectly formed little baby, not a piece of tissue!"

Chloe had the grace to look embarrassed. "I see that. Beautiful, isn't he?" She gazed at the baby several more minutes, then looked up to find Nicole staring at her. "I...I guess I never thought that it would matter too much to get rid of it if that's what the woman wants. I mean, if the government allows abortion, doesn't that make it right?" Her eyes looked agonized. "I feel kind of confused."

Nicole reached up and gave Chloe a sideways hug. "It's okay. I've felt confused over this issue too. But now can you see that it's wrong?"

Chloe wiped at her face; there were a few tears escaping, and she really didn't want to break down. "Well, it certainly makes me think through this in a different way." In a flash she remembered the suggestion she had made to Nicole just yesterday. She gasped and looked at her friend. "I'm so sorry for what I said to you yesterday, Nicole! Really, if you want to go through with the pregnancy, it's up to you." Like she felt she had said enough on the matter, Chloe backed out of the utility room and lightly ran back to work.

Nicole was left alone in the room, looking at the bucket with its precious cargo. With her eyes glued to the fetus, she knew in her heart that abortion is not okay. With a shudder she thought of what would have happened to this little baby had the mother not wanted it and gone for an abortion. Right now it was perfectly formed, whereas in a D & C it would have been torn to shreds. With a thoughtful expression on her face, Nicole returned to work.

∞ ∞ ∞

The next night was uneventful and she was so grateful to return home at 7:30 in the morning. She had four days off! After she woke up she would call Annaliese and they could book their coffee date. Right now she was going to have a nice hot shower and then fall into bed.

Nicole slept a little less than usual so she would still be able to sleep that night instead of going to work. Getting up and moving around, she talked to Shadow who was rubbing up against her legs and making contented sounds.

When she had showered and had eaten a little, she called Annaliese. They decided to make their coffee date for tomorrow morning at 10:00. Nicole would have this day to clean her apartment and do a little bit of grocery shopping after sleeping for a while. Then she planned to sit on Greg's recliner and read. Maybe Shadow would warm her legs with his purring body! Smiling at this last thought, Nicole went to bed for the remainder of the morning.

Vacuuming her room later in the day, she looked up at the opened closet and saw Greg's running shoes. Turning off the vacuum, she stood there and stared. Was it right for her to keep Greg's things the way they were before? Maybe she should consider doing something with all his belongings. Sitting on the bed, deep in thought, her eyes wandered to Greg's bedside table where his Bible sat, same as it had when he was alive. Picking it up, she flipped through some of the pages and found herself in Deuteronomy. Her eyes picked up a portion that Greg had highlighted and she read it with interest:

"I call heaven and earth as witnesses today against you, that I have set before you life and death, blessing and cursing; therefore choose life, that both you and your descendants may live."

Nicole noticed that Greg had written some notes in the margin explaining what this word meant to him. Closing the Bible, she held it close to her heart, both arms folded over to keep it there. With her eyes closed, she prayed, *"Lord, You showed me I should choose life where the baby is concerned. But what about with Greg? This scripture makes me think it's time I choose life. I've been consumed with keeping all Greg's things as they were, but is that life? Or is that death for me? I need for You to lead me through this and into life."*

She got up and with a thoughtful look, she turned on the vacuum and finished the job. There would be time enough during these four days off to make a decision about all this. But the one important thing she concluded as she finished up her cleaning was that the part of Greg that she didn't want to lose was spread out throughout the pages of his Bible with his notes and scribbles. She would take the time to study his Bible more thoroughly on her days off.

Chapter 8

The next morning found Nicole looking forward to her time with Annaliese. She had a few things to tell her! When she was dressed in jeans and long-sleeved t-shirt, she french-braided her hair. Nicole still had an hour before going over to see her neighbour. Hmmm. Maybe she should read her Bible for a bit. Better still, she would read Greg's! Settling on the couch, she pulled his Bible to herself and ran her hands over the cover. This book held many of his hopes and dreams as he had learned more about the Lord. She knew he had scribbled notes in every possible area that had room, explaining the verses he was reading and highlighting his heart's desires.

She wanted to have more faith. How did that happen? Were some people just filled with more faith than others? With a sigh, Nicole opened the book where Greg's bookmark was. She was surprised to find she was in Hebrews where the writer was speaking about faith. Those Christians of long ago sure did have it hard! As she read about Abraham and Sarah, Nicole quietly pondered how faith grows in a person. She knew that in her own strength she was not able to drum up faith. Maybe this would be a question for Annaliese. She was such a wise lady; surely she would know how one can have more faith. Or was each person given a measure of faith and that was his lot for life?

Looking up with a start, she saw it was time to run next door. Putting Greg's Bible aside, Nicole stood up and straightened her clothes. She picked up her own Bible and headed for the door. What would Annaliese's response be to Nicole's pregnancy news?

∞ ∞ ∞

Annaliese, as always, looked lovely. Her short white hair was perfectly in place and her blue eyes twinkled as she opened the door for Nicole. "Come in, come in! I've looked forward to spending time with you, my dear!"

With a smile, Nicole hugged the petite lady before proceeding into the living room. The air smelled of coffee and something sweet which she couldn't identify just then. As she sat down, Annaliese commented, "You are looking better these days, Nicole. I noticed that lately you were looking quite drawn, but you seem more relaxed now." Pouring out the coffee, she looked up. "I have some orange rolls coming out of the oven in just a few minutes. I thought they would be better warm."

Nicole gave her an appreciative smile. "Yum, sounds heavenly!" She sipped her coffee and told Annaliese she was looking forward to trying the rolls. "I haven't felt well for a while, actually. But I thought it was all grief that was playing on my body. Grief can do strange things to a person, just like fear can." Nicole put her coffee down and continued. "The fact of the matter is that when I went home for a few days last week, my dad got me to come into his office for a check-up. He was concerned that I was throwing up so much."

"Rightly so," agreed Annaliese. The sun was shining on her face and she looked comfortably relaxed.

"Well, it turns out I'm pregnant."

Annaliese looked at Nicole with a joyful gleam in her eyes. "I suspected as much, Nicole."

"You did?"

"Do you remember last time we had coffee together you mentioned that you were vomiting? You didn't have the flu and it was at that point that I wondered, but of course I wasn't sure so I didn't want to say anything then."

Nicole's face held a look of surprise. "So this news doesn't come as a shock to you."

"No dear." Just at that moment, the stove timer dinged. Annaliese stood. "So tell me more. Keep talking; I'll just bring those rolls in here. Were you surprised? Or did you suspect as well?"

Nicole placed her free hand over her slightly swollen belly. "Well, to tell you the truth I wasn't thinking that at all. I just thought that my periods were all crazy because of grief. I've had other times when my cycle wasn't very regular, so I just figured my body was going through something." She laughed, realizing what she'd just said. "*Of course* my body was going through something!"

She sat back on the couch, making herself comfortable. Thinking back to her father breaking the news to her, her expression became sober. "I was dumbfounded, actually. I mean, how could this happen when Greg was gone? We were supposed to be parents together!" She swiped at the tears trickling down her face yet again.

Annaliese put her coffee down and sat next to Nicole, enveloping her in a hug. "I know. Sometimes life can sure throw us a curve ball!" They sat there together for a few minutes, while Nicole got herself back under control. Finally with a sigh she pulled out of the hug and grabbed her coffee. Crossing her legs with a sigh, she decided to talk through this whole thing with Annaliese.

"The worst thing is that someone at work suggested I get an abortion, and I was actually considering it!" Nicole looked embarrassed as she peeked over at Annaliese. Her friend was just sitting there quietly, looking at Nicole with concern.

"Go on."

"Well, I came to the conclusion that I could never do that to my unborn baby." Remembering the miscarried baby she had seen a couple days ago, Nicole explained to Annaliese about the twenty week old fetus, and how it had affected her. "So you see, I realized that God had answered my prayer. I had asked Him to show me what to do, and I became aware that abortion could never be for me."

"I'm so glad to hear that, Nicole. You said you were praying. Is that something new?" She looked curiously at her neighbour before buttering a roll and taking a bite.

Helping herself to a hot roll which had finally cooled enough to touch, Nicole told Annaliese about going to Mill Lake after hearing that she was pregnant. She held nothing back. Annaliese might as well know how much she had struggled. When the story ended, Annaliese reached for Nicole's hand. "I am so grateful to the Lord for His mercies which He shows to us every morning!" She smiled at Nicole. "I've prayed for you so much, dear. I knew you were struggling, but it wasn't the right time to say anything. God has taught me that if I am concerned about someone, the first thing I should do is pray. If He tells me to move on it, I do, but most of the time He is the One who does something as I just keep on praying."

Nicole looked at her friend with a new appreciation. How many people would have said they were praying and kept silent about their concerns? This way, she would be sure that God was the One who was changing the person, rather than control getting in the way. Wow! In the same thought, she was awed that God would answer those prayers and work on her own heart. *Thank You, Lord!*

"So what do you think of that thing I felt on my shoulder?"

"You're the one who knows the peace it gave you. Does it matter if it was an angel, or Jesus Himself? It left you with more peace than you had had for a long time. I've heard of things like that happening and I myself have had some experiences with the Lord that only He understands."

"That's what I thought too." Nicole and Annaliese shared a smile and settled back in their seats, content to be quiet together for a few minutes.

"So how far along do you think you are, Nicole?" Annaliese was so short her feet barely reached the ground from her perch on the couch.

"Dad figures I must have been just over three months when I saw him, so I guess I'm heading toward four."

"Wow, only five and a bit more to go!" Annaliese clapped her hands in delight. "I am so happy for you!"

Nicole returned her smile, even though hers was not as bright as Annaliese's. "I have so many decisions to make before having this baby! But I'm not in a rush, so all in good time!"

Annaliese was looking a little more closely at Nicole's belly, trying to not be too obvious. "Are you going to be needing maternity clothes anytime soon? I can't tell if you're bigger or not."

Nicole looked down at her belly, her hands spreading across her abdomen. Glancing up at Annaliese, she responded, "I think I'm okay for the next couple of weeks at least. I mostly see the change in my breasts as they're getting bigger, but my belly is definitely changing, even if it's just a little right now. I can tell because my clothes aren't as loose as they once were."

"Well, isn't that interesting?" Annaliese quietly mulled over all that Nicole had said while drinking the last of her coffee. "Would you like more coffee Nicole? I've just finished my cup and I do have more in the kitchen." Annaliese was already on her feet.

Nicole looked at the small mug in her hand. She looked up with a smile and responded, "I'd love another cup, thanks!"

"So what else has been occupying that pretty head of yours lately?" Annaliese loved spending time with her young friend. And to think that God had so wonderfully answered her prayers!

Nicole smiled self-consciously and reached for her Bible on the coffee table. "Today I was reading Greg's Bible in Hebrews. The saints of old had so much faith, and I have so little faith. How does a person get more? Is it that some people are given a bigger measure of faith than others, and what we have is what we stay with?"

Annaliese picked up her coffee and took a sip. "Well now, that's a good question. Have you ever talked to children who know the Lord? They have so much faith! They absolutely believe that God is going to do what they ask Him to. Is there something different about them than about adults?"

Nicole tilted her head to one side as she considered this question. "I guess I've never thought of that before, but it's true. When I was a teenager I taught Sunday school, and sometimes I was sure that I was learning more from some of those kids than they were learning from me!"

"Beautiful, isn't it? But really, what makes them believe the way they do? Do you think God gives them more faith than He gives us?"

Nicole shrugged her shoulders. This was beyond her.

"I find that if a child has a good relationship with his father, when he learns about God he will automatically see God as a father-substitute. So if the father is kind and considerate and meets his needs, he will automatically believe that God is the same way and it will be second-nature to submit to Him. He won't think twice about praying for his needs to be met, because he'll already know that God is for him."

"So what happens if the father is selfish and angry, or what if he's not home much?"

Annaliese looked sad. "Well, those children usually find faith more difficult because their father wasn't there for them. Even if a father is there physically, it doesn't mean he's there emotionally for the child. Even so, God is bigger than all these problems and knows how to reach a person."

Nicole's mouth formed a perfect "O" as she thought of this.

Annaliese continued, "Another thing is that children find it easier to obey, or some children do, anyhow!" They both laughed. "They don't have their own agenda. And faith grows as we obey the Father. When He tells you to do something, if you hold back and decide to do it your own way, faith won't grow, will it? No, at that point faith is kind of put on the back burner to simmer for a while. If we don't decide to submit to God, the little that is there can be snuffed out." Annaliese paused to let Nicole think this through. "So you see, faith comes by surrendering to God. As you obey, His Spirit agrees with that response in you and faith grows."

"Wow. I never thought of that before."

Annaliese put her mug down on the coffee table and continued. "Children who have faith have a submissive attitude, not an entitlement attitude."

Nicole looked at her neighbour; this was a new concept to her. As her thoughts were beginning to contemplate what entitlement meant, Annaliese broke the silence.

"When my late husband and I were married, we moved into this little studio apartment. It wasn't long before I was pregnant and we were told we would have to move: they didn't allow children in that building. At first I was devastated! Everything was so expensive and we didn't have much money. So we decided to pray. After all, the Bible does say that God will supply all our needs according to His riches in glory through Christ Jesus my Lord! We learned an important truth in those days. We spoke His promises out loud and reminded God about what He'd said He would do. He knew we had to eventually move, but what's more, He also knew where He wanted to move us to! So we decided to submit this to Him and wait on Him. The answer didn't come right away, but then I wasn't too far along so the need wasn't there yet, was it?"

Nicole's eyes were riveted on Annaliese as she continued her tale.

"When I was starting to wear maternity clothes and showing just a little bit, we had Peter's parents over for a meal. His father was very active in going to various Christian activities around the city. That very morning he had run into an older lady he had once known and they began to talk. Eventually the conversation came around to the fact that his son Peter was married and they needed to find a place to live. This lady said that it was too bad she couldn't rent out the other half of her duplex." Annaliese smiled at Nicole and shook her head. "Peter's father found this strange and questioned her more. It just so happened that she had had renters in there who were not good people. They had done some strange things, like trying to light a barbecue in the living room!" Nicole gasped. "In those days there weren't gas barbecues like today and they could be quite messy. There had been so much damage that this lady decided she would never rent it out again...once she finally got rid of them, that is. She was an older spinster, after all, and didn't need that headache. No, she preferred to live in the other half and remain by herself in the building."

Annaliese's eyes had a faraway look as she reminisced. "Well Peter's father decided to see if there was something he could do to change her mind. Her duplex was in south Vancouver, and it would be perfect for Peter and me! So he continued speaking with her, singing the praises of the young people so dear to his heart. At last she agreed to at least meet with them." Annaliese stopped to sip her coffee.

Nicole wanted to hear the rest. "And...what happened?"

"Well that night Peter's father gave us her phone number; he was ever so pleased with himself! The next day Peter set up an appointment with this lady. Miss Dadson was her name. After he was finished work we went over to meet her. She was very fearful, but when we told her we were going to have a baby in four and a half months, she began warming to us. That might have something to do with the fact that she knew Peter's father and felt that his son would be a good fit for the duplex. Gradually she began asking if the size of the duplex would work for us. Now mind you, at this point we were still in her place and hadn't seen the duplex yet." Annaliese was enjoying talking about God's faithfulness. "Eventually we went to see it, and it was perfect: a good size for even up to two children, and a lovely back yard! We were so excited when she agreed to let us move in! The rent she charged us was below the norm for those days in Vancouver, and what's more, she didn't raise the rent the whole time we were living there, which ended up being five years!"

"Wow, what a great story."

"Well actually, that was just kind of the beginning. When it was time to move from there because we had three small children and were bulging out the walls, our faith in God's faithfulness had grown. After all, He had demonstrated so beautifully that He cared. So we became bold in praying about a place to live and He worked it out for us to be able to buy our very own house in Ladner. It was a reasonably large house and we were very happy there for many years. After that, each time we found we had to move, we knew God would direct our path and supply our needs, and He has, every time."

Nicole sat quietly, lost in thought. So faith could grow! That was an encouraging thing for her to hear.

"So you see, Nicole," Annaliese continued, "we must come to the conclusion that we have a need for God in our lives. If we humble ourselves before Him and surrender to Him, He answers our prayers and faith grows in the process. So surrendering means that we know we can't do it without Him; that in fact He has to do it in us. But we can't have a feeling of entitlement in it."

Nicole's eyebrows puckered in a frown. "What do you mean, entitlement?"

"Well now, if you feel that you *deserve* something, that's a feeling of entitlement. But when we come to Christ, we give up our rights and therefore we can no longer have any entitlement. We can't come to Him and say *I deserve that beautiful car over there, even if it's above my ability to pay.* That's not praying by the Spirit, nor is it a need. It's actually greed. On the other hand, if you need that particular car to carry out the work of the Lord, that's a different thing. He will supply all you need to carry out His work, as long as He has told you to do it, and if you wait for Him to do it and not rush in and do it yourself!"

Nicole's head was spinning. There was so much to learn about God! "So if you need something, what is the best way to come to God about it and know He will answer?"

"Have you ever heard of praying according to the Spirit? It's getting your heart in tune with the Spirit of God so that when you pray for something, you already know what His will is in it. As you know His will, you then pray in that direction."

"Wow, so you're saying we can know God's will all the time?" Nicole was incredulous, and her eyebrows shot up in surprise.

"This is a very deep subject, and there is so much to learn about it. But one way that you can know God's will better is to know His Word, and know His character. When you have a clear understanding of these, you then know better how to pray. You are aware of it when your prayers are not quite in tune with Him. He always works according to His Word. If your prayers are for something that is the opposite of what His Word says, you can't expect to get an answer. Or at least, not the answer you're looking for."

Nicole looked pensive. "You mean like if you pray that God would help you win the lottery?" She smiled.

Annaliese returned her smile. "There is nothing inherently wrong in winning the lottery. The problem comes with why you want it. God wants to be our provider. He doesn't want us to look to a big windfall to provide everything we need, because then we might not need Him anymore. But if you look to the Old Testament, you'll find that there are people who were rich and handled it well; sort of like King David. But his heart was in tune with God, and he never put his trust in his riches."

Annaliese reached over for her Bible and found a verse she was thinking about. "Here we go. In Proverbs 11 it says,

"He who trusts in his riches will fall, but the righteous will flourish like foliage."

"God caused King David to flourish because his trust was not in his riches, but in God's mercy and grace toward him."

Nicole was nodding her head in agreement. "I guess sometimes that could be a hard lesson to learn." Thinking back to the earlier part of the conversation, she asked, "So how does one get to know God's character?"

"One thing I remember doing at one point was searching the Bible for scriptures that drew a picture of His character. You could do a search, for instance, on the fruit of the Spirit; use the concordance at the back. And as you read about *LOVE*, for example, you find that the Word talks about God being love. Expand that search and you find that in the New Testament, Jesus says we are to love one another, for God is love and we are to be like Him. So if God is love, would He answer your prayers if you are angry with a co-worker and complain to God about him and ask God to make him lose his job?" Shaking her head, Annaliese continued. "We cannot pray evil onto someone else...that just isn't God's way. So when you know certain things about His character, you know better how to form your prayers for them to be in line with scripture."

Nicole sat back and took a deep breath. "Phew! I should be taking notes!"

Annaliese laughed. "It's good for you to be asking these questions. They show that you are hungry for God."

"Okay, so what are some of the words I should do a search on to find out more about God's character?"

Annaliese pulled out a sheet of paper from her Bible. "Here, I have some things written down from my own time of searching, many years ago. You could start with these." Looking down, she read some of them out loud, "Grace, mercy, love, faithfulness. Actually, doing a search on the fruit of the Spirit would bring you to a good understanding of God's character, because they mirror who He is." She gave the paper to Nicole, who accepted the paper gratefully. She had much to learn, but something told her she would be enjoying this process!

The conversation moved on to other matters, and eventually their visit came to an end. They parted with the promise to get together again soon.

Going back to her own apartment, Nicole found herself thinking of faith. She would be in need of more faith in the days to come, that's for sure!

Chapter 9

Steve was reading quietly in his living room. Finally the kids were all in bed, and he had some time alone while he waited for Jennifer to return from the baby shower she was attending tonight. It was a lovely fall evening and a few windows were still open. He gradually became aware of a loud thumping sound assaulting his ears. She was at it again! Roseanne his tenant was playing her loud rock music. Steve didn't mind so much if she did this in the daytime, but when the kids were in bed he didn't like it. This was so loud it could wake them up!

He had spoken to Roseanne about this before, and each time she looked appropriately remorseful. But the quiet didn't seem to last long before the loud music started up again. He guessed her boyfriend didn't make things easy this way, because when he visited, he liked to have loud music playing.

There just didn't seem to be an easy way out of this. He would just have to start praying about it. He believed God wanted them to have peace in their home, so he would start praying that either Roseanne would change and respect their wishes, or decide to leave. If it says in the Bible that God changed the heart of kings, then surely He could change Roseanne's heart and ways too.

Thump, thump, thump came the steady sound of the bass and drums. Steve resolved to pray more frequently for an answer to this. As the children were woken up more and more frequently, he had to take this in hand and lift Roseanne up to the Lord.

He had just finished praying when he heard their car driving in. Jennifer was home! Walking to the door, he was just opening it when she was about to put the key in the lock. The movement caught her by surprise and she stumbled forward, into his waiting arms. Laughing, they hugged and she began telling him about her evening as they walked back into the living room.

Sitting side by side on the couch was such a luxury these days! Usually there was a smaller body wiggling in between them. Jennifer sighed with contentment after telling him about the shower. She'd been doing all the talking. "So, how was your evening?"

Steve smiled at her as he brushed her blond hair out of her face. Touching her soft cheek was a pleasure he would never tire of! "Do you hear the music?"

Jennifer had not wanted to bring attention to it, but she had noticed it as she got out of the car. With a small frown she answered, "It's getting out of control, isn't it?"

"I would say that. I think the time has come for us to do something about this."

Eyebrows lifting in surprise, Jennifer asked, "Just what exactly are you proposing we do?"

"Pray!" Steve told her what he had felt God speaking to him tonight. The way to get Roseanne to stop or leave was to bring her before the Lord on a regular basis. God had made it clear to him tonight that first he had to forgive her, because his feelings had been heading in the wrong direction lately. Forgiving and blessing her would release God to work on her heart, and he would be free from anger or bitterness. They should keep praying until Roseanne decided to leave, or until God showed them how to get her to move of her own free will. If they prayed blessing upon her, maybe God would give her a different job somewhere far away!

Jennifer agreed with this. "Good plan. Why don't we start right now? I know there is power in a husband and wife praying together. Two people agreeing together makes a big difference."

So once again Steve bowed his head and together they prayed, lifting up this problem to their heavenly Father.

∞ ∞ ∞

Ellen and Stan were walking hand in hand at Mill Lake on this beautiful Sunday afternoon. They enjoyed watching all the different kinds of dogs walking with their owners. Many people stopped to talk if anyone wanted to pet their animal. Ellen loved the friendliness of the people out enjoying the warmth of this gorgeous fall weather. The leaves had just begun to change colour. Even so, there was still plenty of green around, and even a few flowers to take pleasure in.

"Have you spoken with Nicole recently?" Ellen had been too busy with work to call her oldest daughter in the past week.

"As a matter of fact, I have. She's gone for her ultrasound, and all is well. The baby seems to be healthy and it looks like she will be delivering sometime in mid-February."

"That's such good news!" Ellen turned to him with a grin on her face. "Mid-February!" She stopped walking and calculated in her mind what mid-September to mid-February would be in wait-time. "That's only five months away! Oh, I'm getting so excited!" Her eyes danced with anticipation. Grabbing Stan's hand again and continuing to walk, Ellen's smile lit up her face.

Stan was delighted too, but he didn't show his excitement the same way. "The best news is that by now she isn't throwing up anymore. That was a rough patch she went through, and to think she went through it all on her own, without any of us knowing about it." Stan's face was sad. He didn't like the thought of Nicole being so far away at this time. "Do you think she will ever want to come back to Abbotsford?"

"You know, I've been thinking about that too. I would prefer to have her closer, but essentially she has to make that decision on her own. I think somehow this is all wrapped up in her memories of Greg. Maybe she thinks if she leaves that apartment she will lose a part of him. I don't know."

"God has her best interest at heart. She is listening to Him these days, so He'll show her what to do." Stan spoke more confidently than he felt. But he knew it was best for him to leave her in God's hands. If they tried to sway her decision, she might regret moving out here and resent them for it. Somehow she had to see that it was the best thing for her.

Letting her breath out in a big sigh, Ellen thought of Nicole. She would love to be able to spend more time with her right now, maybe go shopping for maternity clothes with her so she could spoil her a little. But God knew their hearts. It was best left in

His hands. Together they walked up the stairs that led to the upper parking lot on Emerson Street. Reaching their car, Stan put his arms around Ellen. "Don't forget that God loves her even more than we ever could. He is fully capable of reaching her and showing her what is the best thing to do."

Ellen understood that. The thing that worried her was that Nicole had made some unwise decisions in the past. Could she hear from God better now than in those days?

∞ ∞ ∞

Julie had come for dinner and was now sitting with Matthew in their parents' living room. Matthew had been telling Julie about some of his classes.

"How much longer do you have to go before you get your degree?" Julie was curious. She had never gone to university and didn't have any idea of how long various programs were.

"I have a year and a half left. Well, that's if I can't manage to squeeze in some courses in the summer. University of the Fraser Valley does offer some summer courses and if I could fit more in I might finish earlier. I'll just have to wait and see, I guess."

"You're certainly learning a lot, that's for sure. Maybe one day you can advise me in starting my own business," Julie's voice was filled with longing. "I would so love to have my own little coffee shop one day!" She sighed.

Matthew was looking at her with his head tilted to the side, pondering what she had just said. "You know, Jules, until you get your own coffee shop there is a way you can start building your customer base, even right now."

Startled, Julie sat up straight and looked at him. "What are you talking about? Any customers we get now would not move over to my coffee shop later. They are Diana's customers. Besides, it'll probably be in a different part of town, which could make it awkward for some of the older folks who love to just sit, drink coffee and chat with their friends."

"We could make you a web page to advertise your cookies, or whatever you're making. And you could offer free delivery for a while until you get more customers. I know all kinds of neat things to incorporate into the web page to make you a data base of customers, and you could send them regular emails telling them what new stuff you're working on. You might even like to put coupons in there for a free cookie or something."

"That sounds like fun! Do you know how to do all that stuff?"

"I've taken computer courses and have learned quite a lot lately with the business end of things. I'm sure I could figure this out for you. I might even be able to use it as a project for school!"

"You know, Nicole mentioned something like this to me last month when she was here. She figured you'd be a good one to help me." She smiled at her brother. She certainly was fond of him and they got along great together. Julie sure did miss seeing him every day, but it was good that he felt free to pop in to the coffee shop now and then.

Matthew stretched out on the couch, plopping his long legs on the coffee table and linking his hands behind his head. "Do you have any idea what you'd like to call your business when you get one up and running?"

"I've given that a lot of thought lately and I think I'll call it the Sweet Tooth Coffee Shop, or would Sweet Tooth Cafe sound better?"

Matthew smiled, "Both are good, but personally I like the first one; it has a certain ring to it. So, do you think you would like to make a web page? I could do a lot of the work, but you would have to be available to make decisions about things."

Pulling her hair out of its pony tail and fluffing up her hair, Julie thought about his suggestion for a bit. Looking over at him, she answered, "I would actually love it. I'm not sure how one drives traffic to a web page, but I'm sure you'll come up with suggestions for that too!" Laughing, she leaned forward to tweak his toes.

"Okay. I'll do some preliminary stuff, you know, decide how to start and all, and then we could meet. How would next Saturday morning sound to you?"

"Wow, you're serious about this!"

"But of course! Nothing but the best for my darling sister!" He made her laugh as he stood up and bowed with an imaginary hat in his hand. Straightening up again, he flipped that hat-that-wasn't-there and settled it on his head. With that done, he tucked his make-believe cane under his arm and helped her to her feet. Julie dove into the fun of acting this out, accepted his offer and arm in arm they walked back into the kitchen to see what their parents were up to. Sometimes it was fun being home again, if even for a short time.

Chapter 10

Matthew was very frustrated. He had been driving all around the place and couldn't find a decent parking spot for his truck. The parking lot at UFV was not cheap if one used it all the time, so he preferred to use the street whenever he could. But this week there had been nothing on the street any of the times he had come to school. This was the fourth day he had to pay for parking. He was not happy!

That night during dinner he happened to mention to his parents about his frustration at the parking situation. They were both secretly amused because parking at the hospital cost so much more than that. However, they knew as a student he didn't have much money, so they agreed with him that this needed a solution. There were no buses near their home, so it wasn't possible to take public transportation.

Suddenly Stan snapped his fingers, "Hey, I have an idea!" He looked so thrilled with this new thought that both Ellen and Matthew burst out laughing. "Why don't you call Grandma and Grandpa and ask them if you could use their second parking spot? It would only be a short walk to the school from their home. And their car is in their garage, so there should be room for your truck in front."

With his head tilted to the side as he liked to do when he was thinking, Matthew considered this option. "Why did I not think of that before? I suppose I could leave them my keys and if they needed to go out, they could move my truck." Matthew was on the phone before he had finished his comment.

As he spoke with Stan's father, Ellen and Stan moved into the living room with their coffees, confident that he would let them know the results. A short while later, he bounced into the living room, a huge grin on his face. "Grandpa said it was no problem. So I'll park closer if I can, but if there's nothing available, I'll go to their place. Thanks for the great suggestion, dad!"

Stan turned to Ellen when Matthew left the room to continue his homework. "I bet when mom knows which days Matthew will be parking at their place, she'll bake in order to give him a tasty snack after school. Won't he love that!" They both laughed, knowing full well that their youngest son would be in heaven if he got fresh cookies, cinnamon buns and whatever else his grandmother chose to bake for him.

With an amused look at one another, Stan and Ellen finished their coffee. Their favourite time of the evening was approaching, when they would go out for a walk and ultimately end up praying for each of their kids and grandkids.

∞ ∞ ∞

Nicole was feeling so much better these days. Her energy was returning, and she was no longer throwing up. What a relief! These days she could easily see the change in her body. Even though she had not yet started wearing maternity clothes, she could see her belly swelling, and her breasts were certainly getting bigger! It wouldn't be long before she had to start wearing bigger clothes, especially for work, as her scrubs were already tight on her.

The phone rang as she was about to grab her keys and head out the door. Looking at the call display, she was delighted to see it was her brother. "Steve! How are you doing?"

"I'm doing well, how about you? Are you feeling better these days?"

"Yeah, I think I've turned the corner on all that vomiting. I'm feeling a little more energetic now, which sure helps out when I'm working!" She laughed. It was so good to hear his voice.

There was some more small talk before Steve tentatively told her the reason he had called. "Say Nic, have you thought any more about moving back to Abbotsford?" he asked her.

"Well, as a matter of fact I have. I just haven't done anything about it yet because I can't decide what to do about a job. There aren't any full time RN positions available at the Abbotsford Hospital that I'm interested in. That's kind of what the whole decision hinges on."

"You mean you don't mind coming back closer to home?" Steve was delighted to hear that.

"No. I have friends here, but it's family I need in the coming months. They're the ones who will help me through as a single mom. Friends are great, but mine are all working full time too. Well, all except Annaliese. I sure will miss her if I ever get back to Abbotsford to live!"

"She's been a real good friend to you, hasn't she?"

"More than you know!" Nicole wasn't about to get into it here, but Annaliese had become a friend who knew how to steer her toward the Lord. She absolutely treasured this! "So, why do you ask?"

"Well, I mentioned to you last time you visited that we were having some problems with Roseanne playing her music so loud late at night. Remember that?"

"Sure." Nicole was wondering what that had to do with her.

"Well, Jennifer and I have been praying for her and asking God to either change her, or move her on. This morning she came over and told us she had found a better job in New Westminster and would be looking for a place to live there. The commute from Abbotsford is just not something she wants to get into right now."

"Oh!" Nicole was beginning to understand. "Do you mean to say that your suite will be available for another tenant?"

"That's exactly what I'm saying. Jennifer and I were wondering if you'd be interested."

Nicole felt her heart jump. Move in right beside Steve and Jennifer? She got along so well with them! This might just be the answer to her living situation. She wouldn't have to be living at home with her parents, but she'd still be close by. In fact, they only lived ten minutes away from Steve and Jennifer.

"I don't remember what the suite looks like. How big is it?"

"Well, that's the beauty of it, Nic. It's got two bedrooms. They're not huge but it would be big enough for you and the baby for a while to come. The other thing is that even though it's called a suite, it's above-ground, unlike a basement suite. There are a few advantages to having a suite separate from the main house. But you know all that, right? Did you ever get to see it when we moved here?"

"I've seen it from the outside. It's a tiny little house on your property, but beyond that I don't know anything about it." Nicole would have loved living in her own little place like that, but when Steve and Jennifer moved into the house and inherited the tenant, she was still in nursing school at Trinity Western University. She couldn't afford to buy herself jeans, let alone live in her own place!

"Once upon a time it was a carriage house. It was built at the rear of the house and made to house horse-drawn carriages and the related tack. Somewhere down the road they didn't need it for that anymore, so someone turned it into a little suite. Roseanne moved in when the previous owners were there, and it seemed right at the time to let her stay on when we moved in."

"Oh, I think you told me this once, but it's all very vague." This suite sounded more and more like a place Nicole would consider moving into.

Steve continued, "I'm not sure when Roseanne will actually be moving out, but we were kind of thinking that if you moved in, we'd re-paint the place and do a few repairs, get it looking nice for you. What do you think?"

"Wow! Well, I need a little time to think about it. I mean, I'm not ready for that just yet. I still have to do something with Greg's stuff."

Steve knew this had been a tough thing...to get rid of Greg's stuff would be so final for her. Gently he spoke, "We could come and help you with that, if you like. We could ask Matthew to babysit one evening and come help you. Just let us know when, okay?"

His offer touched her. To think they would drive all that way to come help her! But she had to work through some of this first. "Thanks so much for the offer. I'll let you know if I come to that."

"I'll tell you what. Roseanne has to first find a place to live in New Westminster, so it wouldn't be ready for you to move in for at least a couple months. We won't rent it to anybody else; we'll just hang on to it and see if you want it later. Maybe by November you'll be closer to it than now."

Warmth filled Nicole's heart at her brother's suggestion. "I'll think about it. I'll pray too, and see if I can give you any kind of answer by the time Roseanne gives you her notice."

"Fair enough. We'll be praying for you too. We miss you over here, you know!" By being so far away she was missing out on a lot of stuff they all enjoyed, like watching his kids grow up. It would be so good to have her close, especially when the baby came. This way they could all help out. "Talk to you soon, then."

"Okay. Bye for now." Nicole hung up the phone with a thoughtful expression on her face. Would it be possible for her to move back to Abbotsford? She took a step into her bedroom and looked at Greg's dresser. She had washed his clothes after his death, but had replaced everything in the dresser, not wanting to make any changes. A part of her felt like he was still around if she saw his dresser with all the paraphernalia on top. She sat on the bed and dropped her head in her hands. Deep down she knew it wasn't a healthy thing she was doing. By now she should have been able to move on. But every time she tried to sort through Greg's belongings, she felt like a traitor. *God I need Your help! I've been trying, but can't seem to move forward with this. Now with a baby on the way, I need to know what You're saying about me moving back to Abbotsford. Is this what You want for me? Please make it clear to me, Lord and give me the courage I need to do something about Greg's things.*

With a sigh, Nicole stood up and dried her tears. She felt curiously deflated. Looking into the closet, she suddenly remembered the scripture God had brought to her attention a while back, "Choose life!" As she considered what this meant, she felt God tell her that a spirit of grief had been affecting her, thereby making it hard for her to make good decisions.

"Woah, now that's strange!" Nicole spoke out loud to her cat. Shadow was sitting on top of her dresser, grooming himself. *Did God say that, or did I dream it up?*

She remembered what Pastor Adam had been preaching on the weekend she had gone home. He had spoken about spiritual beings that were intent on bringing evil to humans, if we let them. Apparently they worked at Satan's bidding. But could she believe that that was what was influencing her and bringing on more grief to keep her in a sad state? Wasn't that just her? Over the years she had heard these kinds of sermons, but she had never really paid too much attention. Recently she had been reading her Bible and doing some praying, yet she was having such a hard time pulling out of the pit of grief.

Nicole walked over to the living room where her Bible was on the coffee table. She opened up the zip cover and reached in for the small notebook she kept in there. Flipping to the last notes she had taken at her home church in Abbotsford, she read that all believers have the authority in the name of Jesus to break the demonic bonds that bound them. Huh! As this came to her, she instinctively knew that a spirit of grief would hold her in a state of limbo where Greg was concerned, and effectively paralyze her from making decisions to move on. And yet, it hadn't been all that long since his death, so she had to be patient with herself.

Nicole knew she had much to think about. She might even run this by Annaliese and see what her friend thought of it all. It was a little scary thinking of dealing with this on her own. Looking down at her notes again, she saw that Pastor Adam had given them the steps they could take to break those bonds when they felt harassed by the enemy. Okay, so she would have to come back to this when she felt more ready.

Putting her Bible and notebook aside, Nicole walked into the kitchen to make her dinner. Tonight she would have spaghetti. She hadn't cooked much in the past few months, had only grabbed a sandwich here and there. But with the nausea gone, she had a renewed interest in food. And spaghetti had long been a favourite of hers.

The next morning found her ready to go to work bright and early. She was wearing her favourite peach coloured scrubs and her hair was in a french braid. Taking one last look around to make sure she didn't forget anything, Nicole laced up her white running shoes, grabbed her lunch and purse, and walked out the door, locking it. Removing the key from the lock she suddenly remembered she had forgotten to add cat food to Shadow's bowl. Unlocking the door, she went back in with a sigh. Grabbing the bag she measured out what she knew her cat would eat today and a little more. Shadow heard the rustle of the bag and came running. With his head in the bowl he watched with interest what Nicole was doing, bringing a smile to her lips. "Were you afraid I would forget you?" She placed the bag on the floor and indulged in a few minutes of petting her cat. Shadow loved the attention and purred like a motorboat.

"Eeep! Look at the time! I'd better run! I love you, Shadow!" Nicole said the last bit as she stuffed the bag back in the cupboard, then ran out the door, juggling her purse and lunch bag.

∞ ∞ ∞

Smiling at Chloe, Nicole sat down to receive the shift report from the night nurse. Did her partner look a little drawn today? She would have to see if Chloe wanted to talk later. Their relationship had gotten better since seeing that fetus together. At least she now knew that Chloe wasn't judging her for her decision to keep the baby. Looking at her friend again, Nicole felt concern as she noticed the dark smudges underneath her eyes. Not wanting to look obvious, Nicole didn't allow her gaze to linger for long, but she determined to find time to talk to her sometime today.

Handing out the last of her afternoon medications, Nicole returned to the nursing station. Today had been an unusually quiet day. What a relief! As she was getting ready to start some charting, Chloe walked into the room. She sat across from Nicole and gave her a smile. They both worked quietly for a while.

Pausing in her work, Nicole turned to Chloe, who looked at her with a question in her eyes. "What's up, Nic?"

"Well, actually that's what I was going to ask you," Nicole said quietly. Looking down at her hands briefly, she prayed for wisdom. "Is everything okay with you? You look so tired and even a little sad today."

Chloe sat back on the chair and sighed. She poked her pen into her hair which was up in a messy bun. Her curly dark brown hair was so unruly, Chloe very rarely wore it down. And her favourite thing to do with her pen to make sure she wouldn't lose it was to stick it in the bun. Nicole waited quietly for her response.

"Barry and I had a big fight last night. I didn't sleep very well."

"I'm sorry, Chloe!" Nicole didn't like to see her friend like this; all of a sudden she looked so miserable. "Do you want to talk about it?"

"I don't think so. Things will get better soon."

"Well, just so you know I'm here for you, okay?" Nicole leaned over so Chloe could look into her eyes and see she meant it.

With a half-hearted attempt at cheering herself up, Chloe smiled and said, "Sure. I know you're there for me. That's what friends are for, right?"

"Yes, just so you know." Nicole had been idly walking her pen through her fingers as she watched Chloe. Bringing it back into the right position, she leaned over the table and continued charting. Something was wrong. She would pray for her friend; even if Chloe didn't want to talk about it now, there might come a time when she would.

∞ ∞ ∞

Several hours later when Nicole was doing her last rounds before going home, the unit clerk called her on her phone; Nicole had a visitor.

"I do?" Nicole was confused. Had she made plans to meet with someone and forgotten? "Thanks for letting me know." Nicole came around the corner and looked over to see Annaliese standing near the desk in her blue volunteer jacket. They saw each other at the same time and smiled. Going up to her Nicole showed her surprise. "Hi Annaliese! What are you doing here? You've been volunteering?"

"Yes, yes, dear. It's just that after my volunteer time was finished today, I went to visit someone from my church who is a patient on the medical floor. I didn't expect to be here so long, but she was doing so poorly, I just sat and prayed with her."

"Is she doing all right?" Nicole knew Annaliese loved visiting with those who were lonely.

"Well actually she passed away just a short while ago. I was with her and she was very peaceful, so that's a good thing."

"Oh, I'm sorry!" Nicole spoke softly. She reached out and took Annaliese's hand in hers.

Annaliese brushed away a tear. "I'm fine, Nicole, truly I am. I am just so grateful that she is with the Lord now. That's all that matters. But it's getting late and I remembered that you were working day shift today. Would you mind very much if I caught a ride home with you?"

Nicole was so pleased she had asked. "But of course not! It would be my pleasure. I just have to give report before I go, though, and it could take a few minutes. Do you mind waiting?"

"Not a bit." Turning, Annaliese saw an empty chair not far away. "I'll just sit here and wait for you. Is that okay? I'm feeling rather weary."

"Great! I'll come back as soon as I can." Nicole found the night nurse coming on shift and began telling her about the key issues that had come up that day. When she was done, she gathered up her purse and lunch bag and made her way toward Annaliese, who was sitting there with her eyes closed, a peaceful expression on her face.

∞ ∞ ∞

In the Jeep, Nicole suddenly remembered something she had wanted to talk with Annaliese about. Stopping at a red light, she turned her head to look at her neighbour and asked, "Annaliese, would you be interested in coming in with me for a bit? I've been thinking about something lately and I'm not sure where to go from here. I thought maybe you would have a better idea what to do."

"That sounds like a splendid idea. Especially if you make me a cup of tea!" They both laughed at her cheekiness. "I'll just pop into my place and deposit my purse and coat, if that's all right with you."

Nicole drove into the underground parking garage and turned to Annaliese when she turned off the engine. "That sounds perfect, actually, because it'll give me a few minutes to freshen up. Just walk right in when you come over, okay?"

Chapter 11

Sipping their herbal teas, the two ladies were a study in contrasts. Annaliese was just barely five feet tall, and as she sat on the couch, her feet didn't quite reach the floor. She was neat and tidy and not one short white hair was out of place. Nicole, on the other hand, was not so tidy. Her hair, which she had put in a french braid before going to work, was unravelling around her face, and her long sleeved Henley was pulled up to her elbows. She was still in her uniform, but had kicked off her shoes. Her crossed feet were up on the coffee table, and she sipped her tea while she relaxed on the couch.

"Mmm. This almond tea is so delicious." Nicole sipped it again and closed her eyes in delight. Suddenly she remembered her friend sitting beside her. "Annaliese, I'm not sure what you think about this, but I feel a little confused and thought maybe you could tell me what you think."

Annaliese encouraged her with a smile while sipping her tea.

"Here, maybe it'll make things easier if I pull out my notes." Opening her Bible cover, she reached in for her notebook. "Last time I was in Abbotsford, Pastor Adam spoke about something that I never really thought much about before." Pausing for a moment to thumb through her notes, Nicole continued. "He said that we could be influenced by evil beings, or demons as he also called them. Is that true?"

Annaliese placed her mug on the coffee table and sat back. "Yes, it's true."

Nicole was surprised but unexpectedly relieved; she had grown to count on her friend's wisdom. "Can you tell me more?"

"Well Nicole, Jesus showed us in the gospels that people can have demonic influence in their lives. But He was able to speak healing into their lives. Do you remember the story in the eighth chapter of Luke about when Jesus and His disciples sailed to the country of the Gadarenes?" Nicole nodded. "Well, there was a man there who was demon possessed. I believe Jesus went over just for that man alone and delivered him; that's how much He wants to see us set free. When He sees someone in need, He is there for that person. But what that scripture shows us is that Jesus has a concern to restore every part of a man's life." Annaliese counted them off on her fingers as she spoke. "He wants to restore our relationship to the Father; He wants to restore our broken personalities and bondages; He wants to restore our broken health and," she put up a finger as though pointing at the heavens, "He wants to rescue us from spiritual death."

Annaliese put an index finger to her bottom lip while she thought. She looked at Nicole with a smile. "When Jesus died, He won the victory at the cross over Satan and every demonic entity. But that doesn't mean that Satan is gone from this world. He is still active and powerful wherever there is sin, and also in our lives if we open the door for him to enter in."

"What do you mean? How can I open a door to Satan?"

"If we get angry for example, Satan will take advantage of our weakness and try to get us to sin by telling us we have every right to be bitter. In that sense he is active. If we listen to him and take a step in his direction, he becomes powerful in our lives to cause us to sin further."

Nicole gasped. "I never thought of it that way."

"Jesus gave us the authority to use His name, that's what the cross means for us. The Name above all names. He defeated sickness and disease, which are often caused by evil spirits."

"They are?" Nicole was surprised.

"Do you remember other stories about Jesus having delivered those who had demonic oppression in their lives? It says that Jesus healed them when they were delivered."

Annaliese took a sip of tea then sat back and continued speaking. "I learned a long time ago that every thought you have is going to have a corresponding chemical reaction in your body. When your thoughts are good, your body releases good chemicals, but when your thoughts are bad, like anger, judgment, or self-rejection, your body releases chemicals that are bad for you. If enough of those bad chemicals build up, over time they will eventually cause your body to malfunction, causing disease."

"Really?" Nicole had never heard it put quite this way before.

Annaliese became animated as she spoke. "Let's say for example you are a very fearful person. Being in almost constant fear puts your body in a permanent 'fight or flight' response. 'Fight or flight' is usually good for your body because if something unexpected happens to frighten you, you suddenly think clearer, you can run faster if you need to and so on. Adrenaline pumps into you to enable you to do these things. But when you are constantly in fear or anxiety, adrenaline as well as other chemicals pump throughout your body all the time and it never has a chance to recover or come back to normal. That is the kind of thing that will trigger disease."

Nicole remembered these things from nursing school. "How come you know about this, Annaliese?"

"Oh I've been studying these things for years. I wanted to be able to help those who needed spiritual healing, so I went to many seminars and took classes." Smiling at Nicole, she sipped her tea.

"Well, how about that? So, okay, I know what happens with fight or flight, but what about the other one? What happens when you think good thoughts?"

"With good thoughts, or when you are relaxed and at peace with yourself or your situation, there's a proper amount of serotonin in your body. I'm sure you've learned that too, yes?"

"Yes, but I guess I never thought of it like that before. Can it be that simple, that these chemicals are controlled by how we think?"

"Why do you suppose God says that we need to have our mind renewed by His Word? Only as our mind gets renewed can we receive that perfect peace God promises us. I believe that perfect peace has corresponding physical, spiritual and emotional components." Annaliese looked thoughtful for a moment. "I know you can have things wrong with your body that release these chemicals in unusual amounts. But the way we think has a lot to do with it too. In fact I found out a short while ago that the medical community is now agreeing that the way we feel about ourselves can play a big part in how healthy we will be throughout our lives."

"Huh." Nicole was processing it all. "So what does that have to do with demons?"

"Like I said, if we continue to respond in the wrong ways, that is, in ways that God doesn't want us to, eventually we will attract demonic activity. It becomes more and more difficult to turn off the bad thoughts and concentrate on the good. Beyond that, it becomes necessary to help the person find the open doors which are allowing the enemy to influence her, and set her free from this oppression before there is a difference in the way she feels physically."

"So this causes disease? All disease?"

"No, I don't believe it causes all disease, but I think it is responsible for a lot of them. Do you remember in the Old Testament when Moses brings the people out of Egypt? God tells them at one point to change their ways and if they continue to follow Him He would put none of the diseases of the Egyptians upon them. This was meant for us today as well. If we keep our thoughts pure before God, we stay free from those diseases that would be caused by the wrong chemicals in our bodies. The New Testament warns us about these things when we're told to avoid being judgmental, bitter, ungrateful, and so on. I think you can find some of that in the book of Romans and the book of James. When we come to Jesus, essentially we are supposed to walk away from Egypt...from all the old or wrong ways and attitudes."

"What kind of diseases are you talking about? I mean, with the bad chemicals." Nicole was still a little sceptical.

"Let's see if it'll make more sense to you this way. If you have a young lady who was abused as a child, she will probably have grown up thinking everything that goes wrong is her fault, and that she is a hateful person. She ends up living with self-hatred because of what was done to her. With this kind of emotion rampant in her mind, do you think her body will stay healthy for long?"

"Hmm. Okay, so if this person hates herself what happens?"

"She continually criticizes herself in her thinking and in her speech and believes she can never do the right thing. This is something God doesn't want us to do; the apostle Paul tells us to not be concerned with what others say, not to compare ourselves with others. God is delighted in who we are, who He has created us to be."

Annaliese took a moment to sip her tea. "If there is something we can change for the better, fine, do it. Like if it's crooked teeth that is making us feel miserable, we can get them straightened. But if it's something unchangeable, we should thank God for making us unique and for loving us in spite of ourselves."

Annaliese paused to put her mug on the coffee table. "So back to this person: if she hates herself, eventually her body will begin to break down. It's a reflection of what is happening in the spirit. Her soul is raging against her, and her body will eventually begin to self-destruct with disease."

Frustrated at her clear lack of knowledge, Nicole sighed. "You mean to tell me you learned all these things by attending seminars?"

"And by ministering to a lot of people through the years. There is a web page I read quite frequently called Nehemiah Ministries. There is so much good information on that web page! I've learned a lot by reading and studying it."

Nicole didn't even know Annaliese had a computer! Surprised, she asked for the web page so she too could look at it when she had time.

Annaliese got a piece of paper from a pad on the coffee table and wrote on it, then handed the paper to Nicole. "There you go. Let me know what you think."[1]

"Thanks." Nicole absentmindedly folded the paper and slipped it into her pocket. Nicole was quiet for a few seconds, assimilating all that Annaliese had said. "I always thought that Christians could no longer be bothered by demons. What you're talking about is completely different from that..."

---

1   To get this teaching, go to www.nehemiahministries.ca

Annaliese was nodding to show she understood what Nicole was saying. "Here, let me draw you a picture of something." She reached over for the pad of paper and drew a large circle. Within that circle was another circle, and then another within that one.

"The small circle represents the spirit of man; it is at the inner core of who we are. The circle outside the spirit is the soul." Annaliese pointed to the middle circle with her pen. "This one, the soul, consists of the mind, the will and the emotions; our five senses are also in that circle." Annaliese placed the tip of her pen on the outer circle and continued her explanation. "The outer circle is the outside or body of man." She looked up at Nicole to see if she was following her explanation. Nicole nodded slightly to show she understood.

"When a person surrenders her life to Jesus, her spirit is renewed and the Spirit of God then resides in there. However, the other parts of that person, namely the soul, the mind, the will and the emotions are still part of the old nature. The Spirit of God does not reside in these, but they can be renewed as you confirm the Word of God when you read and speak what He has said. This is when you will begin to change more into the likeness of Jesus. The things on the outside of the spirit can be influenced by demonic activity if the Spirit of God doesn't yet control those."

Nicole's eyebrows were bunched up in thought. She looked at Annaliese in surprise. "Is that why you can have Christians who respond in the wrong way to things, like in jealousy and rage?"

"Exactly. You will respond according to the flesh or soul in some areas until your mind is renewed and the Spirit of God controls that area. It all takes time."

"Wow, I never understood that..."

"But you know Nicole, not everything we deal with as Christians is going to be caused by the enemy in our lives. A lot of the time we fight the flesh and we think there's demonic activity, but really it's our self-will that's at the bottom of the trouble. We just can't let go of the control and let God do what He does best, which is to direct our lives into freedom."

"Hmm. I'm sure I've seen some of that in my own life. So how do you know that there is demonic activity? I mean, isn't it good to know so you can deal with it? Or *can* we deal with it?"

"Why certainly we can deal with it. Jesus has given us the authority to cast out demons and powers of darkness in His Name. All through the gospels we're told that Jesus cast out the spirits with a word and He healed all who were sick. Now that we have the Holy Spirit, we can do the same. The authority of the believer is given to each one, but not everybody likes to use it. Many prefer to keep begging God to help them, but He now expects us to speak into it because He has provided a way. That's actually what faith is all about."

Nicole's eyebrows shot up. "So, how do you know it's a demon and not the flesh?"

"When it's the flesh, or the 'old man' wanting his way, you can repent and change your ways. You go to God and He forgives you. Then it's just a matter of bringing your mind into alignment with the Word of God so your responses reflect Jesus and God's Word. But when there's demonic activity, you find you are helpless and unable to change. You try and try and it seems like you constantly hit a brick wall. You get frustrated because there doesn't seem to be a way out."

Nicole's eyes were big and round as she considered what Annaliese was saying. Could this truly be her problem?

"Why have you been asking these questions, Nicole? Do you know someone who is struggling like this?"

Glancing down at her hands, Nicole was quiet as she thought through how best to answer her. Looking up, her eyes pleaded with Annaliese. "Well, since Greg died I've been having such a hard time. I cry so much, and even though I know that's normal with grieving, there's more. I...I've been trying to sort through his clothes and stuff, but I can never get myself to do it. I just start crying all over again and think that if I get rid of his things, I'll lose a part of him." Tears slid silently down her face as she put her mug on the coffee table. "Will I never get past this?"

Annaliese reached for Nicole's hand to comfort her. She let a few minutes pass before answering in order to give Nicole time to compose herself. "It's perfectly normal to be sad when you lose your husband. But why were you wondering about demons?"

"Well yesterday I was in my bedroom and going through it all again, wondering how to sort through Greg's stuff, but not being able to. I just started crying. But all of a sudden I remembered Pastor Adam's sermon and it came to me that maybe I was struggling with a spirit of grief."

"Grief does take a long time sometimes, especially if it's in regard to someone who we were very close to. But not being able to move forward is not a good thing. After a while when it has settled in your heart that the person is gone, you should be able to do the necessary things, like give away their clothes or move on. The sadness will remain, but the intense grief passes." Annaliese looked intently at Nicole and thought of all she had been through. "It might just not be the right time for you."

"Do you think there could be a spirit of grief making it more difficult for me?" Nicole's voice was small, as though she was afraid to voice her thoughts.

"It might be." Annaliese thought quietly for a few seconds. "Being influenced by demons is different from being demon possessed. I don't believe Christians can be demon possessed because the Spirit of God resides in them, but they certainly can be influenced by them. They keep trying to find holes in our armour, so to speak, and if they find an open door, they will do their best to trip us up. That means that if we recognize it, we can rebuke them and tell them to leave. I've seen things like this before and it's not hard to deal with."

Reaching for her notes, Nicole showed her what she had written. "Pastor Adam gave us step by step instructions on how to free ourselves from demonic activity. But I didn't want to do this on my own; I was afraid."

"One thing is for sure," Annaliese sat up straighter, "we should not be afraid of demonic beings when God reveals them to us; He wants us to deal with them. And the more you address them, the easier it will get because you will see that they don't have any authority in your life. Often they are there because of ignorance on our part in not knowing what is written in the Word. Jesus gave us some beautiful examples in how to free someone from their grasp, so we just need to address it, and in His Name it will have to go.

He accomplished it and said, "It is finished." That meant we could have freedom for today!"

Nicole was watching her friend, waiting for more.

"The important thing is that we must position ourselves right. When we walk by faith we are no longer the enemy's property. First Thessalonians 5:5 tells us that we are all sons of light and sons of the day. We are <u>not</u> of the night nor of darkness. Satan wants us to be confused but the Word is very clear on who we are in Christ."

Annaliese was quiet for a heartbeat as she thought through what she was saying. "The devil hates all Christians and does everything he can to make them fall or lose their faith. It's his goal to have them not walking with the Lord. He has many helpers to do this, such as rejection, jealousy, anger, death. The root for each one of these is in the powers of darkness."

Annaliese drank some more tea and changed her position on the couch. "The important thing you have to do first is to make sure you have a pure heart before the Father. So that means you don't give in to judgment, or anger, or bitterness; if your heart is not clean, you will have no authority in the spirit world. But if you find that you have been angry or bitter, or whatever, just forgive where it is needed, repent for the wrong attitudes and thank Him for His forgiveness, then move on." They were quiet for a few minutes while they both considered what she had said.

Annaliese opened Nicole's Bible to the book of Isaiah. "In chapter one of this book, there is something very interesting that you should see." She turned to verse sixteen and began reading out loud: *"Wash yourselves, make yourselves clean; put away the evil of your doings from before My eyes. Cease to do evil, learn to do good; seek justice, rebuke the oppressor."* Annaliese gave a moment for the words to sink in, and then she continued. "You see, God wants us to keep a pure heart before Him, but then He tells us to rebuke the oppressor. Who do you think that is?"

Nicole took a guess, "Satan?"

"Exactly, and he is against anything good that God is attempting to do in our lives." She thumbed her way to the fifty second chapter of that book. "Listen to this, Nicole. 'Loose yourself from the bonds of your neck, O captive daughter of Jerusalem.' That means you and me, in fact, it's for everybody who knows the Lord. This isn't only for Old Testament times. And in fact we are told a similar thing in the New Testament in Matthew 18:18. Here it says, "Assuredly I say to you, whatever you bind on earth will be bound in heaven, and whatever you loose on earth will be loosed in heaven."

She flipped to another book toward the end of the Bible. "We're told in Ephesians that we do not fight against flesh and blood, but against principalities and powers, against the rulers of the darkness of this age, and spiritual hosts of wickedness in the heavenly places. So when someone is acting out against you, don't give in to anger or get all defensive with them, but go to a quiet place, forgive them and then rebuke the powers of darkness oppressing that person."

Nicole desperately wanted to believe that this was possible in this day and age.

Annaliese brought the subject back to Nicole's original concern. "Do you feel that you have let grief take control of your emotions? I know it's hard not to at times, but sometimes our feelings drag us somewhere where we know is not healthy."

Pursing her lips together in thought, Nicole could see Annaliese's point. "I probably have. I was so upset by losing Greg. I know there have been times when I've been really weepy and had trouble bringing it under control. Those times I just felt sorry for myself. Other times I knew I shouldn't let myself give in to it, but it actually felt good, in a perverted sort of way. So I just kept on crying."

"Do you believe that God has a good plan for your life, even now, with Greg gone?"

Nicole took a deep, shaky breath. "At first I couldn't see that, but I'm beginning to understand that He doesn't want me to give up, that He has more in store for me." She ended the sentence in a whisper, "I don't know what, but I don't think it's going to be all pain."

With a gentle smile, Annaliese brushed Nicole's hair from her face and away from her brown eyes. "You are so special to Him.

If you were to give up now, what glory would that give Him? No, you're right. And it's as you persevere through these difficult times that you push your roots down deeper into Him. One day you'll see that even through the pain, He was working on your heart to purify it for Himself. And your joy will be in Him because of it."

Looking quietly at her hands, Nicole mulled over how all this applied to her. Then she bowed her head to pray and ask God's forgiveness for giving in to the temptation of feeling sorry for herself. "I'm not really sure I understand it all, but You know how hard it is to stop grieving at times, Lord! I miss Greg so much!" Weeping into a tissue, Nicole was quiet for a moment before continuing. "But I feel like there is a wall preventing me from doing the right thing, and if it's the spirit of grief, I don't want to have any more to do with it!" A fresh onslaught of tears swept over her. "I want to be able to grieve in a healthy way, and not be influenced by anything further than that."

When Nicole had quietened down a little, Annaliese stepped in and prayed for her, rebuking the spirit of grief and commanding it, in the name of Jesus, to leave. Nicole took a deep breath and let out a huge sigh. Annaliese continued with something she felt the Lord was leading her into, "And in Jesus' name I break the powers of witchcraft, and control, and judgment over Nicole!" Still holding her hand, she began to pray for a renewing of Nicole's mind; for peace and a renewed sense of God's presence to fill her. Next she prayed for the baby as well. When Annaliese was finished praying, Nicole was more peaceful.

"Wow. Thank you so much! I feel lighter somehow."

Smiling, Annaliese gave her a hug. "It's always my pleasure to pray with you, my dear. Just keep in mind that grief will try to make you fall again; just resist it and don't give in to it." She picked up her Bible. "Now I should go and let you get to bed so you can go to work tomorrow." Both ladies stood up and hugged once more before Annaliese let herself out the door.

While getting ready to turn in, Nicole thanked the Lord for setting her free, her tears falling once again. But they were tears of gratitude for something had certainly happened to her tonight to bring her closer to Jesus. Now when the time came to do something about Greg's belongings, she hoped that He would give her the strength she needed.

Chapter 12

It was several weeks later, and Nicole knew something significant had happened to her when Annaliese had addressed that spirit of grief. She no longer cried as much as she had before. Whereas any little thing previously had set her off weeping, now she was able to stop quicker; it didn't seem to last as long nor did it control her as easily. Yes, she still missed Greg terribly, but she knew he was with Jesus. For that she was grateful; they would be re-united one day.

Today was her day off. She was looking forward to having a rest from work. Her days off somehow seemed to go quicker than they used to. After cleaning her apartment and taking all of one hour to do so, she was ready to go out and find herself a maternity top. Looking outside she was disappointed to see it was pouring with rain. A typical Vancouver dreary fall day. Wouldn't it be nicer to shop from home? She snapped her fingers as an idea came to her. Chloe had told her about a maternity web page that she had purchased clothes from, saying she got some really cute things for a reasonable price. Why not check it out first?

Opening her laptop, Nicole typed in the web page Chloe had given her, and went shopping.

Picking up her phone, she quickly punched in her mother's cell number. "Hello?"

"Hi Mom, it's Nicole. How are you?"

"Nicole! I've been thinking about you. I'm well, how are you? Are you getting bigger?" Nicole could hear the smile in her mother's voice.

Relaxing against the couch cushions, she took the time to visit before getting her questions answered. "I'm doing just fine, mom. In fact, I've been kind of popping out of my clothes lately. I figure it's about time I get myself something that's bigger or I'm going to have trouble breathing soon!" They both laughed.

"Are you at work, Mom?"

"As a matter of fact, I'm about to leave to go there very soon. Why?"

"Well, you remember Chloe at work, right?"

"The girl who works as your partner now and then?"

"Yeah, that's the one. Anyhow, she gave me a great website to go to to buy maternity clothes. I thought I might order myself a few things and have them sent to your postal box in Sumas. You still use that one for the office supplies, don't you?"

"We do use it. Some of the medical supplies we buy are cheaper through the states, so we have them delivered there. Others are just cheaper in Canada, so they come straight to the office. You don't need my permission to have something sent there, you know that. We'll just pick it up with the other stuff we get, that's all."

"Oh that's great, Mom, thanks. But I actually don't remember the address. Could you give it to me?"

"Sure. Do you have a pen and paper?"

When they were finished with the details Nicole needed, they continue chatting for a few minutes. Ellen asked Nicole to come home soon and promised to take her out shopping for something special. How could Nicole resist such an offer? She promised to go during her next set of days off, a grin working its way up her cheeks.

Putting her phone down, Nicole went back to the web page and ordered the t-shirt. On second thought, she decided to add a zipped hoodie as well. As she got bigger she would have trouble finding something that fit. Digging deeper into the web site, she discovered that they sold something called Belly Bands. She was going to invest in a couple of these and that would help her until she was ready to get a few extra maternity things for the long haul. For now, with Belly Bands and a few tops, she would be okay, at least till she went shopping with Mom.

With extra time on her hands and her shopping done, she wandered into her bedroom and gazed at the closet. Would she have the nerve to start sorting and boxing some of Greg's things now? A shudder went through her. Taking a timid step forward, she found herself touching one of Greg's sports shirts. Even though she had laundered it, it still somehow had his scent. She had loved the cologne he wore just for her. Picking up the shirt, she pulled it in close and inhaled her husband's fragrance. Eyes closed, she stood there several minutes thinking about him. Then putting the shirt back and squaring her shoulders, she decided that today would be the day. She would at least make a start.

Finding an empty box in her dining room, she decided she would put clothes in there. Folding shirt after shirt, Nicole found herself lost in her memories. Here was the shirt he used for painting! It was paint splattered and had a torn sleeve, but he had loved wearing it when they had painted their bedroom last year. Smiling, she thought about the fun they had had. How he had laughed when she had backed up into the wall and inadvertently painted the back of her shirt. He had not stopped teasing her after that. She could never live it down whenever she wore it. Holding his shirt close, she decided this one had too many good memories. She would keep it for herself. Who knows? She might find herself painting again some day, and she could use it then. The bonus was that it would remind her of happy times.

Little by little the box began to fill. When her hand brushed against Greg's guitar case in the back of the closet, she was surprised. Pulling it out, she thought how sad it was that in those last months he had not had much time for this. He had so loved playing, and he was getting pretty good too.

Setting the case on the floor, Nicole opened it up. This guitar had been Greg's since high school. A Takamine acoustic guitar. It was pretty! Sitting back on her heels, Nicole ran her hand along the strings. Then sitting down right there on the carpet, she picked up the guitar to find out how it sounded. She winced as she plucked the strings: a little out of tune! Looking in the case, she found the electronic tuner she was looking for and tuned the strings.

Nicole had played guitar as a teenager. Oh, she hadn't been great at it, but what she did know had helped her to get many hours of simple pleasure. She had often thought she would like to take lessons, but that had never come to pass, what with nursing school and all. And since going to work full time, she hadn't looked back.

But now she had extra time on her hands that she hadn't had before. Maybe she should take it up again. Putting the guitar in the right position, she wrapped her fingers around the neck and tried to remember the chords she had known long ago. There were a few that were still familiar, and she plucked the strings. She laughed when it became obvious she would need to work on the fingering. This sounded pretty bad!

As she was about to put the guitar back in its cradle, she noticed some papers in the bottom and was curious. Were these songs Greg had played? Picking them up, she saw they were helpful scales and chords for guitar. Glancing down at the bottom of the page she found a web page there. Scrawled in Greg's handwriting was written: http://www.guitartipsweekly.com/

Guitar tips online? Maybe she should look these up. It might just get her started back in something she had once loved. Keeping the papers out, she replaced the guitar in the closet for the time being. She had packed one box. That was a good start for her, considering how difficult this had been to come to! With a pleased look on her face, she closed the box and placed it against the wall. She would give that one to the Salvation Army for their second-hand store.

Back at her laptop, she decided to check out the web pages Greg had put in his guitar case. There she found free guitar lessons online! How cool was that! Why had Greg never mentioned this to her? Surely sometime on her days off she should be able to find time to re-learn this instrument, and she might even get better than she had been in her teens. Greg had been improving before things got crazy at work and ate up all his free time.

Looking further down the web page, she found some lessons posted there. Running into the bedroom she hauled out the guitar once more and went back to her laptop. She clicked on one lesson and found it understandable, even though she had much improving to do.

Shadow had been attracted by the sound of music and wandered into the living room. He hopped up on the coffee table and watched as Nicole plucked at the strings. Jumping to the couch, he made Nicole laugh when he stretched out and pawed at the neck of the guitar. Turning the instrument so it was closer to him, she strummed louder, which just made Shadow jump off the couch. He'd be back, she thought with a satisfied grin.

Taking in more lessons and finding the enjoyment of the guitar coming back to her, Nicole easily passed a couple hours. Finally her stomach told her it was time for dinner. With a contented sigh, she put away the guitar for another time. This was something she would pursue!

∞ ∞ ∞

Nicole was back at work. She still hadn't bought any new clothes, even though she had ordered some online. Going in early this morning, she had gone to the operating room first thing to see if she could borrow some of their scrubs. So what if they said 'OR scrubs' on them? She could get a bigger size than she normally wore and that would help her till she bought new ones. So here she was, wearing bright green, a colour she normally would not have been seen in.

Chloe had come back to work today after having taken a few sick days. But she did not look good at all. In fact, Nicole thought she saw some heavy makeup on her face to disguise her appearance, but wasn't sure if she was seeing right, being a few feet away. She would make time later to speak with her.

Later that morning when both Chloe and Nicole ended up at the medication cart to get some pills for their patients, Nicole was able to see the other nurse more carefully. What she saw made her heart sink. She was sure there was a large bruise on Chloe's face which the makeup partly covered. After putting in the combination of the lock to get medications out, Nicole turned to Chloe and put her hand on her arm. Chloe was patiently waiting for her turn, so she turned to Nicole, eyebrows raised.

"Is everything all right with you?" Nicole asked her softly.

Eyes downcast, Chloe responded. "Why do you ask? I'm back at work, so I'm better."

"What was wrong? How come you had to take a few days off work?" Nicole leaned up against the wall, arms crossed, holding the patient's pill cup in her hand.

"Oh, I wasn't feeling good. No big deal."

"Chloe." Nicole spoke her name softly. She didn't believe Chloe had been sick with the flu or whatever. This was something else; she could tell by the marks on her face which Chloe had tried to conceal.

At the sound of her gently spoken name, Chloe winced and turned to Nicole. "Okay, I wasn't sick physically. But I was sick at heart, and that's just as good a reason to take time off as any!" With tears brimming over, Chloe turned to face the cart.

"How did you bruise your face, Chloe?" Nicole asked gently.

With the tears spilling over, Chloe's defence was gone. She turned back to Nicole, imploring her with her eyes, hoping for understanding. "Barry hit me," she whispered. Her hand unconsciously went to the darkened area on her face.

Nicole's heart did a flip-flop. *Oh Father, give me words to say to my friend here. I don't know how to help her, but You know what I should say!* "Do you want to talk about it?"

With a look of frustration, Chloe told her there was no time. She had work to do.

"Nonsense! When there's a problem, we can take a few minutes out of our day to talk. It might even help you to feel better if you can talk about it." After locking all their medications back into the cart, Nicole pulled her into the staff lounge where they would have some privacy at this time of day. "There now, let's sit down for a few minutes, shall we?"

Chloe agreed that it might be good for her to talk. "I've been increasingly suspicious of Barry's hours lately. He's been coming home later and later, and some nights I'm not really sure if he's been there at all; I was wondering if he just showed up a while before I woke up. I was suspecting that he might be seeing someone from his office, but of course I didn't know for sure. Then this week I smelled perfume on one of his shirts in the laundry. I couldn't believe it! I was absolutely dumbfounded." Chloe looked down at her hands. "Anyhow, a few nights ago he did come home and I confronted him with the shirt. He was very angry that I would have the nerve to accuse him of having an affair, so he said. But the thing is that I never said that to him, I just asked him what the perfume was that was on his shirt. He told me the rest with his anger."

She sniffed. "Well, the argument escalated and before I knew what was happening, he had hit me in the face so hard that I fell into the wall." She looked up with tears in her eyes. "When it was over he felt terrible. He kept apologizing for hitting me, but I didn't want him to touch me. I guess I stayed home because I was embarrassed about the bruise, and I didn't think I could work without crying." She finished her account and blew her nose.

Nicole pulled her into a hug and they sat there together for a few minutes. When Chloe's crying was under control, Nicole pulled back enough to look at her friend. "Has he ever touched the kids?"

"No, thank God! I would have surely left him by now if he had."

"So what are you planning to do?"

Chloe looked at her with surprise. "What do you mean?"

"Well, are you going to leave him or something?" Nicole had never encountered physical abuse, but she was sure that if it happened once, it would happen again sometime down the road.

"He said he was sorry!" Chloe did not look happy. Her hands were shredding the tissues in her hands as she thought about her options. "Should I just up and leave him for making one mistake?"

"Well actually, it's two mistakes he made. He went with another woman AND he hit you. Did he talk about what was happening with the perfume?" Nicole wasn't sure how much of this Chloe would want to talk about, but as long as she didn't get angry at her for inquiring, she would keep trying to understand.

"Oh he said someone at work stumbled and fell into him. It sounded kind of lame at the time, but what am I supposed to say to that?"

"He said that?" Nicole's eyebrows shot up with disbelief. "He didn't own up to it? How could someone falling against him put the smell of perfume on his shirt?"

Looking even more miserable, Chloe shook her head. "I don't know. I guess he felt that was a good enough excuse if it's not the truth."

With compassion in her eyes, Nicole took one of Chloe's hands in her own. "Chloe, my place is big enough if you need somewhere to go with your kids for a while. At any time if this should happen again, please call me and come over with a suitcase. We'll figure out where to go from there. Okay?"

The kindness in her voice and concern in her face showed Chloe that she cared. She reached up to her once more and hugged her briefly. Looking at her watch, Chloe gasped. "I have to give out these pills!" Jumping up, she looked back at Nicole, straightened her scrubs up as best she could, then fled the room.

Sitting still for another few minutes, Nicole prayed for her friend. Her heart felt heavy. Too many of her patients had been physically abused. She knew this was not what she wanted for Chloe. But Chloe would have to make the decision to leave on her own.

Chapter 13

Nicole was on her days off and this afternoon she was going to go to Abbotsford for a few days. She was looking forward to the break with a great deal of anticipation. For one thing, the maternity clothes she had ordered online should have arrived by now, and her mother had promised to take her shopping for more clothes. There was a maternity store in the Little Oaks Mall; she had been in there with Jennifer when she was pregnant and loved their clothes.

Humming as she went about the business of cleaning out her small apartment, Nicole spoke to her cat as she went. "Now you will be a good boy for Annaliese while I'm gone, right Shadow? And don't you worry; before you know it, I'll be back." Shadow was sitting on the small counter beside the stacking washer/dryer combination and watching as she piled laundry into the washer. Putting in the soap, she closed the door, made her selections and turned on the machine. The sound made Shadow jump down from the counter. He sat where he was and began grooming himself. With a smile on her lips, Nicole watched him for a moment. He was such a precious cat! She could depend on him to give her his brand of cat affection every day. And when she really needed loving, he was there, purring on her lap. She bent down and petted him, loving him.

∞ ∞ ∞

Nicole grinned and waved at her father's receptionist. Walking through, she found her mother's office and peeked her head in the door. Ellen, as manager of this busy medical practice, was working at the computer. She glanced up when she saw a shadow cross her vision. "Nicole, it's so good to see you!" She stood and gave her daughter a hug, then pulled her into the room. "Look what came for you this week," she said as she reached for the parcel on the bookshelf beside her desk.

"It came?" Nicole was delighted. Ripping open the package, she pulled out the items she had bought from the maternity web page. "Mom, do you know what a Belly Band is?" she asked with a twinkle in her eye.

"A belly who?" Ellen had a bemused expression on her face.

Nicole laughed. "A Belly Band, and this is it." Holding up the strip of fabric, she showed her mom and explained how it would help. "How about I put it on right now? Then we'll both see how it works." Pulling on the elasticized fabric, she placed it over her jeans and opened the zipper. "Ah, it feels better already." Nicole wasn't really big, but she was definitely heavier in the belly than her normal size. She adjusted the band so it completely covered the upper part of her jeans. Then pulling on the light blue maternity t-shirt, she modelled it for Ellen. "There, what do you think?"

Ellen was amazed. That band really did look good! And it surely would help Nicole to wear her normal pants longer. "You look great!" she said. With a frown, she remembered something. "Does that mean you don't want to go shopping with me tomorrow?"

"No way! Of course I want to go shopping with you. This is all the maternity stuff I have. It'll be good for a bit, but I'm not comfortable any more in my tops. Besides, we have a date, right?" she asked her mom, eyebrows raised in a query.

Sitting down again, Ellen smiled. "I wasn't really worried. A woman can use all the maternity clothes she can get when she's pregnant. But I was...and am...still looking forward to our time together."

Nicole grinned at her as she folded up her clothes and put them in the package she had received. "So, what time did you want to go, then?"

"Well, I figure we can have a leisurely breakfast and head out to the stores by the time they open, around nine or nine-thirty. What do you think?"

"Sounds good to me. Say, would you like me to head home and start dinner? That way it could be ready when you and dad get home."

"Thanks, Nicole, but I prepared us some beef stroganoff last night and it's in the crock pot now. It's been cooking all day so it should be perfect when we get home. We'll just have to add sour cream, cook a few noodles and we'll be all set. Why don't you go say hi to your father? I'm sure he'd love to see you if he's in between patients."

Just at that moment Stan poked his head in the door. He was wearing a white lab coat over his coffee-coloured dress slacks and beige button-down shirt. "I thought I heard voices. Hi Nicole! You look wonderful, honey!" Pulling her to himself, he gave her a big bear hug. "You're staying for a couple of days?" he inquired, a smile on his face.

Nicole pulled back from his hug and looked at him fondly. Her father was ageing nicely, with salt and pepper hair and blue-gray eyes.

"I'll be with you for three whole days this time."

"Now that's something to look forward to, isn't it honey?" he turned and spoke to Ellen, his arm still around Nicole. Smiling back at him, Ellen agreed.

∞ ∞ ∞

"Phew, I'm exhausted! I didn't know shopping could be this tiring!" Nicole dropped into a chair and put her feet up. "I think we bought everything I'm going to need for the rest of this pregnancy, don't you, Mom?"

Ellen was on the couch, taking a much-needed break. "I sure hope so. That was why I wanted to be with you, so I could treat you to a few nice things."

"Thank you so much!" Nicole said with a grin. "How did you know 'Pro One Uniforms' was in Abbotsford?"

Ellen looked at her. "Well, our Medical Office Assistants buy their uniforms there. I'm so glad they had a few maternity things for you. They're not like the plain scrubs you get at the hospital, but much nicer, as far as I'm concerned."

Nicole agreed. "Hospital scrubs are great because they are so comfortable. But they aren't anything special to look at. Oh, they're practical and all. But these other uniforms they carry at that store are so cute! And they'll certainly go a long way to make me feel prettier than the OR scrubs I've been wearing, especially as I get bigger." She sighed with contentment. All in all, she was very happy she had come home for a while.

∞ ∞ ∞

Nicole looked at all the cookies on display. How could she choose only one? Waffling back and forth, she finally chose two different kinds and bought a coffee as well. Speaking to the cashier while the sale was being rung up, Nicole peered through the window into the kitchen to see if her sister was there. "Is Julie busy right now? Do you know if she could come out and say hi?"

The young lady behind the counter gasped and responded, "I thought you looked familiar! Let me go get her for you." Poking her head in the door of the kitchen, she sang out, "Julie, your sister is here!"

Nicole was sipping her coffee when Julie came bounding through the door. Catching a glimpse of Nicole, she jogged over and threw her arms around her sister. "You didn't tell me you were coming! How are you?" Pulling away from Nicole and taking a close look at her, she smiled. "You are looking good! Look at the maternity clothes!" She patted Nicole's tummy. Bending down and speaking to the slight bulge, she whispered, "Can't wait to meet you, little one." Straightening up, she grinned at Nicole. "I see you have some coffee already. Just a sec and I'll get myself one too. It's time for a break." She went behind the counter and in less than a minute she was leading the way to a booth.

Julie took a long swallow of her coffee and looked inquiringly at Nicole. "So how are you doing these days? Are you still throwing up?"

Nicole laughed and said, "No, I'm not throwing up, thank God! That was not a fun part of this pregnancy."

"So you're feeling better now?" Julie began munching on her favourite cookie, Cappuccino Melts. She was wearing the brown trademark apron of Diana's coffee shop over her khakis and white shirt which was rolled to the elbows. Her light brown hair was pulled back in a french braid today and her eyebrows went up as she questioned her sister.

"Yeah, physically I'm better." Nicole looked down at her cookie, lost in thought for a moment.

"Is something wrong?" Julie thought Nicole didn't look too happy.

Looking up, Nicole shook her head. "No, there isn't anything wrong, not really."

"But...?" Julie figured she should try to pry this out of her sister.

Nicole glanced up with an embarrassed look. "It's just that I still worry, you know, about what will happen after the baby comes. How will I handle being a single mother? Where will we live? I guess I'm just scared, that's all. It's an awful lot of responsibility to have all by myself." Nicole's chin quivered, showing that she was very close to losing it.

With a look of compassion on her face, Julie took one of Nicole's hands in hers. "Oh honey, I know! You wouldn't be normal, I don't think, if you didn't worry about these things." She just wished she could be a bigger help to her sister. What a scary time this must be for her!

Nicole looked at Julie with a distracted air. "I feel better and that's a good thing. But there are still so many things I struggle with where Greg is concerned. Next month will be his birthday. How will I get through that?" The tears escaped again and tumbled down her face before she wiped them away with the back of her free hand. Releasing her other hand from Julie's, she turned and reached for her purse which was on the bench beside her. Opening it, she rummaged around inside till she found a tissue to wipe her nose. With a sigh she sat back and continued drinking her coffee.

Julie didn't have a clue how to respond. She began to pray in her heart for wisdom to know what to say. She wanted to be a help, not a hindrance in Nicole's pain. After allowing a short silence between them, Julie spoke. "I know you wish Greg was here to enjoy this with you. I know you wish he would be there for the birth, to see the baby's first step and so on. I feel for you, I really do."

Nicole reached out and squeezed her hand. "Thanks, sis. I know you care." Looking down, Nicole struggled with herself, wondering if she should be honest with Julie. Making up her mind, she spoke, "Someone at work suggested I should get an abortion."

"An abortion! Whatever for?" Julie was surprised.

"Well, so I don't end up being a single parent, I guess." Nicole looked somewhat distracted.

Julie watched her for a moment, wondering what to say. "Please don't tell me you're considering that, are you?" She didn't want to be pushy, but after all, this baby was wanted in the Graham family!

As Nicole looked at Julie, a sigh escaped and made her sound so weary. "No, I'm not considering it...anymore."

"But you did consider it?"

Nicole was only able to continue because she knew her sister loved her and wasn't judging her. "I thought about it for a while. But then something happened at work which made me see that this little baby is not just a hunk of tissue, but a real live baby." Nicole took a sip of her coffee.

Julie had heard enough stories from the medical people in her family to know anything could happen in a hospital. "So what happened?"

"One of my patients had a miscarriage at twenty weeks and the fetus came out whole and intact. We had it in the utility room for a bit and I got to see it." With an intense look on her face, begging her sister to understand, Nicole continued. "Oh Julie, you should have seen it. It was a perfectly formed little baby, just so very tiny. As I looked at it, I suddenly felt myself drawn to the baby inside me." She looked down at her folded hands on the table. "I guess for the first time I saw how selfish I was being in considering ending this, thinking it would give me freedom."

Julie took Nicole's hands in her own before speaking. "I'm so glad you came to that conclusion, Nic. I know it can't be easy for you. But you know, this precious baby is very much wanted and looked forward to in the Graham family!" She smiled at Nicole. "We're all so excited and can't wait to meet him or her."

Nicole was grateful for the support. And it felt good somehow to get the abortion thing off her chest.

"You know, Nic, something just occurred to me. Your baby might look a lot like Greg. Wouldn't that be a comfort to you? To be reminded of him each time you see your baby?"

Nicole looked like she'd been punched in the gut. "I guess I didn't think about that. You know, I don't know if it would be a comfort, or just painful to be reminded of Greg every time I see the baby. Don't you think it would just remind me of the accident and everything I've lost?" Nicole looked pleadingly at Julie.

"Maybe. But don't forget that you will have several more months to work through the grief before this baby comes on the scene. By then it just might be a consolation rather than a reminder of bad things. I don't know, I guess I just thought it was possible, that's all."

"Thanks, I know you're trying to be helpful." Nicole had pulled her hands from Julie's and her fingers were now intertwined. She had finished both her cookie and coffee, and didn't know what to do with her hands during this discussion.

Suddenly Julie gasped and snapped her fingers. "I just had an idea!"

Nicole smiled at her excitement. "What's that?"

"Well, I thought if you were interested, I could come with you for the delivery. I could be with you for the whole time, help you. Maybe we could go to prenatal classes together or something!"

Nicole's face flushed. "You would do that for me?"

"Of course I would! And I would enjoy every moment. Mind you, it would be easier if you were closer, that's for sure. I mean, it would take me an hour or more to get into Vancouver, so if you're still there I would need to know as early as possible. But I'm still totally willing, it doesn't matter where you're living or which hospital you go to."

Nicole was so touched by the suggestion, she found herself tearing up again. "Thanks, Jules. I would really love that."

Smiling at one another across the table, the two sisters felt a connection like never before. They had been close growing up, but there had been so much competition all the time. It wasn't until Nicole left home that she knew how much she really did love this girl! And to think Julie was willing to give up her time this way for Nicole. It was amazing to her! "I still have four months to go, so there's still a little time left. I don't know how easy it is to get into prenatal classes at this point, but in any case, I have a friend who works in maternity at St. Paul's Hospital. She might be able to give us some pointers. Maybe I should invite her over one day when you can come over too. How would that work?"

"Even better! We'll get individual assistance this way!" They both giggled.

"You know, Julie, I really am trying to get things together to move to Abbotsford. I have made a start with putting away Greg's things. It's going slowly, but the important thing is that I've begun." There was silence for a couple beats. Nicole continued, "Did you know Steve has asked me to move into his suite when Roseanne leaves?"

With a happy smile on her face, Julie nodded. "He mentioned it to me. Do you have any idea what the hold-up is? Hasn't it been a little while since she mentioned she wanted to go?"

Nicole sighed long and deep. "She needs to find somewhere to live closer to her new job. But apparently the prices are pretty steep the closer you get to the city. She hasn't found anything that comes close to what she has now at Steve's."

"Well, why don't we pray that God will help her find something? He can guide her to just the right place." Looking at her watch, Julie made a moue of distaste. "Coffee break is up; I must get back to work. Will I see more of you before you head back?"

"I'm staying at Mom and Dad's so just pop on by. You know my cell number too, so just call if you're not sure I'm there."

Both ladies stood up to leave. Hugging as they stood near the booth, Nicole held on a little longer than usual. Whispering into her sister's ear, she said, "Thanks for the offer. I'll see what I can do." With that she gave one last squeeze and walked to the door as Julie returned to work.

∞ ∞ ∞

Having dinner with her parents and Matthew the following evening, Nicole mentioned what her problems were in finding a job at the Abbotsford Hospital. She didn't want twelve hour shifts, and would prefer to not work nights either. "How could anyone find a full time RN job with those limitations?"

Stan was the first to comment. "You know, honey, you don't have to work full time. You don't even have to work part time. Why don't you try to find a casual position for the time being? Even if you just work one day a week, that would still keep your hand in, but would still give you plenty of time with the baby when he comes."

"He?" Nicole teased her father. "Do you know something I don't?"

"Come on, honey, you know that's just a figure of speech." He grinned. "But it would be fun having a little boy baby again. It'll be fun having a little girl baby too; as long as it's a healthy baby, I'll be happy."

Nicole sobered a little. "I know what you mean. Actually, I don't care one way or another either. Right now I'm not ready for this baby. I have a few more things to work through before I feel strong enough emotionally to see this child!"

Stan reached over and gave her a hug, which wasn't difficult to do as she was at the end of the table and he was right beside her.

"Thanks, Dad. I've never thought of working as a casual before. Are there many positions for casuals in the hospital?"

"I'm sure they need them here and there. The only thing is that you'll probably run into twelve hour shifts in the main hospital, whatever you apply for. But if you want eight hour shifts, you could apply for a position in Worthington or the Cottage, where they have the long term care patients as well as General Rehab. I think they work eight hour shifts there." Lost in thought for a moment, he continued as an idea came to him, "You know, I think General Daycare and Surgical Daycare also have eight hour shifts. You could try those too."

"Oh really? That's a good idea. I'll have a look on the Fraser Health web page and see if there's anything available." Nicole was surprised at how excited she was getting. This was definitely something that would work out better for her. As a casual she could choose her own hours.

Ellen jumped into the conversation. "You know if you got on as a casual, you don't necessarily have to stop working nights. I don't know if you like working those or not. But maybe we could help you with the baby if you worked then. The other thing is that they need extra staff so much on weekends. I bet if you offered to work Saturdays or Sundays you would get all the work you want. And you could work whatever shift you want too because we could chip in with the baby, no problem."

Nicole's eyes glowed. Things were starting to come together, in her mind at least. "I'll let you know what comes up." With that she stood up to help clear the table. They were planning on playing Apples to Apples tonight and she wanted to get the show on the road!

∞ ∞ ∞

Nicole had already filled in her resume online at Fraser Health in anticipation of something coming available for her. Tonight she was scanning the available jobs and found that there were several casual positions that might be possibilities for her. Sitting there thinking about it all, she wondered if she should go ahead. Finally, with her mind made up, she clicked on the site and sent off her application for all the available positions. There! It was done. Now she would wait and see what opened up for her.

∞ ∞ ∞

Walking in a half sleep the following morning, Nicole heard voices in the kitchen before she got there. Rounding the corner, she saw Julie and Matthew at the nook, his laptop opened between them. "You can choose from these wallpapers for your site, but I would recommend you use one that is appealing to the eye, like maybe this one," Matthew said as he clicked the mouse. Julie was looking on with such rapt attention she didn't even see Nicole walk into the room.

"There, what do you think of these colours?" Matthew asked her. Looking up he saw Nicole and grinned at her. "We're working on making a web page for Julie so she can start her own business right now, even if it's in a small way."

Nicole looked over and saw that there was coffee in the pot. "Is the coffee fresh?"

Julie nodded her head. "I just put it on about ten minutes ago. Get a mug and come sit with us, Nic."

Pouring milk into the mug, Nicole moved slowly. She hadn't fully awoken yet. In fact, she was still in her pyjamas. Good thing there were no strangers here! She smiled at her own silliness. Her parents often had friends over for meals, but breakfast wasn't one of those meals. "Where are Mom and Dad? Have you seen them?" She asked as she perched on the chair beside Julie, sipping her coffee.

"Oh, they ran over to Costco. Mom said something about looking for a new elliptical trainer for their gym. The one they have is not working well," Matthew answered her absentmindedly while he continued to click on the screen with the mouse. When he was done, he turned the laptop over so Nicole could see what he was doing. "Have a look, Nicole. This is just the beginning stages, but Julie's going to have a great webpage."

Taking a peek at the screen, Nicole found she was quite stunned by what was there. There was a banner across the top with colourful swirls. 'Sweet Tooth Cafe' was written in the midst of the colours; it was all very appealing. Lower down the page there were pictures of cookies, muffins and other sweet things. She looked over at Matthew. "You've done a good job so far."

She turned to Julie with a grin. "I didn't know you were this far ahead. You were serious about doing this!"

"But of course! And having Matthew helping me has been really great. He even got a web designer from India to make this banner for me for very little money! Doesn't it look good?" She was beaming with delight.

Nicole agreed with her. Even so, she could see there was still lots of work to be done. "I guess it'll be a while before the web page is up and running, huh?"

"It's a work in progress." Matthew agreed. "But the good thing is that I'm using it as a school project. So it'll be finished by the end of the semester." Glancing at Julie he continued, "I just hope Julie likes the end result."

Swatting him on the arm, Julie laughed. "Of course I'll like the finished project. After all, I'm helping you with it, right?" They all laughed.

"You know, Julie, my prof will want something specific for my project, but we can always go in and change anything you like afterwards. That won't be a problem."

Having finished her coffee, Nicole got up and stretched. "I guess I'd better go take a shower. I'll see you guys in about fifteen minutes, okay?"

"Sure thing, Nic. Don't rush, just make sure you do a good job," teased Matthew.

Giving him a dirty look, then throwing a grin over her shoulder at him as she flipped her hair back, Nicole made her exit.

∞ ∞ ∞

Nicole was sitting with Jennifer in their kitchen. She was there for dinner, but she had arrived early so they could talk for a bit.

"You look cute in those maternity duds, Nicole." Jennifer admired her clothes. "You know, I still have a few things left from my last pregnancy. If you wouldn't mind giving them back when you're done, I'd be happy to loan you a few things."

"Really?" Nicole hadn't even thought of that, but she had loved some of Jennifer's maternity clothes. "That would be great!"

"Good. When I've gotten the kids into bed later on, I'll dig them up for you, okay?"

Nodding at her in delight, Nicole bent down to pick up Leila who had just toddled over to her. "Look at you! You are getting so big!" Nicole was acutely conscious of all she was missing by being so far away. Wasn't it only yesterday that Leila was born? And here she was already walking holding on to things! She picked up the little girl and gave her a hug, then settled her on her lap.

"NicNic," Leila said in her baby voice. She was waving a cardboard book in Nicole's face as if to say 'Read this to me'.

Picking up the book, Nicole began reading with great inflection and wiggling of her eyebrows to amuse Leila. When both of them were giggling, Jennifer stood with a pleased smile on her face. "I'll finish dinner while you two get re-acquainted."

Suddenly Nicole's breath caught in her throat. As she gazed at Leila and smelled the clean baby smell, she was suddenly brought face to face with the fact that at this time next year she would have a little bundle of her own to take care of, all by herself. It was a scary thought, but as she regarded this little cherub, she was actually looking forward to meeting the infant who would be a perfect Philips/Graham combination. Picking up the book again, she continued reading to Leila.

∞ ∞ ∞

Nicole found herself sitting in the living room with Steve while Jennifer stayed a few more minutes with the kids as they were falling asleep. "I love your kids, Steve," she said wistfully. "I hope my baby will be as much fun as yours are."

Steve poked her feet with his foot while they were propped on the coffee table. "Of course yours will be as much fun. Why wouldn't he? Kids are all such a gift from the Lord. Just wait, when your baby comes you'll find you've fallen in love all over again."

"Do you think so?" Nicole asked him hopefully, a tentative smile on her lips.

"Of course I think so. Jennifer and I were the same with all three kids. It's amazing how you can love kids and play with them, but when it's your own that comes into the world, everything changes. All of a sudden this protectiveness comes up in you too, and it mixes in with the awe of who this little person is. There is nothing like it! The love you feel is quite overwhelming."

Nicole was watching his face carefully. "Overwhelming, that's kind of how I feel this whole thing is."

"You know, you can read about babies and children and all that stuff, trying to prepare yourself for this new little baby. But in the end, you can't really prepare yourself. The only way to learn is to dive right in. But when your baby is born, God gives you a special love for this helpless little creature. You're aware this is a product of your love together, and the 'overwhelmed' part is different. I didn't mean it as a bad word...it's like you get a new appreciation for how God looks at us. I remember feeling such gratitude toward God for this remarkable blessing."

"Huh. Do you think it'll be the same for me? I mean, you had Jennifer there too. I'll be on my own." Sadness filled Nicole's face.

Steve dropped his feet to the ground and scooted closer. Putting his arm around her, he comforted her. "Of course it will be different for you, but there will be many similarities too. And you won't be alone. If you want, we'll all come!"

She looked up at him and laughed. What a funny picture that made in her mind, having all the Grahams in the delivery room with her! "Actually, Julie has offered to be there with me through the labour and delivery."

"That's super, Nicole! We'll still come if you want us to though."

She smiled and said she would think about it. "By the way, what's happening with Roseanne these days?"

Stretching out with his arms on the back of the couch, Steve answered her question. "Her new job has different hours. She doesn't seem to be here as much as before, so that's good for us. But she's still looking. I'm not sure if she's looking all that regularly. It sure would be nice to see her go so we could prepare the suite for you." He looked over at her and sighed.

"Julie and I have both agreed to pray for her to find something soon. After all, God knows where the available places are and He can lead her to them, don't you think?"

"I sure agree with that one. We'll pray too."

At that moment, Jennifer walked in carrying an armful of clothes. "Here are the things I was talking to you about, Nicole." She dropped the bundle on the chair beside the couch and blew the hair out of her face.

Nicole jumped up, "Really? All these?" She began sorting through the clothes with much oohing and aaahing. Holding up every outfit one by one, Nicole gave them a preview of what they would look like on her. She was so excited! She could put all her regular clothes away till after the baby was born now, even the pants she had worn the Belly Bands with. "Do you mind if I go try these on?" she asked, holding up a pair of jeans and a pink lacy top.

"Go for it. You'll look great in them, I'm sure, but come out and show us, okay?" Jennifer dropped into Nicole's place on the couch and nuzzled up to her husband with a grin. After a few minutes of quiet, she looked up at him and whispered, "I sure hope Nicole can move out to Abbotsford before the baby arrives!"

Agreeing with her, Steve put a finger to her lips. He could hear Nicole returning. In she walked wearing Jennifer's maternity clothes. They were different colours than she ordinarily wore, but she liked them and they did look good on her.

With a whistle of appreciation, Steve told her he liked them. "There's only one thing though, Nicole. You better bring them back when you're done with them. I have a feeling Jennifer might need them by that time." He teased Nicole, grinning over at Jennifer who was blushing sweetly beside him.

Chapter 14

Nicole had been home from her parents' place for a week now. She had already worked and was on her days off again. Today she was determined to learn a little more about the guitar. She had bought a stand to sit it on instead of keeping it in the case all the time. This way she was reminded more frequently to pick it up and play a little. Her fingers had been sore for a bit as her fingertips grew the necessary calluses to play, but now playing didn't hurt anymore. She had sent away for a special DVD from that guitar web page and was learning some good things. The most basic and recent thing she had learned was the name of each string. They were labelled E, A, D, G, B and E. She had never been able to keep these straight before, but on the DVD she learned an easy way to remember them: Eddie Ate Dynamite, Good Bye Eddie. This made her laugh to herself every time she tuned the guitar with Greg's electronic tuner.

Suddenly she thought of Greg. How happy he would be to see she had taken his guitar and begun playing it. As Nicole sat on Greg's easy chair, she ran her hands along the arms. He had sat here not all that long ago. Her eyes glazing over, Nicole was lost in her memories of Greg. He'd had a way of making her laugh with his playing, and remembering it brought a smile to her lips. Greg could compose a song at a moment's notice. He often had her in stitches with one of her favourites: a song about a cow named Daisy. As the song grew, the cow became rambunctious and sounded more and more human.

Now and then Greg would sing her a love song he had composed just for her.

As she thought back to those days, an intense longing gripped her heart. How she missed him! Turning her head, her gaze fell on one of their wedding pictures. Nicole lost what little composure she had left. Tears blinded her as she stumbled into the bedroom to get some tissue. Then falling onto her bed, she wept for what she knew could never be.

Some time later she woke up to find she had fallen asleep and her pillow was wet with tears. Looking in the mirror, she saw lines on her face. If she didn't think of why she had been on her bed in the first place, she might have laughed at the markings on her face. But it was best not to go there today. She couldn't afford to cry like that too much.

Nicole knew what she should do. She would make herself a cup of tea and read her Bible. Maybe God would have some comfort in there for her. She would turn to the Psalms. King David had cried out to God in his need so many times; it was an encouragement for her to see that others had suffered the same kind of problems.

Reading Psalm 62, she felt her heart quicken. Verses five to eight took her breath away.

"My soul, wait in silence for God only, for my hope is from Him."

Nicole knew that her hope had to be in God. She knew that she was not able to do anything to change her situation, and the more she relied on God, the better she would be.

"He only is my rock and my salvation, my stronghold; I shall not be shaken."

She had tried over the years to save herself in other things, but that didn't bring peace. As long as God was her stronghold, she would not be shaken.

"On God my salvation and my glory rest; the rock of my strength, my refuge is in God. Trust in Him at all times, O people; pour out your heart before Him; God is a refuge for us."

She knew it was only in Him that she would make it through this difficult time of mourning, when she remembered Greg in everything she saw and did. Reading the verses over and over, Nicole knew that this portion of scripture was a beautiful promise for her. Pulling out her highlighter, she made the words pop out of her Bible. She wanted to remember this! Even as she sat there reading, a melody began going through her head, intertwining with the words she had just read.

Scrambling to get the guitar off its stand, Nicole sat down with her Bible nearby. Playing the tune that was in her head, she worked at it until the song had taken shape. As she sang, tears of gratitude to God flowed. Annaliese had once told her that there was healing in the Word of God. If that was the case, she would have to take it deep into her heart. As she sang this new song[2] into being, an excitement hummed within her. This would be the way to memorize special verses that God gave to her!

Nicole looked at the words and chords she had written down. It was simple, but it touched her deeply. God was indeed her stronghold. Since that day at Mill Lake, she had been finding out just how faithful He was to her. He was always listening to her when she prayed. Oh, she didn't always get her prayers answered in the way she would like, but she was learning how to pray according to the Spirit instead of through the flesh, and it had made a huge difference in her Christian walk.

Looking at the verses again, she thought about what it meant to not be shaken. In her circumstances, it must mean that He would guide her through the quagmire of grief into peace, His peace. She didn't have that peace all the time, but she was starting to feel that it might be possible one day.

With a contented sigh Nicole put away the guitar and closed her Bible. God had really met with her today! With a quiet and tranquil heart, she went about her chores, talking to her cat as she worked.

∞ ∞ ∞

Nicole was heading home from work, and didn't feel like making herself dinner. She was just too tired. But the problem was that she was also hungry. She thought about what she would like to eat, and decided she was actually craving Chinese food. So turning her Jeep around, she headed toward the other part of town and some Chinese take-out!

Nicole balanced her purse, lunch bag and dinner in her arms and shut the door of her Jeep. Locking it with the key fob, she started walking in the direction of the stairs. In an effort to remain fit she had been using the stairs. Tonight with all the packages she carried, she ended up at the elevator. She would treat herself to a ride upstairs for once.

---

2   To hear the song "My Soul Wait in Silence", go to http://www.oliveboettcher.com

Juggling with all the bags in her arms, Nicole unlocked her apartment and dropped everything inside. Once the door was shut, she greeted her cat by bending over and petting him. Shadow adored it when she did that, so he sauntered in and out of her legs, enjoying the rubdown and meowing his approval.

Standing up with a laugh, she put her bags in their proper place and brought dinner to the kitchen. She could smell the pineapple chicken and the aroma was divine! Pulling out a dinner plate, Nicole settled herself at the table and took a grateful whiff before eating her meal. When there were just a few crumbs left on the plate and she felt like she might burst, she pushed it aside and had a cold drink of milk. Ahhh! That felt better.

Looking around for one of Shadow's toys, she spotted the laser pointer on the corner of her kitchen counter. Shadow couldn't resist this little red spot on the ground, and Nicole enjoyed watching him run to catch it. This would give him a little exercise. He crouched down low to the ground, his pupils dilating while he got ready to pounce; then with a leap he attacked the red, dancing spot. When Nicole turned it off, Shadow looked at the laser pointer. *What a smart cat*, she thought. *He knows the light is coming from the pointer.* After having gone around the apartment a couple times, she spotted the 2 meter-long cord Shadow also played with. She put down the pointer and started dragging the cord over furniture and all over the apartment. Shadow tried to catch it as she walked with the cord behind her. She teased him with it then pulled it just out of his reach so he would keep going. *Okay, that's enough. We've both had some exercise, now it's time to relax.*

Nicole curled up on Greg's chair with Shadow sitting on the arm. She had borrowed a Dee Henderson book from her mom and it was time to start it. She kept yawning through the first chapter, and pretty soon her eyelids were drooping too much to understand what was on the written page. She put the book down and got ready for bed. As soon as her head hit the pillow, she was dead to the world.

Nicole awoke with a start at two o'clock in the morning with her telephone ringing. *Who could be calling at this time of night? It must be a wrong number*, she thought as she scrambled for the receiver.

"Hello Nicole?"

The whispered voice sounded like Chloe, but she didn't sound right. "That's me. Is that you, Chloe?"

A hard blow from a nose told her Chloe had been crying. "Yes, it's me. Oh Nicole, I didn't know what to do anymore so I called you!" She began crying.

"It's okay, Chloe. Tell me what's wrong. Are you hurt? Do you need help?" Nicole was sitting up in bed gripping the receiver by now. This didn't sound good.

"I…I'm a little hurt. And I don't want to stay here anymore. He might hurt me again when he wakes up."

"Do you want to come over with the girls? I could come and get you right now." Nicole was thinking fast. Where would she put everybody? She only had one extra room and it was pretty small with a single bed in it. Never mind, she would work it out.

"Could you? I'd be forever grateful to you!" and Chloe sobbed again.

"Hang tight. I just have to throw some clothes on and I'll come right out. I should be there in fifteen minutes, okay?"

"Yes. I'll go get the girls ready and I'll be waiting with them at the door. Thanks so much, Nicole!"

Nicole's heart was beating fast. She wasn't sure what had happened tonight, but there was plenty of time to find out the details once she had Chloe and the girls safe in her own apartment. In her haste she put on two different coloured socks. Oh, who cared? It was the middle of the night and she wasn't going to a fashion show! Off she ran for her Jeep and turned it in the direction of Broadway and Granville.

Parking near the entrance of Chloe's apartment, Nicole ran for the door. Chloe was huddled against the door with sleepy one-year-old Christine in her arms, and four-year-old Brittany beside her. She had a hastily packed bag with baby essentials and a few clothes for her and Brittany. Nicole stole a quick look at her friend. She looked awful! Her nose looked crooked and there was blood running down to her chin which she had not properly mopped up yet. Bruises were quickly developing on her face. Compassion forced her to wait with her questions. She huddled the little troop into her Jeep and took off for home.

Once there she made a rapid decision about bedding. She found some blankets and made a bed for both little girls to sleep together on the floor, and told Chloe she could have the bed. After the sleepy girls were settled, Chloe joined Nicole in the kitchen. There was herbal tea made and a welcoming scent of almond in the air.

Nicole watched her friend slowly take a seat. She must be in pain. Getting up, she motioned for Chloe to lift her sweater. Nicole gasped at the sight that was before her. Chloe's back was a kaleidoscope of colours with contusions and bruises all along her left side. No wonder she was in pain! "I'll be right back. You just sit here and drink some tea." Nicole went to get some Advil. This would help with the inflammation. Getting back to the kitchen, she handed the pills to Chloe, who gratefully accepted them and took them down with a sip of tea.

Sitting down beside the young battered woman in her kitchen, Nicole spoke softly. "Okay, tell me what happened."

Chloe's chin wobbled as she fought with the tears. "Barry came home tonight after having been gone two days on a business trip. When he came in the girls were still up and they were carrying on, happy to see their daddy again." Chloe blew her nose in the tissue Nicole gave her. "When I finally put them to bed, Barry was sitting in the living room, watching something on TV. I wanted him to talk to me. After all, he had been gone and I was happy to see him too."

Two large tears slowly ran down her cheeks as she continued. "I asked him how his business trip had gone, and before I knew what was happening, he was angry with me and yelling that I should mind my own business. I didn't know what to do. He started telling me I was meddling and stupid. I was still standing, and before I had a chance to explain that I was just curious about his business trip, he hauled out and hit me in the face. He got my nose, which explains the blood. But I fell over the coffee table and hurt my back. I was crying and asking him to stop when I heard Brittany crying from the hallway. She had seen it all!"

Chloe swallowed convulsively for a couple beats. "I was so afraid he would hit her too. She came running to me, calling 'Mommy, mommy!' I grabbed her in my arms and held her tight. He would have to get through me first before hitting her. But I think just seeing her made him sort of wake up to what he was doing. He gaped at her, then at me, and he pounded off to the bedroom and slammed the door. I didn't know what to do, so I stayed on the floor, telling Brittany that it was going to be all right. I don't know how long we were there for. Brittany fell asleep in my arms and I sat there, trying to figure out what to do. Then I thought of you!" Chloe implored Nicole with her eyes. "I couldn't stay there tonight, I hope you don't mind!"

"Oh honey, I'm so glad you called. And as you can see, it'll work out fine with you here. The girls will love sleeping on the floor; we'll tell them it's like going camping." She took Chloe's hand in hers. "Do you have any family you could go to in a few days when you're feeling a bit better?"

Chloe was shaking her head back and forth. "My father was abusive toward me and my sister. My brother left home before I was in tenth grade; he's older than me. My sister lives in the states and he lives in Toronto. My parents, well, they're home but I'm not going there. I already said a little about my dad; my mom is an alcoholic, probably to insulate herself from dad's abuse."

Concern filled Nicole's voice as she spoke. "Well, don't worry. You can stay here as long as you need to. We'll make it work."

In the silence that followed, Nicole thought of something else. "Do you want to press charges? We should probably call the police."

Chloe drew back and fear filled her face. "No, don't call the police. They don't need to get involved. I don't want them here."

"But Chloe, what if he comes after you? Wouldn't you prefer to have a restraining order on him?"

Her face crumpling in despair, Chloe wailed quietly. "I still love him! Isn't that the crazy thing? How can I love such a brute! But I don't want to bring the police into this; Barry doesn't need that!"

Nicole could see that she would not be able to change her mind. She let the subject drop for the time being. "Come on, Chloe. Let's get you cleaned up and settled into the bedroom. You look like you need a good sleep." Lifting her to her feet, she led her to the bathroom where together they cleaned up the worst of the blood. Nicole would prefer to have that nose looked at and straightened, but she wasn't going to suggest going to the hospital now. Chloe's eyes were droopy with fatigue and emotion, so Nicole gave her a nightshirt and tucked her into bed. As she closed the bedroom door, she wondered what she should do next. She didn't have any experience with abusive spouses.

Getting down on her knees beside her bed, she cried out to God for wisdom and strength for what lay ahead.

Chapter 15

It was early in the morning and Nicole was knocking on Annaliese's door. She peered behind her shoulder to see if anyone was watching from her own apartment before entering.

"Nicole, you look awful!" Annaliese had never seen her look so tense, not even when Greg had died, as she hadn't seen Nicole then until his funeral was over. "What has happened, dear?"

Nicole followed her into the living room and sat down on the couch. "Annaliese, I need your help. I got a phone call in the middle of the night from a co-worker of mine. She has mentioned in the past that her husband had beaten her and I had offered her my place for a while should she need it." She paused to catch her breath.

Annaliese was alert and listening carefully. "Okay, carry on."

"Well she called at two in the morning because he had beaten her again. This time her four year old daughter saw it happen. Chloe is afraid to stay with him right now, so I went to get them and they are sleeping in the spare bedroom." Nicole took a deep breath. "The thing is... I don't know anything about abuse. I don't know how to help her. Do you have any experience with something like this?"

Annaliese was very concerned. "Stay right there; I'm getting you a glass of water." She returned in a couple of minutes with a tall glass of cold water which Nicole drank like she was parched.

"Well first of all, did she leave him permanently? Is this a separation, or is she going to divorce him?"

"I don't know if she has thought through all that yet." Chloe might be upset with Nicole for telling Annaliese, but she was desperate.

"Did you call the police last night? Do they know what's happening?" Annaliese asked her quietly.

"Chloe wouldn't let me call them. She says Barry doesn't need this complication in his life."

"Sounds to me like she's in denial. The man is clearly abusive and it's dangerous for her and her child."

"There's actually two little girls, and I know it's dangerous. That's the reason I came here; I don't know what to do next. They're all sleeping right now so I took the opportunity to come over here." Nicole was a little calmer because Annaliese's unruffled manner encouraged her.

"Hmm. I know there are some good shelters for abused women and children around. Actually, there is a group connected with our church that deals specifically with abuse but I'm not sure of the details because I haven't had anything to do with them. Would you like me to make some calls and find out what they recommend in this situation?"

Nicole was relieved. It was a start. "Oh yes, please. I just don't know where to go from here."

"Why don't you go on back in case they wake up...they're still sleeping, aren't they? I can call you when I have some answers. Right now the church isn't open, but it will be in another hour."

Standing up and giving Annaliese a big hug, Nicole felt like she was holding on to a life preserver. Walking to the door together, Annaliese looked up at her and smiled. "Let's be praying about this, shall we?"

"You bet!" answered Nicole, feeling better for having someone else involved.

∞ ∞ ∞

Walking into her apartment, Nicole could hear little-girl voices coming from the spare bedroom. The mere sound of it put a smile on her face because it was so endearing; but in the same moment she sobered, thinking about how their home life had just been torn apart.

Knocking at the door, she opened it a crack when Chloe said to come in. Making sure there were no small bodies near the door, she opened it completely and let herself in. "Good morning everybody!" she said with a smile.

The girls looked at their mother with uncertainty. When Chloe nodded to them, they greeted Nicole likewise. "How did you all sleep? Did you girls have fun camping out on the ground?"

They giggled and jumped on their blankets. A pillow flew off the makeshift bed. Chloe's sad eyes lit up with fondness at their antics. "Girls, this is Nicole. We are going to stay with her for a few days."

Both Christine and Brittany stopped their bouncing and looked at her. Brittany appeared to be the spokesperson for the children. "Will daddy be coming here too?"

Chloe shook her head. "No, daddy won't be coming here."

Brittany asked her mother where the bathroom was. Chloe stood up and took the girls' hands to lead them there. In the meantime, Nicole said she would make coffee and headed to the kitchen. She would have to get some food that children liked. Maybe they would welcome some Cheerios or other cereal for breakfast. Today would be a shopping day. Good thing she was off.

All three trooped into the kitchen several minutes later. The baby was able to walk, but could easily lose her balance, so Chloe and Brittany each held a hand.

"What are your plans for today?" asked Nicole as she poured the coffee into a mug for Chloe.

"I don't know." Chloe was moving even slower than yesterday; she most certainly had to be hurting physically as well as emotionally. The bruises on her face were dark and angry looking.

"Would you like some more Advil?" Nicole reached for the container which she had placed on top of the fridge. Shaking out two, she handed them to Chloe. "If that is really sore, you can take a couple of Tylenol at the same time; together they make a really good pain killer."

"That's not a bad idea!" Chloe would take all the help she could get today.

Nicole got her some Tylenol. She hated seeing her friend suffering like this. "So now, what do you girls like to eat for breakfast? How about I make us some pancakes?"

Her suggestion was quite a popular one, judging by the amount of cheering going on. So Nicole got to work.

When breakfast was done and Chloe had taken the girls into the bathroom to brush their teeth, Nicole cleaned up the dishes. While she was drying the last ones, the shrill sound of the telephone made her jump. "Good morning."

"Hi Nicole, it's Annaliese."

"Oh Annaliese, I'm so glad to hear from you! Did you find out anything?"

"As a matter of fact, I did. There is a group for battered women affiliated with our church, but they're somewhere else downtown. I got the phone number for you so you can call and find out what to do."

"How can I ever thank you, Annaliese?"

"Oh, I'll think of something!" Annaliese answered airily, making them both laugh. On that note, they both said goodbye and hung up.

∞ ∞ ∞

Nicole was working day shift again, and instead of Chloe working with her, there was a new Licensed Practical Nurse called Marianne. Chloe was still very bruised and sore, so she had called in sick. Good thing she had a bunch of sick time saved up from having worked as an LPN for several years.

While receiving report at work, Nicole got a glimpse of what working with Marianne was going to be like. She was downright surly this morning and Nicole couldn't say anything right. When she spoke, Marianne either ignored or frowned at her, effectively cutting off any further conversation with Nicole.

Nicole went about her day. She tried a few times to ask Marianne for help with some of her heavier patients. Working with Chloe had become a real team effort; if either of them needed help, they both felt free to ask. But every time Nicole asked Marianne, she was told it was not a good time, she was too busy with her own work. So Nicole made do on her own.

As she pondered what to do, Nicole's anger intensified toward Marianne. *How dare she treat me like this? Doesn't she realize that in nursing it's always better to work as a team? What have I done to make her so angry at me?* Nicole stewed in her anger for a while, making it doubly difficult to go back and speak with Marianne.

As noon was approaching, Nicole took a few minutes to bring the situation to the Lord. *I can't seem to do anything right with her, Lord. She hates me and I have no idea why! What do I do here?*

An impression came to her ever so gently. She felt the Lord was telling her to forgive Marianne. *What? Forgive her? I'm so angry, how can I forgive? And why does Marianne deserve that anyhow?*

As long as Nicole resisted God's voice, she had no peace. She continued her work, her mind swirling with criticism toward Marianne. The two were paired, but there was no teamwork. In fact, Marianne was just barely civil with her.

Taking a bathroom break, Nicole closed the door, leaned her forehead on it and began to pray quietly. *Okay, God, I'm ready to listen. You want me to forgive her. In my own strength I can't do that. I just want to strangle her! So Lord, I pray that You would give me Your love for Marianne. Help me to see her through Your eyes. What do you see when You look at her?*

As Nicole stood there quietly, listening for the voice of the Lord, in her mind's eye she saw a picture of the cross with Jesus hanging there, all bloody and disfigured. The picture took her breath away. Pondering what it might mean for her just now, it suddenly dawned upon her that Jesus died for Marianne too. That angry and bitter lady just didn't know it right now.

Nicole's heart felt squeezed. *Lord, I don't know what happened in her life to make her so bitter, but I forgive her and bless her. I'm sorry for the anger and criticism I've had toward her. Maybe one day You'll give me the opportunity to make a difference in her life. Have mercy on her, Lord.*

When Nicole was finished her business, she flushed the toilet, washed her hands and left to continue her work.

Mid-afternoon found her at the nursing station once again, and Marianne was there sorting out her medications. She went and stood beside the new LPN. "Marianne, could I speak with you for a minute please?" she asked with much trepidation.

Marianne swung around so fast she nearly spilled the drugs she was sorting. "What is it? Make it fast, I have to go give out my meds." Her snapping voice sounded like she was spitting out the words at Nicole.

What the heck? She is so angry; I don't know what I've done now. Help me, Lord!

"Are you okay today? I don't know you, but I get the feeling something is wrong. Is there anything I can do to help?" While she was speaking, Nicole took a careful look at Marianne. What she saw gave her compassion. The other nurse looked downright harried. "Is there anyone you need help with? I have a little time right now."

With a look of impatience toward Nicole, Marianne continued what she was doing. "There's nothing wrong. Now can I get on with my work? You're holding me up!"

Nicole's mouth dropped open in surprise. She didn't know what to do next. As Marianne turned her back to her and continued her work, Nicole pulled her mouth closed with a snap and turned on her heel. Well, there would be no truce today, that's for sure! She felt like yelling, "Time out!" with her hands in the international signal. Little good that would do! Marianne was in her own ugly little world right now.

With a sigh, Nicole went back to work and finished the day with a cloud of unhappiness clinging to her.

∞ ∞ ∞

When she got home after stopping to get a treat for the girls, Nicole looked around to see where her guests were. She found all three of them in the little bedroom. The children were petting Shadow, who loved every moment of it. Chloe was teaching them how to do it gently. Their little-girl voices were raised in excitement when the gray cat purred. "Mommy, he's making strange sounds!" Brittany exclaimed.

Chloe smiled. "That's called purring, honey bunch, and cats do that when they're happy. See? He must be really happy to have you pet him so gently."

Nicole smiled at the picture as she leaned on the door frame, her arms crossed. She could hear Shadow's purring from the door.

Christine was crawling around trying to get a better vantage point on this petting thing, when she looked up and saw Nicole. "Mama," she said, and pointed at Nicole.

Chloe glanced over and grinned. "They're having such fun with your cat. He is a patient one, isn't he?"

Pushing away from the door frame, Nicole walked into the room. "He is that. He's good with kids too, don't you think?"

"This is really nice for the girls. They've never been able to have pets because Barry is allergic to them." She sighed at the mention of his name.

"I went shopping and bought you girls a treat! Want to come and see?" Nicole took a hand from each and together they went into the kitchen. Pulling out a container of ice cream from the freezer, Nicole looked at Chloe, eyebrows raised in query, even if a little late.

"Oh look girls, she bought you some ice cream! Do you want some?" Chloe asked.

"Yay, ice cream!" Brittany answered in delight. Christine was making enthusiastic noises too. So they all sat down and had some ice cream.

"How was your day?" Chloe asked Nicole. She thought her friend looked tired.

Looking at Chloe briefly, Nicole shook her head. "You are the best partner anyone could hope to have, you know that? I sure felt lost without you today. I had a different partner, someone I've never met before. Her name is Marianne and she made my day miserable!"

Chloe's mouth dropped open in surprise. "What do you mean, she made your day miserable?"

"Well for one thing, she never wanted to help me with anything, never needed any help either, so we pretty well did our own thing all day. There was no team work whatsoever and if I tried to talk to her, she was so rude!"

Chloe narrowed her eyes in thought. "Is she like about six feet tall? With shoulder length brown hair and a rather plain face?"

Nicole gasped, "That does sound like her all right. How did you know? "

"A few months ago I took a course offered by the hospital called Prevention and Management of Aggressive Behaviour. There were about thirty of us in the class, and in the part where we practiced what we had learned about protecting ourselves, I was teamed up with Marianne. She was reasonably new."

"Oh my, it must have been terrible to be partnered with her. How did you manage?"

Chloe's eyebrows rose in surprise. "To be quite honest, it wasn't too bad because we had to learn together. She wasn't friendly, but she did do what she was supposed to do."

"Huh."

"After the class I went out for coffee with some of the other LPNs who were there. We started talking about Marianne, probably just because only a couple of us had ever seen her before. I feel so sorry for her, Nicole!"

"Why, whatever for?"

Chloe looked sad. "Well, one of the gals having coffee with us has worked a fair bit with Marianne at the Vancouver General. Apparently, as the story goes, a few months ago her father had a major heart attack and died." Chloe took a deep breath.

"Oh, no!"

"That's not the worst of the story though. Her mother has been sick with Alzheimer's for many years. Marianne's father was looking after her at home, and now the responsibility is left to Marianne. She had to move back home and everything. But she had just started her job here and didn't want to lose it, so she hired a nurse to stay with her mother during the day, and Marianne has her in the evening and at night. Terrible, isn't it?"

"Oh Chloe, that's dreadful!" Nicole was shocked. No wonder the poor girl was angry and bitter. Life had dealt her an awful blow! "She must be exhausted. Alzheimer's can be so all-consuming." Well one thing for sure, Nicole would have more compassion for her now.

"That doesn't excuse her behaviour, but it might give you a little more insight into what's bugging her. And I'm so sorry it was an awful day. I hope I'll be able to go back soon."

"Yeah, you and me both!"

There was quiet for a few moments while they considered Marianne and the anger that fuelled her behaviour.

The children had finished their ice cream and were now sitting in the living room, looking through books. Brittany was attempting to read to Christine, making up the story as she went along.

Chloe looked away from the girls and back to Nicole. "I would like to go back in a couple of days. By then I should be better, at least enough to cover some of these bruises with makeup. I need the money."

"I'll be so glad to have you back!" Nicole was so emphatic that both of them burst into laughter. It felt so good to laugh after so much sadness.

When they were able to get their breath back, Chloe spoke, "I'm not sure what to do with the girls when I'm at work. When I was living at home, I had a daycare close by and just hopped on the bus to work from the daycare. But I don't have a car to go back there. Do you know a reliable daycare in the West End?"

Pursing her lips in thought, Nicole tried to find a solution. She had heard others say their kids were in daycare, but she didn't remember where they were.

At that moment, there was a knock at the door. Chloe's eyes flew to Nicole's face, then to her girls, fear clearly showing what she'd been through in the past couple of days. Nicole put her finger to her lips so Chloe wouldn't say anything, and she rose to answer the door. Peering through the peep hole, she breathed a sigh of relief. She opened the door. "Hi Annaliese, how are you? Come on in."

Annaliese stepped across the threshold, and Nicole quickly shut the door again. She turned toward Chloe and motioned for her to come meet her friend. As Chloe walked slowly over, Annaliese told Nicole she had been thinking about her and just wanted to say hi. With a smile, Nicole introduced Chloe to her. Chloe's face was a myriad of colours, but Annaliese hid her surprise well, never making mention of it. Christine and Brittany were called over so the visitor could meet them as well.

Annaliese loved the girls. Before the others knew what was happening, she was settled on the couch with one girl at each side, and she was reading them stories. The little ones were enthralled as Annaliese changed her voice for the different characters in the book.

Chloe looked at the clock with surprise. "It's getting late! I must put the girls to bed. Annaliese, thank you so much for reading to them. They loved it." The girls echoed their delight to Annaliese.

Chloe gathered her brood together and off they went to the bedroom.

In the meantime, Annaliese and Nicole were left alone in the living room. "Say, Annaliese, do you know of a good daycare around here? Chloe would like to return to work in a couple of days, but she doesn't know what to do with the girls."

"They're such darlings, aren't they?" Annaliese's eyes twinkled. She clearly had enjoyed her time with them. Placing a finger on her bottom lip in thought, Annaliese considered Nicole's question. "I've personally never had to use a daycare." Nicole smiled. There had been no daycares when Annaliese was a young mother. "However, there is a young lady at my church that I'm quite friendly with. She has a baby and needed to find somewhere to bring him when she went back to work. I don't know if she found what she was looking for, but would you like me to speak with her about it?"

"Sure. I don't have a problem with Chloe not going back to work until next week. She's been quite beat up. So that would give you the weekend and you could speak with your friend on Sunday. Would that work?"

"Perfect. I'll make sure I speak with her then, and I'll come back for another visit with my news, okay?"

Nicole nodded. Chloe was already coming back into the room.

"I guess I'd better get going back. I was only just popping in for a few minutes." Annaliese was already standing up. "It was lovely to meet you, Chloe. Maybe I'll see you again?"

"That would be nice." Chloe responded shyly. Annaliese had been so good with the girls. She wondered if this little lady was a grandmother.

Chapter 16

Chloe still hadn't returned to work. Nicole really missed her as she walked onto her ward that morning. Looking up at the assignment board, her heart sank when she saw she was teamed up with Marianne again. Her next thought was of guilt that she should have automatically expected the worst. Squaring her shoulders in determination, she decided to make the best of this day.

Marianne stomped into the nursing station with a chip on her shoulder. She scowled at Nicole, making it clear that she was just as unhappy with today's assignment. She threw herself into a chair, ready to read the shift report.

Nicole watched her warily while making her notes for the day. When her notes were taken, Marianne stood up and sulked out of the room. Nicole's deep sigh expressed her frustration. The chatter at the nursing station momentarily blocked out, she closed her eyes and tried to focus on taking deep breaths. Marianne was not a happy person, but that didn't mean Nicole had to be miserable as well.

Standing up when she was ready to begin work, she stretched her arms over her head. As she did so, she accidentally hit someone across the cheek. She turned in surprise with an apology on her lips. Blair Mackenzie, the registered nurse in the team next to hers, was standing right beside her. He must have started moving at the same time she did. He grinned at her and told her not to worry, he had another cheek in case she wanted to hit that one too. Blair could always make her laugh, and she certainly appreciated it this morning. Smiling in return, Nicole began the job of organizing her day and got to work.

One of her patients today was a heavy woman who weighed close to four hundred pounds. She had had surgery the day before, so she would still be very sore and unable to help herself too much.

With trepidation, Nicole found Marianne and asked her if she could help her later with this lady.

Marianne looked at her with surprise. "I've got so much of my own work, I don't need to be doing yours as well. Find someone else to help you." Abruptly she turned away.

Nicole had kind of expected this response. Even so, it didn't make it any easier to stomach. By keeping her eyes and ears open, she had concluded that she was not impressed with the quality of work this irate female was doing, nor was she a team player.

Oh well, she would just have to find someone else. Nicole rounded the corner and asked Blair if he would come help her in a half hour. "Sure! I'll just finish these meds and come right on over." He smiled before turning away.

Comforted by his attitude, she finished up a few things while waiting for him to appear. Together Blair and Nicole worked efficiently and quickly. While they worked, Blair kept Nicole and the patient laughing by telling them something that had happened on his days off. Before long, the lady was washed and sitting in a chair for breakfast. What a relief to not have to do her alone! Nicole thanked Blair for his help. Just as he was about to leave, a thought occurred to Nicole. "Say Blair? Could I speak with you for a moment?" She had worked with Blair ever since she started at St. Paul's and she respected him.

The tall young man turned back to her. "Can we talk right here?"

Thinking fast, Nicole decided it was best spoken in private. "The utility room will be better."

Blair swung open the door for Nicole to walk in first. Turning toward him, she asked if he had worked with Marianne before.

With one eyebrow raised, he leaned against the wall and crossed his arms. "Is this your first time with her?"

"No, my second."

"Are you having a few problems?"

"Oh, just a few." Nicole wasn't sure what he was thinking because he looked so serious. Should she go on?

Both his eyebrows raised in surprise at this point, so Nicole took the bull by the horns. "Actually, I don't have any idea what to do with her. She refuses to help, insists she doesn't need my help, and is always angry and mean. There, I said it!" She blew her hair out of her reddened face. She hated gossiping, but she needed help.

Blair's deep blue eyes softened as he listened to her. "Yes, I have worked with her and she's a monster! I couldn't do anything right, and it's just like you said, she doesn't believe in team work."

Nicole was surprised to find out he understood what she was going through. "So what would you suggest I do?"

"I don't know if there's anything you can do about Marianne. There are unhappy people in every profession and she just happens to be one of them. If Marianne doesn't want to help you, don't go to her. If I'm working, just come to me; I'll give you a hand with whatever you need. She's not worth the effort."

"Really? You'll come help me?" Relief flooded her. "Thank you so much, Blair! I promise I won't overextend you, but that heavy lady will have to be returned to bed sometime and I would prefer to not do her alone."

Blair waved a hand in dismissal. "Don't you worry about it. Just come get me, okay?" He waited until she had responded before he took his leave. They both had a lot of work to do today!

Later that morning Nicole had her coffee break in the staff room. Several minutes later, Karen, the patient care coordinator, walked in and plugged the kettle in for tea. Looking around to make sure they were alone, Nicole asked her if she could swing something by her. "Sure. Just let me make my tea and I'll come right over," responded Karen.

When she came to sit on a chair beside her, Nicole had worked up enough nerve to bring up the subject. "I'm having an awful lot of trouble working with Marianne. Have you had any other complaints about her?"

Dodging the second question, Karen asked her what kind of trouble she was having. So Nicole went into an account of what it had been like working with Marianne last time and also this morning.

Karen listened politely while drinking her tea. When Nicole was finished, Karen explained that she was indeed concerned about this problem. However, it was up to the staff members to get along, and they should work at it until things got better. She would not step in and intervene. This was Nicole's problem to deal with.

Nicole's heart was beating fast. She couldn't believe this problem had effectively been swept under the rug! Nicole's face was red with embarrassment and anger. *I should never have talked to her about this! Some help she turned out to be!* When Karen got up to leave, Nicole had to get her anger under control.

In the meantime, Marianne continued her belittling ways toward Nicole, refusing to lift a hand to help or work as a team.

∞ ∞ ∞

By the time Nicole arrived home, she was an emotional mess. She was so glad she could hear Chloe bathing the children in the bathroom. At least she wouldn't have to face her right now.

She went into her room and closed the door. Kicking off her shoes, she suddenly burst into tears. *Lord, I know You want me to forgive Marianne, but she is absolutely despicable! How can I possibly forgive her?*

Even as she prayed, Nicole once again saw the cross in her mind's eye and Jesus hanging there. This time though, she was reminded of the rejection and pain He suffered, and yet He never retaliated, never got angry. He even asked the Father to forgive them because they didn't know what they were doing. Wow! What an example He was! But how could she do this too? She wasn't perfect like Him.

Nicole was quiet for a while, sitting back on the pillows at the head of her bed. Rousing herself, she picked up the guitar and began strumming quietly. Eventually this grew into an old song she had learned in church and had recently figured out on the guitar. The song spoke of Nicole's love for Jesus and stated that He was holy and worthy of her praise.

Tears were running down her face when she was finished. She realized that when she had Him in her life, the problems that were there didn't seem to be as devastating. The most important thing was to know He was there and He loved her.

While Nicole was pulling herself together, there was a little-girl knock on her door. "Cole, can we come in?" Brittany had heard her sing.

Rubbing her sleeve over her face, Nicole told her to come in. Both girls skipped into the room in their nightgowns. They were pink-cheeked from their bath and so cute. They hopped onto the bed and giggled. Chloe walked into the room slowly, not wanting to disturb the girls and Nicole.

"What's that?" Brittany asked, pointing to the guitar.

"It's a guitar; it's a musical instrument."

"What's a istrumit?" Brittany had so many questions!

Nicole explained as best she could, then said, "Let me show you what it does." And she played *Old MacDonald Had a Farm.* The girls giggled and bounced on the bed, singing with her. Chloe stepped in and told them to sit down if they wanted to sing along. They promptly obeyed, wanting Nicole to sing more.

Nicole thought for a moment, and then began *Jesus Loves Me this I Know.* The girls had never heard it before, but it wasn't long before they knew it.

"Who's Jesus?" Brittany clearly hadn't been to Sunday school.

"Okay girls, that's enough. It's time for bed." Chloe ushered them into their own room and read them a bedtime story before tucking them in.

Nicole knew that at some point she would get to talk to the girls about Jesus, but obviously it wouldn't be tonight. Her spirit felt lighter than it had coming home. She got up and walked into the kitchen. She would make Chloe and herself some hot chocolate before they both went to bed.

When the hot chocolate was almost made, Chloe entered the kitchen. "I made us a drink to warm us up before bed." Ladling the brew out of the pot and into mugs, Nicole spilled some on the counter. With a sheepish grin on her face, she looked at Chloe. "I guess I'm not too coordinated after work, huh?"

Chloe laughed and accepted the mug. "Home-made hot chocolate!"

"Oh wait, I forgot the best part!" exclaimed Nicole. Rummaging through her cupboards, she finally found what she was looking for: mini marshmallows. Putting a handful in each of the mugs, Nicole then closed the bag and put it away.

Sitting at the table, Chloe had a thoughtful look on her face. She could see that Nicole had been crying. Rather than bring up the reason why, she decided to get her to talk about Greg. There might be comfort in the memories for Nicole. "I've never heard the story of how you met Greg. Would you feel bad talking about it? I'd love to hear the story."

Startled, Nicole was taken off guard. Recovering quickly from the surprise, a gentle smile tugged at her lips as she thought back.

At the beginning of her last semester of nursing at Trinity Western University, Nicole had been invited to a hockey game the TWU Spartans were playing in. The game had been in Langley, BC, not far from school, so Nicole decided to go. Her friends had met others they knew there at the game, so she was introduced to Greg, who happened to have come along for the fun. He was a vibrant young man who took an instant liking to Nicole.

"I guess we kind of hit it off. He was so interesting! He was just completing his training as an officer for the Vancouver Police Department. In fact, he was going to start work the very next week." Nicole played with her hair, finding pleasure in thinking back.

Chloe sat watching Nicole, sipping her hot chocolate.

"We all went out for coffee afterwards, and Greg chose to sit beside me. We could have talked for hours!" She looked at Chloe. "I remember thinking that his hair matched his personality. He had thick red hair, and he was such fun!" Nicole's gaze fell on Shadow, who was sleeping peacefully on the rug in front of the kitchen sink. He had all four paws up in the air and he looked like he was completely at peace with the world. Nicole smiled. What a funny cat!

Chloe pulled her back to the moment with her question. "Was he handsome?"

"I thought so. He was about six foot two and slim. When I found out he was going to be a policeman, I remember thinking how attractive he would look in his uniform. Oh, and he had a dimple in his chin. I had never really known anybody with a dimple in their chin before!" Nicole grinned at the memory.

Continuing with her story, she said, "All too soon the evening was over and we had to part ways. But Greg asked me if he could have my email address and he gave me his. He wanted to keep in touch, he said." Nicole laughed. "I got a message from him the very next day, and boy, was I surprised! I didn't really think he'd want to email me. I thought he was just being polite."

Chloe had her chin in her hand, a dreamy smile on her lips.

"It wasn't long before an email here and there became a daily occurrence. Then one day he asked me for my telephone number. We talked for hours. Even when he became a policeman, he would find out what my schedule was so he could call me when I was free." Nicole's hot chocolate was nearly finished. Her hands were wrapped around the base of the mug.

"Where were you at with school at that point?" Chloe was trying to set a timeline in her mind.

"I was in my final year. I graduated in May of that year, and Greg came out for it. I was so excited to have him there. That's actually when he met my family. We all went out for dinner after, and he got along really well with everybody. By that time we had been out on a few dates." She sighed. "Do you want to know all this? Isn't it boring for you?"

Chloe sat up straighter and replied, "Boring? It's a beautiful love story! Go on..."

Nicole quirked her eyebrows at her. "You're sure? Well, let's see. I got a job at the Langley Hospital soon after I graduated, so at that point Greg and I were both on shift work. It was more challenging to spend time together on the phone. Every weekend that we were both free, he came out to visit. Did I tell you he was living in Vancouver at that point?"

"I kind of guessed that he wasn't too close if you had to talk on the phone and through emails," Chloe responded.

"I remember one weekend we were both free I went and spent Saturday with him. We rode bicycles around Stanley Park and had a wonderful time."

"That would have been fun," Chloe agreed.

"In August that year he asked me to marry him. Of course I said yes, because by that time I was head over heels in love with him. We got married the following February. I really didn't think too much of the fact that I would be moving away from my family and going to Vancouver. I was in love! And I figured I'd probably be able to get a job at one of the hospitals in town. It was all such a great adventure with Greg. Besides, I knew it wasn't all that far by car, so I'd still get to see my family occasionally."

"Where did you go for your honeymoon?" Chloe wanted all the details.

"We went to Hawaii. I had never been out of North America before so it was a big deal for me. Greg planned everything. He just told me to get my passport, and pack for warm weather. It was dreamy! I loved every minute of it..."

"Sounds so romantic!" Chloe smiled at her, encouraging her to go on.

"Well as you know, we found this apartment, and I've been here ever since." Nicole heaved a sigh. "Greg was such fun. I know you only met him once or twice, and briefly at that. It's too bad you never got to know him." Nicole looked wistfully at her friend. "And now he's gone."

Chloe took her hand in hers. "You had a great marriage, and you both loved each other very much. That's something special to remember."

Nicole looked down at the table. *Yeah, but it doesn't help on those lonely nights....*

Looking at her watch, Chloe suddenly stood up with a gasp. "I've kept you up so long! You have to work tomorrow. Sorry, Nicole."

Nicole smiled at her and told her not to worry. It had done her good to reminisce. She didn't want her memory of Greg to fade.

Saying goodnight, they each went to their separate rooms. Nicole realized she hadn't even told Chloe about Marianne!

Chapter 17

Nicole was sitting in the cafeteria, eating a cookie and drinking coffee. She had about ten minutes left before having to return to work. Lost in her thoughts, she didn't hear Anna come up beside her. "Hi Nicole! I haven't seen you in such a long time! How are you doing?" Anna had a huge grin on her face when she bent over to give Nicole a side-hug. She settled her coffee cup and took the seat in front of her friend. They used to work together until Anna took a special course to work in Maternity. She had been there for six months and loved it. "What a delight to see you! I don't see you often enough." Watching her friend, she scrutinized her appearance. "I know it's kind of rude for me to say this, but are you gaining weight?"

With a start Nicole realized Anna didn't know all that had been going on in her life recently. Had it been that long since they'd seen each other? "There's something you don't know about me, Anna." She stopped and looked down at her hands.

Anna was curious and smiled at Nicole in encouragement. "Yes?"

Looking up with a sigh she said, "I'm pregnant."

Anna's mouth dropped open. "Are you serious?" When she got over the surprise, her eyes danced. She grabbed for Nicole's hands and squeezed them. "I am so happy for you!" Then suddenly she remembered that Greg had passed away six months ago. "Oh..." She sat back, deflated. "But Greg is gone. Are you okay with this?" Her eyes searched her friend's face.

Nicole looked down at her mug. "I'm getting there. I must have gotten pregnant right before he died. It's been tough, but I'm hanging in there." She gave Anna a small smile. "I actually was talking to my sister about you a while back."

"You were? Whatever for?" Anna probed.

"She offered to come to the hospital with me when I deliver and be there for me. She thought it would be a good thing to take some prenatal courses beforehand, but she lives in Abbotsford and of course I'm here in Vancouver. I just thought maybe you could give us some pointers, seeing you work in maternity and help women deliver babies every day." Nicole was really hoping she would say yes.

Anna was taken aback. "Well now, that's a tall order. What exactly would you want me to help you with?"

"Well, I've seen babies born before, but Julie has no idea. I guess it would help for her to know how to help me. You know, all the breathing stuff and that sort of thing."

Anna's eyes twinkled. "That wouldn't be hard to do. How would you like to arrange it?"

Nicole smiled, grateful for this good friend. "I thought I would have you both over for dinner when we're all free. When we're done eating, you could give us a whirlwind class of sorts. What do you think?"

Anna grinned. "I would love to! And I just happen to have my schedule here in my leg pocket." She pulled out her little calendar and the two of them compared notes. They decided that they both would be available in three weeks.

Nicole wrote the date down on a piece of paper she had in her pocket. "I'll call Julie to make sure she's all right with those dates. Then I'll let you know."

It was settled. Oh that felt good! Nicole was pleased to have that out of the way. "Thanks so much, Anna! It's a relief for me to know we'll go over all the pertinent things together before the baby comes."

"Are you planning on having the baby here?" Anna was hoping she would also be on shift.

"That's all kind of in the air right now. I would prefer to be in Abbotsford closer to my family, but I'm waiting for my brother's suite to become available and it doesn't appear to be moving very fast. I think I would get more support from my family if I was closer."

Anna tended to agree with that. Still, she would love to have Nicole deliver the baby here. "Are you planning on working after the baby is born?"

"Well, that whole thing is kind of a blur to me right now too. I've been looking at jobs in Abbotsford, and I actually applied for one. But I'm not sure what to do."

"When exactly are you due?" Anna pulled out her calendar again.

"Around the thirteenth of February, if all goes according to plan."

Anna looked up from the calendar. "Are you taking maternity leave?"

Nicole looked confused. "I don't think I can if I'm moving, do you?"

"Have you absolutely decided you're moving?" Anna looked disappointed. "According to our union you don't get full coverage if you don't return to a permanent position. Would that sway you enough to make you want to stay in Vancouver, if it would mean you'd have a year off then go back to work?"

Nicole looked doubtful. "I haven't really thought this through much..."

"You've been working full time for a couple of years and it's your right to take a mat leave when your baby arrives. I guess you'll just have to figure out if having a year off this way is more important to you. Do you think you would want to work full time once the baby is a year old?"

Nicole sat back, all kinds of emotion flitting across her face. "I don't really know. Right now I think being a single parent will be difficult enough as it is without me adding to it. The only people in Vancouver I really know are those I work with. Who would be there to support me in this new role? It would be different if Greg was still alive...."

Anna's compassion for her friend showed on her face. "I know what you mean. It would be very lonely here with a baby and no family around."

"So you see my dilemma with taking maternity leave. They won't grant it to me unless I return here. Right now I don't see that as a very real possibility. And you know, Anna, Greg's life insurance with the police left me quite comfortable. I don't really have to work full time; not for a while, anyhow." Nicole was quiet for a couple heartbeats. "And if I should have to return full time and have a difficult time making ends meet, I think I could probably work something out with my parents. Maybe I could have part of their basement or something."

"You're right, Nicole." Anna was nodding her head in agreement. "Something will work out for you, even if you don't take maternity leave." The girls contemplated each other and slowly smiled, enjoying the friendship they shared.

Suddenly Nicole looked at her watch. With a gasp she jumped up from the table. "Yikes! I've taken a half hour more than I should have! I have to run...talk to you later." She called over her shoulder as she ran out of the cafeteria.

Riding the elevator up to the tenth floor, she thought through all they had discussed. Maternity leave would have been perfect if Greg were still with her. But his death had changed everything in her life.

∞ ∞ ∞

Ellen had had a very busy day sorting through some problems at the clinic. She was glad her work day was over. They had just cleared the dinner dishes, and now it was time to relax. She was sitting in her favourite chair, reading a Karen Kingsbury book. The gas fireplace was giving out nice warmth and she was enjoying the quiet. Matthew was doing homework, and Stan was at Steve's house helping him with a project.

The phone rang and Ellen got up to answer it. "Hello?"

"Mom! I felt the baby move today!" It was Nicole, and she sounded excited.

"Oh honey, that's wonderful! What an exciting time for you." Ellen was thrilled for her. She slowly walked back and made herself comfortable in her chair while listening to her pregnant daughter.

"I wasn't sure what it was at first, and then it happened again. This little chickadee is active," she ended with a laugh.

"How have you been feeling lately? I haven't spoken to you in a week or so." Ellen hated the distance that was between them. She sure wished Nicole lived closer.

"I've been feeling fine, just a little tired, that's all. Those maternity clothes you bought for me are getting lots of good use!"

"Do you have enough? It seems to me we didn't get you all that much."

"Oh, as I get bigger I might order a few more things from that maternity web page and have them sent to your postal box again. But right now, I mostly work or relax at home, so I don't need much. But thanks, Mom." Nicole sounded tired now that the initial excitement of the baby kicking had worn off. "And Jennifer gave me some of her clothes on loan, so I have a nice assortment."

"Is everything going well at work? Were you there today?"

"Yeah, I was working today. Chloe hasn't been working lately because she's had some problems. Actually, she's recently separated from her husband and is now living with me for a short while. She and her two little girls."

"Isn't that too much for you, honey?" Ellen sounded concerned.

"No, I don't think so. Chloe is good about helping out here, and her girls are little gems. I like having them around because the place isn't so quiet and lonely."

"I can understand that the company would be nice. Have you made any plans about where you'd like to have the baby?"

"Actually I've been thinking about it a lot. I think I want to be living in Abbotsford by that time. Steve told me his suite should become available one of these days. I know it doesn't make sense to wait for it when I have a time limit myself, but I'm not sure what to do. Would you keep your eyes open for me to see if anything becomes available in Abbotsford? I don't need a big place, but two bedrooms would be nice."

"Sure, I'll keep a lookout for you. When were you hoping to come out?" Ellen was so relieved to hear this news. The rest of the family would be delighted!

"I have some vacation time coming up. I thought I would take the last three weeks in December for that, then I'll see how I feel. It would be really nice if the suite was available then for me to paint and stuff and then I could just move out, but that's all kind of up in the air right now." Nicole paused for a moment. "If I end up moving and still need to return to work after Christmas, I can commute. It wouldn't be for that long before the baby was born anyhow. What do you think, Mom?" Nicole hadn't finalized her decision yet, so it was good to have a sounding-board in her mother.

"Well, I think that works out okay. I'm not too crazy about the commute for you, but as you say it wouldn't be for too long." Ellen was quiet for a few seconds. "Nicole, I understand that you'd prefer to have your own place, but would you consider moving back home until Steve's place becomes available? You could have your old room back, and we could store your stuff in Julie's old room."

"Oh! You would let me do that?" Nicole sounded surprised.

"Of course. And I'm pretty sure your father would be thrilled to have you back home for a bit too."

"Let me think about it. In the meantime, if Steve's suite becomes available, I'll move in there. But your place is a pretty good option for me if it doesn't. Thanks so much, Mom!"

"You're welcome. So, we have good things to look forward to in the next couple of months! It'll be a delight to have you closer, honey."

"It'll be good for me too, Mom. But first I have to make sure everything works out for Chloe. I feel kind of responsible for her. She's had such a hard time."

"Would she consider coming out this way too if something became available?"

Nicole thought that was a fantastic idea. She would have to swing that by Chloe, but first let her mom see if there were suites available out there and what the prices were. "Would you look for her too in the Abbotsford paper?"

"I'll do that. I'll email you if there's anything that comes up."

"I'll check my email every day, just in case. Thanks again, Mom. I'm not sure if Chloe will go with the idea, but if I move out there, maybe she'll be happy to do that too."

"Okay, we'll be in touch then. Have a good sleep, honey."

"You too, Mom. Bye for now."

Chapter 18

Today was Nicole's first day off. She finished working nights a short while ago, so there wasn't much on the agenda for the day except sleeping and taking it easy. Chloe had decided that it would be best to take the girls out so Nicole could sleep. The three of them were going to Stanley Park for the day. They would take in the Aquarium and Zoo and see what else they wanted to do.

The girls were all dressed in their jeans and sweaters, ready for their adventure when Nicole returned from work. Their excitement brought a smile to her face. It was good for them to spend time with Chloe doing something fun. Chloe had already asked to borrow Nicole's Jeep for the day, seeing she'd be sleeping. "Here are the keys, Chloe. There's plenty of gas in the tank, so don't worry. Just have yourselves a really fun time." She handed the keys over.

Their plan was to first go for breakfast at White Spot, before starting their fun day. "Do you have a camera?" asked Nicole. "I have a great digital camera you could borrow if you want to."

Chloe admitted she didn't have one. She hadn't brought much from her home, and she hadn't wanted to go back for fear of running into Barry. Nicole looked around to find the camera, saw it on the bookshelf in the living room and handed the case over. "It's not difficult to figure out. Here, let me show you how it works." She pulled it out of the case and showed Chloe the basics. "Tonight we can download all the pictures into my laptop and we can have a little slideshow of your day. That way I can still kind of have a part in your fun. Sound good?" Chloe's eyes glowed at the thought of having good memories of today with her girls.

"You bet!"

With a hug for Nicole, Chloe and her little chicks were off with a flurry of little voices laughing and chatting, and Chloe leading the pack like a mamma duck with her ducklings.

Nicole returned from waving them off in the hallway, and walked into her kitchen to make some toast for breakfast. She would wait on the coffee till she woke up. She needed to get a few hours of sleep so she could function, but she didn't want to sleep all day or she would never sleep tonight.

∞ ∞ ∞

At noon Nicole was laying in bed, just enjoying being lazy, when the phone rang. It was Annaliese, saying she had gotten some information for her regarding the daycare.

"That's great, Annaliese. I'm just about to take a shower. Why don't you give me half an hour and then come over? I'll be ready for my coffee by then and I'm sure you'll probably want one too."

"Well now, that sounds delightful. See you soon."

∞ ∞ ∞

"This is the phone number of the daycare. It's actually not that far from the hospital, and Chloe could easily take the bus to work or walk. My friend says she trusts the people who run it; they're great with kids."

Nicole took the number and put it under one of the fridge magnets right away so she wouldn't lose it. "Thank you so much, Annaliese. Maybe she can return to work next week then. That sure would be nice for me, because the person replacing her is just awful!"

"Awful? What do you mean, Nicole?"

"She hates me and makes it very obvious. I can't ask her anything, she is rude and obnoxious. She won't help me and doesn't want any help with her patients. That's not good either because I'm technically responsible for them, so I need to know how they're doing. But she makes it very clear that she doesn't want me to butt in unless she calls for me, which she never does. I'm just so tired of it all. And to make matters worse, my patient care coordinator has told me that we all need to learn to get along. As if it was just that simple or up to me only!" The frustration of the past few days was showing on Nicole.

"That does sound difficult! How have you been handling it?" Annaliese wanted to help, so maybe talking about it would give Nicole the opportunity to figure it out.

"God told me to forgive her. The first day I was able to do that, but then it seemed to escalate and I've just kind of washed my hands of her. All I want now is to have Chloe back. She makes working there so much nicer." Nicole blew her hair from her face. She hadn't intended to talk about this disturbing subject with Annaliese. She just wanted to relax, not get all upset. She was on her days off after all! She sighed and reached for her coffee.

Annaliese regarded her with thoughtful eyes. "Sometimes it's easier to forgive someone if we first repent of anger and criticism toward that person. I know you have good reason to be angry, but that is not what God wants for you because it brings strife in your own heart. He wants us to be able to walk through these difficult things in our lives with His peace. His peace will not come if there's anger, blame or other ugly stuff. And in saying that, I'm not saying you are bad to feel them, Nicole. It's just a human response. But it's not God's response, that's all I'm saying. You know, Jesus gave us a beautiful example of that when the people who crucified Him were mocking and taunting Him, beating Him and spitting on Him. He asked the Father to forgive them because they didn't know what they were doing. They had no idea that He was indeed the Son of God, and that God the Father would judge them for it. But Jesus asked for forgiveness for them. That's powerful stuff."

Nicole sat quietly assimilating all that Annaliese was saying. She knew Annaliese was right. She had a lot of resentment toward Marianne, and that had to go. "Thanks for the reminder, Annaliese. You're right. I'll be sure to pray when I'm alone. I need some time with the Lord to bring a measure of peace because it sure hasn't been there lately!"

Annaliese reached over and patted Nicole's hand. "He is *for* you, Nicole. Just remember that. There are actually many different portions of scripture that are standing out in my mind right now in light of this. Would you like me to read them to you?"

"Please."

"The first one is from Psalm 140. David was crying out to the Lord and he says,

"Deliver me, O Lord, from evil men; preserve me from violent men, who plan evil things in their hearts; they continually gather together for war. They sharpen their tongues like a serpent; the poison of asps is under their lips.'"

"Does that sound a little bit like this lady you've been working with?" asked Annaliese.

"You bet it does! She doesn't go to war physically, but her tongue sure gives that impression!"

"Well David cried out to God and fully believed that He would deliver him from evil men. And God did, right? That's the way it was in the Old Testament; they had to cry out to God for deliverance. But today, in the New Testament, it is different. Here, let me flip to the other portion." Annaliese thumbed through the Bible and found the spot she was looking for. "This is in the second chapter of Ephesians." She came closer to Nicole so they could read it together.

"And you He made alive, who were dead in trespasses and sins, in which you once walked according to the course of this world, according to the prince of the power of the air, the spirit who now works in the sons of disobedience..."

Nicole pulled back and raised one eyebrow in query. She wasn't sure she understood where Annaliese was going with this.

"What this portion means is that today, because of Jesus, God has made us alive. We used to be dead in our trespasses and sins, just like everybody who has not chosen to walk with Jesus. They are all influenced by Satan, or the prince of the power of the air; they are all sons of disobedience. But today, God doesn't require that we beg Him for deliverance. He *has* made us alive in Christ. It's His will that you be protected from the wiles of the enemy, which will often come through people."

Timidly Nicole answered, "Okay." She was still not too sure where this was going. She looked at her friend with uncertainty.

Annaliese sat back and attempted to clear up the confusion. "Satan knows that God has made us alive. He knows that all we have to do is accept it and speak out the truth. As long as we aren't sure of what is legally ours, we won't make a stand. But when we know that we are seated together in heavenly places with Him, we know that Satan has no business harassing us." Annaliese made a slash into the air with her pointed finger to emphasize what she was saying.

"As we rebuke the oppressor, we are set free because he flees. Now in your case, this lady is being used by the enemy. Oh I don't mean that she is aware of that. No, her response to whatever anger is boiling inside her is wrong as she lashes out at you. This is sin. But the important thing to note is that the powers of darkness are bringing out this response in her."

Annaliese flipped to the end of the book she was open to. "At the end of Ephesians it tells us that we fight not against flesh and blood, but against principalities and powers and so on. It's not her you're warring against, but the powers that are operating in her." She looked up at Nicole. "Once you've forgiven her for treating you with such anger, you can take authority over that anger because God doesn't want you to be harassed that way."

"Are you serious?" Nicole was finally beginning to see where Annaliese was going, and she was getting excited at this new truth she was learning.

"Very much so. When you know your position in Christ, the enemy of our souls can't come at you with destruction. It's when you don't know who you are in Christ that he does what he wants because you aren't walking in the faith that indeed you are the apple of God's eye, and He protects His own."

"Woah! That's pretty heady stuff!"

"Well, actually it's just the truth. In another place it tells us that God wants us to be the head and not the tail. When you know who you are in Christ and you operate in authority, you are the head. When you don't know and therefore don't speak into the situations around you, you are in fact the tail because anything can happen to you. It's like God's shield of protection around you has a hole in it which the enemy can penetrate."

"Wow! So how do you address something like this? How would you suggest I pray?"

"Before you go to work you could take authority over the anger and judgment in that lady. It's always good practice to take authority over the powers in your workplace anyhow. When you know what they are, you can name them, which is the effective ingredient to breaking their power in that place." She took a breath. "But one thing you must know: authority doesn't come right away. The first time you speak to break the powers around you, you might not feel anything. But your authority will grow as you learn who you are in Christ."

Both ladies were lost in their own thoughts for a bit, digesting these truths from the Bible. Annaliese continued as something occurred to her. "This doesn't mean that nasty things won't happen to you anymore. It's just that if your response is in Christ, that is, if you are walking in humility and righteousness every day, He will make all things to work together for good because you love Him."

While they were both quietly sipping their coffee, Annaliese regarded Nicole sitting in the easy chair near her. "So tell me, dear, how have you been doing since we prayed together? Do you think it made a difference to pray last time?"

Nicole was quick to respond. "Oh yes, I've seen a change in me. For one thing, I've started packing Greg's stuff. Well, I kind of got sidetracked with that because Chloe and the girls are here, but it's a start. And now when I speak of Greg, I still feel very sad, but I don't get shattered with grief."

Annaliese smiled at Nicole, grateful for the change in her. "That's marvellous, praise the Lord!"

"Yes indeed, He is the One who changed me."

The two ladies looked at one another and suddenly they both burst out laughing. "Isn't God good?" commented Annaliese with joy. There was a moment of pleasure shared between the ladies as they thought of all God was doing to bring peace into Nicole's heart regarding Greg's death.

"There are so many things yet to decide regarding this pregnancy, but I'm beginning to see that God cares and wants to be involved in my life. It's actually kind of exciting, don't you think?"

"Every time I see God at work it's exciting for me." Annaliese sat back and crossed her legs. She was a pretty picture in her light pink wool sweater and maroon slacks. Her white chin-length hair was a perfect contrast to the colour she wore.

They drank together companionably for a minute.

"You know," said Nicole, "it's amazing to see God at work. But even with what He has done in my life, I sometimes still find it hard to relax and let Him do it, or even believe that He will."

"That's very perceptive of you, Nicole. Letting go of control isn't always easy, that's for sure, but the first step is always agreeing that you're struggling with that, and turning to Him."

Nicole was thinking about the past few days. "I was doing so much better until these problems at work came up. Now I'm wondering how everything is going to work out and whether I deserve to have that freedom."

"My dear, none of us deserves to have it. That's the beauty of it all. Yet, because Jesus shed His blood for you, for me, we have access to that freedom in Him. It's not because of anything you or I can do, but all because of the sacrifice He made on that cross for us. Not one of us measures up, that's why Jesus had to pay the ultimate price."

"Huh." Nicole was looking at Annaliese, one eyebrow raised. She didn't have any difficulty believing these things for other people; she just had doubts that they could be for her.

Annaliese sensed Nicole's struggle. She stopped for a couple of heartbeats. "Faith is an outflow of a relationship with Jesus, and the application of the Word of God to our everyday lives. Faith is of the Spirit." She stopped briefly to think.

"If you're in unbelief, you say, *'I can't do it, it's impossible.'* But when you have faith, you say, *'I can't do it, but Christ can do it in me, or through me.'* God extends grace to every person who believes in Jesus. Grace says, *'I can do it through you.'* That's God speaking.

He wants to do it through us, not have us feel that we have to make the changes in ourselves, because that's impossible. It's only as we submit to God that He is free to change us and make us more like Jesus." Annaliese stopped speaking. Reaching for her cup, she took a sip of coffee.

"Really?"

"The secret of the New Testament is not that I walk with Christ, but that He walks in me – and He gets the glory for the change in me."

Nicole sat back in her chair. "Okay, it's beginning to make more sense." Reaching for her Bible, she pulled out her little notebook. "Let me write these things down. I want to remember this." She tucked her legs under her and began writing. Shadow jumped up on the back of the chair, enjoying being near Nicole. He sat there grooming himself as she began to write.

Annaliese loved an eager student! What a charming picture this was in front of her: Nicole in her jeans with a blue oversized Vancouver Police sweatshirt, writing furiously in her notebook, and Shadow, her gray, short-haired cat, sitting as close to her as he could without actually being on her. She smiled and continued speaking. "It's in the abundance of grace that we stand. Jesus changed everything for us when He rose victorious over the powers of darkness. But the results depend on our response to it all. I once heard it said that responsibility is our response to His ability. Isn't that beautiful? It really shows us that it's the condition of our heart that matters. He can work through us if we let go and let Him do it."

Nicole stopped writing and looked up at Annaliese. Her right hand still held her pen, and she had it up in the air as she thought of something. Annaliese waited for her thought to form. "That whole thing about Jesus going to the cross confuses me. I mean, why did He have to die anyhow? Was there no other way for us to get salvation?" Nicole's face puckered in a frown. She wondered if Annaliese would get angry with her for asking such a bold question, but it really bothered her.

"Tell me something, Nicole. Do you think that Jesus going to the cross was from God, or from Satan? I mean, do you think that Satan demanded that sacrifice?"

Looking confused, Nicole's mouth dropped open. "I'm not really sure. I've heard some people say that it was Satan's idea, you know like in the book *The Lion, The Witch and The Wardrobe,* but I'm not sure what I really believe."

"Remind me about what happened in that book."

"Well, at the end, the witch is the one who calls the shots, and tells Aslan the lion that he has to die in order for the others to be set free. If you take that as a picture of what happened in the Bible, then I guess Satan is the one who decided that Jesus had to go to the cross and die."

Annaliese nodded. "Okay, now I see where your confusion is coming from. In actual fact, God the Father is the One who said that blood had to be shed, and Jesus volunteered for the job. It was never Satan's decision. Actually, even when Jesus was dying on the cross Satan thought he had won a tremendous victory, because he didn't foresee what would happen when Jesus rose from the dead."

Annaliese opened the Bible near the end. "Here, let me read out of chapter two in Colossians."

"And you being dead in your trespasses and the uncircumcision of your flesh, He has made alive together with Him, having forgiven you all trespasses, having wiped out the handwriting of requirements that was against us, which was contrary to us. And He has taken it out of the way, having nailed it to the cross. Having disarmed principalities and powers, He made a public spectacle of them, triumphing over them in it."

"How do you figure Jesus disarmed them? It was by the flowing of His blood. When the blood comes, the devil must lose his hold on us. We are free because of the blood of Jesus. That's in the legal sense; it is finished. But the enemy of our souls wants us to believe we are still in bondage. He knows that if we speak up and break his power over us, we will indeed be free. As long as we remain ignorant about what actually happened at the crucifixion, Satan can bring defeat, fear and all kinds of other undesirables into our lives."

Nicole was nodding, showing Annaliese that she was following, but her brows were puckered, demonstrating that she was still confused about some issues.

"Until you understand what the cross is all about, it's difficult to appropriate what He has accomplished for you. Let's see if I can explain that for you." She put her index finger against her lower lip as she considered what to say. "Do you remember that in the Old Testament, when the people of God sinned, He required that they have a blood sacrifice in order for their sins to be forgiven?"

Nicole nodded. She did remember that and had never understood it.

"It's all about the blood. God required the animal sacrifice because blood had to be spilled to bring life. Now let me take a different direction here for a minute. God is a holy God. He cannot abide sin of any kind. There is no sin in Him whatsoever. Man, however, is sinful from birth. We inherited that sinful nature because of Adam and Eve and their disobedience to God. Because of that, there is now a great chasm between God and man, and it's impossible to bridge that gap in human terms because none of us is holy. None of us can be righteous through works, it's impossible. We can try, but we'll never achieve holiness in our own strength. Jesus knew that the sacrifice of blood was necessary for redemption, and He offered Himself as the ultimate sacrifice. By shedding His blood, He was guaranteeing that man could now come to God. Why was that?"

Nicole had her head tilted to the side, thinking. "I'm not sure..."

"Blood had to be poured out for sin to be forgiven. Jesus had no sin in Him, and He loved the Father so much that He gave Himself willingly, knowing that He would defeat the powers of darkness that harassed man if He gave Himself. In doing this, He fully satisfied the demands of God. Now we don't live in the wrath of God because of sin that's in us, but we have life everlasting through Jesus' sacrifice."

"Okay. So what was it that you were saying earlier, that we need to a – app - appriate it?"

Annaliese smiled. "It's a different word, isn't it? It's actually *appropriate*. And it means that legally, because of Jesus' sacrifice, all these things belong to us. But the enemy still roams the earth and tries to make us agree with him that we don't actually have those things. Appropriation means that we stand on the Word of God and speak in faith that all His promises are yes and amen for us today."

"I sort of understand you..."

"Let's put it another way. Let's talk about the owner of a very large estate. This man has two sons. One day the owner dies and his will is read. Legally he left all he owned to his two sons. However, one of them refused to appropriate it and remained poor. His friends spoke negatively to him about going to the bank and identifying himself; they made it sound like it would be a stupid thing to do and he listened to them. As a consequence, he didn't bother going to the bank, even though that was where his money was. He felt it should be his right there where he was, and he didn't *feel* rich, so he wasn't. Had he gone to the bank, he would have had all he needed to rid himself of such worthless friends."

" The other son believed that it was true that all his father's riches were now his legally, so he went to the bank where the proof became alive in him and he received all that was his. He lived in his father's riches from that time on. Now all the other son had to do was to identify himself at the bank, that is, speak out who his father was, and declare that he had received an inheritance. But he never did and eventually he died, a bitter man who believed his father never loved him."

Nicole's face was a mixture of emotions. "So that's what appropriate means?"

"In a nutshell." Annaliese sat back; she had been sitting forward to help get her message across.

"Wow!" Nicole was speechless. She had never heard it put quite that way before. The death of Jesus on the cross made more sense now. "Is that why there isn't much healing for today?"

"There *is* healing for today! I see healing all the time! I believe that Jesus paid the price for us to receive healing, and so that's how I pray. In my church we have regular healings. Some churches don't know how to pray according to the Spirit, so they give up and don't pray for healing. When that happens, there won't be any."

"Well, you've certainly given me a lot to think about." Nicole slowly put her notepad and pen on the coffee table. She was thinking through it all.

"He is *for* you, Nicole. That's what the cross was all about. He loves you so much He gave His only begotten Son to be nailed to the cross." Looking at Nicole, she felt enough had been said for today. "Let me pray for you, okay?"

Nicole agreed and bowed her head.

Annaliese began praying out loud, "Dear heavenly Father, You know all that we've been discussing here today. I pray for your Spirit to give Nicole clarity of mind and the understanding to take in all that has been said. In the name of Jesus I break the power of confusion over Nicole, and I speak peace to her mind, peace to her spirit, in Jesus' mighty name. Let Your Word bear much fruit in her as she seeks to understand, Lord. Amen."

There were a few tears on Nicole's face when she said, "Amen." But she looked up and smiled at Annaliese. "Thank you so much, Annaliese. Maybe this will help me to grow in faith more." The two hugged and Annaliese bid her goodbye.

While she had everything reasonably clear in her mind, Nicole sat back on the couch and began to pray, lifting her heart to the King of kings and Lord of lords.

Chapter 19

Nicole had today and tomorrow off. There was still time to do what she could to help Chloe out. She had received a couple of phone numbers from Annaliese, and now was the time to call and see if they should go visit them.

Picking up her cell phone, Nicole punched in the numbers for the abuse-against-women group. Speaking with a counsellor there, she felt it would be a good idea to bring Chloe in and meet them. As the woman was speaking, Nicole made her decision. She would make an appointment for tomorrow afternoon and ask Annaliese if she could babysit the children for an hour.

Her next call was to the daycare; they could drop in tomorrow and meet the owner. It would be a busy day!

Leaving her room, she walked into the kitchen to make her morning coffee. Chloe was there ahead of her and the smell of fresh brewed coffee reached out its tantalizing odour to Nicole. *Mmmm, how nice!* She smiled at Chloe and said good morning. Getting a mug from the cupboard, she thanked Chloe for making the coffee. She could get used to this!

Sitting down at the table with Chloe, Nicole explained to her about the phone calls.

Chloe's eyebrows rose higher on her forehead. "The daycare sounds nice. What time would you like to go tomorrow morning?"

"Oh, let's wait and see what time we get up. We can plan to go when we've eaten breakfast and everybody is ready to leave. Does that sound good?"

Chloe smiled. "Of course. I'm looking forward to seeing this daycare." Her smile slipped a little and her voice quavered as she spoke. "But I'm not sure what to think of the place for abuse-against-women. Do you really think I need to go there?" Chloe looked scared.

Nicole came to a perfect standstill and looked at Chloe. Why had she not thought of that before? Chloe was afraid. She probably still hadn't allowed herself to fully admit that Barry was one who beat up on women, a bully. If she did go there, she would have to own up to the fact that she had failed and chosen the wrong person to marry. That's a hard pill to swallow!

Gently, Nicole spoke, "Chloe, there's nothing to be afraid of. You can speak to someone there, and if you feel it's all wrong, we'll just leave. I'm not pressuring you here. I just thought they might be able to help. Wouldn't it be good to find out what resources are available for you?"

Chloe was looking solemnly at Nicole. "Do you think so?"

"Well, let me see. For instance, the daycare could be a great place, but do you think they'll be open for you to bring the girls when you're working night shift?"

Chloe's mouth dropped open. "I hadn't thought of that!" She looked distressed. "What will I do about my job?" she wailed.

Reaching out to her, Nicole attempted to comfort her friend. "That's one reason I thought it would be good to go there. They might know of someone who could help you out with that. Who knows? They specialize in helping women who need some assistance." She ended with a smile and a shrug of her shoulders.

Chloe thought about this for a moment. Timidly she spoke, "Okay, I guess we can go." She ended in a rush, "But if I don't feel comfortable, we can leave?"

"Absolutely! I'll stay with you if you want, or sit and wait for you, whatever works. But at any time, just say the word and we'll come home."

"All right then."

∞ ∞ ∞

The next day found Nicole waking up bright and early. She lay in bed, thinking about the day and how it might unfold for them. Punching her pillows into submission behind her, she sat back against the headboard and pulled her Bible to herself. Today she would need God's wisdom and guidance. She had been reading various scriptures that were outlining God's character. That she was precious in His sight was still a fairly new concept to her, and as she had surrendered to His love, felt that it also meant He would protect His property. His property! *Imagine that*, she thought. This reflection sent goosebumps up her spine. Somewhere along her Christian walk she had heard these things before, but she had never really thought about it meaning her. Now she was learning that God never lies, and that all the promises in the Bible were meant for her. It was amazing to consider this, if even a little confusing as to how to see some of that come to pass.

As Nicole was finishing up praying for wisdom for the day, she heard the children stirring in the other bedroom. She got up and padded into the kitchen and found Chloe had gone ahead to prepare breakfast.

Brittany and Christine walked bleary eyed into the kitchen. Christine went over to Nicole and climbed up on her lap, and Brittany did the same with her mother. Both women cooed over the children for a while, enjoying their company before getting on with their day.

∞ ∞ ∞

Chloe and Nicole were sitting in a room with comfortable chairs. Speaking to them was a well-dressed and attractive lady named Abigail. She had been telling them about the resources they have for women who have been abused, and now she was asking Chloe some very personal questions. Chloe was not ready to admit that Barry was an abuser; she preferred to think of him as a nice man who had anger problems. It might even have been all her fault to begin with!

Abigail saw that Chloe was not being entirely honest with herself, so she changed the topic. "I started this centre because I had been abused by my common-law husband. I was with him for ten years. Throughout a good part of that time, if I didn't do what he wanted me to, he would beat me. It was after I ended up at the hospital with a broken jaw that I allowed myself to see that something was dreadfully wrong."

Chloe gasped at Abigail's admission. "What happened at the hospital?"

Abigail looked at her with kind eyes. "Well for one, the nurses looking after me didn't believe that I had slipped and fallen down the stairs, then hit my jaw on the way down. Even though I wouldn't tell them the truth, they were gentle with me, and I gradually became ashamed that I was lying to them. I had to get my jaw wired. It was a good thing I hadn't been able to have children, because it made it easier to run out and go to the hospital rather than try to nurse my wounds."

Chloe looked down at her hands. She knew what it was like to run with children.

Abigail got her attention again when she described what Allan had done to her and how he was always filled with remorse after the fact. But Abigail had had enough. That night, after he assaulted her, as soon as he thought she was sleeping, he went out. Abigail only had fifty dollars in her purse, but she did have her own credit card. As quickly as she could with the pain she was in, she packed a few essentials and crept out of the house. She took a cab to the hospital, determined she would not call Allan or let him know where she was. Not yet, anyhow.

The nurses got her in touch with Susan the social worker, and it was she who had eventually found out the truth of what happened to Abigail. Susan told her about a home run by a Christian couple; they took in women who had been abused by the men in their lives, and helped them get back on their feet. Abigail had lived there for six months; in the meantime she had found a job in a different part of town and eventually moved into her own apartment. She was young enough at that point that she knew if she was ever to be a help to others in the same plight, she would need formal schooling.

She worked to save some money, and then the day came when she started school. She had never looked back. When her formal education was officially over and she had a degree in counselling, she got a job helping abused women.

Chloe looked at her open-mouthed. She would never have dreamed that this lovely lady was also a survivor of abuse.

"Tell me Chloe, do you think your relationship with Barry has been healthy?"

"What's healthy?" Chloe's eyes were downcast and she looked a little ashamed to not really know the answer to her own question. Her own family was so dysfunctional, she had never learned the right behaviour from watching her parents.

"Well now, let's see. A healthy relationship is one where both people are free to speak their minds without the other being physically or emotionally abusive. It's where there is mutual respect and love, and where you can go to after work and feel safe, secure and accepted." Abigail stopped and looked kindly at Chloe.

Chloe looked up and she tried several times to speak. "I...he... it's not...um, I guess my relationship with Barry isn't like that. I feel so confused!" Chloe's frustration and shame was plain to see.

Nicole felt sorry for her and yet she knew that in order to get help, Chloe had to be honest with herself. She put her arm around her friend.

Abigail spoke before Nicole could say anything. "It's okay to feel confusion. You have a lot to think about. I too didn't want to admit that Allan was abusive. I had chosen him, after all, so what did that say about me? But in order to get any help, you have to be willing to look at the situation in an honest fashion. Do you understand what that means?"

Chloe nodded yes, her eyes looking miserable.

"How about we change the subject for a bit. I think it's time I tell you about some of our services."

Both Nicole and Chloe nodded their appreciation.

When Abigail was finished speaking, Chloe had found out that if she wanted to she could move into a similar home that Abigail had been in. There was one in the Greater Vancouver area, although not in the West End where Chloe worked. Even so, she could still take the bus to work. The good thing was that other young mothers with one or two children were also in that home and she could make new friends who understood what she was going through.

Abigail stood up and extended her hand to Chloe, then to Nicole. "That's about all I think you can take in for today. Why don't you go back and think through all this? You can come back next week if you like. If you want to move into this home, I can arrange it all for you then. How does that sound?"

Chloe smiled for the first time since their chat had begun. "I would like that very much."

They made an appointment for the week after, then Nicole and Chloe took their leave.

∞ ∞ ∞

Back in the Jeep, the two nurses were quiet for a while. Chloe was the one who broke the silence. Turning to Nicole she asked, "Do you think I should move into that place?"

Nicole stole a look at Chloe before answering. "It does sound good. We could ask Abigail if we could go look at it before you make a decision. That might give you a feeling one way or the other."

"Oh, what a good idea! Maybe I'll call her back tomorrow. Thanks Nicole." Chloe turned forward once again, lost in her thoughts.

They had gone to the daycare that morning. Chloe was surprised to find it was in a woman's house, but it was plain to see that she was well set-up for a daycare. There were only four other children there at the time, and the mood had been peaceful even though the children were playing. Christine and Brittany had gone over to the children immediately, and had lost any shyness they had walked in with. The beauty of this place was that Chloe could easily take one bus to work from there and the lady was willing to keep the girls till Chloe finished her day shift. So that might just work for her. She didn't think it was all that far from the home Abigail had described to them just now. She sat back and wondered if she was doing the right thing. What would she do when she worked nights? And what if Barry wanted to get back together? Would she agree?

Nicole was also lost in her own thoughts. She was really hoping that Chloe would file for divorce. She didn't think Barry would ever change and she didn't want to see her friend hurt again. At the very least it was important for them to have a formal separation for a while. Moving into the house offered by the centre would be a good step in the right direction. Chloe would be sending the message to Barry that she was committed to succeeding on her own.

∞ ∞ ∞

Several days later, Chloe was packing up the few belongings she had accumulated at Nicole's for herself and the girls. Tomorrow they were moving into the house Abigail had told them about. Chloe had gone over and met the other ladies, and had been impressed with how nice everybody was. One shy young lady named Johanna had brought them tea while they chatted with the owner of the house. As she placed the tea and cookies in front of them, the story had unfolded that Chloe was a nurse and worked night shift half the time. The difficulty of finding someone to mind her children during those hours was the topic of conversation for a few minutes.

Watching Christine and Brittany playing with the other children, Johanna had a smile on her face. She didn't have any children of her own and would have dearly loved some had her boyfriend not turned out to be so deceiving and cruel. Making up her mind, she spoke up, "You know, Chloe, if you move in here maybe we could work something out for when you work nights."

Looking up at her in surprise, Chloe's eyes lit up with hope. "What do you have in mind?"

Johanna hesitated. She suddenly realized all eyes were on her and that made her uncomfortable. Pressing through, she spoke. "Well, if we're both living here, maybe they could come sleep in my room when you're working night shift. We could make a little bed for them on the floor. I would love to look after them. They're so sweet. What do you think?" Johanna looked at Chloe with pleading in her eyes.

Chloe snapped her mouth shut. It had fallen open while Johanna spoke. Was this a godsend or what? "Are you sure?" she queried, looking from Johanna to Nicole, wondering if the latter also thought this was a good idea. "I would be willing to pay you what I pay the daycare," she added when she saw an approving look on Nicole's face.

"You would?" Johanna was surprised and pleased. So far she had only been able to find herself a part-time job at a local print shop. Any extra cash was always welcome.

So they had settled it all and planned for Chloe and the girls to move in. Of course, it would be much better to have a job that required only day shift, but she didn't know where that would be. She was planning on looking as soon as she was able.

Chloe came back to the present and the job at hand. She had thought about it long and hard, and had decided to file for divorce. Just separating from Barry was not the answer if he didn't change. She had yet to hear from him on the matter.

Brittany and Christine were playing with dolls nearby while Chloe packed. She could hear them talking in their little-girl voices, and every now and then they included her in their conversation.

The front door opened and Nicole called out, "I'm back!" in a sing-song voice. Brittany and Christine dropped their dolls and Brittany ran while Christine toddled along to say hello. Nicole was struggling into the door with grocery bags in tow. She laughed at their enthusiasm upon seeing her. "Hi girls. How are you doing this afternoon?"

"We're okay. We're playing with our dollies," replied Brittany. "Want to come and join us?" she asked hopefully.

"Oh honey, sorry but I have to put away these groceries. You can help me if you want. I have a surprise for us for supper too." This was their last dinner with her while living in her home, and she wanted it to be special for all three of them.

Brittany and Christine hopped up and down in excitement. "What is it, what is it?"

Chloe stepped in, smiling. "Now girls, it wouldn't be a surprise if Nicole had to tell us what it is ahead of time, would it?"

They stopped their jumping and looked at Chloe. "Okay, mommy, we'll wait. We'll be good." Brittany said. Taking

Christine's hand, she headed back to the bedroom. "C'mon, Chrissy, let's go back and play. We'll let mommy and 'Cole make dinner, okay?"

Christine walked with Brittany. She really was getting better at this walking thing! Pretty soon their voices could be heard as they resumed their conversation with their dollies.

Nicole shooed Chloe out as well, wanting to prepare everything for dinner in a special way. "Go finish your packing. Dinner won't be too long and we'll talk then, okay?"

With a smile on her face, Chloe retreated to the bedroom and joined her girls.

Nicole was going to put a tablecloth on the table, and they would have candles too. She had a special chicken dinner planned, and for dessert she would let the girls make their own ice cream sundays. She knew they were going to love that!

$$\infty \; \infty \; \infty$$

Nicole and Chloe jammed the last box into the Jeep. This in effect was going to erase the last traces of Chloe's and her girls' stay at Nicole's apartment. Nicole's heart felt heavy. She knew Chloe would be happier at the house where there were other children to play with, and Chloe would make friends. It was just going to be hard having the apartment so quiet again. With a sigh she closed the back and they all piled into the Jeep which, by this time, was loaded to the gunwales. Chloe had gone back home when Barry was at work and had returned with more of their belongings.

Driving to the house was actually fun because the girls were so excited. They had met another little girl there and they were eager to play with her again. Chloe and Nicole were quietly enjoying their chatter. Soon Nicole was pulling into the driveway. "Okay folks, here we are."

Nicole began pulling out boxes while Chloe unbelted the girls and together they went in to make their presence known. Chloe came back out with Johanna, who wanted to help with the move, having left the girls inside to play with their new friend.

When all the boxes were safely stowed in Chloe's and her girls' new room, Nicole crouched down to give them both a hug. "Don't forget me, okay?"

Brittany and Christine thought that was funny and their peals of laughter rang down the hall. How could they possibly forget her? Nicole grinned at them and ruffled their hair. She stood up slowly, ever mindful of her growing belly and gave Chloe a big hug. "You know my phone number. If you ever need me, please call!"

Chloe's eyes were moist. "I will. And I'll see you at work in two days!" Nicole was delighted to be reminded of that wonderful fact. They would be working together again! With a final wave, Nicole turned around and headed for her car.

The ride home was quiet, so Nicole put on a CD. She sang along with Brian Doerksen as he sang, "From everlasting to everlasting, You are God!" Before she knew it her heart had been uplifted by the words in the song. Once again she knew that God was in control. Even if it wouldn't be the same to have Chloe gone, Nicole knew this was better for Chloe. And it wouldn't be all that much longer before she herself could move to Abbotsford. Now she wanted that day to come quickly!

Chapter 20

Nicole was seven months pregnant. Ripping off her nightshirt and about to jump in the shower, she suddenly stopped in front of her closet doors. The sliding doors were mirrors, and showed perfectly just how much Nicole had grown in the past couple of months. She hadn't stopped to look much, and now as she reached her hands down to cradle the belly bump, she caressed the rounded mound, thinking of her baby. She had read recently that at seven months the baby was the size of a good head of cabbage. How funny! Unexpectedly she felt a kick and she laughed with delight. This little one was feisty! As she stared at her changing body, tears started trickling down her face. *Oh Greg, how you would love seeing these changes in me!*

Nicole's back was against the mirrors and she slid down to the carpet. Overcome by grief once again, she struggled with her thoughts. She realized she was standing on a fence, so to speak, and could easily fall to either side. One side held peace in God, the other total despair.

As she sat there she was nudged into thinking of something she had read that morning. She reached out for her Bible which was on the floor by her bed, and thumbed over to the book of Romans. In chapter eight she read that all things work together for good for those who love God and are called according to His purpose. *Huh. How are You turning this for good, Lord?*

While brooding over this and wiping the last tears off her face, Nicole was drawn to a bookmark that was half out of her Bible. Flipping over to Matthew ten, she read the highlighted section near the end. *"Are not two sparrows sold for a penny? Yet not one of them will fall to the ground apart from the will of your Father. And even the very hairs of your head are all numbered. So don't be afraid; you are worth more than many sparrows."*

Nicole allowed this truth to sink into her heart. Even as the tears flowed again, it registered that she was precious to God. Why was it that she could so easily forget this? Total assurance that He would look after her washed over her soul once again, and peace settled there.

Nicole recognised that something was different here. She was coming out of the anguish quicker. She remained sad, but was not overcome with grief. She must be getting better! With her head on her knees, she began to pray. *Help me Lord to understand why this happened. It's such a struggle! I don't like being alone. But thank You Lord that You're showing me You are with me through it all.*

Nicole sat quietly on the carpet, thinking. Then closing the precious book, she stood up and made her way to the bathroom to shower. She would wait and see. Right now there didn't seem to be any good in it, but maybe one day she would see it.

Opening the shower doors, Nicole smiled at Shadow who was sitting on the rug directly in front of her, waiting for her to come out. He loved to lick the water that dripped down the door after her shower. She had tried to break him of this habit, but to no avail. Oh well, he was an animal after all. He would do what he wanted to do.

When Nicole was towelling herself dry, Shadow meowed, letting her know he still loved her. She smiled and bent down to pet him. He truly was a good friend!

Looking through her clothes, Nicole chose to put on her jeans with the belly band. Next she covered it with a pretty mauve maternity shirt her mother had bought her. Tonight she was having Anna and Julie over for dinner! She had planned lasagne, salad and garlic bread for the main course. They could have their prenatal teaching after they had eaten their dessert of Chocolate Pavlova, something she had made for Greg once and he had raved over.

Nicole knew Julie was excited about getting some prenatal teaching and she herself was looking forward to the refresher. She had learned a fair bit in nursing school, but of course she had not been pregnant then. It was much more relevant to her now and she was pleased about practicing with Julie.

∞ ∞ ∞

Anna had just left and the two sisters were cleaning up the dinner dishes while talking about the evening. Julie had decided to stay the night. She didn't have to be at work early the next day, and it was pouring quite hard outside. Better to go home in the morning.

"That was all so interesting, don't you think, Nicole?" Julie asked her.

"It was that. She taught me a few things I didn't already know about childbirth. Now it all feels like it's coming fast!"

"I know. Before we know it you'll be going into labour. Oh I'm getting so excited!" Julie's eyes danced and she reached over to give Nicole a side hug. "Have you decided where you're going to have the baby?" Her hands went back into the dishwater to scrub the lasagne pan.

Clearly Julie had not spoken to her mother in the past week. At least, she hadn't spoken about Nicole. "Yes, I've decided to have it in Abbotsford."

Julie slapped both hands over her mouth to stifle a shriek of glee and promptly got her face soaked in dishwater and soap bubbles. Both girls broke into fits of giggles. Julie had suds dripping from her chin, making her look like she had a white beard.

When the laughter had died down, Nicole explained what she planned to do. "I have three weeks of vacation left, so I'll take that the second week in December. I hope to be able to move out then. I'll just commute back and forth to Vancouver for the short time I'll have left at work before the baby is born."

"What if Steve and Jennifer's suite isn't available in December? What will you do?"

"I spoke with Mom. She said I could move in there until Roseanne moves out."

"You won't mind being back at home? Would you rather move in with me?"

Smiling at her sister, Nicole appreciated her thoughtfulness. "That's kind of you to offer, Jules. I think it's better if I'm at home. You have such a small apartment, and once the baby comes it would be too disruptive for you. No, I'll be fine at home. And my old room is at the opposite end of the house from Mom and Dad's room, so hopefully the baby won't disturb their sleep too much."

"I heard that Roseanne was having car trouble. She does have a long commute right now. Maybe she'll get fed up with the situation and get serious about looking."

"Yeah, I hope so." Nicole turned back to drying the dishes. "I can bring everything from my apartment instead of putting some in storage. Mom said I could stuff everything I don't need in some of the other bedrooms."

Julie had a relieved look on her face. "That will work out well for you. That was nice of Mom, don't you think?"

Nicole nodded. She knew it would put their home in a topsy-turvy mess until Nicole could move out, but her parents were willing to put up with that. She really did have great parents!

After a few moments of each thinking their own thoughts, Julie spoke. "Say Nic, I don't have to leave here tomorrow until around noon. Would you like me to help you pack some things in the morning?" She looked so eagerly at her sister that Nicole grinned. "We'll have to get some boxes first, but I know just where to get them."

"All right!" They high-fived one another. The dishes were done and they were ready to put their feet up for a little while before going to bed.

∞ ∞ ∞

The next morning found them at the local liquor store, scrounging for empty boxes. These ones would be ideal for books; they were small enough for them to lift yet strong enough they wouldn't break with the weight.

Driving back to the apartment, they hooted over the load of boxes they had managed to collect. Looking over her shoulder at the boxes in the back of the Jeep, Nicole laughed. "At this rate we might get more than just the books packed before you head home today!"

∞ ∞ ∞

Matthew was commuting through the driving rain, trying to find a parking place on King Road before his first class of the day. There was one! As he headed toward it, a Smart Car scooted right in from the opposite side of the street, doing a perfect U turn and nabbing the only parking available. Slamming his hand on the steering wheel and muttering under his breath, Matthew fumed at the lack of street parking.

Suddenly he remembered his grandfather's offer. His face lit up with a grin. He pressed on the accelerator and zoomed off for their townhouse. Once he was situated in their driveway, Matthew gathered his backpack and jacket, then ran to ring their doorbell. He was scrambling into his jacket when the door opened and his grandmother pulled him inside out of the rain. "Hi Grandma. Do you think I could park here today? There's nothing available near the school."

"Of course, Matthew. It's so nice to see you, even though you're dripping wet!" They both laughed. "You must be in a hurry to get to class so I won't detain you. But I do have a favour to ask of you though."

Matthew's eyebrows rose on his forehead. "Sure, Grandma, just tell me what it is."

"When will you be back?"

"My last class finishes around three, so if all goes well I should be back around three-twenty."

With a satisfied smile on her lips, Margaret spoke, "Just come in for a little visit when you come back, would that be okay? I might have a surprise waiting for you."

"I would love to have a visit with you after, Grandma. I'll make sure I have enough time."

Turning her head and raising her voice, Margaret spoke to her husband who was in the living room. "Harold, would you mind running Matthew over to UFV? It's pouring outside and he doesn't want to be late for school." Then turning to Matthew with a twinkle in her eye, she said, "Wait just a minute. He'll get you there faster than if you run."

Matthew dropped his backpack to the ground. Leaning against the door frame, he crossed his arms in a relaxed position and smiled. "I can wait a bit."

Harold came around the corner with his jacket half on. "Matthew! I was wondering when we would get to see you. Boy it's a real doozy out there today. Good day for you to park here. Tell you what, when you're finished your classes, just call me and I'll come get you, okay?" He finished putting his jacket on and plopped his hat on his head. "All right, let's go."

"Say Grandpa," began Matthew, "How about we use my truck to drive to school? I'm parked in your driveway," he said with a sheepish grin.

"No problem. I'll just bring it back and park it right there after."

"Thanks so much, Grandpa! Wow, the ride there and back will make a significant difference for me today. For one thing I won't be as wet as I thought I would be for class."

Giving him an amused look, Harold said, "When an old retired man can't drive you back and forth once in a while to a school that's so close by, there's a problem!" He laughed and slapped Matthew's shoulder. They climbed into the truck and off they went.

"If I know your Grandmother, she'll have a snack prepared for you when you come to get your truck. Come back with an appetite."

Matthew grinned. "No problem there, Grandpa. And I'll call you when I'm done for the day."

Shortly after three that afternoon, Matthew called Harold to let him know he was done his classes. "Okay, Matthew, I'll be there in a few minutes. Should I pick you up where I dropped you off?"

"Sure, that's a good place. I'll be there waiting for you. And Grandpa...thanks so much!"

"My pleasure."

∞ ∞ ∞

Matthew opened the passenger door and slipped his backpack onto the floor of his truck, then he climbed in beside his grandfather. "Your grandma has baked you something for a snack before you go home," he announced. Matthew's mouth began to water before they arrived, knowing that whatever his grandmother had made, it would be good. His beaming face showed Harold how delighted he was with this development.

Walking into the house they were greeted with the luscious smell of cinnamon buns. As Margaret was walking toward them, Matthew took a whiff with his eyes closed. "It'll still be a while before you eat dinner, so you might as well park yourself at the table here and have your fill."

He eagerly obeyed and sat down. Reaching for the pan, he thanked her for going to all this trouble.

Margaret smiled as she watched her grandson fill his plate. "You know I love to bake, but it's a challenge for just your grandfather and me because we always have so much left over. It's a pleasure to bake for you. I'll try to do this every time you park your car here, if it isn't too much trouble for you to stay a little while."

With his mouth full, Matthew shook his head that it wouldn't be any trouble at all!

When he was satisfied with his snack and sitting back drinking his milk, Margaret kept the conversation going. "So tell me about school. What are you doing right now and do you like it?"

With a final gulp of his drink, Matthew set the glass down. "Actually right now I'm doing a computer course that I really enjoy. I'm going to build a web page for Julie for one of my projects. You knew that she wanted to get her own business eventually, didn't you?"

"I heard about that. So you're building her a web page?" Margaret wasn't sure what this was all about. She had never even turned on a computer.

Matthew smiled as an idea occurred to him. "Hang on, I'll go get mine and show you what I'm doing." He retrieved his Mac Book Pro from his backpack near the door. As he sat down again, he hooked into a neighbour's internet, then quickly found his way back to what he had been doing for Julie, explaining to his grandmother about the webpage. She was fascinated.

"And you think you can get her some customers in Abbotsford through this?" Margaret asked sceptically.

"Why sure! We'll just make her a business card and put the web page on it. We'll do a bunch of advertising too. She already has customers that say they come there because of her cookies, so that's a good start."

A small ding alerted Matthew that he had a new email coming in. Margaret asked him what that sound was and he explained to her. Before he knew it, he was showing her all about emailing and the fun she could have with something like this. She already knew how to type, so the rest was easy as pie.

Margaret was fascinated. She was thinking how much easier this would be than writing an actual letter. She might be able to keep better track of her friends this way.

Looking at his watch, Matthew was surprised to find he had stayed so long. He needed to get home to do some homework! Apologizing for having to run out in such a hurry, he put on his jacket and gave his grandmother a kiss. "Thanks again for the treat, grandma!" Turning to his grandfather he gave him a hug and stepped outside. It wasn't raining anymore, but the sky remained overcast. Typical Abbotsford weather!

Climbing into his truck, it dawned on him that he had a good deal in this parking spot! He smiled as he drove away and toward home.

Chapter 21

Nicole was back at work and today Chloe was working with her. It was such a relief for her to not have to work with Marianne anymore! Even as these thoughts went through her mind, Nicole felt sorry for the LPN. She was making life so much harder for herself with her attitude.

Grinning and waving at Chloe who was working down the hall, Nicole went about her business with a spring in her step. Her heart felt curiously lighter, like a heavy load had come off her shoulders. She had already arranged for her vacation and she had two weeks to go before having that time off.

Later in the day when both Nicole and Chloe were sitting near each other doing their charting, Nicole decided it was time to tell Chloe. "Harumph!" she cleared her throat. Chloe glanced up with a distracted look, her mind filled with the words she was writing. "I have something to tell you, Chloe."

Chloe put her pen down and gave Nicole her full attention.

"I've arranged everything for going on vacation in two weeks. I'm really hoping Steve's suite will be ready by then, but if it isn't, I'll move into my parents' house till the suite is ready."

Chloe's mouth dropped open. "So soon?"

"Don't worry. After my vacation I'll continue working here till I have the baby. The commute will suck, but not for very long. I think I can handle it for a short time."

Chloe looked embarrassed. "I thought you were going for good in two weeks. I'm just selfish, that's all. I don't want to see you go!"

Nicole smiled. They made such a good team. "There will be someone else for you to work with when I do leave, and you'll be just fine."

Chloe agreed with a wan smile. "I know that. I'll just miss you, that's all."

Nicole reached over and gave her friend a hug. "I'll miss you too. Maybe you and the girls could come out to visit me in Abbotsford. After the baby is born you could take the West Coast Express out and I'll come pick you up in Mission. How does that sound?"

"Hey, that sounds like fun! The girls would love to be on a real train, and that one is two levels high. We could sit on the top floor and see everything around!" They laughed easily together. Chloe would be fine.

"I'll let you know when the baby comes. Your girls would love to see a small baby, don't you think?"

Chloe agreed. It would certainly be special for them. "We're getting along really well with the other ladies in the home. Brittany and Christine love having the other kids around to play with too."

Nicole was pleased for her friend. "That's fantastic!"

"When we go on night shift this week, Johanna will take care of the girls in her room until I get back from work."

"I know you don't believe in having a relationship with God, but I've been praying that things would get better for you. I really believe He's had a hand in how well it's all working out, don't you?"

Chloe looked uncertain. "I didn't know. Huh, maybe God really is interested in me, after all."

"Oh I know He is. If you ever want to hear more, just let me know. He's waiting at the door of your heart, knocking. I'll explain how you can open that door and let Him in."

Chloe smiled at the picture this painted in her mind. "Okay, I'll think about it." She returned to her work and Nicole watched her for a minute. She didn't want to forget this special friend. When she had a good picture in her mind of Chloe with her curly, unruly brown hair and a grin on her face, she too bent her head to the work at hand.

There was a blinking light on Nicole's phone when she returned home. A message? Who could it be? Pushing the button she found out it was the Abbotsford Hospital, wanting her to come out for an interview. She had forgotten all about having put in her application online!

The following morning when she had her coffee break, she returned the call. They wanted her to come as soon as possible. She arranged the interview for her second day off after this set of shifts. She might even stay at her parents' overnight. Even though she wasn't sure when she would be ready to start work in Abbotsford, she had decided to go for the interview anyhow because she wanted to know what her chances were of getting casual employment after the baby was born.

While she was planning all this, Nicole noticed she had a nagging headache. She didn't get headaches often so this was a surprise. She had been tired lately; maybe that was the reason for the headache. The baby was getting bigger and keeping her awake more at night. Nicole sighed. It would be a while now before she got a proper night's sleep.

∞ ∞ ∞

A few days later, Nicole was driving on the freeway to Abbotsford. When she came up on the crest of the hill and saw the sign for Mt. Lehman, she found the scenery breathtaking. In the distance was Mount Baker, a ten thousand foot high mountain covered in snow and brilliantly white against the blue sky. It was in Washington State, but looked so much closer. Nicole became quite emotional while revelling in the beauty in front of her. It was unusual to have clear blue skies in early December in the greater Vancouver area, and here God was giving her something to take her breath away before she got to the interview. Her heart suddenly felt uplifted somehow, like God was smiling on her. Her faith rose as she continued driving. Maybe things would change for her now. She knew that moving to Abbotsford was the right thing to do.

Nicole was surprised with how bright and beautiful the hospital was. She had heard good things about this new hospital, but she hadn't expected it to be so nice. The lobby was huge with lots of sunlight brightening everything up. There was even a drugstore in the atrium, and a Starbucks! She crossed over to the volunteers' desk and after getting instructions on how to find her destination, she headed in the right direction.

∞ ∞ ∞

After the interview when she was back at her parents' house, Nicole called Julie and asked her to come over for the evening. She left a message on her cell phone and hoped Julie wasn't working tonight. Punching in the stop button to disconnect the line, Nicole heard the front door open. Matthew came into the kitchen a few minutes later and found her sitting at the table, drinking a cup of herbal tea.

He sat down with her and began telling her about parking at their grandparents' townhouse. "The odd thing is," he continued, "that Grandma has taken such a liking to emailing. She didn't have her own computer, so I brought her to the library and showed her how to use one there. Now she goes to the library on a regular basis in order to use the computer. She's gotten in touch with friends of hers who never wrote before but somehow also love using the computer. It's funny!" Matthew grinned while shaking his head. How amazing that he was the one responsible for getting her started!

"Grandpa thinks it's hilarious that they go to the library so often. His nose is firmly planted in a book, while Grandma is plugged to the computer! Anyhow, believe it or not, tomorrow after school I'm going to pick her up and we're going to Future Shop to get her her own laptop."

Nicole laughed. For her generation, computers were a necessity. For Grandma's generation they sometimes were more of a headache than anything else because they hadn't grown up with them and they so easily got frustrated with the problems that arose in using computers. "Well good for her! I'll have to tell her I'm proud of her next time I see her!"

"Why don't you send her an email? She'd be really tickled if you did." Matthew scribbled his grandmother's email address on a scrap of paper and handed it over to Nicole. "I think I'm going to try to convince her to go for a Mac. She'll have less trouble with it, and more fun. I can show her how to download photos and she can go whole hog when the baby arrives!" Nicole giggled. Her grandmother the computer queen! Somehow that was a hard one to wrap her brain around.

Nicole's cell phone announced Julie with a special ring tone she had assigned her. "Hi Jules! How are you?"

"I'm fine. I just finished work so I'd love to come over for the evening seeing you're at Mom and Dad's. Is this invitation for dinner or just for the evening?"

Nicole told her to hang on for a second. She turned to Matthew and asked him when Mom and Dad would be home. He replied that they were actually in Seattle for a conference, so they wouldn't be back until tomorrow night. Woohoo! Julie could come for dinner too and it would be just the three of them! Not that she didn't enjoy being around her parents. But it was fun being with only her siblings too.

∞ ∞ ∞

An hour later, the brother and sisters were making pizza together. Matthew was chopping up the green peppers and olives, Nicole was mixing the dough in her mother's big mixer, and Julie was looking in the pantry for spaghetti or pizza sauce. The group project didn't take long to complete, and soon they had two good sized pizzas in the oven.

While eating the pizza together later, they talked about what they would do for the evening. "I have some homework I need to finish, but I think I could spare an hour. Want to play a game?" Matthew asked.

"Sure. What do you suggest?" replied Julie.

Dropping his piece of pizza into his plate and wiping his hands on his serviette, Matthew walked into the living room where the cabinet was crammed with all their games. "How about we play CSI? Mom bought it last month and it's fun to play!"

"That sounds good to me. Let's clear the dishes first and then we can go to it."

The evening was spent with lots of laughter as the siblings spent time together. When Matthew had gone to his room to complete his homework, the girls were left alone.

"So what happened at your interview today?" Julie was curious.

"Well they were very nice. They thought I wanted to get a job now and I told them I would stay at St. Paul's till the baby was born. But I did mention that once the baby was old enough I'd be interested in working for them on a casual basis."

"So what was their response to that?" Julie wanted the whole story.

"The lady who seemed to be the leader of the two gave me her card. She wants me to call her when the time is getting close. She'll know if there is a casual or a regular position available at that point. I'll have to re-apply online, but at least now I'll have that personal touch."

Julie smiled. "That's great. So there should be something for you to do round about the time when you feel you are ready to start up again."

Nicole agreed. It had taken a load off her mind.

∞ ∞ ∞

Nicole stopped at the coffee shop the next day. She was heading home in the afternoon, but wanted to see Julie a little more before going.

Julie was busy in the kitchen mixing a new batch of strawberry rhubarb cookies. She had taken Matthew's challenge to heart. He wanted her to come up with a good recipe, and she thought this might just be it! "Come sit with me in the kitchen," she spoke to Nicole from the counter. "You can be the first one to taste my new creation."

Nicole couldn't resist that offer. She followed Julie into the industrial kitchen, knowing by the smell that these cookies would be really good.

"I couldn't come out to sit with you because these cookies mustn't burn. I want to watch them carefully. I'm not too sure how long they'll take to bake properly so I've got them on for twenty minutes right now; I might have to change that."

Nicole didn't see a problem with this arrangement. She still got to sit, and better still, she could watch her sister roll the dough into little balls for the cookies.

"I'd still like you to come and live with me until Steve's suite is available, Nic. But I think you're right. Mom and Dad's is bigger, for sure. It'll be easier for you to get around in there with a baby than in my little two-by-four apartment." They both laughed. Julie's apartment wasn't only two-by-four feet, but sometimes it didn't feel much bigger. She lived in a studio, so her bed was actually in the living room with a partition to make a division so it looked like two rooms.

"Thanks for understanding, Julie. But if you want, I'll let you do some babysitting after the baby comes!"

Julie's eyes lit up. "Really? I would love that. If you're tired and need a nap, or if you need to pick up some supplies, or groceries or something, whatever you want, I'll give you time to do it in and I'll babysit the little critter."

That made Nicole smile. Suddenly she stood up and walked to Julie. She took her hand and placed it on her belly, right where the baby was kicking. With a gasp, Julie realized what she was feeling.

"Is that the baby kicking?" she cried.

"You betcha," replied Nicole. She looked proud as Julie's face took on a look of rapt attention.

"Wow! That's amazing. Does it hurt?" Julie was concerned. "That seems like a strong kick."

Nicole laughed. "No, it doesn't hurt. It only bothers me when I'm trying to sleep and this little one wants to stay up."

Julie giggled. God's creation was so amazing.

Nicole suddenly frowned. Putting her hand up higher up her belly, she spoke, "This is strange. The baby must have turned awfully fast, or he's punching me because I feel something like kicking up here now. How can that be?"

The sisters were both touching Nicole's swollen belly, enjoying the feel of the little one, even if only through his or her kicking.

All of a sudden they were interrupted with a ding from the timer. The cookies were ready! As they were slipped out of the pan onto cooling racks, Nicole's mouth watered. These cookies might just be Julie's best ones yet. When they were cool enough to handle, she reached for one. It just melted into her mouth, and the combination of strawberry, rhubarb and chocolate was divine!

"Do you ever give out your recipes, Julie? These are fantastic!"

"I don't give them to just anybody, but to you, dear sister, I would give it out." Reaching into the binder she kept with recipes and notes, Julie took out a blank piece of paper. She copied the recipe on it and handed it over to Nicole.

Strawberry Rhubarb Surprise

Ingredients:

1 cup cornstarch
1 cup icing sugar
2 cups all-purpose flour
½ tsp. cinnamon
1 ½ cup butter or margarine, softened
¼ tsp. vanilla
¼ cup strawberries (chopped in small pieces)
¼ cup rhubarb (chopped in small pieces)
1 cup chocolate chips

Sift together cornstarch, icing sugar, flour and cinnamon. Mix in butter until soft dough forms. Add vanilla, strawberries, rhubarb and chocolate chips.

Drop dough with a spoon 1 ½ inches apart on ungreased cookie sheet. If dough is too soft to handle, refrigerate for an hour prior to placing on cookie sheet.

Bake in 325° F oven for 20 minutes or until the bottom is lightly browned. Makes 2 dozen cookies.

Nicole read it over, smacking her lips throughout. "This looks good, Julie. It's an easy recipe, yet it tastes so good. How do you do it?" she asked her sister with a smile.

"Well, it's a shortbread recipe with a few extra things added in." Julie came close and they looked at the recipe together.

"Did you start with this complete recipe, or did it change as you went along?" Nicole was curious.

"I started with basic shortbread. But it felt like something was missing. And the more I thought of it, the more it had to be chocolate. Don't you think the chocolate chips are the finishing touch?" Julie's eyes twinkled. She was a true chocolate lover, so she never had any problem adding it to her recipes.

"I'll say!" Nicole took another bite. Mmmm!" She closed her eyes and pretended she was swooning. Then laughing, she finished the cookie she was eating. "They just wouldn't be the same without the chocolate."

∞ ∞ ∞

When she left the coffee shop, Nicole drove straight to Steve and Jennifer's. Jennifer was at home with the children, and all were happy to see her. Jennifer placed her hand on Nicole's growing belly, and with a knowing smile she patted it. "Can't wait to meet you, little one!" she said.

Nicole perched herself at the counter on the island in the middle of the kitchen. Once settled there, she explained to Jennifer about her upcoming vacation and her hopes of moving out at that time. She was planning on starting her packing the day after she finished work. In any case, she would be spending Christmas with her family.

"So where will you stay?" Jennifer looked distraught. Why was Roseanne taking so long to leave?

"I'll stay at my parents' house for the time being. I can have my old room back for a while."

"Oh Nicole, I'm so sorry we can't offer you the suite yet!"

Jennifer looked like she was going to cry. They so wanted Nicole to move in, but short of kicking Roseanne out there wasn't much they could do. Or was there? Jennifer became perfectly still for a minute as it dawned on her there was one thing left they could do, that is, if Steve agreed with her. She would talk with him about it tonight.

"Should we plan to come out and help you pack? We'll certainly be there the day you move. Have you got a truck lined up for moving with?"

"I was going to talk to Dad about that. Maybe he could arrange one. I don't want to drive a U-Haul or something big. But maybe one of the men in the family would be okay with that."

"Hey!" Jennifer exclaimed. "I just remembered that Steve's friend Will has a truck. Maybe Steve could borrow it for the day. Of course we'll need more than that, but it's a start, right?"

Nicole thanked her. They chatted some more for a while, until it was time for Nicole to drive back to Vancouver.

As Nicole got back on the freeway heading west, she was feeling pretty good about everything that had happened that day. Oh, it certainly would not be easy leaving St. Paul's Hospital. She had made some good friends there. But she knew that her life was changing, and she had to adapt and change with it. Getting a different job was not the scary thing she had thought it would be. Over the past few months she had felt like she was getting itchy feet, wanting to do something else. She just hadn't had any particular direction she felt she should go in. This might just be good for her.

∞ ∞ ∞

When Steve got home from work, Jennifer was waiting for him. The kids had all been fed early and were now ready for bed. But these parents were going to have a candlelight dinner all to themselves.

The children were jumping all around, excited to have daddy home and tell him their adventures for the day. When they had all been rounded up and put to bed with a couple of stories, Jennifer placed the dinner on the table while Steve washed up. She was standing at the kitchen sink, washing the pots so she wouldn't have to do it later, when Steve walked in and placed his arms around her waist, nuzzling her neck. "Mmm," he said, "I could get used to this."

Turning around and laughing, Jennifer kissed him back, then led him to the beautifully laid table. With one eyebrow raised in query, Steve looked at his lovely wife. "Why the candlelight?"

"Well I don't know if you noticed, but the children are all in bed. This is our evening alone!" With a grin as his stomach rumbled with hunger, Steve sat down beside her.

After praying over the food, they told each other about their day while dishing up the food in their plates. When it was Jennifer's turn, she told him about Nicole's visit and how bad she felt about not being able to offer her the suite.

"I know you don't want to upset Roseanne, Steve, but we've been waiting long enough for her to move out. Do you think there's anything else we could do to get her to go more quickly?" Jennifer's forehead was creased as she asked the question.

With a huge sigh, Steve thought about it for a moment. "I really don't know what we could do. We've prayed and she still hasn't gone. I know her car is giving her problems and she doesn't like the commute. But what can we do? Do you have any suggestions?" As he looked at her he grinned. He could see she had something up her sleeve, but was just waiting to see if he would come up with something first. How he loved this charming lady!

"We've been talking about having more kids. Maybe we could tell her that this is the time when we want to upgrade the suite before we get pregnant again. And that we can only do it when it's empty!"

Steve looked at her. She was serious. "You mean kick her out?"

Jennifer looked slightly uncomfortable. "Not really. But we could let her know that we no longer think it's cool that she stays as long as she wants. The painting we do for Nicole will get it ready for after we have our next baby. I was thinking that maybe we could use it as a home school when Nicole eventually finds a bigger place. We could put all the supplies we need in there and it's so close to the house it would work." Jennifer looked eagerly at him. She had been a teacher before the kids came along and she certainly would be able to home-school when the time came, at least for a few years.

"That's not a bad idea, Jen. Maybe we could put a note on her door and ask her if we could speak with her together on Saturday."

Jennifer's eyes danced. "I'll do it tomorrow. Thanks, Steve! Maybe we can pray later that this will give her the push she needs to leave."

Chapter 22

Nicole was parked on the street in front of the house where Chloe and her girls were living. The residence was a pretty two-storey light blue house with white window trim and doors. There were flowers and bushes placed strategically in the front yard to make it look welcoming and peaceful.

Sitting there, Nicole was once again struck by how much she would miss Chloe and the children when she moved to Abbotsford. With a sigh, she opened the driver's door and climbed out of her Jeep. Walking toward the front door she could hear the joyful sound of children at play and figured they must be in the backyard. She was so happy for Chloe. Things seemed to be working out better for her since going to the Centre for Abused Women.

Nicole rang the doorbell and waited patiently for someone to answer. She grinned when she saw Chloe through the small window in the door, and a moment later it was opened wide.

Throwing her arms around Nicole, Chloe cried, "It's so good to see you! Come in, come in!" Then pulling her inside, she enthusiastically introduced her to the other ladies. After a round of introductions and a mini tour of her new home, Chloe poured two mugs of tea from the teapot which was buried under a tea cozy. From the kitchen they could see and hear the children at play in the backyard. With Christine and Brittany were two other small children, a boy and a girl. They were playing in the sand box with cars and trucks and small shovels. "Do you mind if we sit outside to watch the children?" Chloe asked Nicole. There was a patio swing for them to sit on and they could keep an eye on the kids while they chatted.

"Not a bit. It's such a beautiful day."

The two ladies bundled up and brought their tea outside as well as a blanket for their laps. They were quiet for a few seconds as they watched the children at play.

"I haven't had a chance to ask you how things were going lately. We don't always have much time for chit chat at work," began Nicole.

Chloe smiled. "Things couldn't be better, actually. I've got someone to watch the girls when I work nights now, and the daycare is working out well during the day. I'm finally relaxing a little."

Chloe certainly did look better, thought Nicole. Her smile came easier, and she wasn't fidgeting like Nicole had seen her do when she was nervous. A peaceful quiet descended upon them.

Nicole was enjoying just sitting with her friend, swinging gently and watching the antics of the girls. Finally she broke the silence. "I was just wondering something: would you ever consider getting back together with Barry? When we were at the Centre for Abused Women you didn't seem too sure."

Chloe allowed herself to reflect for a few seconds before answering. "I've had long enough to think it through. I don't want to get together with him again. I see now that there was all kinds of abuse throughout our time together. It wasn't just him hitting me that changed my mind. He could be demeaning in so many ways. All it took was for him to come home unhappy because something happened at work, and he would put me down. Towards the end, as you know, he started hitting me and I was so afraid he would eventually hit the girls." Chloe looked sad. "So I thought you'd be interested to hear that I filed divorce papers with Barry last week. I just don't think he is capable of changing."

Nicole looked up in surprise. She didn't know Chloe had thought it all through to that extent. "Really? So how did he take it?"

"He actually took it better than I thought he would. He's been going to anger management classes." She looked down at her hands wrapped around her mug. "He says he feels really bad for what happened and wants to change, but I'm not convinced he can be faithful to that. He didn't seem too broken up over the fact that the girls are living with me." Chloe suddenly looked up with a sigh.

"I'm not sure I trust him. He might try for a while, but I think if we get back together, we'll end up in the same boat."

Nicole was nodding, understanding Chloe's comment. "It's hard to change ourselves or get rid of bad habits."

"Yeah, well he says he wants to change, but now I've come to the conclusion that my girls deserve better than that. They were always so afraid that Barry would come home angry. Right now they are so happy. Just listen to them!" They both turned their gaze to the children playing. There were peals of laughter coming from the girls as they raced their cars with the other children. One of them was making a mountain out of the sand, and another was crashing a car into it. Their cheeks were flushed with delight as they amused themselves. They looked healthy and happy.

Nicole's eyes softened as she watched their excited chatter. "I'm so pleased for you, Chloe," she spoke softly. "You certainly have gone through a rough time and deserve to be happy with your girls."

Chloe responded in the same tone, "Yeah, I know. When we were living at your place I never dreamed that something like this would be possible. We'll probably still be here for another couple of months. At least until something more permanent comes around for us."

"Good. I'll know where to reach you then."

"Barry is talking about selling the house and splitting the proceeds with me once the divorce is finalized. I don't know how much money that will be, but maybe I could buy a smaller house for the girls and me. We don't need something big, just enough for us to live in. I'd actually be happy in an apartment too, depending on where it ends up being. I think that would help us feel like we're starting anew."

"That would be nice."

"He actually offered to have the girls and I stay in the house, but I didn't want to have any bad memories for them. I think it's best we move altogether. What do you think of that?" Chloe took a sip of tea and watched Nicole over the rim.

"I think it's a good idea. Starting fresh after a painful time like you've been through is always a good idea. Say, would you consider moving out to Abbotsford? I'll be living there next month, and you could look into getting a job at the hospital there too!"

Chloe wasn't sure what to think of this suggestion. She hesitated as she answered, "It would be nice to live close to you again, but it's so much to consider right now. Abbotsford just seems so far away, you know?"

"Oh don't worry about it. I just wanted to ask, that's all. Besides, it'll be easier for you to think of the future once the divorce goes through. Think about it though, would you please? My mom has been looking for suites in the area and has been able to find some decent ones at cheaper prices than Vancouver has." Nicole pleaded with Chloe. "I could look around and see what kind of jobs are open to LPNs. I'm sure they are in as much demand as they are here."

Chloe smiled at her friend. "I'll let you know if I'm ever ready for you to look for me. The ideal thing would be if I could find a day job, but they aren't easy to find for LPNs."

∞ ∞ ∞

Nicole drove home, her head pounding. What on earth was going on? She had never had headaches much before, and all of a sudden through the last few weeks she had had them regularly. Mulling over what it could mean, Nicole drove herself the rest of the way home and parked her Jeep in the underground garage.

Back in the apartment, she striped off her jacket and hung it up in the closet. Sitting on the couch with Shadow, she noticed that her feet were slightly swollen. Was this a normal thing when one was with child? She knew it was common to retain fluid during pregnancy; but the headaches too? Fatigue washed over her as she considered what might be happening to her body. Pulling her feet up on the couch and curling herself into a comfortable position, well, as much as was possible when she felt like she had a football attached to her belly, she pulled Shadow close and they both fell asleep.

∞ ∞ ∞

Briiiing! Nicole was startled awake by the telephone's insistent ring. "Hello?" She was still kind of sleepy and it showed in the lazy sound of her voice.

"Nicole! It's Steve. How are you doing?"

Steve was calling her during the day? What time was it? Nicole quickly looked at her watch and saw that she'd been sleeping for three hours. It was already dinnertime. That explained it. Steve must be home. "You just woke me up from a long nap. I'm okay, how are you?"

"Great. Say, I have some good news for you."

"You do?"

"Yup. Jennifer and I had a long talk with Roseanne and she's now moving out in mid-December."

"Really? What did you do to get her to move? Did you kick her out?"

Steve laughed. "No, nothing like that. We realized as we were chatting with her that she was feeling an unreasonable pressure to stay here because she liked us and didn't want us to not have a tenant. Funny, huh? When she figured out we actually wanted the suite empty, she was happy. She had seen a few places she liked already, so it didn't take long for her to secure one for herself. So she found a basement suite in New Westminster. She says it's bright and has lots of room. She's actually pretty excited. She'll be paying a little more than here, but she'll be saving on gas, so she's all right with that."

"Steve, that's great news!" Nicole was finally wide awake. Her heart was beating a steady excited rhythm as she considered what this meant for her.

"I knew you'd think so," Steve said with a smile in his voice. "So actually, Jen and I have decided that once she's gone, we're going to repaint the whole place. Would you like to help us choose the colours?"

"Are you serious?" Nicole hadn't ever had the opportunity to choose colours for her own place. When she and Greg had married, the walls in their apartment were neutral in colour. They had only done small paint jobs in the same neutral tones when necessary as a touch-up. This might be fun! "How much are you going to paint? I mean, which rooms?"

"Well it's been years, so it wouldn't hurt for us to do it all. There's a few plumbing problems that need to be repaired, and I believe there are a few patch-up jobs that need to be done to the walls. And right now Roseanne does her laundry at the Laundromat, so we thought it would be a good idea to put in a stacking washer/dryer for you. I think it will need a complete make-over. Are you up for it?"

"Wow," Nicole's voice sounded thoughtful. "I don't know how much I'll be able to do to help you. I mean, by that time I'll have a fairly large bump out front. I'm already feeling quite top-heavy..."

"Oh I didn't mean that you'd have to do the work yourself. We'll ask Julie, and Matthew should be out of school for the holidays at that point. Maybe he'll give us a hand too. Who knows, maybe Mom and Dad will help out as well. What we need from you, though, is the colours that would suit you for each room. Have you thought of what you would like for the baby's room, for instance?"

Nicole blew the hair out of her face. "I haven't given much thought to that yet because I wasn't sure if I would still be at Mom and Dad's house when the baby came. So I'll give it some thought and get back to you. Are you in a hurry to get those answers?" she asked anxiously.

"No, no hurry. I just wanted you to start thinking about it. Maybe you could drop into a paint store and get some swatches of different paint colours that you like. You know?"

"Oh yeah, those little paint chip samples. I could do that. I actually don't have much put together for the baby yet. I've been so busy with work, and it's taken me a while to start moving forward with my life since, well you know, since Greg..."

"I know. It's been a difficult road for you," Steve's voice had softened with emotion. He took a deep breath and continued, "But we're all here for you. Jennifer and I can loan you a bunch of our baby stuff, so don't worry about what you have and what you don't have right now. We'll work it out. There's still time."

Nicole was finding it hard to speak with the lump in her throat. "Thanks, Steve. I'll get on to those paint samples tomorrow. It's my last day off before my last set of shifts, and then I'll have three weeks off."

"Mom and Dad mentioned it. Let me know when you are ready to move. One of my friends has a truck that would work well with all your stuff." He paused. "Actually, we could come out this weekend if you'd like us to help you pack."

"I've done a little so far, but I just don't have the energy when I'm working. How about when I'm finished work we plan on a day to do that, okay?" Nicole just couldn't push herself these days; she was just too tired.

"That's fine. Don't forget to let us know. I'd better run now. Looks like dinner's ready. Take care and we'll talk soon, okay?"

"All right. G'bye for now." Nicole hung up the phone with a thoughtful expression on her face. She was going to choose the colours for her "new" place! Where would she start?

Getting up and looking at the kitchen, she noticed she had lots of blue things. Opening the cupboard, she pulled out one of her dinner plates. Turning it over, she found the name imprinted on it: Pfaltzgraff Summer Breeze. She loved this pattern with its yellows and blues. With a thoughtful look on her face, Nicole set the plate aside. She would bring this in to the paint store. If she brought the thing with her that she loved the most about her kitchen, namely her dinnerware set, she would be better able to choose colours that would match.

It would sure help if she could remember the colour of the kitchen cabinets and layout in Steve's suite. Oh well, she would bring home lots of different paint colours so she could run them by Steve and Jennifer. That way she would be ready for anything. With a smile on her lips and a song in her heart, she began making herself something to eat.

∞ ∞ ∞

On the last of her days off, Nicole managed to drive around town and find quite a few empty boxes. Once they were all in the apartment she set about packing. She already had the books done. Now was the big job of starting with the kitchen. There were some items she wouldn't need at all till she moved into her new home, so she could easily pack those now. Her waffle-maker and mix-master were the first small appliances she packed. She hadn't used them since Greg had died. Would she ever use them again? With a heavy sigh she loaded them in separate boxes and protected them with old newspapers.

Sealing the openings with tape, she chuckled when Shadow hopped on top of the first box and pounced on the tape as she was sealing the box. "This isn't one of your toys, Shadow," she tried to scold him, but the laughter was still too evident in her voice. Shadow would certainly not listen to her this time, she thought with wry amusement.

The day passed by fairly quickly as she went from one room to another. She had gotten into the groove of packing and had only one box left. She decided to use it to pack some more of Greg's things. When she was done, she had a box of items for the second-hand store. She would drop it off tomorrow evening on her way home from work.

Nicole had been thinking about Greg's bicycle for a while. It was still busted up, but she didn't have the heart to part with it. He had paid so much money for that thing! Taking the elevator to the basement, she made up her mind that today she would make her decision when she saw it again.

Once in the storeroom in the basement, Nicole had to push some boxes out of the way before she saw the beat-up bike. Taking a closer look, she thought the only thing that appeared wrong with the bike was that the front tire was crooked. It certainly was not rideable as it was, but she didn't think it would cost too much to repair it. Greg's pride and joy had weathered the accident better than she remembered. Maybe Matthew would like to have it! Come to think of it, she would offer Matthew all of Greg's bicycling paraphernalia. Greg had loved the speedometer and other items which made riding fun for him.

Nicole was kneeling on the ground, looking through the box with Greg's bicycle things. He would have loved to have seen Matthew with his bike. That was it; she would call her brother tonight.

She stood up straight and dusted off her hands. Placing them on the lower part of her back, she leaned backward a little to relieve the pressure on her back. Only a few tears had fallen as she had worked on Greg's belongings, even though sadness permeated her soul. She was healing.

Chapter 23

Nicole was on her last day shift. She was heading into her two last night shifts tomorrow and the night after. On her breaks she usually stayed in the staff room on their ward, but it filled up very quickly and sometimes got noisy. Today, however, she was tired. She rummaged into her backpack and found her book. She would go to the cafeteria, sit by herself and read.

Sitting in a booth in a quiet area, Nicole sipped her coffee and enjoyed the quiet. Her feet were propped on the bench in front of her and she was comfortable. She was holding her book up to partially hide her face; she didn't want to have anyone come sit with her right now as she needed the silence.

Being completely absorbed in her book, it took a few minutes for the sound to reach Nicole's ears. The woman's loud complaining was getting closer. Nicole moved her book slightly and peeked from behind it. Coming toward her was an elderly lady walking with a cane. Immediately behind her was a younger woman who looked like a younger version of the elderly one. They settled themselves in the booth in front of Nicole. At that instant, Nicole gasped in recognition. The younger lady was Marianne! This then must be her mother, the one she had heard had Alzheimer's. Marianne was explaining to her mother that they were early for her appointment, so they would sit here while they waited. She placed her belongings on the bench beside her and told her mother to wait while she got them both a cup of tea. "Now don't go anywhere, mother," she said, standing up. "I need for you to sit right here and wait for me. I won't be long. Can you do that?"

"Of course. I'll be right here. You run along. A cup of tea does sound good."

Marianne left to get their tea, and for a few minutes her mother sat there quietly. Nicole was amazed. Marianne could actually be nice when she wanted to be.

Suddenly the elderly lady stirred, and looking around she began to mutter to herself. As Nicole watched, she fidgeted in her seat. Marianne was taking a little longer than her mother could understand, what with the dementia and all. She swung her legs out from under the table, and stood up.

At that instant, Nicole decided she would do what she could to help Marianne. Compassion filled her as she watched the mother. Standing up, she reached Marianne's mother in two strides. "Hello there!" she said eagerly.

Marianne's mother looked up at her, confusion and curiosity mirrored in her face. "Do I know you, young lady?" Then her eyes took in Nicole's uniform and she said, "Oh, you're a nurse. Do you work here?"

Nicole smiled at her and said, "Why yes, I do work here. In fact I've worked with your daughter before."

"My daughter?" Her brows puckered in concentration.

Nicole helped her along a little. "Marianne, your daughter. She's just gone to get you a cup of tea. I heard her say she would be right back. Why don't you take a seat and wait for her? I could just stay and chat with you if you like." Nicole smiled to put the woman at ease.

"Oh, if you say so, dear." She re-settled herself in the booth.

"Are you a nurse? You look like you might be one." She smiled back at Nicole, the fear and concentration gone for the moment.

"I am. Are you a nurse?" Nicole knew she couldn't possibly be one now, but who knows, maybe she had been one at some point. The easy forgetfulness of Alzheimer's was very evident in this poor lady. Nicole was beginning to understand what Marianne must be going through in taking care of her.

"Oh no, dear. I'm not a nurse. I'm a librarian. I love working with books. Do you like to read?" she queried, looking at Nicole.

"Yes I do. One of my favourite pastimes is reading. What kind of books do you like?"

"What kind? Now let's see... there are so many different kinds. But I do love those ones that talk about a person's life; what are they called? It's interesting to read about someone who has gone through hard times and how they came out of it. Don't you think so?"

"Oh yes, I completely agree with you. They can be so encouraging. And those books are called biographies."

"Mother, here's your tea!" Marianne came up so quickly she surprised them both. She looked at Nicole with suspicion. "Who is this with you, mother?" Marianne had recognized Nicole but wondered what she was doing with her mother.

"Marianne, this young lady is a librarian too. We both love to read biographies. In fact, you work here, don't you?" she asked Nicole. "Isn't this the library?"

"Mother, we're at the hospital. We've come here for some tests which you will take in a little while. But let's have our tea while we're waiting, shall we?" Marianne sat across from her mother and looked over at Nicole, who was still standing. Nicole wondered if she should tell Marianne why she was speaking with her mother. Taking a look at her unfriendly face, she decided she would gracefully bow out. "I'll be leaving you, then. Have a good day!" She smiled at the two ladies and went back to her own booth.

Sitting there with her book in her hands once again, Nicole wasn't seeing any of the words on the page. All she could think of was Marianne and her mother. How draining it must be to take care of someone with Alzheimer's. At least if Marianne could go home after her day's work, it would be different. But this wasn't a job. This was her life. She was beginning to see that the anger simmering on the surface of Marianne's personality had a deeper root. Praying for both women, Nicole found herself losing her frustration for Marianne. This must be her way of dealing with the blow life had given her. She prayed that God would pour His grace and mercy upon Marianne, that He would reveal Himself to her. Ultimately what Marianne needed was to know Jesus Christ as her Saviour. Only when that happened could she let go of the anger that was eating at her.

Nicole's time was up, break was over. She walked back to the elevator with a thoughtful expression on her face. She knew that God had prompted Marianne to sit in that very booth so Nicole could see what life must be like for her. She suddenly realized she had judged Marianne and knew now that she had been wrong. What was it they said? One mustn't judge a book by its cover...

∞ ∞ ∞

Nicole was doing her charting, sitting at the nurses' station. Her head was pounding. She pulled her hair out of its elastic, releasing the silky mane around her shoulders. Putting her head in her hands, she sat there quietly for a few minutes.

Chloe was sitting a couple of seats away from her. She looked up and saw Nicole with her head in her hands. Concern covered her features as she pushed her chair back and walked over to her friend. "Are you okay?" she asked, putting her arm across Nicole's shoulders.

Startled, Nicole sat back and smiled at Chloe. "Hi. Actually, I have a headache again." She sighed and threw her pen onto the chart she was working on.

Chloe hadn't had any problems with her pregnancy, but she remembered all the research she had done with each one. She had wanted to be prepared if anything came up. These headaches Nicole was having didn't sound good, not for someone who had never really had headaches before. "Come over to the back, Nicole. I want to take your blood pressure." She took Nicole's hand and led her to the back room.

"Is this necessary?" Nicole looked embarrassed to have such a fuss made over her.

"Yes it is. If nothing else, it'll give me peace about how you're doing. So sit!" Chloe brought the blood pressure machine close as she spoke. Wrapping Nicole's arm with the cuff, she turned on the machine. As the cuff pumped up, both women watched the numbers. "What's your normal blood pressure, do you know?" Chloe sounded very business-like.

"Hmm. I think it was 120/75 last time Dad took it."

With the musical note signalling that her blood pressure was completed, the machine displayed the numbers 154/88. Nicole sat there stunned. Could this indeed be the reason for the headaches?

Chloe watched her, thinking the same thing. "You need to go see your obstetrician, Nicole. You can't let this wait."

"It's too late in the day to go see anyone right now. Besides, I don't have an obstetrician in town here. My Dad is the one who's been taking care of me during the pregnancy."

"Nicole, I'm telling you right now that you have to go see someone. I guess you can't really go to emergency with this, but please, could you at least call your father tonight? Tell him about your headaches and blood pressure."

"Okay, I'll call him when I get home. Is there something else we could check here that would help him? You're the expert on pregnancy. What do you think?"

Chloe was quiet while she removed the blood pressure cuff from Nicole's arm. Her lips were pursed together in thought. "One thing I read a lot about is preeclampsia. You seem to have some of the symptoms, and I wouldn't want to see you end up with something worse. The blood pressure needs to be under control or this could escalate. You just don't want to go there Nicole. I'm telling you, take this seriously, okay?" Chloe pleaded with her friend.

Chloe's beseeching surprised Nicole and she found herself getting scared.

"We could check your urine for proteins. That too would be an indication of preeclampsia." She went into the supplies room and took out a little bottle with numerous small multi-coloured squares on it. Opening the cap, she pulled out a stick which also had the same coloured squares. "Go pee in a bottle. I'll check your protein."

Nicole returned a few minutes later, and in doing the test they found she had a some protein in her urine, although it was only slightly elevated. Her heart sank. She had a suspicion her father would tell her to not return to work. Chloe's eyes sought hers, and Nicole knew she too was thinking the same thing.

"Oh Nicole!" Chloe moaned. They stared at one another in silence and suddenly embraced as friends, knowing they might not work together again.

"I'll call Dad tonight when I get home," Nicole spoke quietly.

"Call me tomorrow and let me know what he says?" Chloe begged her friend.

"You bet." Nicole sat in silence for several minutes. She was going to do her own research when she was home. If this was preeclampsia, she wanted to do what was best for her baby.

Chloe and Nicole returned to their charting, Nicole's pregnancy uppermost in their minds.

∞ ∞ ∞

Nicole was home sitting on Greg's recliner, her feet up in the air. "What do you think it could be, Dad?"

Stan didn't want to commit himself without examining Nicole, but he was worried about her and the baby. "I think it *could* be preeclampsia. We don't want to jump to conclusions, though. I do need to see you. How many shifts do you have left?"

"Two night shifts starting tomorrow."

"Hmm. How would you feel about calling in sick for them?"

"For both?" Nicole's heart sank. She had suspected he would say that.

"I think so, honey. Your health and the health of your baby are of primary concern to me. I'd like to see your blood pressure come down to more normal numbers, and I don't think that working on a busy surgical floor is going to do that. So what do you think?"

"Yeah, I see your point." Nicole was quiet for a moment. "I never got to say goodbye to the people I work with," she said wistfully.

"It's hard, I know. Maybe you could pop in sometime just to say goodbye. But definitely not to work, okay?" Stan's voice wasn't stern, but Nicole knew he meant business.

"All right, I'll do it. Can I pack while I have the time off?" Nicole was joking. She knew she was going to have to take it easy, but how was all this work going to get done?

"Absolutely not! I would be happier if you could just lie on the couch for a good part of the day. Of course you can make yourself something to eat, but don't do any housework right now, okay? I'll get in touch with the rest of the family, and we'll arrange everything for you, don't worry. I'll see what I can do, and call you back tomorrow."

Nicole agreed with a sigh. When she hung up the phone, she stared into space for a while. Finally she roused herself and made the call to let work know she wouldn't be there for her next two shifts.

∞ ∞ ∞

The next day found Nicole spending time in the morning reading her Bible and pouring out her fear to God. *"How am I going to pack all my things, Lord? If work makes my blood pressure rise, I won't be able to do anything; and I have to be out of this apartment at the end of the month!"* Nicole blew her nose. She had already been crying so much today, her eyes were puffy and her nose red.

"And what about my baby? I know that at first I fought this pregnancy; I wasn't sure I wanted to have a baby on my own, but You know I've changed and really want to have it! Please protect my baby!" Nicole was overcome with anguish as she considered what could happen in the next month or so.

When Nicole quietened down, she opened her Bible to Deuteronomy chapter thirty one. God had been speaking to her recently through the plight of the Israelites. Their unbelief and constant turning away from God showed her that she wasn't all that different from them.

As it turned out, God spoke clearly to her that day about not being afraid. While drying her tears, Nicole remembered her newfound joy in writing songs. She knew she needed to remember this passage, and the easiest way was to put it to music. Pulling the guitar toward her, she began strumming different chords, playing with the sound. As she looked at the words, a tune popped into her head. She began singing it, tweaking it here and there. When she was satisfied with the way it sounded, she sat back on the couch.

Her heart was full as she thanked God for giving her the gift of this song.[3] Singing it again, peace washed over her.

> *"The LORD is the One who goes ahead of you.*
>
> *He will be with you, He will be with you;*
>
> *He will not leave you nor forsake you.*
>
> *Do not fear, do not fear nor be dismayed.*
>
> *Do not fear, do not fear nor be dismayed."*

Nicole was quiet for a while, allowing this new peace to wash over her. She would definitely remember this song.

Suddenly the silence was shattered with the ringing of the phone on the coffee table next to her. The sound took her by surprise. "Hello?"

"Hi, honey." It was her father. "I've spoken with the rest of the family, and we're all coming out on Saturday morning. Is that okay with you?"

That was in two days. Nicole was surprised, but happy. She hadn't expected anyone to come until the following weekend because she was supposed to be working this coming weekend. How things can change! "Sure, Dad. What are we going to do?"

"*We're* going to move you back home, what do you think? I don't want you to do the packing on your own. Please let us do it for you. It'll go faster, you'll have company, and you and the baby will be safer." her father said with a smile in his voice. "The only one not coming is Leila. We figured she'd just get in the way, so Steve and Jennifer's neighbour will babysit her for the day. The other kids are thrilled; they can help carry small stuff out to the truck."

"Oh, Steve'll be able to borrow the truck from his friend?"

"He sure will. He figures we should be able to put as much of your stuff in there as possible, and split the rest up into all our vehicles."

"Wow." This was being taken completely out of her hands. But with the fatigue she had lately, she really didn't mind if they

---

3   To hear the song "Do Not Fear", please go to www.oliveboettcher.com

did most of the work. "Okay Dad. I'll see you guys in a couple of days." She felt like she was riding a whirlwind.

So they arranged the time, and Nicole hung up the phone with both trepidation and excitement vying for attention in her mind. She would have to tell Annaliese.

How would she ever be able to say goodbye to her favourite neighbour?

As she was about to pick up the phone again, she heard a melodious sound from her laptop announcing she had a new email. Curiosity got the best of her and she pulled it close, clicking the mouse in order to read it. It was from her grandmother! Nicole grinned. This was going to be fun. She had written an email to her grandmother after Matthew had given her the email address and this was her response.

Reading it eagerly, Nicole felt a warmth wash over her. Grandma was expressing concern over her working full time and looking forward to having her back in Abbotsford where they could all dote on her and show their love during this pregnancy. Nicole quickly answered the email, telling her grandmother she was moving back into her parents' house in two days. That would make her happy!

Picking up the phone again, Nicole dialled Annaliese's number. The answering machine came on, so Nicole left her a message, explaining that things had changed with her pregnancy and she would be moving out to Abbotsford in two days. Her whole family was coming out to do the work for her. She ended the message on a tearful note. "Please pop in and see me when you can!"

Chapter 24

"Would you like me to come with you for moral support?" Chloe offered Nicole as they discussed going to say goodbye to the staff on their floor at the hospital.

"Oh, I don't know if that's necessary. Although it would be nice to see you again too."

"I'll tell you what. I have to go to the Centre for Abused Women later today. How about I pop in after and we can go together."

"Are you sure?" Chloe sounded like she really wanted to see Nicole.

"Absolutely. I'll be at your house around three thirty. See you then." And with a quick goodbye, they hung up.

∞ ∞ ∞

Nicole and Chloe had just walked onto their ward. It was quiet and there weren't many staff members around. "Come on, let's go see if someone's in the staff room," Chloe said.

As they came near, Chloe stopped to tie her running shoe, allowing Nicole to be the one to walk in first. She opened the door and "Surprise!" came the joyful shout from twenty or so people spread out around the room. Nicole gasped. The whole room was decorated with balloons, gifts and baby things. Many of her co-workers were there, as well as others who had heard she was leaving and wanted to say goodbye.

Nicole stood at the door, her hand to her mouth, tears biting her eyelids. Chloe came up from behind her, grinning, and pushed her into the room. She looked at Chloe, her eyes round. "You knew about this?"

"You betcha! It was all planned!"

The group erupted with laughter and joyful chattering as they led her to the chair of honour, which was decorated creatively with ribbons and balloons. Nicole was amazed as she looked around the room. How had they pulled all this together? Even some of the doctors were there. Emotion welled up within her. But before she could begin to cry, they each took a turn bringing her their special gift. Marcie was the first to hand her a gift bag. Thanking her, Nicole took a peek inside and pulled out the tissue paper. Inside was a tiny pair of jeans and a t-shirt. "Oh, this is so cute!" She smiled at Marcie and thanked her.

Barbara, another registered nurse, came close and put a wrapped box on her knees. Chloe looked at her and thanked her for coming. As they chatted, she tore through the wrapping paper, exposing a plain white box. Nicole shook it to try to figure out what was inside. With a curious look on her face, she opened the box and nestled into tissue paper was an exquisitely knitted sweater and booties set in pale yellow. With a gasp, Nicole said, "Oh my, this is beautiful! Thank you so much, Barbara!"

"When I found out you were pregnant, I started knitting and just kept adding pieces. There's more underneath." She helped Nicole pull out the pieces. There was a little hat and also a blanket. What a set!

As Nicole was putting the items back in the box, several doctors came forward with their gift. It was a car seat with a huge bow attached. "You'll make a great mother," Dr. Sullivan said, grinning at Nicole while she figured out how the car seat worked. What a blessing this gift would be. Nicole smiled at each one of them and thanked them profusely.

The gifts kept coming until she had quite a pile beside her. There were baby blankets, soothers, cute clothes that would work for either boys or girls. In the pile was also a great diaper bag which Chloe had given her and a box of diapers from the cleaning lady. Nicole was so touched. When all the gifts had been given and there was still a lot of chatter in the room, she looked around at each person. How could she leave such a wonderful group of people to go work elsewhere?

But before she could get all teary eyed, they pulled her up and over to the table which was laden with good food. In the centre was a beautifully decorated cake which looked like a baby carriage, complete with a small plastic baby inside!

While the food was happily being consumed, Nicole mingled with each group of people, thanking them again for the fantastic gifts. There was a whirlwind of hugs, farewells and promises to keep in touch, and suddenly Nicole was alone with Chloe, the others having all gone back to work.

She stood there looking at her gifts, wondering how she was going to get all this home. But Chloe had thought of all that ahead of time. "This is the reason I came over, Nic. I'm going to help you get all this to your apartment. Don't worry, you won't have to do a thing." She spoke quietly, understanding that Nicole was close to tears for the emotion of the moment. Walking across the room, Nicole embraced her friend and clung to her. What would life bring in the next couple of months?

Finally pulling away from Chloe, Nicole looked at her friend with a shaky smile. "You fooled me!"

Grinning, Chloe began to gather the gifts into boxes and bags. "Yeah, we sure did surprise you, didn't we? It was fun! You should have seen your face!" She laughed at the memory. "We actually began planning it a couple of weeks ago, but brought the date closer when we found out you were leaving earlier."

Blair, one of the registered nurses, had taken lots of pictures and promised to send them on to her. She had given him her email address; good thing his camera was a digital.

Just as they had gathered everything together, Blair came back into the room. He was pushing a small trolley on wheels. "I'll help you ladies bring all this down, if you want."

"Oh what a fabulous idea! Thanks for bringing the trolley!"

"No problem. And it's fairly quiet right now, so I can leave for a few minutes."

They worked together to pack all the gifts onto the cart. Chloe told Nicole she could bring the rest of the cake home, but Nicole opted to leave it for the staff instead. "I don't have to tell you how nice it will be for the staff to have something to munch on during the night," Nicole said to Chloe, with a smile on her face, knowing her friend would also be the recipient of that snack. So into the fridge the cake went.

All the other gifts were finally loaded onto the trolley. Chloe said she would push it, and Blair could carry the car seat.

Once everything had been safely stowed into the Jeep, Blair came around to give Nicole a hug. "You take care of yourself, you hear?"

She hugged him back, thanking him for everything. Climbing into the Jeep, Nicole and Chloe waved and off they went.

∞ ∞ ∞

Chloe had refused to let Nicole carry anything into the apartment. She had settled Nicole on the couch, and then made several trips from the garage to the apartment. They were sitting together with a cup of herbal tea, looking through the gifts and exclaiming now and then when a little treasure was discovered again.

With a happy sigh Nicole settled deeper into the couch and took a sip of tea. "That was so lovely. I don't know how you pulled it off, but I want to thank you."

Chloe beamed at her. "It was my pleasure. It's not every day that an important member of our staff leaves!"

When Chloe had finished her tea, she looked at her watch and exclaimed. "I need to get home. I'll just have a couple of hours to nap before I have to get back to work."

Handing Chloe her car keys, Nicole spoke up. "I won't need these tonight. Why don't you use the Jeep to go home? You can always return it tomorrow morning after your shift is over."

"Are you sure?" Chloe was surprise, but also touched by her friend's generosity.

"Most definitely. Here, take them." And Nicole put the keys into her hand.

As they stood together, Nicole once again enveloped her friend in a hug. They laughed at the big bump that was between them. Nicole giggled and grabbed her belly as the baby kicked toward

Chloe. "I think this baby's had enough hugs for one day! Here, put your hand right here and you'll feel it." Nicole took Chloe's hand and guided it where the baby was kicking.

They both laughed as another kick came. "Wow, I think you might have a little soccer player in there, or maybe that's a punch! Maybe there's a boxer or wrestler in there, Nic!" she said with a laugh. Sobering, she looked at her friend. "Remember to call me with any news. I'll be waiting to find out what happens."

"You can call anytime once I've moved. I've given you my phone number at my parents' house. And of course you can always call my cell phone."

"I'll do that. Well, I'd better run. See you in the morning, Nicole." Chloe gave her one last hug and rushed out the door.

The phone rang as Nicole was walking back in from the entryway. It was Annaliese. They arranged to get together the next morning. "Don't you worry about a thing. I'll bring us something to eat and you can just relax, okay?"

"I look forward to it, Annaliese. It's so good to hear from you; thanks for calling."

∞ ∞ ∞

Later that day while she was resting on the couch, Nicole decided to call her mother.

"How are you doing, honey?" Ellen asked after answering the phone.

"Oh, I'm doing okay. I went to work with Chloe today and they had a surprise baby shower for me."

"What fun, Nicole! I'm glad you were able to get in to say goodbye. Your father mentioned to me that you were hoping to do that. What did they give you?"

Nicole gave her a run-down on the gifts. "And the biggest one yet was a car seat that a few of the doctors went together on. Just wait till you see all this stuff, Mom!"

"I'm looking forward to it. You didn't carry all those things into your apartment yourself, did you?" Her mother sounded worried.

"No Mom, Chloe came with me and brought everything in so I wouldn't have to lift a finger."

"She's a good friend, huh?"

"You got it. I'm sure going to miss her." There was a pause and then Nicole continued. "Mom, could you bring a bunch of boxes when you come over on Saturday? I've done some packing, but there's still a fair bit to do. I've gone through all my boxes."

"Okay. I'll go out tomorrow and see how many I can round up for you. I'll ask the others too. Maybe we can throw them all into the truck Steve'll be driving."

"That's a great idea. I might ask Annaliese if I can rest at her place when the last of the furniture is being loaded in."

"I like that. You make sure you ask her."

"Okay, Mom. I'll see you Saturday then."

"Right, dear. You try to rest now."

When she hung up the phone, Nicole looked around the room. She had done some packing, but now because of the party she had more to pack! Oh well, so be it.

Chapter 25

Chloe had dropped off Nicole's Jeep and Annaliese and Nicole were once again sitting on Nicole's couch, sipping coffee and munching on apple coffee cake. Nicole had just told her about her possibly having preeclampsia and how this could affect her and her baby.

While they were discussing that, Annaliese asked Nicole pertinent questions about how she felt and where she was at with God in this new development.

Brooding over the questions, Nicole took her time in answering. "My relationship with Jesus is so much better than at the beginning of all this. Even so, I'm finding it really hard sometimes. I mean, I've already been through so much. Why do I have to have more problems?" Nicole looked beseechingly at her friend.

"I know dear, it's not easy to understand why these things happen. But the important thing is not so much that you're going through a difficult time, but what your attitude is in the meantime. Are you able to keep your eyes on the Lord through it all?"

"Oh, sometimes yes, sometimes no," Nicole responded with an embarrassed swipe at her bangs to get them out of her face. Would she ever come to a place of rest in her faith?

Annaliese looked at her thoughtfully. "You know in the book of James we are told to consider it all joy when we encounter various trials, because it's as we walk through them that endurance is produced in us. These are the things that mature us in Christ, as we keep our faith in Him. Every one of us is going to have trials. But we don't have to fear, because Jesus has promised to be with us in it all."

Nicole just looked at her friend. She had heard this before, but she wasn't sure how to be joyful when she and her baby were in danger with this preeclampsia.

Annaliese continued in the same vein. "We are also told in the same passage that we are to ask God for wisdom through the difficulties. Have you asked Him how to pray in regards to this new problem?"

"No, I never thought of that," Nicole answered.

"Why don't you ask Him right now? Then we can just pray through this problem, okay?" Annaliese looked at Nicole enquiringly.

With a nod, Nicole agreed. She put her coffee cake on the table and wiped her hands. Bowing her head she began, "Lord Jesus, please protect my baby! Please keep me safe and for my baby to be born safely even through this new development!" She ended on a strangled note.

After a few seconds of quiet, Annaliese opened her eyes and pulled her Bible to herself. She reached inside for some notes she had made. "Nicole, God has given us His Word to guide us through these difficult times. In the Old Testament the children of God saw Him as one who brought pain as well as joy into their lives. But those who actually had a relationship with Him, like King David, knew that He was loving and totally trustworthy. He wanted to be their Father. Those who don't have a relationship can't see Him as a Father, but when you've felt His touch and know His faithfulness, you can see that He wants to keep you through difficult times, if you will let Him."

"Sometimes I can see His faithfulness to me. Other times I don't see it, nor do I feel that I deserve any of it." Nicole wasn't sure where to go from there.

"Thank you for telling me that, Nicole." She placed a hand on Nicole's arm in comfort. "It's a struggle, but you need to know that no one deserves His faithfulness. That's what grace is all about; it's getting something we don't deserve. None of us deserves God's love, His faithfulness, His protection. But the beauty of it is that God already knew this and that's why He provided Jesus."

Annaliese put her hands in her lap and continued. "You see, it's because of the sacrifice that Jesus was willing to endure on our behalf that has now broken down the wall of separation between us and the Father. Now when we are in Jesus, we can come boldly to the Father and thank Him for all His promises that are in the Bible because they are without a doubt meant for every one of His children. God is not a respecter of persons, that is, He loves each one the same and all the promises are equally for them all. But how do we come to a place where they really are working in our lives?"

"Good question. I hope you will help me find the answer," Nicole spoke with a smile.

Annaliese smiled back. "When you know that the Bible is God's love letter to you, you can take the portions that speak directly to you and say them out loud to yourself. As you do that, you are convincing your soul that this indeed is for you. Your spirit already knows, but sometimes it takes convincing for your soul to get with the program!" They both laughed at that. "The more you read it, knowing God will do this for you, the more faith rises in your heart until you know, that *you know,* that this is indeed for you."

"Could you give me an example? I'm trying really hard to understand this concept."

Annaliese placed a finger on her lower lip as she thought of an example for Nicole. Pointing her finger up to heaven, she signalled that she had her example.

"The Bible tells us that Jesus defeated the powers of darkness at the cross. In fact it says that He made a spectacle of the principalities and powers and triumphed over them in it. That's found in Colossians. He died to set us free from sickness and disease just as much as for salvation. Isn't that what we see Him doing the most during His earthly life? Healing all the people who were around Him?"

"Okay," Nicole said, not sure where Annaliese was going with this.

"Sometimes healing can come from speaking to the issue in prayer. When we ask Him for wisdom, now and then He shows us something that we are doing wrong, for instance if we are judging others, or angry. That is when He expects us to deal with the issue before we move on to pray for healing. Other times all we can do is trust that He will provide the peace that we need while we walk through the difficulties. But I don't believe He wants us to beg

Him for anything. You see, everything is laid out so beautifully in His Word, all that is ours in Christ. He wants us to appropriate it into our souls. The Word of God is tremendously encouraging, and brings change in our lives when we trust that it will do what it is meant to do." Annaliese stopped to take a sip of her tea.

Looking up, she saw the confusion on Nicole's face. "Oh dear, I don't think I'm making this too clear. Let's see...in the New Testament, because of all that Jesus has accomplished on the cross for us, we can pray with boldness that which is in His Word because we know that all His promises are yes and amen through Christ Jesus our Lord for us today." She picked up her Bible and opened it to the book of Luke. "Do you remember how Jesus rebuked the wind and the waves so they wouldn't drown when they were in the boat?"

Nicole nodded her head. She remembered that story well.

"Okay. Jesus didn't beg God to protect them from the waves, He went directly to the root cause of the problem...the waves and the wind. He wants us to do the same today. He rebuked them for their unbelief and showed them how to do it. He was actually expecting them to speak out in faith, and when they didn't, but cowered in fear, He showed them how it should be done. When we see issues that come up in our lives, He wants us to speak the Word or address the powers directly. We need wisdom to know what to rebuke, and through prayer God does show us what the root problems are."

Annaliese adjusted her position on the couch. "I have these friends in Kelowna. Do you remember the terrible forest fires they had there a few years ago?"

Nicole nodded. Those fires had been well documented in the papers and on television.

"Well, when the fires were coming closer to their home, they knew they had to act. It tells us in the Bible that God's thoughts toward us are for good and not for evil, to give us a future and a hope. Taking the truth of the Word to mean that God didn't want their house burned down, they stood on a hill overlooking the fire and declaring this truth in God's word, they then spoke to the wind to change direction away from their little community. They rebuked the fire in the name of Jesus."

Nicole had a surprised look on her face. "So what happened?"

"The wind changed direction and their home didn't burn down." Annaliese said with a triumphant voice. "You see, Nicole, God is for us, not against us. We need to do as He tells us in the Bible when we are praying."

"So how exactly would you pray if you were in my shoes?" Nicole queried.

"Can you see that it is a sin to allow the fear of preeclampsia to control you? In doing that, you can't hear from God anymore as the fear grips you."

Nicole thought through this for a few heartbeats. Finally she answered, "Yes, I see that."

"All right. Why don't I pray and you can repeat it after me?" Annaliese asked her.

"Okay." Both ladies bowed their heads.

Annaliese began, "I repent Lord for allowing this preeclampsia to bring stress and anxiety into my heart. You want me to be at perfect peace in You, knowing that You are holding me and my baby in the palm of Your hand. Lord I don't believe this preeclampsia is from You. Your Word says that You are for me, not against me. So in the name of Jesus I rebuke this infirmity. I speak to my blood pressure to come into line with God's Word now and be corrected."

Nicole was careful to repeat after Annaliese. First she repented for allowing the fear in, and then continued.

"I thank You Lord that You say in Your Word that Your protection is upon me and upon my baby. You are looking after us even through this. I speak Your life into both of our bodies now, in Jesus' name. Thank you for Your forgiveness and thank You for Your peace that passes all understanding, even in the midst of trials. Amen."

"Amen," repeated Nicole. She opened her eyes and looked at Annaliese. "I think I understand better now. When we beg God, we are in fear of what could happen. When we thank God that He is working all things for good in our lives, we are able to rest there, knowing that He will do what He says in His Word He will do. Wow, it's quite an important truth, wouldn't you say?"

"Most definitely. Can you see the difference in praying? When you beg God to do something, you are not left with a victorious end. You don't really know one way or the other what He's going to do. But when you speak to the issue...repenting of anything you need to repent of and then dealing with the powers, speaking the Word, you are left with a victorious faith that knows He is for you and He will protect you. Alleluia!"

Nicole's eyes glowed with new understanding as she looked at her friend.

"Do you remember when I told you we had to learn to pray by the Spirit?"

Nicole nodded.

"Well, when a prayer is not connected by the spirit of faith, it becomes a desperate prayer. If you're not convinced that God has you in the palm of His hand and is watching over you for good, you pray a prayer of desperation, not victory. Always remember: no faith, no receiving!"

Nicole picked up her notebook and pen. She needed to remember this!

"Here, I just thought of something else. Can you turn to Psalm ninety one?" Annaliese was already thumbing her way there.

Nicole grabbed her Bible and turned to the passage Annaliese had just spoken of. "Okay, I'm there." She looked up at her friend, her hand on her open Bible.

"Look at this:

"He who dwells in the shelter of the Most High will rest in the shadow of the Almighty.

I will say of the LORD, "He is my refuge and my fortress, my God, in whom I trust."

Surely he will save you from the fowler's snare and from the deadly pestilence.

He will cover you with his feathers, and under his wings you will find refuge;

His faithfulness will be your shield and rampart.

You will not fear the terror of night, nor the arrow that flies by day,

Nor the pestilence that stalks in the darkness, nor the plague that destroys at midday.

A thousand may fall at your side, ten thousand at your right hand,

but it will not come near you."

"No, it will not come near you because you have put your faith in the Lord!" Annaliese looked up with a twinkle in her eye. "I'm going to jump around here..."

"If you make the Most High your dwelling — even the LORD, who is my refuge-

Then no harm will befall you, no disaster will come near your tent.

For he will command his angels concerning you to guard you in all your ways;

They will lift you up in their hands, so that you will not strike your foot against a stone.

You will tread upon the lion and the cobra; you will trample the great lion and the serpent.

"Because he loves me," says the LORD, "I will rescue him;

I will protect him, for he acknowledges my name.

He will call upon me, and I will answer him;

I will be with him in trouble, I will deliver him and honour him.

With long life will I satisfy him and show him my salvation."

She sat back with a contented sigh. "You see? The Word of God tells us that when we love God and put our faith in Him and call upon Him, that He will deliver us. It doesn't necessarily mean He will take away what besets us, but indeed He will guide us safely through it. And in the process we will have matured more in our faith."

Nicole kept reading the Psalm. Wow, this was so encouraging! She had never really looked at it this way. She had thought that the Psalms were for days gone by. But there were important promises in there! She felt an assurance grow in her heart as she contemplated all that was spoken. What a treasure Annaliese was to her! Looking up, she smiled at her friend. "That is beautiful. Thank you so much. Once again you've helped me understand something pretty important to my faith."

"My pleasure, Nicole. God has given so much to me, and I want to give back to others where I can."

Nicole felt uplifted in her faith. Even so, she was not looking forward to saying goodbye to Annaliese.

Sensing that the time was quickly approaching, Annaliese made a suggestion. "Tomorrow when your family is here packing, why don't you come over and rest on my couch? You're not supposed to be doing any of the work, are you?"

"Oh, I was going to ask you about that!" Nicole smiled. "Probably that would work best toward the end, especially when they are loading up the furniture. It wouldn't do for me to be glued to the couch when they are trying to put it in the truck!" They both laughed at the picture.

"Okay, I'd be really happy to come over then. In the meantime, if you want to come over and say hello to my family, please feel free to do so. In fact, I know they would be glad to see you again." Nicole suggested, hoping Annaliese would take her up on it.

"So it's not goodbye yet. We'll save that for tomorrow, all right?" Annaliese reached up to Nicole and enveloped her in a hug. "Oh my," she laughed at the big bump in between them. Placing her hand on the bump, she spoke to the baby. "Peace from the Lord Jesus Christ to you, little one." And with that she turned and took her leave. "Till tomorrow then."

Chapter 26

Nicole was pulling on her blue maternity long-sleeved t-shirt when she heard a knock at the door. The gang was here! She flew to the door, opening it wide. A grin creased her face when she saw Matthew lounging on the door frame. "Hey there, Mr. Nonchalant, come here!" She pulled him to her for a hug. Once again the big-bump-that-was-her-belly got in the way, and Matthew laughed.

"Hi there Nicole... and baby bump! The others are all slowly making their way up here, but I ran ahead. How are you doing?" He peeked around the apartment, trying to get a gauge on how much work needed to be done.

"Great now that you're here." She turned around and looked at him. "But seriously, it's not a nice place to be in when you have to move and can't do any of the work." She pouted at him.

With a chuckle he swatted her on the rear. "Trust my sister to get a handle on that one. If I ever have to move, what excuse will I come up with?" He jumped out of the way before she could swat him back. They were giggling like school children when the others came walking into the apartment.

"Hi Nicole!" The chorus sounded good to her ears. How she loved her family!

One by one they hugged her, commenting on how big she was getting. "Well now, that's not a nice thing to say to a lady!" she answered playfully.

Steve took her hand and led her to the living room windows. Peeking out, she saw a big truck parked there. On the street scattered here and there were other family vehicles. "That there," he pointed, "is what we'll have to fit everything that's in here." He looked around the apartment. "We're going to work until it's done, but you, my dear, are not allowed to lift a finger, do you hear?" He raised his eyebrows at her in query.

"Yes sir, loud and clear." She saluted him in jest, but she knew he was right; she shouldn't do any work today. "Maybe I'll just park myself on the couch and direct the flow of traffic. How does that sound?"

Julie came up behind her, surprising her. She hadn't seen her yet. "Sounds good to me. If you're good I might park right beside you and keep you company for a while, too."

Nicole laughed and grabbed her sister in a hug. Julie pulled her down onto the couch.

"Okay everybody," Steve began, "There's a ton of boxes in the truck. How about the first thing we do is bring them all upstairs?"

Nicole's parents were the first ones out the door, ready to roll up their sleeves and pitch in. Jessie and Andrew accompanied them. They would be a help with the smaller boxes.

After the flurry of activity out the door, Nicole turned to Julie. "So what's new in your life?"

"Let's see. Matthew has my web page up and running. What a lot of work it was to finish that, I'll tell you!"

"Once we're all back in Abbotsford you'll have to show it to me."

"Don't worry. I'm so proud of that web site with my name on it that I'll be sure to show it to you. I've gotten business cards made up too and have been handing them out all over the place. I've gotten a few sales out of that already."

"Have you? That's great!"

"Actually, my biggest sale so far is to a local furniture company. I deliver a couple dozen cookies to them every week."

"That's fantastic, Julie! Congratulations!"

"Well, it's not much yet, but it's a good start. Speaking of cookies, I brought some along for our coffee break."

"Oh yum! What kind did you bring?"

"Cappuccino crisps. It's a new recipe I'm trying out."

"Can't wait to try them." Nicole smiled at her sister and pulled her feet up onto the sofa. Good thing she had a long couch. Her sister was on the other end and Nicole's feet just touched her.

They heard some noise and voices coming from the hallway, and suddenly several of them burst into the apartment with boxes in tow. Throwing them to the ground, they promptly turned around and went back for more. Nicole and Julie looked at each other with raised eyebrows. There would soon be a mountain of boxes in here.

Pretty soon they had distributed boxes throughout the apartment, and they all set to work. Matthew parked himself in the living room with the girls. Julie got up to help him take apart the stereo and make sure all the cables were safe in a labelled box. As they worked, he gave them a running commentary on what he was doing. "Say, have you heard my latest joke, Nicole? What's the difference between a roast beef and pea soup?"

Nicole looked at him with an incredulous look on her face. "Can't say that I know..."

"Anyone can roast beef."

As understanding dawned on her, Nicole's laugh bubbled out of her. "Oh my, that's pretty bad, Matthew. Hahaha." She looked at Julie to find her also grinning. Apparently she had heard that one before.

Julie spoke with gooey sweetness, "Be good, Matthew, or I won't let you have any of my cookies when we have a break!"

He stopped and put both hands to his heart. "You know how to go right for the jugular! I'm devastated!" He bent to the work at hand with an exaggerated sigh. The girls looked at each other and smiled. Matthew worked in silence for a few minutes. Then, out of the quiet came a small voice, "Do you know what kind of coffee was served on the Titanic?"

"Hot coffee?" Nicole spoke before it dawned on her answer wasn't funny. That couldn't possibly be the answer, knowing Matthew.

"Sanka." Matthew continued working as his two sisters groaned.

"That's nasty," Julie said. "Careful or I'll get a towel and flick it at you!"

"Oooh, I'm really scared!" Matthew grinned at her. "Okay, I have one final one. What's the difference between a bad golfer and a bad skydiver?"

"What? Between a bad golfer and a bad skydiver?" asked Nicole, scrunching up her face in thought. "I give up."

"A bad golfer goes, 'Whack! Dang', but a bad skydiver goes, 'Dang! Whack!'"

"Ouch!" Julie exclaimed amidst their giggling. "Enough! Get back to work, wretched slave!" And with that she flicked a dishtowel towards Matthew's rear end.

Just as he was about to grab it from her, their father walked into the room. "So, how's it going in here?"

"It was going just fine until Matthew decided to bore us with his bad jokes." Julie laughed when she spoke, showing she really enjoyed Matthew's sense of humour, even though she wasn't saying it.

Stan put his hand on Nicole's shoulder. "You doing okay?" he enquired.

She covered his hand with hers. "Yes, Dad. I'm fine. These two are keeping me entertained."

"Good. Mom and I are going to work in the kitchen. Is there anything I need to know about what's left to pack in there?"

"No, everything's good to go."

"All right, so we'll be in there till we're done then."

∞ ∞ ∞

They had been at it for a couple of hours and everybody was getting a bit tired. Matthew arrived just in time with Tim Horton's coffee for the adults and juice boxes for the children. Julie pulled out her cookies and everybody found a place to sit down. As they munched and sipped coffee, they chatted about how to best organize the rest of the work. When that was all taken care of, Stan commented on the cookies. "Julie, these are really tasty. Are they your finished version?"

"They will be if everybody likes them well enough. What do you all think?" She looked quizzically around the room at her family.

Ellen spoke up. "I think these are really good. I love the big crunchy sugar on top."

"Truly?" Julie was pleased at her mother's observation.

Jennifer and Steve both gave her a high five; they loved the new cookie recipe. "It's great, Jules. I'll be sure to come to you when I think of a different kind of cookie I'd like to try."

"Please do. Sometimes it's hard to come up with ideas for my cookies. So if you guys tell me what you'd like, that will make things easier for me." She glanced around the room with a smile on her face.

"Thanks for bringing food for our coffee break!" Nicole brushed the crumbs off her jeans and took a drink of coffee. "Yum," she said with a smile.

Holding up one of the cookies and looking carefully at it, Matthew said, "You know, I think there's just one thing you could do to make your strawberry-rhubarb cookies better."

Julie looked at him in surprise. "What's that?"

"Add a drizzle of chocolate on the top. Now that would make them truly special!" he said with a grin and stuffed the whole cookie into his mouth.

"Not a bad idea, Matthew." Julie agreed. "That's just what I'll do. In fact," she snapped her fingers as the thought occurred to her, "I'll make it their trademark with the way I drizzle it on. Thanks, Matthew!"

"Okay," said Ellen. "I think our break is over if we want to get this finished today. Shall we get back to work?" she enquired, looking around at each one.

"The master bathroom is finished. All I have to do is bring all the boxes and stack them in here," Jennifer announced.

"Oh good," said Julie. "In that case, I'll start cleaning in there. Is that okay?"

"Sounds good to me," replied Nicole. "Maybe I'll bring one of the cushions in there and sit on the floor while you work. That way we can still chat."

"Great! Let's go then!"

When they broke for lunch, both bathrooms and the guest bedroom had been packed and cleaned, and there was a mountain of boxes in the hallway. Following their break, some of them began stacking boxes in a dolly and carting them downstairs to the truck, while the others stayed behind to continue working.

Julie was now cleaning cupboards in the kitchen and Nicole had retired to the couch again. This time Andrew sat with her and she was reading him book after book. "Auntie Nicki, you are so good at reading stories. I like that you make animal sounds and everything. It's so cool!" Before long his eyes began to get heavy. He moved his position so he was laying beside her, and several minutes later they were both asleep on the couch.

Nicole woke up before Andrew did. She lay there with him, brushing the blond hair out of his eyes, loving the feel of this little boy. She was looking at him dreamily when Julie came and plopped down on a chair beside her. "Phew, I'm getting tired!" she stated, wiping the sweat off her brow.

"Sit with me a few minutes then."

"You don't have to twist my arm, that's for sure." While they sat there in silence, Julie noticed it was possible to hear quite a few sirens from this apartment. "Do you get used to the sound?" she asked Nicole.

"Well, yes and no. I don't stop and wonder anymore who's in the ambulance and what's wrong. And they don't wake me up anymore either, but when I'm awake I haven't ever learned to tune them out. I guess some of that is because I've been in one and have an idea of what's possibly happening in there."

Julie was surprised. "You've been in one? Why?"

"I was near the end of my shift a while back and getting ready to go home. The site leader called our ward and asked if there was a nurse who would be interested in accompanying a patient to the Royal Columbian Hospital. I figured I had nothing to lose, so I volunteered."

"So what happened?" Julie was hanging onto every word.

"I went to Emergency because that's where the patient was. She had a perforated abdomen and was being transported for immediate surgery."

"Why go all the way there? Couldn't they operate at St. Paul's?"

"Her surgeon was at the Royal Columbian and it was a very complicated case. So that's where we went. When I got to Emergency I saw the paramedics standing waiting, so I went over to help the nurse get her patient ready for transport. Before long, we were loaded into the ambulance and off we went."

"That must have been exciting!"

"Well, yes and no. I was sitting on the hard bench beside the patient, so it wasn't a terribly comfortable ride. Also, I was checking her and trying to keep her talking. She wasn't doing too well at that point."

"Did they have the siren on?"

"It was a Code 3, so they had lights and siren. When it's a Code 3 there has to be a nurse along as well in case something goes wrong." Nicole gave a laugh. "It was right in the middle of rush hour too. It was a strange feeling to be in the ambulance and watch the traffic part in front of us. Sometimes it was a wild ride as the ambulance had to weave in and out of traffic."

"Sounds exciting!"

With another laugh, Nicole explained the worst part of being in that traffic. "I was actually surprised, you know. Since our new cell phone law stating we can't use a cell phone without it being hands-free in the car, there were a surprising number of people on their cell phones who didn't know what to do when the ambulance appeared right behind them. The worst offenders were those who stopped their cars where they were, whether they were on the side or in the middle. I don't have any idea how they figured we would get around them when they were in the middle of the road. The driver of our ambulance was really good; he'd just get right behind them and they sooner or later realized that he couldn't move, so they gradually slid out of the way." Nicole laughed, shaking her head. "Unbelievable!"

When she finished speaking, she saw that it was getting kind of dark in the apartment. *It must be after four o'clock!* she thought. And sure enough, when she looked around she saw that the bulk of the boxes had already been taken out, and the furniture was all that was left.

By that time Andrew was awake too and stretching beside her on the couch. "I think I'll go see what mommy and daddy are doing."

"You do that, buddy. I'll see you later. Thanks for keeping me company!" And she reached down to plant a kiss on the top of his head. With a cheeky grin he ran off to find his folks.

"I think it might be time for me to wander over to Annaliese's apartment. That way the furniture can be taken out too."

As she was speaking, her father walked over to the couch. He heard her last comment. "That's good, Nicole, because I was going to mention that we were nearly ready to start loading the big stuff."

Standing up, Nicole straightened her clothes. "Right! So you'll know where to find me. She's in the apartment to my left, okay?"

"All right."

Nicole walked over and rang Annaliese's doorbell. Opening the door, she gave Nicole a big hug and pulled her inside. "You people have been really busy today. I've been keeping track by watching out the window now and then."

They smiled at each other. "Here Nicole, you can have the couch. I'd rather sit here in my rocker. How are you holding up?"

"Well it's not like I've been doing any work or anything. Everybody is working so hard, but it's just a small apartment. I think they'll be done in the next couple of hours. They'll have to figure out what items to put in the cars. There are a few boxes left over and I have a couple of plants, so I guess those will be put in the cars too."

"Yes, moving can be such a lot of work. I don't envy you, my dear."

They chatted for a while, and as always when Nicole was with Annaliese, the time moved swiftly by. Before she knew it, it was time to say goodbye and she was dreading it.

"Oh Annaliese, I'm going to miss you so much!"

"I'll miss you too, Nicole. But you know that you can call me any time. I'd be happy to continue our conversations on the telephone if you think you'd like that."

Nicole was so touched. "I don't know what to say! That's exactly what I would like to do. Thank you, Annaliese!"

"We could arrange it for a specific time, so it would be best to let me know ahead of time, and I'll be sure to make myself available. Would that work for you, Nicole?"

"Sure it would! I was actually dreading saying goodbye to you because I didn't want to stop our visits. You have taught me so much about the Lord in the past few months. That's so valuable to me, you know?" She looked wistfully at Annaliese.

"My pleasure." Annaliese smiled at her young friend. "Oh, and I have a small baby gift for you. Would you mind waiting for a moment while I go get it, dear?" She stood up and walked into her bedroom. A moment later she came back out carrying a very large box all wrapped in light green coloured wrapping paper with a big bow on top.

Nicole looked surprised and gasped.

Annaliese placed the gift on the coffee table and smiled at Nicole. "Go ahead, open it," she nudged her.

Glancing at her friend, Nicole pulled tentatively on the tape. Then she got into the spirit of it and ripped all the paper off, revealing a plain white box. Curiosity filled her face as she figured out how to open it. As the lid was lifted, Nicole gasped. She pulled out the most beautiful baby quilt she had ever seen. There were letters of the alphabet, as well as just plain boxes and rectangles. The colours were yellows and greens, perfect for either a boy or girl. Nicole's eyes filled with tears as she opened the quilt and looked at each lovingly sewed part. "Annaliese, this is so precious!" she whispered. "How did you ever find the time to make this?"

"Evenings are long in the winter. I'm glad you like it. I made some for all my children, and lately I'd been thinking I would like to try my hand at one again. So you gave me the perfect opportunity."

They stood there looking at the quilt which was draped across the couch. Finally Nicole folded it with a contended sigh and placed it back in the box. "I'll treasure this," she said and turned to give her friend a big hug.

As they broke apart, Annaliese spoke, "Well now, let me carry this next door for you and we'll see how close your family is to being done, shall we?" And off they went.

∞ ∞ ∞

Julie and Nicole were in Nicole's Jeep. Shadow was in the back seat inside his crate, and the rest of the vehicle was mostly filled. Nicole thought they were going to need a giant shoe horn to get the door shut, but they got it all. Before she knew it, she was waving at Annaliese and they were pointed east, driving towards Abbotsford in a procession of Grahams. Nicole was driving and for the first few miles they were chatting. As they got closer to the freeway, she became quiet. Emotion was welling up in her throat as she saw the city getting smaller in her rear-view mirror. Julie knew Nicole had to be struggling. There were so many things that must be going through her mind, like Greg and all that had happened in the past year. Also her leaving Annaliese was difficult for her. Julie reached over and put her hand on Nicole's hand, which was resting in her lap. "You'll be just fine, Nic," she said softly.

Nicole looked at Julie incredulously. How did her sister do that? How could she read her mind like that? With a strangled sob she turned her eyes back to the road and put both hands on the steering wheel. "I know. It's just there are so many good memories here in Vancouver for me." She paused for a moment. "Come to think of it, they're not *all* good, are they?"

"That's true, but there were a lot of good ones."

They sat in silence while the Jeep ate up the miles. "There will be good memories for you in Abbotsford too." Julie reminded her.

235

"You'll be starting anew with your baby, and we'll all be there to help you."

Nicole smiled tearfully at her sister. "I know. Thanks. Please don't think I don't appreciate all you guys are doing. It's just that this is a very emotional time for me, that's all."

"I know. Don't worry about it, I understand." Julie was quiet for a few moments. A new thought occurred to her suddenly. "You know Nic, this is the end of a chapter for you. Today you begin a new chapter in your life. That's kind of exciting, don't you think?" She looked at her eagerly.

"Good try, Jules. It's true. And this time my faith is stronger, so I know God is with me too. That makes all the difference."

Chapter 27

Nicole's belongings were now stored in Julie's old bedroom, which had been empty for a while. She was now comfortably settled in her own room and in the corner near the window she was collecting all the baby stuff she had been given. There was a car seat, a diaper bag, soothers and blankets, bibs and stuffed toys as well as all kinds of clothes. Steve and Jennifer were lending her their crib, and Annaliese's quilt was folded into it, waiting for the baby.

Nicole was sitting on the bed, folding her laundered clothes when Matthew walked in from school, carrying his backpack. He had been touched when Nicole had offered him Greg's bike, seeing it had been an expensive one. It was a tempting offer; he had been looking for a bike just like it, even if it was a little bent.

After they greeted each other with a smile, Matthew pulled off his ski jacket, sat down on the chair and set his backpack on the floor. "Nicole, I've been thinking about the bike."

She looked up from the small stack of clean clothes she was working on and held his gaze for a moment, trying to figure out what he was going to say next. "Okay..."

"Well the thing is, I love that bike and everything, and I know it's fixable so that's not the problem."

"You don't want it?" Nicole seemed disappointed.

"It's not that I don't want it. I'm trying to think about you in this. How do you think you'd feel every time you see me ride it? Don't you think it would bring back memories of Greg's accident? I'm just concerned that it might not be the best thing for you, that's all." He ended in a rush, willing her to understand where he was coming from.

Nicole's mouth dropped open. She hadn't even considered how she would feel seeing that same bike being ridden by Matthew. And she knew if it was his, she wouldn't be able to avoid seeing it. "Wow, I never thought of that. You have a good point."

"I just don't want to see you struggling more than is necessary, that's all."

Nicole felt warmed by his caring of her in this way. A rush of emotion propelled her to her feet and she stumbled toward him. He met her part way and they embraced in a long hug. "You're such a good brother," she whispered. "Thank you for thinking of me this way." She pulled back and wiped the tears that had begun trickling down her face. Matthew was right. She would forever be reminded of how Greg died if she saw him riding the bike.

Sitting back down on the bed, she looked at him. "So what should we do with it?" she asked in a small voice.

Making himself comfortable on the chair again he answered, "I'll still fix it. I know I can make it good as new again. But then I'll sell it for you. Maybe I can put it on Craigslist or something. I'll think it through better and let you know. But you don't need to worry about it."

"What do you think you could get for a bike like that?"

"I'm not too sure what they go for second-hand, but they're pretty expensive new. I'll check it out and let you know what I'll sell it for. Once it's sold I'll give you the money."

"No way. If you sell it, you keep the money."

Matthew opened his mouth to protest, but Nicole raised her hand to stop him. "I appreciate the fact that you want to fix it and sell it for me. But if it was just up to me, I'd throw it out, so don't even think twice about this. Besides, that money would come in handy to pay for school, don't you think?" she asked him with a gleam in her eye.

As he gazed at her in silence, Matthew was very grateful for her generosity. He certainly could use help with school fees. Still, he felt badly because this could end up being a couple thousand bucks, if not more. That was a lot of money to give away!

As she watched him think it through, Nicole read him right and responded. "If you don't feel good about taking all the money, how about we look at it as an investment?"

Matthew's eyebrows rose in query. "Huh?"

She patted her swollen abdomen and smiled. "Well, there will soon be a small Greg or Nicole to take care of. Maybe you could babysit for me sometime when I'm in desperate need of getting out. What do you think of that?"

Matthew's broad grin showed her what he thought. "You know I'll be a great uncle!"

The funny thing was she did know that. She had watched him with Steve and Jennifer's kids often enough to know that he would dote on this little one as well. Nicole smiled at him. It was settled. She felt so good about this decision. He would be fixing the bike, so he should benefit from the work he would put into it.

"I can't actually start fixing it until after we've finished painting your suite. And if I run out of time and need to go back to school, I'll wait and fix it in the spring. That might be the best because it should be nice enough by then for me to do the work outside." He stood up to leave and picked up his jacket and backpack. "There's no rush. I think I'll store the bike in my room in the meantime; it's a better place than the garage right now. I don't want it cluttering up the space where Mom and Dad park their cars. Is that okay with you?"

"Absolutely. And Matthew," she said as he started walking out the door, "Thanks!"

"You're welcome, sis." He grinned at her and left the room, whistling.

∞ ∞ ∞

"Isn't it interesting that the colours Annaliese used for the quilt are actually colours I was thinking about for the baby's room?" Nicole was having coffee with Jennifer, who was trying to pin her down to specific colours for the suite so they could get started on the painting soon.

239

"You must have mentioned to her what you were thinking of, even if you don't remember specifically doing that. She's a smart lady; she probably stored that information away for use later on." Jennifer was amused that Nicole found the whole thing so amazing. Of course Annaliese must have known and planned it that way to bless Nicole.

On the table in front of them were different paint colours they could choose from. It was a good thing the suite was not big or they would be at this forever! This job was frustrating for Nicole because she was not able to do any running around. But Jennifer had been very kind in picking out the paint samples with Nicole's basic ideas in mind, and she had brought home at least a hundred different colours and shades to choose from.

"I'm leaning toward one of these two blues for the kitchen. Do you remember my dishes set?"

Jennifer nodded. "Uh huh."

"These blues both match. Which do you think would work?"

With a thoughtful look on her face, Jennifer looked around the table for another colour. When she found it, she said, "Ah hah!" and pulled it toward the blues Nicole had chosen.

Nicole looked from the blues to the soft yellow and back to Jennifer.

"Well, didn't you say you loved the colours in your dishes? If you used both these colours, you could incorporate the colours from your dishes into the walls. Wouldn't that be fun?" Jennifer's eyes twinkled.

"But how would you use them? You can't have one blue wall and one yellow wall, can you?"

"I don't know about that. But what I was thinking is different. I thought you could have the blue around the white cupboards, and on the far wall we could put a chair-rail moulding halfway up the wall, around waist height. The bottom could then be painted blue, and the upper part could either be yellow or we could find a wall paper with a similar yellow in it, maybe with flowers or something."

Nicole's mouth opened in surprise. "Hmm, that does sound interesting. Are you sure that wouldn't be too much trouble?"

"The only thing is that we'd have to get that chair rail moulding, but it shouldn't be expensive for such a narrow wall. Putting up wall paper isn't hard, I've done it before. And that wall is small enough we could get it done quickly."

"Sounds like fun. Okay, let's do it!"

"All right, that's one room out of the way. I think that's enough for today. We can do a little more next week, okay?" Jennifer didn't want to tire Nicole out and they'd been at this for an hour.

When Jennifer left, Nicole lay on the couch with the blue paint colour she had chosen. She put it against the yellow and thought about her kitchen. With a dreamy look on her face, she set the colours down. She was going to love this suite when it was done!

∞ ∞ ∞

The following week they finished choosing the colours for Nicole's new place. Jennifer had brought more paint samples home, and the two of them had chosen by putting different ones against Nicole's furniture. Now it was all done and they just needed to buy the paint and get started.

Roseanne had moved out, and Steve had managed to do the necessary repairs to the walls. He was currently working on the electrical that needed upgrading in the bathroom, but they could start painting in the kitchen. He had bought the paint and all the supplies were waiting in the suite.

Matthew was now off school for Christmas. He picked up Julie and headed for Steve's house. They were both in their 'ugly' clothes, so it didn't matter if they got paint splatters on them. Jennifer had picked Nicole up a little earlier. All was set.

When Matthew and Julie walked in, Nicole was settled on a bunch of cushions on the floor like the Queen of Sheba. The children had gathered around her and she was reading them a story. Jessie and Leila were on one side, and Andrew sat on the other. Nicole could no longer put Leila on her lap as there was no longer any lap left. She had grown in the past few weeks!

With Nicole watching the children, Jennifer, Julie and Matthew began painting the kitchen. They had each taken a specific job and were well into it when Matthew decided they needed comic relief. "So what do you call cheese that isn't yours?"

"Huh?" Nicole looked up from the book she was reading, confused. "Cheese that isn't mine? What are you talking about?"

"Just that. What do you call cheese that isn't yours?"

"Oh, I get it. Another joke." She rolled her eyes at him.

"Nacho cheese," he said with a flourish.

"Clever!" Nicole said with a laugh. The other two ladies just groaned.

"What do you call four bullfighters in quicksand?" Matthew wanted to know. He was standing on the ladder and the paint roller was dripping paint onto the plastic sheets below.

"No idea," replied Jennifer, "But I'm sure you're going to tell us," she ended with a smile.

"Quattro Cinco."

The girls guffawed. Where did he get his jokes?

"Okay Matthew, you've had your fun, now let's get back to work," Julie tried to bring a semblance of order to the group.

"Just one more, please?" He held up the paint roller and put his hands together in a pleading manner.

Nicole laughed at his silliness. "Oh all right. Make it quick."

"What do you get from a pampered cow?"

"A pampered cow..." Jennifer said slowly. Finally she gave up.

"Spoiled milk!"

Julie had had enough. She splattered Matthew with paint as he laughed at his own joke. He ended up with a blue streak in his hair, making him look a bit like a psychedelic skunk. Laughter erupted as they saw how much paint was on him. There was more paint on Matthew than on the wall at present. Hopefully they would be able to paint the walls as well.

With a smile on their lips, they all turned back to the work at hand.

∞ ∞ ∞

Day by day they made more progress till the suite began to look quite lovely. Nicole was very pleased with her paint choices. She knew her furniture would look great in here. She was certainly looking forward to moving in, but she had no idea when that would happen. She was still supposed to be on "bed rest", something which she obeyed kind of loosely. She was lying down right now, but the important thing was that she wasn't stressed and she was off her feet. With a sigh she realized it would be better for her to stay at her parents' house until after the baby was born. If she moved in before the baby came, she would be tempted to put her home together, and that would not be good.

Chapter 28

The living room was all painted and her brothers had brought some of her furniture over. Nicole was laying on the couch, admiring the job everyone had done. Jennifer was sitting on a chair opposite her and the two were commenting on the paint colours. They had chosen well; the place looked good. There was just the bedroom to finish up and then it was ready to move into. She knew she wouldn't do that for a few weeks, but it felt good to know the place was ready for her.

Tomorrow the stacking washer and dryer were being delivered. Jennifer was planning on being home all day so she would be there when they arrived. Steve was still planning on putting up some shelves in the little laundry area, but there was no rush.

Julie was coming over tonight to help put the kitchen things in place. Nicole could move them around where she wanted to once she moved in, but for now they would just put everything where they felt was best. The boxes with the pots and pans and dishes were already here.

Nicole was quiet as she thought of all the work everyone was doing for her.

"What are you thinking, Nicole?" asked Jennifer. She was perceptive and knew that Nicole was struggling through this change.

Nicole looked up in surprise. "Oh, I was just thinking how frustrating it is to not be able to help with any of this."

"I thought you might be thinking about that. Isn't it funny how it is so much easier to give than to receive?" Jennifer asked her.

"I never thought of it that way before, but it's true. It's so much easier to help someone who is struggling than to have others do your work for you."

"But you know, sometimes it's necessary. I believe God wants us to be at peace with whatever happens. If we can help, so be it, but if we can't, we should be able to allow others in to do what's needed." She stopped and looked embarrassed. "I know it's easier said than done, and if it was me in that boat I might not like it at all. Sorry, Nicole."

"Oh, don't worry about it. I know what you mean. It's always a conflict to allow others to do your own work. People don't necessarily do it the way you want to, right? But God has been teaching me in this too. I've had to give up control and let Him bless me the way He sees fit. And I'll tell you, if it wasn't for my family I certainly wouldn't be looking at such a cute home right now!"

They both laughed. Jennifer was glad that Nicole's attitude was so good in this. And once the baby was here and Nicole moved into the suite, she could change things around to better suit herself then.

∞ ∞ ∞

Nicole was well into her eighth month. The baby was growing and so was her belly. She wondered how much more she was going to grow; it didn't seem possible for her to expand any more; her skin was already taut as it was.

She was sitting on the couch with her guitar in hand. She was playing one of her recent songs when the front door opened and Julie popped her head in. She came in quietly, hearing the guitar and Nicole humming to the tune she was playing.

With a look of delight on her face, Julie greeted Nicole, who looked embarrassed to be caught playing the guitar. As she moved to put the guitar away, Julie spoke up. "No, please don't put it away. I didn't know you could still play! When did you start up again?"

Gazing at Julie, Nicole felt a smile tugging at the corners of her mouth, "When I was cleaning out Greg's stuff I found his guitar. On a whim I decided to start playing and found it very soothing with all I was going through."

"That's wonderful, Nicole!" Julie was so pleased.

"Anyhow, Greg apparently had been taking on-line guitar lessons. I found the web page[4] and have been learning too, so I'm still at it."

Julie looked from the guitar to Nicole in surprise. How come this was the first she was hearing about it? Was Nicole shy about her playing? "What were you playing just now? It sounded so pretty."

Nicole's face flushed at the unexpected praise. "Oh, just something I put together." She was quiet for a heartbeat and then began telling Julie about the day God gave her Deuteronomy 31:8 in song. She had been feeling frightened about being a single mother, feeling the responsibility weighing on her. "And as I read the verses, the tune just kind of popped into my mind. This song reminds me of God's faithfulness in my life and the fact that He will be there for me through it all."

Julie was looking at her sister with a look of compassion. Suddenly she realized Nicole was moving to put the guitar away. "No, don't put it away please. Could you sing it for me?" Julie pleaded with her.

"All right." Nicole sat down again and placed the guitar on her receding lap. Strumming the strings softly she launched into the song. "He will be with you, He will be with you, He will not fail you nor forsake you. Do not fear, do not fear, or be dismayed." Nicole sang till she finished the song.[5]

When the last sounds died down, Julie looked up, her eyes bright with unshed tears. "That is beautiful!" she said softly. "I have goosebumps, seriously Nicole, I love it."

Nicole looked shyly at her sister. "Thanks. Singing scripture helps me to stay focused on the Lord rather than on my circumstances."

"I know you didn't really want to sing it to me, but I really appreciate it. Thanks!" Julie leaned over and gave her sister a hug.

---

4   www.guitartipsweekly.com
5   To hear the song "Do Not Fear", go to www.oliveboettcher.com

Nicole was laying on the couch, hot chocolate in hand. Matthew, Julie and their parents were decorating the beautiful fir tree her parents had gone out to find. The lights had been put up and now they were working on the decorations. Each item had special significance for their mother, who had been collecting them for years. Some decorations were small and dainty, and many had been bought somewhere else in the world while they were vacationing or given to her as gifts. Ellen had collected quite an assortment over the years, and she was pulling them out of their boxes with a smile on her face. There was a story behind each one; bringing them out once a year was like seeing old friends again.

Matthew was up on a ladder placing the angel on the top. Right now it was leaning precariously to the left and Nicole started laughing at the sight. He heard her and kicked up his antics, just so he could make her happy. He loved hearing Nicole laugh. He had felt every bit of her quietness in the months after Greg had died. She was gradually coming out of her shell again. He tilted his head to the side, gazing at the angel. "I think I'll leave her that way, what do you think, Nicole?"

"Well, if we all bent our heads a little she would look normal. And we'd all have a crick in out necks for Christmas!"

He laughed. "Yeah, I guess a crick in the neck isn't really a good Christmas present now, is it?"

He reached up and tugged on the angel's skirt to straighten her a little more. "Okay, you have to admit that this is better, right?" He swung his head over to look at his sister. "Yeow!" he exclaimed, as he felt himself lose his balance.

Nicole gasped and held her breath. Keeping her eyes on her brother, she started getting up to lend him a hand. Stan stood up and moved towards Matthew in an attempt to prevent a crash. With a hand to her mouth Nicole suddenly she started giggling. Matthew's arms were wind-milling in an effort to establish good balance on the little step stool. His face had a surprised look as he toppled over onto the floor with a thump. On his way down his body rubbed against the tree and now as he was trying to get up, the long fragrant branches swayed and threatened to free themselves from their decorations. Once the surprise had worn off, Matthew lay where he had fallen, a sheepish look on his face.

Ellen stood a little to the side, hands on her hips and a tolerant look on her face. "Matthew!" she quietly chided in a good-humoured way. Stan was still standing, hand outstretched toward Matthew as though frozen in a moment of time.

As Matthew attempted to straighten himself out, a few pieces of tinsel caught onto his head, draped on him like long silver hair. His sisters giggled. Turning to look at them both, he grinned. "No harm done." He stood up and brushed off his jeans with a flourish. As he turned his head, the tinsel swung around him, causing Julie and Nicole's mirth to erupt into loud laughter. Wondering at the sound, Matthew cut his eyes to the side and he saw the tinsel wrapped around his ear. With a grin he took more off the tree and placed it on his upper lip, giving him a silver moustache. He twitched his mouth from side to side, causing the tinsel to swing, at the same time wiggling his eyebrows up and down. The picture was more than the girls could handle and they found themselves clutching their stomachs, tears coming down their faces as they laughed in abandon.

When the hilarity was over, they all sat down, their chests heaving from the laughter. Didn't the Bible say that laughter was good medicine? It certainly had filled the room with joy.

This was why Matthew enjoyed making his family laugh. He knew this Christmas was going to be a tough one for Nicole. Actually, it would be a tough one for everybody because they had all loved Greg and this would be their first one without him.

As they all fell into a pensive quiet, Nicole suddenly gasped. Bringing her hand to rub the upper part of her swollen belly, she started speaking to the baby, "What woke you up, little one? That was such a hard kick!" Turning to her father she said, "This baby has a powerful kick!"

They had occasionally heard Nicole say the baby was active, but this suddenly became a family affair as they all gathered around her, each touching her belly to feel the kicking. Matthew had his hand a little to the side when he jumped back, surprise etched on his face. "Was that a kick? Was that the baby I just felt?" he exclaimed in wonder.

Nicole looked at him happily. "So now what do you think? Is it going to be a soccer player, or what?"

Matthew was still so shocked at what he had felt. He had never had the nerve to put his hand on Jennifer's belly when she had been pregnant. What did he expect? There was a real baby in there, after all. But he just hadn't expected to find such force to the kick. "Either that or a football player! Wow, that was strong!" He grinned at his sister, his hand rubbing the back of his neck. He hadn't felt attached to this baby until now. He knew Nicole was pregnant, but to feel life that way somehow made the little one more real. He could hardly wait to meet this infant!

Even though the decorating wasn't finished, they took a break. Ellen went to make some hot apple cider for them all, and Julie pulled out the cookies she had brought over for the occasion.

Stan reached over and selected a pumpkin chocolate chip cookie, promptly putting half of it in his mouth. "Hmmm," he mumbled. Swallowing, he spoke again, "Yum, Julie!" He smiled his appreciation to her.

Ellen came back into the room carrying a tray laden with mugs of apple cider. They each took one and began sipping the hot drink, munching on their cookies. They would finish decorating the tree soon enough.

∞ ∞ ∞

It was Christmas morning and everybody was going to be here for breakfast. Nicole had allowed herself to sleep in. She had not slept well the night before, thinking about Greg again.

As she was getting dressed, she thought about where she had come from in the past eight months. Her relationship with Jesus certainly had changed. Before Greg's death she had believed in Him but hadn't spent too much time with Him, expecting that as she got older there would be more opportunity for that.

But in the months following Greg's death, she had at first been angry and bitter toward God. How could a loving God allow her wonderful husband to die so young?

Gradually she had thawed and her icy silence toward God had changed. It was at that point that she realized He was changing her, bringing her closer to Himself. Now He was her Friend, her Lord again.

But that didn't stop the ache deep in her heart. There were many more "firsts" for her to live through after Greg's death: the first wedding anniversary date without him, her first birthday without him and so on. Today was her first Christmas without her beloved husband. How was she going to make it through the day?

Nicole looked at herself in the mirror. There was sadness in her eyes that had never really gone away since that terrible day when she had received the phone call about Greg's accident.

Her eyes took on a faraway look as she reminisced. Greg had been so much fun last Christmas. He didn't always get the holiday off from work, but last year it had worked out. They had come out Christmas Eve and slept here in her bedroom for a few days. It was last Christmas, when they had gone out for a walk alone, that they had decided it would be a good time to consider getting pregnant. But for some reason, several months had gone by without success. Still they were patient, expecting that at any time they would succeed. Greg had been ready to become a father. He loved Steve and Jennifer's kids, and when they talked about parenting he was always hopeful, looking to the future.

With an audible sigh she swiped at the tears that were falling. She would not bring her family down on this important day. They would all be together to celebrate the birth of their Saviour. After all, it was a day to rejoice, wasn't it?

$$\infty \infty \infty$$

Ellen's brunch, as always, had been a delight. Now the adults had all pushed away from the table, slowly sipping their coffee while the children played nearby. Harold and Margaret, Stan's parents, had joined them for this special meal. The turkey was in the oven, and Ellen would be preparing the rest of their Christmas dinner later today, but Jennifer and Steve would be with her family. As a result, the best time to have the whole family together was for brunch.

Nicole couldn't help but notice the emptiness Greg's absence created in her. She pushed away from the table, ready to start the cleanup and load the dishwasher; she hoped that no one would notice she was on her feet as she needed time alone. Her heart felt so heavy. As she rinsed the plates and stacked them prior to loading into the dishwasher, she felt the tears prick at her eyes. She stopped what she was doing and gripped the side of the sink, closing her eyes. The pain and heaviness in her soul was threatening to overwhelm her.

Suddenly she felt a hand on her shoulder, and a soft voice spoke into her ear, "It's a hard day for you, isn't it honey?" She turned to find her grandmother standing close, empathy all over her face. As Nicole brushed the hair out of her face, the tiny shreds of strength that were keeping her from breaking down evaporated. Margaret reached for her and Nicole felt the grief paralyze her soul as she wept for what could never be. Gut-wrenching sobs shook her frame. Nicole was lost in the moment, not aware of the rest of the family gathering around her, arms reaching to comfort and support her. There were tears in everybody's eyes as they felt the intense pain of the moment for Nicole.

Gradually her sobs eased and she became quiet, being occasionally shaken by the remnants of her weeping as she took deep breaths to quiet herself. She became aware of the others there with her in a tight embrace. Nicole closed her eyes as her father began to pray, speaking God's comfort and strength to her during this time of grief.

A hush came over the group as Nicole gradually allowed herself to relax. "Come on, honey. Come into the living room and lie down on the couch," Ellen took her hand and led her to a comfortable spot. As Nicole looked around at the concerned faces all around her, she felt grateful for their care and sensitivity. "Thanks, everybody," she said shakily. Her eyes were puffy and red, but there was a measure of peace in her heart again. "Thanks for being there for me." She closed her eyes momentarily. The hush in the room showed that even the children had been affected by Nicole's grief.

After a few minutes, Matthew looked at the beautiful tree with all the presents stuffed under it. "Why don't we open up our gifts? Isn't it a good time for that?"

A general agreement rippled through the room.

"Jessie, you're the oldest of the kids. Would you like to hand out the presents?" asked Stan.

"Oh yes, grandpa!" she exclaimed, her blue eyes round and shining, her toothless grin bringing a smile to each one, including Nicole. She rushed over to the tree, and Matthew sat himself down next to her on the floor, ready to help her should she have difficulty reading a name.

There was a flurry of activity as each one opened up their gifts, exclamations of surprise and delight filling the room.

Nicole gazed around her at this precious family. To think that there was a time when she was chomping at the bit to get away from them! God had changed her heart, and she was so grateful. They had helped her through the difficulty of this day. The pain was still there, but not as pronounced as it had been since last night. She sighed, knowing that she would eventually get through the worst of the grieving.

Chapter 29

It was mid January. Christmas and New Years had gone by in a blur for Nicole. She was feeling as big as a tent! Good thing her blood pressure was only a bit higher than at the beginning when they had discovered she had preeclampsia. She was still getting headaches, but now that she could rest more, they were under control.

Nicole's father had spoken to her about being under an obstetrician's care in case something went wrong with the delivery. She had agreed and he had set up a meeting with a co-worker of his.

Nicole had gone in to the appointment feeling nervous. But Dr. McLean put her at ease right away. He was an older gentleman with a South African accent who reminded her of her dad in so many ways.

After he examined her, he explained to her about preeclampsia. "Your blood pressure is not dangerously high right now, but as you get closer to term it could rise. If this happens, both you and the baby will be at risk. The next step would be that you would develop eclampsia. I sure don't want that to happen."

Nicole was feeling nervous again. "What is eclampsia?"

"It's a complication of severe preeclampsia. One of the main problems with eclampsia is the convulsions. We want to avoid that. And for sure, at this point we can control what's happening so it doesn't develop into something worse."

Nicole gasped. Convulsions! She suddenly felt scared. "So what are you suggesting?"

"Well, I think it would be good to book you for a C-section ahead of your due date. This way we could head it off at the pass, so to speak."

"A C-section?" Nicole asked weakly. She had felt throughout her pregnancy that she would have a natural delivery.

Dr. McLean answered her gently, yet firmly. "It would be the best thing for both you and the baby."

Nicole began to cry. Julie wouldn't be able to be with her then, or would she? "My sister had planned to be with me for the delivery. I need someone with me!" She fumbled in her purse for a tissue.

"That would still be possible, Nicole." She looked up, tissue half-way to her nose. "Our operating room is set up so that the father or support person can be there for the delivery. We can give you an epidural or spinal anesthetic so you can be awake and aware through the whole thing if you like. We rarely put the mother to sleep these days; it's better for her to be awake so she can meet her baby right away."

"Really?" Hope was beginning to rise again.

"Most definitely." He smiled at her. "So how do you feel about this? Should I go ahead and book it?"

"When would it be?"

The kind look on his face showed Nicole that Dr. McLean cared about what was happening to her. But right now his top priority was safety for both Nicole and the baby.

"I think it would be prudent to do it in two weeks. I would need for you to still be on bed rest until then, but we'd have a better chance through the delivery if it was earlier."

With a gasp Nicole realized it would come upon her very fast. She was mentally counting to see how far along she would be at that point.

Finally she responded to his question. "My dad really trusts you as a good obstetrician. I guess I need to do the same." She took a deep breath and resolved to do what was required of her. With a nod of her head, Nicole spoke, "Okay, let's do it."

"All right then. I'll set it up and get my receptionist to give you a call with the date and time. Have you pre-registered at the hospital for the birth?"

"No. I thought I still had time to do that," Nicole said with a sheepish look on her face.

"No worries. You go ahead and pre-register at the hospital, and I'll set up your pre-admission appointment with a nurse."

"All right."

With that, the appointment was over and Nicole returned home. She called Julie to tell her all about the C-section, but there was no answer. Julie must be at work. Nicole left a message for her sister to call her back; she had news about the upcoming birth. With another sigh she closed her phone and started up her Jeep. *"Greg, you should be here!"*

Back home at her parents' house, Nicole went to her room; she felt emotionally drained. With no one else in the house it was easy to just give in to the tiredness. Nicole slowly walked over to her bed and fell onto it completely dressed, exhaustion filling her soul.

Two hours later she woke up to the sounds of dinner being prepared in the kitchen. Mom must be home! Nicole got up as quickly as she could with the extra weight she was carrying. She poked her head into the kitchen to see her mother chopping vegetables.

"Mom!" Nicole surprised her with the outburst. Ellen swung around, knife in hand, mouth open in surprise.

"Nicole, I forgot you were home!" She smiled at her daughter, then caught herself when she saw the look on Nicole's face. Her smile slipped as she dropped the knife on the counter and embraced her daughter. "What's wrong, honey? You don't look so happy!"

Tears threatened to fall as Nicole related to her mother all that had taken place at the doctor's office. When the story had been told, Nicole allowed the emotions to take over and she wept on her mother's shoulder.

"There, there, Nicole. Everything will be all right." She patted her on the back and waited for the sobs to die down. "Here, let's sit down. I'll make you a nice cup of herbal tea and we'll just have a good chat. Sound okay?" Ellen peered at Nicole's face and was cheered by the fact that the sobs had ended.

"It was such a surprise, Mom. I had really felt that I would have a natural delivery, and that Julie would be with me. This pregnancy hasn't turned out to be anything I wanted from the beginning!"

Ellen looked at her daughter with compassion. "I know you were surprised by the pregnancy, but you've done remarkably well considering." She sipped her tea, a thoughtful look on her face. "You know, having a C-section is not the worst thing that could happen. And it means that there would be fewer unknowns, less danger for you and the baby."

Nicole looked at her mother. "I guess I see that. I just felt so confused; I thought it was a bad thing. But Dr. McLean explained to me that Julie can still be with me. It's just that she won't be helping with the birth, that's all." She sipped her tea and thought some more. "I guess I'll be okay," she murmured with a small smile.

"That's my girl!" Ellen reached over and patted Nicole's hand. "Life can throw surprises at us, but it's how we handle them that makes a difference." Ellen was quiet for a heartbeat, and then she continued, "You know, Julie will be helping with the birth, just in a different way than you had thought. She'll be there with you as a support, and I'm sure she'll help out with the baby after too. Try to look at the silver lining in those clouds."

Nicole gazed at her mother. Yes, it was all in the way you looked at it! There were still positive things to see in this situation. She smiled at Ellen and in her heart asked God to help her see the good things in life, rather than only dwelling on the bad.

As they were finishing the last of their tea the telephone rang. "Hello!" sang Ellen into the receiver. She spoke for a while and then handed the cordless telephone over to Nicole, mouthing "Julie" at her.

"Hi Jules. Did you get my message?" The conversation continued on. Julie had indeed received the message and she was concerned for Nicole. She just wanted Nicole to be all right with the C-section. She was relieved to hear that Nicole was doing better. "So you'll let me know as soon as you hear from Dr. McLean about the date, right?"

"You bet. I'll be counting on you to be there with me." Nicole by now had accepted that she would have surgery instead of a natural birth. And when she thought of it, it wasn't such a bad outcome after all. Here was one more thing happening in her life that she was losing control over, and she hadn't been ready for that. But as she prayed, God gave her peace.

She was ready.

∞ ∞ ∞

The days following Nicole's appointment with the specialist were filled with visits from her family, reading books and listening to music. Her favourite so far was a Hillsongs CD Matthew had given her for Christmas. The music was so worshipful and never failed to bring her into the presence of the Lord, especially if she was struggling. She wasn't playing her guitar much these days; she had gotten much too big for that. Oh well, she thought, she could pick it up again once the baby was born.

The days had flown by and she was scheduled to go into the hospital today for her c-section. Julie was picking her up in half an hour. Nicole's bag was packed and she was resting on the couch, talking to her mom who was sitting close by.

"The surgery's scheduled for eight-thirty, Mom. Will you and Dad be by sometime after?"

Ellen smiled warmly at her daughter. "Of course we will! We wouldn't miss this for the world! I'll talk to your dad about it, but I'm thinking we'll probably be there just before you go in."

Nicole returned her mom's smile. "It would mean a lot to me if you did. Thanks, Mom!"

∞ ∞ ∞

Nicole was laying on a stretcher, dressed in the operating room gown, hat and socks. She was ready for this. Dr. McLean had popped his head into her room to say hello, and to make sure all was as it should be. His check of Nicole and the baby had shown that nothing else had gone wrong; they were set to go!

Her parents arrived just before she was to leave for the operating room. They hugged and kissed Nicole, telling her they would be praying. They were both excited to meet their newest grandchild!

"We're going downstairs for a cup of coffee at Starbucks, but we'll return before you get out of the recovery room." Her father leaned down and kissed her forehead. Snuggling in close to Nicole's ear, he whispered, "I am very proud of you, honey! You are doing so well. I know God has everything under control."

Nicole looked up at him with teary eyes, but there was a happy look in her eyes. She grabbed onto his hand. "Thanks, Dad. Just think, you'll get to meet the newest member of our family in a couple of hours!" They grinned at each other and then the porter came in to transport Nicole to the operating room. "Bye, see you soon." Nicole was getting butterflies in her stomach. *"Do not fear or be dismayed."* Her song played over and over in her mind. She knew God was with her; she and the baby would be okay.

Julie was walking beside her as she was wheeled to the operating room. She was dressed in bright green OR scrubs provided for the patient's partner, her hair in a funny paper hat and her feet covered in blue paper hospital slippers. Her face was flushed with excitement. She was going to watch Nicole's baby being born today! The OR porter chatted with the girls as she deftly wheeled Nicole into the operating room and parked her near the unit clerk's desk; there she waited for a few minutes until the OR nurse came to get her.

∞ ∞ ∞

Nicole was all set up on the operating room table. Julie was sitting down on a stool at her head. There was a little camera in the nose of the big light directly above Nicole's belly. Julie could easily watch the surgery while it was projected onto the huge TV screen on the wall, but Nicole had averted her gaze and was watching the anesthetist. Julie's face, however, was turned to the screen so she could track what was happening with the operation.

Nicole's left hand had an intravenous dripping into it. Nicole watched while the anesthetist put some medication into the IV. "Do you want to watch?" he asked Nicole.

"I don't think so," she responded tentatively, not sure what she should do.

Suddenly Nicole felt scared and looked over at her sister who seemed to know what she was thinking. Julie reached over and gripped her right hand. "You'll be just fine," she whispered, holding eye contact until she felt her relax. Nicole closed her eyes and imagined it was Jesus holding on to her hand. She felt her whole body relax.

The doctor had cut Nicole open and was now reaching in for the baby. With a blue screen in front of her face, Nicole couldn't see anything that was happening. All she felt was some pressure; there was no pain whatsoever. "Tell me what's happening, Julie," she whispered.

Julie found herself holding her breath. Her attention was focused on the TV screen in anticipation. "He's just about to pull the baby out," she whispered back. Julie was fascinated by the drama taking place in front of her. Suddenly she straightened up, excited. "The baby's coming out!" she told Nicole. Seconds later, she gasped and exclaimed, "Oh my goodness, you should see all the red hair!"

At the same moment Dr. McLean's voice broke through with, "Nicole, you have a beautiful baby boy. Congratulations!" And then the baby's wail was heard as they continued working on him, cutting the cord and preparing him to meet his mother. Julie laughed at the joy of the moment, and she was tickled pink with the fact that this little boy was red-faced with outrage at being taken out of his warm home. He made his discontent known by screaming at the top of his lungs.

Suddenly the room erupted in laughter, followed by the anesthetist bending over Nicole with a grin to tell her the baby was peeing on the surgeon. Nicole and Julie looked at each other and giggled, and before Nicole turned back the baby was placed on her chest, all covered in a blanket and wearing a little hat. With her arms wrapped around her precious boy, Nicole couldn't get enough of him.

A boy! Nicole was engulfed with emotion too deep to verbalize. A red-headed boy! Tears trickled down the sides of her face and into her ears.

When the baby was placed on her chest, she felt overwhelmed with joy mingled with grief that Greg wasn't there. This little boy was definitely a copy-cat of her husband, down to the little dimple in his chin. Nicole's face softened as she gazed at him in wonder. Her hand reached out to stroke his soft face. He had found his hand and was sucking it with all he had, his bawling having been replaced with loud sucking. She looked over at Julie, choked by the realization that God had given her a little boy so like her own husband.

"I know," Julie whispered to her. "He looks like Greg. Isn't God good?" she verbalized Nicole's thoughts. Julie laughed in delight, taking pictures of mom and babe.

When the nurses took the baby away to weigh him, Julie spoke up. "So what do you think you'll name him?"

Dr. McLean's assistant was sewing Nicole up, but she felt no pain. "Greg's name was Gregory Robert Philips. I think I'll name this little one Robert Greg Philips. What do you think, Julie?" She looked over at her sister, eyes round with wonder.

"I think that's a great idea! You'll still have Greg's name without actually calling him Greg. Do you think you'll stick with Robert, or will you shorten it?"

"Oh, he'll be Robbie," Nicole responded with a smile. She sighed with pleasure. She closed her eyes and savoured the moment. She was a mom!

∞ ∞ ∞

Julie and Nicole were back safely in her room on the maternity ward. Their parents had just arrived and there was a flurry of voices as they met Robbie, who at the moment was snuggling in Nicole's arms. As they were chatting amongst themselves, Matthew arrived, flying into the room with a huge bouquet of flowers for his sister, a grin covering his face with delight. "A little boy! Congratulations, Nicole!" He reached her and engulfed her in a tender hug, careful not to hurt the baby.

They all oohed and aahed at Robbie's red hair that had the cutest little curl to it. "Robbie, welcome to the family," Matthew said as he put his index finger into the baby's hand. Robbie promptly curled his fingers around the bigger one, making a tight little fist. Matthew chuckled in delight.

Nicole happily gave permission for each of them to hold the newest member of the family. While one held Robbie, Julie took pictures and the others continued chatting amongst themselves.

When it was Matthew's turn, he sat down on the rocking chair and spoke quietly to Robbie, "I'm going to teach you how to play soccer, and anything else you want. Although I think you are a born natural, judging by the kicking you've been doing inside your mom!" He grinned at Robbie, who had once again taken a hold of his finger and was now sucking his fist with the larger finger attached. "Sorry there's no milk in that finger, little fella. You'll have to go to your mom for that!" Matthew looked up with a grin as a photo was taken of this special moment.

Ellen stood back from the commotion, watching and praying in her heart. *Thank you Jesus for Your mercies which You have bestowed upon us today. Thank you that this gorgeous little boy looks so much like his daddy. Thank You for the blessing he will be to our family! I pray for Nicole, Lord, that You will envelope her in Your comfort. Even though there is so much joy, she has to be hurting that Greg isn't here.*

∞ ∞ ∞

Nicole was dressing Robbie in his first little outfit, getting him ready to go home. She felt like she was playing with a doll as she put him in the light blue pants and sweater outfit she had received as a gift.

When Julie poked her head in the door, she smiled as she saw Nicole sitting on the rocker, eyes closed and with Robbie in her arms. There was a peaceful look in Nicole's face and Julie wanted to memorize the moment. She leaned back on the door frame, arms crossed, watching her sister. Eventually Julie made her presence known with a light cough. Nicole looked up in expectation. "Today's the day!" she said with a smile.

"You betcha," agreed Julie. "I have his car seat all strapped into my car and it's all ready to go. What can I bring to the car for you before taking our precious cargo down?" she looked at Nicole, one eyebrow raised in query.

"I guess we'll have to bring all the flowers down first, and my bag. How about we ask the nurse if we could borrow a cart so you could bring it all down at once?" Nicole reached over and pressed the call bell.

The cart materialized and Julie filled it quickly. When she was gone, Nicole stood up and placed Robbie, who was snacking on his fist, on her bed while she finished getting ready. He looked so tiny! She watched him for several moments, completely in love with her little boy.

When Nicole heard Julie returning, she snapped out of her daydreaming and looked toward the door. "You mean I have to ride in that?" she asked and pointed at the wheelchair Julie had pushed into the room, not sure what to do.

Julie grinned at her. "Your chariot awaits, m'lady." She flipped the brakes on and walked over to pick up Robbie.

"Huh. Okay, let's go then." Nicole looked around the room to make sure she hadn't forgotten anything, then gingerly sat down in the proffered seat, putting her arms out to hold the baby, who was now sleeping peacefully.

Chapter 30

Nicole was now in her little suite on Steve and Jennifer's property. She and Robbie had settled in well and were establishing a breastfeeding routine. Robbie had done well from the beginning and Nicole's heart was full with thanksgiving to God.

She still missed Greg terribly, but for the most part she was kept so busy with a newborn that she didn't have too much time to dwell on it. The most difficult time for her was that first week after they got home because she was still trying to set up some kind of breastfeeding schedule.

Today she was feeding Robbie and sitting quietly in the rocking chair, giving him all the time he needed. When she was burping him on her shoulder, her cheek nestled against the softness of his hair, she was hit by sadness. The strong maternal love that welled within her for this little boy reminded her of how proud Greg would be of him. Holding Robbie close, she found the tears coming easily.

"I wish Greg could be here, Lord. How proud he would be of his little boy!" Her hand stroked his back and revelled in the feel of his softness. Even as she grieved for Greg, she was reminded that Robbie was God's creation. He was wonderfully knit within her womb, and God knew him very well. This brought comfort to her heart. *"Thank You, Lord. I know grieving is normal and I'll continue to feel sad that Greg's not around. But thank You for Your love, thank You for Your guidance and for Your faithfulness in my life. Thank You that You love Robbie and You will continue to be faithful in our lives. I praise You Lord, for Robbie is fearfully and wonderfully made by You!"*

Nicole rocked for a while with Robbie nestled in her arms, allowing God's peace to wash over her. How would she have managed through all this without her family? She was so grateful it had been possible for her to move back to Abbotsford. Her family was very good in taking turns coming over to help her. So far she had been able to get naps, which was a great godsend, because she was up at least once during the night feeding Robbie.

For the first couple of weeks at Nicole's new home, Julie had moved in with her to help out where she could. She was due to move back to her own apartment tomorrow.

This morning Nicole was preparing for a special visit. Annaliese had called to congratulate Nicole and was coming out today by bus to visit for several hours. Nicole was so excited to see her again. And introducing her to Robbie was going to be fun.

In preparation for the visit, Nicole had asked Julie to make some of her cookies so they could have nibbles. Arranged on a pretty plate on the kitchen counter were two of Julie's most popular cookies, and the coffee was brewing in anticipation. Annaliese was due any minute.

Nicole was breastfeeding Robbie. Just as she was about to put him down, there was a knock at the door. She yelled out, "Come in!" and quickly placed Robbie in his car seat. She looked up to find Annaliese beaming at her from the door. She was wearing a periwinkle blue winter coat; her head and hands were covered in white fleece hat and gloves.

Nicole grinned and sprinted over to her friend, wrapping her arms around her in a long hug. "Oh Annaliese, it is so good to see you!"

Chuckling in delight, her friend returned the hug. "Same here, Nicole. I sure have missed you." Pushing Nicole away and scrutinizing her appearance, Annaliese smiled broadly, "You look wonderful, my dear!"

"And you are such a sight for sore eyes. How was your trip out here?" Nicole asked as she took Annaliese's outerwear to hang in the closet, and led her to the couch.

"Fine. It's still pretty cold out there, but I'm hopeful that we'll be seeing spring soon. Oh, this must be Robbie!" she exclaimed, bending down to have a better look at the sleeping baby before her.

"Yes," beamed Nicole. "I just fed him. Here, let me take him out of his seat." She reached down and picked him up.

Annaliese sat down on the couch and reached up her arms, waiting for Nicole to give Robbie to her. When he was safely within the shelter of her arms, Annaliese watched him settle in with a smile on her face. Eventually she looked up at Nicole and breathed out, "He's beautiful, Nicole! And look at that red hair! And the dimple! Now who do you suppose he reminds me of?" she asked playfully, eyes twinkling.

Nicole smiled shyly at her friend. "I know, he looks like Greg, don't you think?" She paused for a heartbeat. "But he has my nose!" They laughed at her confession.

Annaliese eyeballed Nicole and then turned her gaze back to Robbie. "I'm sure you'll find other ways he resembles you as he gets older. What a delight he is!" And she sighed in contentment, rocking him gently in her arms.

Nicole got up to get the coffee. "I've got treats for us this morning, made especially by my sister Julie. I'll just get the coffee and that will warm you up." As she gathered the necessities, Nicole could hear Annaliese cooing at Robbie from the living room. Smiling to herself she loaded up her tray and carried it in.

"Here we are. You can put him back in his seat if you'd like to have your hands free to eat," Nicole offered.

"Oh please, no! I want to hold him as much as possible. I haven't forgotten how to do this, you know," Annaliese responded with a twinkle in her eyes. She lay Robbie down on her knees and accepted the coffee from the young mother.

Taking a sip, she said, "Thank you. This hits the spot!"

Smiling contentedly, Nicole sat down beside her.

They chatted for a while about motherhood and the delivery. Annaliese wanted to know all the details. When that topic was exhausted, they were quiet as they gazed at the sleeping baby.

"How's your relationship with the Lord been through all this, Nicole?" Annaliese asked her softly.

Nicole answered with a smile. "It's been good. Although with a baby it's not always as easy as it used to be to find time to read my Bible. Sometimes it's a real challenge, but I'm learning." She paused for a heartbeat. "You know, when I look back at my life in the past few years, I see God's fingerprints all through it even though I didn't even think He was interested in me."

"How so, Nicole?" Annaliese was intrigued.

Nicole looked down at her hands and searched for the right words. "Well, when Greg was alive I kind of lost my interest in Jesus. I wasn't really interested in nurturing a relationship with Him, although when I look back, I see there was a thread of faith in me. It reminds me a little of Matthew 12:20. In that verse Jesus says, *"A bruised reed he will not break, and a smouldering wick he will not snuff out..."* She turned to her mentor with a beseeching look on her face. "You see, Annaliese? When I really didn't have the time of day for Jesus, He didn't leave me because deep down there was a tiny little thread of faith in my heart. He wasn't going to quench that, but wait for the day He could cause it to grow."

Nicole took a deep breath. "It wasn't until after Greg died that Jesus began to fan it into flame. He used my inability to change my circumstances to bring a hunger in me for Himself, and this in turn caused my faith to grow so I would have more assurance of who I am in Christ. That makes all the difference to me now in how I respond to difficulties that come up."

Annaliese was touched. "That's beautiful, Nicole. That thread of faith was your anchor to Him, even if it was flimsy at first. And I see that He has caused it to become a beautiful tapestry to His glory!"

Nicole's eyes were filled with unshed tears, but they mirrored her joy in the Lord, not sadness. "Amazing, isn't it?"

They were both quiet for a few seconds as they contemplated the workings of God in a willing heart.

Nicole sighed, a smile growing on her pretty face. She looked at Annaliese with thankfulness to God for this friend who had been so willing to pray for her and spend time explaining the Word to her.

"And how are you managing without Greg?" Annaliese knew how to ask tough questions.

Putting her drink on the coffee table, Nicole sat back. "It was a mixed blessing to see that Robbie looked so much like Greg. I was grateful to the Lord for the gift He had given me, but I was so sad that Greg couldn't be there." She took a deep breath. "Greg would have been so proud to be his daddy!" Grabbing a tissue from the box near the tray, she dabbed at her eyes.

Annaliese had one hand on Robbie's tummy, and she put her other hand on Nicole's shoulder, extending comfort and understanding in the gesture. She looked at her friend in compassion. Life sure wasn't easy at times! "I'm making you cry. I'm sorry."

With a forced laugh Nicole answered, "Aww, that's okay. I seem to have bouts of crying every now and then. It's nothing new." She blew her nose and looked over at her friend. "My family has been great in helping out. Julie's been staying here for a couple of weeks until I could settle in with Robbie. She'll be leaving tomorrow, but I'm sure if I need her again she'll come back." Nicole looked up with a smile. "And Steve and Jennifer are only a few feet away."

"They are all such a good support to you." Looking around, she commented on Nicole's new home. "This is a really nice home you have, by the way. I love the colours you chose for the paint."

Nicole beamed. "That was my so-called support system again. They all came over and painted the place for me before Robbie was born."

Annaliese remembered why Nicole had been on bed rest. "And how is your health doing these days? Are there any further problems since you were put on bed rest?"

"No. I'm happy to report that my blood pressure has gone back to normal. It's a relief to know everything's fine now, and we didn't have any problems through the surgery." Robbie stirred and Nicole picked him up, placed him on her shoulder and began gently rubbing his back. When he gave a small burp they both giggled. Nicole handed him back to Annaliese, who was delighted and reached out for him.

Eventually the conversation returned again to the Lord. Nicole had a question for Annaliese. "Do you remember when you taught me how to pray in faith? I was reading in my Bible recently and this is what I found," she said as she searched for the correct passage.

"In the fourteenth chapter of John, Jesus says to His disciples, *"Most assuredly, I say to you, he who believes in Me, the works that I do he will do also; and greater works than these he will do, because I go to My Father."*

Nicole stopped reading and looked at her friend. "I was thinking, do you think this applies to praying in faith? I mean, before I didn't know how to do that. My praying was often a bunch of pleading with God because I didn't really know what His will was for me. But as I've learned more about the Bible and started praying in faith, I see that I can speak into issues with greater understanding."

Annaliese smiled. "I believe that's true, dear. It's so exciting for me to hear you say that! It shows that God is guiding you, leading you into a closer walk with Jesus." She smiled at Nicole. "When you pray in faith, you are doing greater works than if you don't really have any idea how to pray. Your prayers get answered more readily and you feel a connection with God that wasn't there before."

Nicole sat back and pondered her friend's words. "What do you think Jesus meant when He told His disciples that they would move mountains? Are those real mountains, or do you think He meant something else?"

"Good question, Nicole!" Annaliese beamed at the young mother beside her. "The mountains He speaks about are difficulties that arise in our lives. They're not real mountains, like the Rockies." She smiled at Nicole. "They are problems and issues you grapple with on any given day. But rather than dealing with them in the natural, Jesus points us to dealing with them in the Spirit. In this way alone can we move mountains!"

Nicole's eyes were bright. "Okay, that makes more sense." She turned and grabbed a chocolate chip cookie from the plate. As she began munching, she continued thinking about what Annaliese had said. "I want to learn more and more to pray this way." Turning to her friend she was suddenly sad. "But how can I learn if you live so far away?"

Annaliese laughed. This child was such a delight in her love of the Lord! "God tells us in His Word that we have no need for any man to teach us, but His Spirit teaches us. As you seek Him and take time to spend with Him on a regular basis, He will lead you into the right way. After all, He wants you to succeed even more than you realize!"

Nicole's eyebrows rose on her forehead. "Oh, I never thought of it that way before!" She smiled, relieved. "Thanks, Annaliese. I needed to hear that."

"In Ephesians there's a verse that says, *"Not of works, lest anyone should boast. For we are His workmanship, created in Christ Jesus for good works, which God prepared beforehand that we should walk in them."* Annaliese had been reading from the open Bible in front of her. Now she looked up at Nicole and continued. "You know, those good works which He has prepared for you to walk in include learning how to pray in the Spirit. Imagine, He has prepared the way for you to walk this way. That means He will protect what He is doing in you so you will walk His way."

Nicole was touched. To think that God was leading her as a Father, wanting her to succeed!

The two ladies continued visiting and before they knew it, it was lunch time. They made a simple lunch together and continued their chatting. The hour soon grew late and Annaliese had to return home. The bus ride back into Vancouver would take her a couple of hours.

As she stood up to leave, she reached out to her friend and enveloped her in a long hug. "You are doing so well, Nicole. I am very proud of you. And any time you need to talk, please call me. Leave me a message if I'm not there, and I'll call you back as soon as I can."

Nicole clung to her, not wanting to say goodbye. "You're always such an encouragement to me, Annaliese. You are one of the reasons I'm sad I left Vancouver. I'll have to call you often!" There was general laughter as the two ladies pulled away from the hug.

"I'll come out again, Nicole," Annaliese didn't want to leave her with a negative taste in her mouth. "It's not that far, really. I rather enjoyed coming out on the bus."

Nicole smiled. "Maybe next time we could plan it a little better and you could stay out here for a couple of days. How would that sound?" She looked at Annaliese with hope in her eyes.

Annaliese was touched. Her eyes gentled as she gazed upon her friend. "Let's do that, shall we? I'll bring a little suitcase and stay a bit longer."

Clapping her hands together with delight, Nicole looked like a burden had been lifted off her shoulders. They agreed to speak on the telephone soon, and with that Annaliese was gone.

Nicole knew it was possible for God to teach her, but it was so inspiring and encouraging to have Annaliese help her along. She was relieved that she would see her again. She sat on the couch and pulled out her guitar, strumming a few chords for Robbie who was sitting close by in his car seat. Shadow, who had moved with her from her parents' house, was on the floor near the couch, grooming himself in preparation for a nap.

The three of them made an entrancing picture as this young mother sang to her infant son's benefit while she worshipped the God she loved with all her heart. Nicole's heart was full and she could only express it in song. She knew life was going to be all right for her and Robbie, and of course... for Shadow.